HIGH COTTON:

Selected Stories of Joe R. Lansdale

GOLDEN GRYPHON PRESS
2000

"The Pit," first published in *The Black Lizard Anthology of Crime Fiction*,1987.

"Not From Detroit," first published in *Midnight Graffiti*, Fall, 1988.

"Booty and the Beast," first published in *Archon Gaming*, 1995.

"Steppin' Out, Summer, '68," first published in *Night Visions*, 8, 1991.

"Incident On and Off a Mountain Road," first published in *Night Visions*, 8, 1991.

"My Dead Dog, Bobby," first published in *The Horror Show*, Sum. '87.

"Trains Not Taken," first published in *RE:AL*, Spring 1987.

"Tight Little Stitches in a Dead Man's Back," first published in *Nukes*, 1986.

"Dog, Cat, and Baby," first published in *Masques* #2, 1987.

"Mister Weed-Eater," first published by Cahill Press, 1993.

"By Bizarre Hands," first published in *Hardboiled* #9, 1988.

"The Fat Man and the Elephant," first published in *By Bizarre Hands*, 1989.

"The Phone Woman," first published in *Night Visions*, 8, 1991.

"Letter from the South, Two Moons West of Nacogdoches," first published in *Last Wave*, #5, 1986.

"By the Hair of the Head," first published in *Shadows*, #6, 1983.

"The Job," first published in *Razored Saddles*, 1989.

"Godzilla's Twelve Step Program," first published in *Writer of the Purple Rage*, 1994.

"Drive-In Date," first published in *Night Visions*, 8, 1991.

"Bob the Dinosaur Goes to Disneyland," first published in *Midnight Graffiti*, Fall 1989.

"The Steel Valentine," first published in *By Bizarre Hands*, 1989.

"Night They Missed the Horror Show," first published in *Silver Scream*, 1988.

Copyright © 2000 by Joe R. Lansdale

LIBRARY OF CONGRESS CATALOGING–IN–PUBLICATION DATA
Lansdale, Joe R., 1951–
    High cotton selected stories / of Joe Lansdale — 1st ed.
        p.   cm.
    ISBN 0-9655901-2-7
        I.   Title.
PS3562.A557H54   2000
813'.54—dc21   00-028806
    ISBN 1-930846-17-7

First Softcover Edition 2003.

CONTENTS

For Karen, Keith and Kasey,
years of mental madness consigned to paper.

FOREWORD

ROWING UP IN EAST TEXAS, I KNEW EARLY ON that I wanted to be a professional writer, even though I wasn't exactly sure what a professional writer was. I began to write stories at a very early age. Perhaps as early as seven, though I can't be certain of that, as family stories vary. I know that when I was nine I was seriously trying to understand how stories were told, and I even put together a book of stories, poems, and my interpretations of Greek and Norse myths. I also included, for some unknown reason, the ancient Greek alphabet that I had copied out of an encyclopedia.

When I was old enough to sort of understand what a writer did to make a living, and I began to entertain the idea seriously, I thought that I would be a science fiction writer. I read all the time, and not just science fiction, but there was a time in my life where science fiction—and keep in mind I lumped fantasy, horror, science fantasy, weird adventure, ghost stories, anything odd, under that label—was my main source of reading matter, coupled with supposedly non-fiction books about things like flying saucers, Big Foot, ghost, and Fortean activity.

When I finally began to write a true novel, it was in the Edgar Rice Burroughs vein. Somewhere, I hope, those efforts still exist.

They are either in the library where my work is kept, or in my study, or, heaven forbid, I may have destroyed them. I remember thinking about it. I feel sentimental about those old pieces, and about ten years ago, when I last saw them, I took them out and was surprised to find they weren't really too bad, considering a kid, not even teenage yet, had written them.

But they were never finished. They just sort of went on and on in composition notebooks, but I didn't know how to reach a peak in the books, and then wrap them up. When I began to write novels with serious intent in my mid-twenties, I discovered I still hadn't learned that trick. The idea of novels became daunting. I decided I'd write something shorter, and in my mind easier, so I turned to short stories.

I had always read short stories, but for some reason it had never occurred to me to pursue them seriously. I had written a few, but none were any good, and I just assumed novels were where it was at. I began to review stories I had read and loved. Stories by Poe, Doyle, Bradbury, Bloch, others, and I began to read them more carefully, and I expanded my reading. I had read stories by Hemingway, Fitzgerald, Faulkner, and others of that ilk that I had enjoyed, but now I began to study them seriously. And then, I began to write.

I once spent about three months writing a story a day—no kidding. I sent each one out to several markets, and all of them came back. Over a period of time—more than three months—I probably got a thousand rejects. I kept the stories and the rejects for years, and then, when we moved from Starrville, Texas to Nacogdoches, Texas, I had a ritualistic burning of stories and rejects. A few of the rejected stories survived, and were revised later and published, and some were published in a book I did of early writings, designed for the fan of this sort of thing; a book designed primarily to show that everyone has to begin somewhere.

But, I got hooked on the short story, and pretty soon, they were all I wanted to write. They were much harder than I ever expected. In fact, harder than novels. But, still, there was less of an investment in time, and therefore I could get something to market relatively soon; I could see an end in sight when I was working on them, and I could change moods and genres rapidly. That was appealing to me, since, essentially, I have a short attention span.

I became enraptured with short stories, and no longer just science fiction. I had expanded my reading, and now I expanded the type of stories I liked to write. When I finally began to sell my stories, I found I no longer wanted to write novels. I found short stories just too satisfying.

Still, since I wanted to be a full-time freelance writer, I knew I had to eventually write novels. I almost regretted when the novels began to sell; my excuse to write short stories began to evaporate. By the early nineties I was writing fewer and fewer short stories. Some of the energy I had invested in them went into the novels, and into comic book and film scripts. It wasn't that I had lost interest in short stories, but it was as if I got up one day feeling like I had met certain goals in the short story world, and now I was ready to see what I could do elsewhere.

Short stories, and novellas, are still favorites of mine, but I have really learned to appreciate the novel. And since I get paid more for novels these days than I used to, it has allowed me to return a little more frequently to short stories.

I doubt I will ever be a full-time short story writer again. That was hard, though I did pull it off for a time. But, it wasn't exactly more than a hand-to-mouth living. Now that I can get more for my short stories, I also make more for the novels, so it's easy to see which one I give the time. Besides, I like doing novels as much as short stories now. That said, I think short stories taught me how to write tighter, better novels.

These stories are the ones that I think taught me the most. They are personal favorites of mine. I could have added a few stories to this collection, replaced one with another in some cases, but these stories are the ones I think best reflect my work.

Growing up in the South, there's an expression you hear. "He's in high cotton now." "I felt like I was in high cotton."

This is taken from the fact that in the Old South, when cotton was good, it stood rich and tall and full. It was called high cotton. If you made your living from cotton, this was a good thing. The expression has carried over to include things that have nothing to do with farming or cotton.

Short stories, for example.

I can't say that this is the best cotton grown. But in my personal field, this is the best cotton I've grown in the short form.

I hope, that as you pluck it from my field, you will enjoy the work better than those who pluck actual cotton, and I hope the product, once plucked, is satisfying.

I have been a published writer for nearly twenty-seven years now, and these stories were written in the last seventeen. They are fewer and farther between these days, but I hope that long before another twenty-seven years, there will be yet another book produced from my field, and if talent, luck, ambition, and hard work stay with me, perhaps the cotton produced will stand even higher.

Joe R. Lansdale
Nacogdoches, Texas
February, 2000

HIGH COTTON:

SELECTED STORIES OF JOE R. LANSDALE

I read an article in GEO *magazine — a magazine I believe has come and gone — about dog fighting. It struck me as horrible and cruel. I had heard it compared to boxing, a comparison I don't buy. Boxers can choose to get in the ring or not, and they are taught how to protect themselves and there are referees. Dogs do it for the love of their masters and for something to eat. For a reward, when they lose, they are most often killed or abandoned. These dog-fighting guys don't want losers.*

I thought about that, added in another story told me by a friend. Supposedly, back in the late fifties or early sixties, there was a small town where a black man's car broke down and he was captured and made to pull a wagon around the town square, and was fed axle grease on crackers. Finally, he escaped.

Swear. That's the story. I'm not saying it's true, but it was told to me as the truth and it was given to the teller as the truth. If it did happen, I have no idea where this took place. North, South, East, or West. But it got the story wheels turning. My thoughts about dog fighting, boxing, and this supposed incident, all came crashing together, and became "The Pit." This was about 1982 or 1983. I sent it out, and no one bought it. They didn't know what the hell it was. All the standard horror markets — there were a number of them then — thought it wasn't horror, and they were probably right. Some wanted it to have a twist ending, or another ending. One editor wanted me to give it a positive spin. I wouldn't. I pulled it. It lay in a file drawer for several years.

By the mid-eighties I was beginning to develop a name, and when I was asked for a story for a crime/mystery anthology being published by Black Lizard, I sent the editor this. He accepted it and later it appeared in my first short story collection, By Bizarre Hands. *That's been many years ago and though it's been reprinted several times, it still hasn't gotten the exposure I modestly think it deserves. Maybe this collection will help.*

THE PIT

SIX MONTHS EARLIER THEY HAD CAPTURED HIM. Tonight Harry went into the pit. He and Big George, right after the bull terriers got through tearing the guts out of one another. When that was over, he and George would go down and do their business. The loser would stay there and be fed to the dogs, each of which had been starved for the occasion.

When the dogs finished eating, the loser's head would go up on a pole. Already a dozen poles circled the pit. On each rested a head, or skull, depending on how long it had been exposed to the elements, ambitious pole-climbing ants and hungry birds. And of course how much flesh the terriers ripped off before it was erected.

Twelve poles. Twelve heads.

Tonight a new pole and a new head went up.

Harry looked about at the congregation. All sixty or so of them. They were a sight. Like mad creatures out of Lewis Carroll. Only they didn't have long rabbit ears or tall silly hats. They were just backwoods rednecks, not too unlike himself. With one major difference. They were as loony as waltzing mice. Or maybe they weren't crazy and he was. Sometimes he felt as if he had stepped

3

into an alternate universe where the old laws of nature, and what was right and wrong did not apply. Just like Alice plunging down the rabbit hole into Wonderland.

The crowd about the pit had been mumbling and talking, but now they grew silent. Out into the glow of the neon lamps stepped a man dressed in a black suit and hat. A massive rattlesnake was coiled about his right arm. It was wriggling from shoulder to wrist. About his left wrist a smaller snake was wrapped, a copperhead. The man held a Bible in his right hand. He was called Preacher.

Draping the monstrous rattlesnake around his neck, Preacher let it hang there. It dangled that way as if drugged. Its tongue would flash out from time to time. It gave Harry the willies. He hated snakes. They always seemed to be smiling. Nothing was that fucking funny, not all the time.

Preacher opened his Bible and read:

"Behold, I give unto you the power to tread on serpents and scorpions, and over all the power of the enemy: and nothing will by any means hurt you."

Preacher paused and looked at the sky. "So God," he said, "we want to thank you for a pretty good potato crop, though you've done better, and we want to thank you for the terriers, even though we had to raise and feed them ourselves, and we want to thank you for sending these outsiders our way, thank you for Harry Joe Stinton and Big George, the nigger."

Preacher paused and looked about the congregation. He lifted the hand with the copperhead in it high above his head. Slowly he lowered it and pointed the snake-filled fist at George. "Three times this here nigger has gone into the pit, and three times he has come out victorious. Couple times against whites, once against another nigger. Some of us think he's cheating.

"Tonight, we bring you another white feller, one of your chosen people, though you might not know it on account of the way you been letting the nigger win here, and we're hoping for a good fight with the nigger being killed at the end. We hope this here business pleases you. We worship you and the snakes in the way we ought to. Amen."

Big George looked over at Harry. "Be ready, sucker. I'm gonna take you apart like a gingerbread man."

Harry didn't say anything. He couldn't understand it. George was a prisoner just as he was. A man degraded and made to lift huge rocks and pull carts and jog mile on miles every day. And just so they could get in shape for this—to go down into that pit and try and beat each other to death for the amusement of these crazies.

And it had to be worse for George. Being black, he was seldom called anything other than "the nigger" by these psychos. Furthermore, no secret had been made of the fact that they wanted George to lose, and for him to win. The idea of a black pit champion was eating their little honkey hearts out.

Yet, Big George had developed a sort of perverse pride in being the longest-lived pit fighter yet.

"It's something I can do right," George had once said. "On the outside I wasn't nothing but a nigger, an uneducated nigger working in rose fields, mowing big lawns for rich white folks. Here I'm still the nigger, but I'm THE NIGGER, the bad ass nigger, and no matter what these peckerwoods call me, they know it, and they know I'm the best at what I do. I'm the king here. And they may hate me for it, keep me in a cell and make me run and lift stuff, but for that time in the pit, they know I'm the one that can do what they can't do, and they're afraid of me. I like it."

Glancing at George, Harry saw that the big man was not nervous. Or at least not showing it. He looked as if he were ready to go on holiday. Nothing to it. He was about to go down into that pit and try and beat a man to death with his fists, and it was nothing. All in a day's work. A job well done for an odd sort of respect that beat what he had had on the outside.

The outside. It was strange how much he and Big George used that term. *The outside.* As if they were enclosed in some small bubble-like cosmos that perched on the edge of the world they had known; a cosmos invisible to *the outsiders,* a spectral place with new mathematics and nebulous laws of mind and physics.

Maybe he was in hell. Perhaps he had been wiped out on the highway and had gone to the dark place. Just maybe his memory of how he had arrived here was a false dream inspired by demonic powers. The whole thing about him taking a wrong turn through Big Thicket country and having his truck break down just outside of Morganstown was an illusion, and stepping onto the Main Street of Morganstown, population sixty-six, was his crossing the river Styx and landing smack dab in the middle of a hell designed for good old boys.

God, had it been six months ago?

He had been on his way to visit his mother in Woodville, and he had taken a shortcut through the Thicket. Or so he thought. But he soon realized that he had looked at the map wrong. The short cut listed on the paper was not the one he had taken. He had mistaken that road for the one he wanted. This one had not been marked. And then he had reached Morganstown and his truck had broken down. He had been forced into six months hard labor alongside George, the champion pit fighter, and now the moment for which he had been groomed had arrived.

They were bringing the terriers out now. One, the champion, was named Old Codger. He was getting on in years. He had won many a pit fight. Tonight, win or lose, this would be his last battle. The other dog, Muncher, was younger and inexperienced, but he was strong and eager for blood.

A ramp was lowered into the pit. Preacher and two men, the owners of the dogs, went down into the pit with Codger and Muncher. When they reached the bottom, a dozen bright spotlights were thrown on them. They seemed to wade through the light.

The bleachers arranged about the pit began to fill. People mumbled and passed popcorn. Bets were placed and a little fat man wearing a bowler hat copied them down in a note pad as fast as they were shouted. The ramp was removed.

In the pit, the men took hold of their dogs by the scruff of the neck and removed their collars. They turned the dogs so they were facing the walls of the pit and could not see one another. The terriers were about six feet apart, butts facing.

Preacher said, "A living dog is better than a dead lion."

Harry wasn't sure what that had to do with anything.

"Ready yourselves," Preacher said. "Gentlemen, face your dogs."

The owners slapped their dogs across the muzzle and whirled them to face one another. They immediately began to leap and strain at their masters' grips.

"Gentlemen, release your dogs."

The dogs did not bark. For some reason, that was what Harry noted the most. They did not even growl. They were quick little engines of silence.

Their first lunge was a miss and they snapped air. But the second time they hit head-on with the impact of .45 slugs. Codger was knocked on his back and Muncher dove for his throat. But the experienced dog popped up its head and grabbed Muncher by the nose. Codger's teeth met through Muncher's flesh.

Bets were called from the bleachers.

The little man in the bowler was writing furiously.

Muncher, the challenger, was dragging Codger, the champion, around the pit, trying to make the old dog let go of his nose.

Finally, by shaking his head violently and relinquishing a hunk of his muzzle, he succeeded.

Codger rolled to his feet and jumped Muncher. Muncher turned his head just out of the path of Codger's jaws. The older dog's teeth snapped together like a spring-loaded bear trap, saliva popped out of his mouth in a fine spray.

Muncher grabbed Codger by the right ear. The grip was strong and Codger was shook like a used condom about to be tied and tossed. Muncher bit the champ's ear completely off.

Harry felt sick. He thought he was going to throw up. He saw that Big George was looking at him. "You think this is bad, motherfucker," George said, "this ain't nothing but a cakewalk. Wait till I get you in that pit."

"You sure run hot and cold, don't you?" Harry said.

"Nothing personal," George said sharply and turned back to look at the fight in the pit.

Nothing personal, Harry thought. God, what could be more personal? Just yesterday, as they trained, jogged along together, a pickup loaded with gun-bearing crazies driving alongside of them, he had felt close to George. They had shared many personal things these six months, and he knew that George liked him. But when it came to the pit, George was a different man. The concept of friendship became alien to him. When Harry had tried to talk to him about it yesterday, he had said much the same thing. "Ain't nothing personal, Harry my man, but when we get in that pit don't look to me for nothing besides pain, cause I got plenty of that to give you, a lifetime of it, and I'll just keep it coming."

Down in the pit Codger screamed. It could be described no other way. Muncher had him on his back and was biting him on the belly. Codger was trying to double forward and get hold of Muncher's head, but his tired jaws kept slipping off of the wet neck fur. Blood was starting to pump out of Codger's belly.

"Bite him, boy," someone yelled from the bleachers, "tear his ass up, son."

Harry noted that every man, woman and child was leaning forward in their seat, straining for a view. Their faces full of lust, like lovers approaching vicious climax. For a few moments they were in that pit and they were the dogs. Vicarious thrills without the pain.

Codger's legs began to flap.

"Kill him! Kill him!" the crowd began to chant.

Codger had quit moving. Muncher was burrowing his muzzle

deeper into the old dog's guts. Preacher called for a pickup. Muncher's owner pried the dog's jaws loose of Codger's guts. Muncher's muzzle looked as if it had been dipped in red ink.

"This sonofabitch is still alive," Muncher's owner said of Codger.

Codger's owner walked over to the dog and said, "You little fucker!" He pulled a Saturday Night Special from his coat pocket and shot Codger twice in the head. Codger didn't even kick. He just evacuated his bowels right there.

Muncher came over and sniffed Codger's corpse, then, lifting his leg, he took a leak on the dead dog's head. The stream of piss was bright red.

The ramp was lowered. The dead dog was dragged out and tossed behind the bleachers. Muncher walked up the ramp beside his owner. The little dog strutted like he had just been crowned King of Creation. Codger's owner walked out last. He was not a happy man. Preacher stayed in the pit. A big man known as Sheriff Jimmy went down the ramp to join him. Sheriff Jimmy had a big pistol on his hip and a toy badge on his chest. The badge looked like the sort of thing that had come in a plastic bag with a cap gun and whistle. But it was his sign of office and his word was iron.

A man next to Harry prodded him with the barrel of a shotgun. Walking close behind George, Harry went down the ramp and into the pit. The man with the shotgun went back up. In the bleachers the betting had started again, the little fat man with the bowler was busy.

Preacher's rattlesnake was still lying serenely about his neck, and the little copperhead had been placed in Preacher's coat pocket. It poked its head out from time to time and looked around.

Harry glanced up. The heads and skulls on the poles—in spite of the fact they were all eyeless, and due to the strong light nothing but bulbous shapes on shafts—seemed to look down, taking as much amusement in the situation as the crowd on the bleachers.

Preacher had his Bible out again. He was reading a verse. ". . . when thou walkest through the fire, thou shalt not be burned; neither shall the flame kindle upon thee . . ."

Harry had no idea what that or the snakes had to do with anything. Certainly he could not see the relationship with the pit. These people's minds seemed to click and grind to a different set of internal gears than those on *the outside*.

The reality of the situation settled on Harry like a heavy, woolen coat. He was about to kill or be killed, right here in this dog-smelling pit, and there was nothing he could do that would change that.

He thought perhaps his life should flash before his eyes or something, but it did not. Maybe he should try to think of something wonderful, a last fine thought of what used to be. First he summoned up the image of his wife. That did nothing for him. Though his wife had once been pretty and bright, he could not remember her that way. The image that came to mind was quite different. A dumpy, lazy woman with constant back pains and her hair pulled up into an eternal topknot of greasy, brown hair. There was never a smile on her face or a word of encouragement for him. He always felt that she expected him to entertain her and that he was not doing a very good job of it. There was not even a moment of sexual ecstasy that he could recall. After their daughter had been born she had given up screwing as a wasted exercise. Why waste energy on sex when she could spend it complaining.

He flipped his mental card file to his daughter. What he saw was an ugly, potato-nosed girl of twelve. She had no personality. Her mother was Miss Congeniality compared to her. Potato Nose spent all of her time pining over thin, blond heartthrobs on television. It wasn't bad enough that they glared at Harry via the tube, they were also pinned to her walls and hiding in magazines she had cast throughout the house.

These were the last thoughts of a man about to face death? There was just nothing there.

His job had sucked. His wife hadn't.

He clutched at straws. There had been Melva, a fine looking little cheerleader from high school. She had had the brain of a dried black-eyed pea, but God-All-Mighty, did she know how to hide a weenie. And there had always been that strange smell about her, like bananas. It was especially strong about her thatch, which was thick enough for a bald eagle to nest in.

But thinking about her didn't provide much pleasure either. She had gotten hit by a drunk in a Mack truck while parked offside of a dark road with that Pulver boy.

Damn that Pulver. At least he had died in ecstasy. Had never known what hit him. When that Mack went up his ass he probably thought for a split second he was having the greatest orgasm of his life.

Damn that Melva. What had she seen in Pulver anyway?

He was skinny and stupid and had a face like a peanut pattie.

God, he was beat at every turn. Frustrated at every corner. No good thoughts or beautiful visions before the moment of truth. Only blackness, a life of dull, planned movements as consistent and boring as a bran-conscious geriatric's bowel movement. For a moment he thought he might cry.

Sheriff Jimmy took out his revolver. Unlike the badge it was not a toy. "Find your corner, boys."

George turned and strode to one side of the pit, took off his shirt and leaned against the wall. His body shined like wet licorice in the spotlights.

After a moment, Harry made his legs work. He walked to a place opposite George and took off his shirt. He could feel the months of hard work rippling beneath his flesh. His mind was suddenly blank. There wasn't even a god he believed in. No one to pray to. Nothing to do but the inevitable.

Sheriff Jimmy walked to the middle of the pit. He yelled out for the crowd to shut up.

Silence reigned.

"In this corner," he said, waving the revolver at Harry, "we have Harry Joe Stinton, family man and pretty good feller for an outsider. He's six two and weighs two hundred and thirty-eight pounds, give or take a pound since my bathroom scales ain't exactly on the money."

A cheer went up.

"Over here," Sheriff Jimmy said, waving the revolver at George, "standing six four tall and weighing two hundred and forty-two pounds, we got the nigger, present champion of this here sport."

No one cheered. Someone made a loud sound with his mouth that sounded like a fart, the greasy kind that goes on and on and on.

George appeared unfazed. He looked like a statue. He knew who he was and what he was. The Champion Of The Pit.

"First off," Sheriff Jimmy said, "you boys come forward and show your hands."

Harry and George walked to the center of the pit, held out their hands, fingers spread wide apart, so that the crowd could see that they were empty.

"Turn and walk to your corners and don't turn around," Sheriff Jimmy said.

George and Harry did as they were told. Sheriff Jimmy followed Harry and put an arm around his shoulders. "I got four hogs riding on you," he said. "And I'll tell you what, you beat the nigger and I'll do you a favor. Elvira, who works over at the cafe has already agreed. You win and you can have her. How's that sound?"

Harry was too numb with the insanity of it all to answer. Sheriff Jimmy was offering him a piece of ass if he won, as if this would be greater incentive than coming out of the pit alive. With this bunch there was just no way to anticipate what might come next. Nothing was static.

"She can do more tricks with a six inch dick than a monkey can with a hundred foot of grapevine, boy. When the going gets rough in there, you remember that. Okay?"

Harry didn't answer. He just looked at the pit wall.

"You ain't gonna get nowhere in life being sullen like that," Sheriff Jimmy said. "Now, you go get him and plow a rut in his black ass."

Sheriff Jimmy grabbed Harry by the shoulders and whirled him around, slapped him hard across the face in the same way the dogs had been slapped. George had been done the same way by the preacher. Now George and Harry were facing one another. Harry thought George looked like an ebony gargoyle fresh escaped from hell. His bald, bullet-like head gleamed in the harsh lights and his body looked as rough and ragged as stone.

Harry and George raised their hands in classic boxer stance and began to circle one another.

From above someone yelled, "Don't hit the nigger in the head, it'll break your hand. Go for the lips, they got soft lips."

The smell of sweat, dog blood and old Codger's shit was thick in the air. The lust of the crowd seemed to have an aroma as well. Harry even thought he could smell Preacher's snakes. Once, when a boy, he had been fishing down by the creek bed and had smelled an odor like that, and a water moccasin had wriggled out beneath his legs and splashed in the water. It was as if everything he feared in the world had been put in this pit. The idea of being put deep down in the ground. Irrational people for whom logic did not exist. Rotting skulls on poles about the pit. Living skulls attached to hunched-forward bodies that yelled for blood. Snakes. The stench of death — blood and shit. And every white man's fear, racist or not — a big, black man with a lifetime of hatred in his eyes.

The circle tightened. They could almost touch one another now.

Suddenly George's lip began to tremble. His eyes poked out of his head, seemed to be looking at something just behind and to the right of Harry.

"Sss . . . snake!" George screamed.

God, thought Harry, one of Preacher's snakes has escaped. Harry jerked his head for a look.

And George stepped in and knocked him on his ass and kicked him full in the chest. Harry began scuttling along the ground on his hands and knees, George following along kicking him in the ribs. Harry thought he felt something snap inside, a cracked rib maybe. He finally scuttled to his feet and bicycled around the pit. Goddamn, he thought, I fell for the oldest, silliest trick in the book. Here I am fighting for my life and I fell for it.

"Way to go, stupid fuck!" A voice screamed from the bleachers. "Hey nigger, why don't you try 'hey, your shoe's untied,' he'll go for it."

"Get off the goddamned bicycle," someone else yelled. "Fight."

"You better run," George said. "I catch you I'm gonna punch you so hard in the mouth, gonna knock your fucking teeth out your asshole . . ."

Harry felt dizzy. His head was like a yo-yo doing the Around The World trick. Blood ran down his forehead, dribbled off the tip of his nose and gathered on his upper lip. George was closing the gap again.

I'm going to die right here in this pit, thought Harry. I'm going to die just because my truck broke down outside of town and no one knows where I am. That's why I'm going to die. It's as simple as that.

Popcorn rained down on Harry and a tossed cup of ice hit him in the back. "Wanted to see a fucking foot race," a voice called, "I'd have gone to the fucking track."

"Ten on the nigger," another voice said.

"Five bucks the nigger kills him in five minutes."

When Harry backpedaled past Preacher, the snake man leaned forward and snapped, "You asshole, I got a sawbuck riding on you."

Preacher was holding the big rattler again. He had the snake gripped just below the head, and he was so upset over how the fight had gone so far, he was unconsciously squeezing the snake in a vice-like grip. The rattler was squirming and twisting and flapping about, but Preacher didn't seem to notice. The snake's forked tongue was outside its mouth and it was really working, slapping about like a thin strip of rubber come loose on a whirling tire. The copperhead in Preacher's pocket was still looking out, as if along with Preacher he might have a bet on the outcome of the fight as well. As Harry danced away the rattler opened its mouth so wide its jaws came unhinged. It looked as if it were trying to yell for help.

Harry and George came together again in the center of the pit. Fists like black ball bearings slammed the sides of Harry's head. The pit was like a whirlpool, the walls threatening to close in and suck Harry down into oblivion.

Kneeing with all his might, Harry caught George solidly in the groin. George grunted, stumbled back, half-bent over.

The crowd went wild.

Harry brought cupped hands down on George's neck, knocked him on his knees. Harry used the opportunity to knock out one of the big man's teeth with the toe of his shoe.

He was about to kick him again when George reached up and clutched the crotch of Harry's khakis, taking a crushing grip on Harry's testicles.

"Got you by the balls," George growled.

Harry bellowed and began to hammer wildly on top of George's head with both fists. He realized with horror that George was pulling him forward. *By God, George was going to bite him on the balls.*

Jerking up his knee he caught George in the nose and broke his grip. He bounded free, skipped and whooped about the pit like an Indian dancing for rain.

He skipped and whooped by Preacher. Preacher's rattler had quit twisting. It hung loosely from Preacher's tight fist. Its eyes were bulging out of its head like the humped backs of grub worms. Its mouth was closed and its forked tongue hung limply from the edge of it.

The copperhead was still watching the show from the safety of Preacher's pocket, its tongue zipping out from time to time to taste the air. The little snake didn't seem to have a care in the world.

George was on his feet again, and Harry could tell that already he was feeling better. Feeling good enough to make Harry feel real bad.

Preacher abruptly realized that his rattler had gone limp. "No, God no!" he cried. He stretched the huge rattler between his hands. "Baby, baby," he bawled, "breathe for me, Sapphire, breathe for me." Preacher shook the snake viciously, trying to jar some life into it, but the snake did not move.

The pain in Harry's groin had subsided and he could think again. George was moving in on him, and there just didn't seem any reason to run. George would catch him, and when he did, it would just be worse because he would be even more tired from all that running. It had to be done. The mating dance was over, now all that was left was the intercourse of violence.

A black fist turned the flesh and cartilage of Harry's nose into smouldering putty. Harry ducked his head and caught another blow to the chin. The stars he had not been able to see above him because of the lights, he could now see below him, spinning constellations on the floor of the pit.

It came to him again, the fact that he was going to die right here without one good, last thought. But then maybe there was one. He envisioned his wife, dumpy and sullen and denying him sex. George became her and she became George and Harry did what he had wanted to do for so long, he hit her in the mouth. Not once, but twice and a third time. He battered her nose and he pounded her ribs. And by God, but she could hit back. He felt something crack in the center of his chest and his left cheekbone collapsed into his face. But Harry did not stop battering her. He looped and punched and pounded her dumpy face until it was George's black face and George's black face turned back to her face and he thought of her now on the bed, naked, on her back, battered, and he was naked and mounting her, and the blows of his fists were the sexual thrusts of his cock and he was pounding her until—

George screamed. He had fallen to his knees. His right eye was hanging out on the tendons. One of Harry's straight rights had struck George's cheekbone with such power it had shattered it and pressured the eye out of its socket.

Blood ran down Harry's knuckles. Some of it was George's. Much of it was his own. His knuckle bones showed through the rent flesh of his hands, but they did not hurt. They were past hurting.

George wobbled to his feet. The two men stood facing one another, neither moving. The crowd was silent. The only sound in the pit was the harsh breathing of the two fighters, and Preacher who had stretched Sapphire out on the ground on her back and was trying to blow air into her mouth. Occasionally he'd lift his head and say in tearful supplication, "Breathe for me, Sapphire, breathe for me."

Each time Preacher blew a blast into the snake, its white

underbelly would swell and then settle down, like a leaky balloon that just wouldn't hold air.

George and Harry came together. Softly. They had their arms on each others shoulders and they leaned against one another, breathed each others breath.

Above, the silence of the crowd was broken when a heckler yelled, "Start some music, the fuckers want to dance."

"It's nothing personal," George said.

"Not at all," Harry said.

They managed to separate, reluctantly, like two lovers who had just copulated to the greatest orgasm of their lives.

George bent slightly and put up his hands. The eye dangling on his cheek looked like some kind of tentacled creature trying to crawl up and into George's socket. Harry knew that he would have to work on that eye.

Preacher screamed. Harry afforded him a sideways glance. Sapphire was awake. And now she was dangling from Preacher's face. She had bitten through his top lip and was hung there by her fangs. Preacher was saying something about the power to tread on serpents and stumbling about the pit. Finally his back struck the pit wall and he slid down to his butt and just sat there, legs sticking out in front of him, Sapphire dangling off his lip like some sort of malignant growth. Gradually, building momentum, the snake began to thrash.

Harry and George met again in the center of the pit. A second wind had washed in on them and they were ready. Harry hurt wonderfully. He was no longer afraid. Both men were smiling, showing the teeth they had left. They began to hit each other.

Harry worked on the eye. Twice he felt it beneath his fists, a grape-like thing that cushioned his knuckles and made them wet. Harry's entire body felt on fire—twin fires, ecstasy and pain.

George and Harry collapsed together, held each other, waltzed about.

"You done good," George said, "make it quick."

The black man's legs went out from under him and he fell to his knees, his head bent. Harry took the man's head in his hands and kneed him in the face with all his might. George went limp. Harry grasped George's chin and the back of his head and gave a violent twist. The neck bone snapped and George fell back, dead.

The copperhead, which had been poking its head out of Preacher's pocket, took this moment to slither away into a crack in the pit's wall.

Out of nowhere came weakness. Harry fell to his knees. He touched George's ruined face with his fingers.

Suddenly hands had him. The ramp was lowered. The crowd cheered. Preacher—Sapphire dislodged from his lip—came forward to help Sheriff Jimmy with him. They lifted him up.

Harry looked at Preacher. His lip was greenish. His head looked like a sun-swollen watermelon, yet, he seemed well enough. Sapphire was wrapped around his neck again. They were still buddies. The snake looked tired. Harry no longer felt afraid of it. He reached out and touched its head. It did not try to bite him. He felt its feathery tongue brush his bloody hand.

They carried him up the ramp and the crowd took him, lifted him up high above their heads. He could see the moon and the stars now. For some odd reason they did not look familiar. Even the nature of the sky seemed different.

He turned and looked down. The terriers were being herded into the pit. They ran down the ramp like rats. Below, he could hear them begin to feed, to fight for choice morsels. But there were so many dogs, and they were so hungry, this only went on for a few minutes. After a while they came back up the ramp followed by Sheriff Jimmy closing a big lock-bladed knife, and by Preacher who held George's head in his outstretched hands. George's eyes were gone. Little of the face remained. Only that slick, bald pate had been left undamaged by the terriers.

A pole came out of the crowd and the head was pushed onto its sharpened end and the pole was dropped into a deep hole in the ground. The pole, like a long neck, rocked its trophy for a moment, then went still. Dirt was kicked into the hole and George joined the others, all those beautiful, wonderful heads and skulls.

They began to carry Harry away. Tomorrow he would have Elvira, who could do more tricks with a six inch dick than a monkey could with a hundred foot of grapevine, then he would heal and a new outsider would come through and they would train together and then they would mate in blood and sweat in the depths of the pit.

The crowd was moving toward the forest trail, toward town. The smell of pines was sweet in the air. And as they carried him away, Harry turned his head so he could look back and see the pit, its maw closing in shadow as the lights were cut, and just before the last one went out Harry saw the heads on the poles, and dead center of his vision, was the shiny, bald pate of his good friend George.

This was inspired by a scene in The Nightrunners. *When I wrote the book in the early eighties and it went out to sell, no one bought it. I thought it was dead, so I began to cobble stories out of it. Some were merely lifted, most were inspired by scenes in the book. This one is one of the inspirations, though there are many lines and moments taken directly from the book. As I recall, Richard Christian Matheson told me his father, the great Richard Matheson, was story editor for the television show* Amazing Stories, *and I should try something on him. I did a synopsis of a story I had written based on a scene in* The Nightrunners *and sent it to him. He liked it, suggested the song at the end of the story. But the powers that be didn't like the story. Maybe Spielberg axed it himself, as he was the producer for* Amazing Stories. *I like to think I was accepted by one of the best, and rejected by one of the best.*

Whatever, it didn't become an episode of Amazing Stories, *though I still feel it would have been excellent for that show. I decided to use the synopsis and revise the original story which I had titled "A Car Drives By." The reason for the complete revision was I didn't like the original story, which had appeared in a literary magazine called* Mississippi Arts and Letters. *The result of the rewrite, based on a scene from* The Nightrunners, *the original story and the synopsis, was a better story. I kept Matheson's idea of the song at the end of the tale. I think it adds a nice touch.*

The Nightrunners, *the inspiration for so many of my stories, as well as a children's book (Go figure!) eventually did sell, and as of this writing is still in print in paperback.*

NOT FROM DETROIT

OUTSIDE IT WAS COLD AND WET AND WINDY. The storm rattled the shack, slid like razor blades through the window, door and wall cracks, but it wasn't enough to make any difference to the couple. Sitting before the crumbling fireplace in their creaking rocking chairs, shawls across their knees, fingers entwined, they were warm.

A bucket behind them near the kitchen sink collected water dripping from a hole in the roof. The drops had long since passed the noisy stage of sounding like steel bolts falling on tin, and were now gentle plops.

The old couple were husband and wife; had been for over fifty years. They were comfortable with one another and seldom spoke. Mostly they rocked and looked at the fire as it flickered shadows across the room.

Finally Margie spoke. "Alex," she said. "I hope I die before you."

Alex stopped rocking. "Did you say what I thought you did?"

"I said, I hope I die before you." She wouldn't look at him, just the fire. "It's selfish, I know, but I hope I do. I don't want to live on with you gone. It would be like cutting out my heart and making me walk around. Like one of them zombies."

"There are the children," he said. "If I died, they'd take you in."

"I'd just be in the way. I love them, but I don't want to do that. They got their own lives. I'd just as soon die before you. That would make things simple."

"Not simple for me," Alex said. "I don't want you to die before me. So how about that? We're both selfish, aren't we?"

She smiled thinly. "Well, it ain't a thing to talk about before bedtime, but it's been on my mind, and I had to get it out."

"Been thinking on it too, honey. Only natural we would. We ain't spring chickens anymore."

"You're healthy as a horse, Alex Brooks. Mechanic work you did all your life kept you strong. Me, I got the bursitis and the miseries and I'm tired all the time. Got the old age bad."

Alex started rocking again. They stared into the fire. "We're going to go together, hon," he said. "I feel it. That's the way it ought to be for folks like us."

"I wonder if I'll see him coming. Death, I mean."

"What?"

"My grandma used to tell me she seen him the night her daddy died."

"You've never told me this."

"Ain't a subject I like. But grandma said this man in a black buggy slowed down out front of their house, cracked his whip three times, and her daddy was gone in instants. And she said she'd heard her grandfather tell how he had seen Death when he was a boy. Told her it was early morning and he was up, about to start his chores, and when he went outside he seen this man dressed in black walk by the house and stop out front. He was carrying a stick over his shoulder with a checkered bundle tied to it, and he looked at the house and snapped his fingers three times. A moment later they found my great-grandfather's brother, who had been sick with the smallpox, dead in bed."

"Stories, hon. Stories. Don't get yourself worked up over a bunch of old tall tales. Here, I'll heat us some milk."

Alex stood, laid the shawl in the chair, went over to put milk in a pan and heat it. As he did, he turned to watch Margie's back. She was still staring into the fire, only she wasn't rocking. She was just watching the blaze, and Alex knew, thinking about dying.

After the milk they went to bed, and soon Margie was asleep, snoring like a busted chainsaw. Alex found he could not rest. It was partly due to the storm, it had picked up in intensity. But it was mostly because of what Margie had said about dying. It made him feel lonesome.

Like her, he wasn't so much afraid of dying, as he was of being left alone. She had been his heartbeat for fifty years, and without her, he would only be going through motions of life, not living.

God, he prayed silently. When we go, let us go together.

He turned to look at Margie. Her face looked unlined and strangely young. He was glad she could turn off most anything with sleep. He, on the other hand, could not.

Maybe I'm just hungry.

He slid out of bed, pulled on his pants, shirt and houseshoes; those silly things with the rabbit face and ears his granddaughter had bought him. He padded silently to the kitchen. It was not only the kitchen, it served as den, living room and dining room. The house was only three rooms and a closet, and one of the rooms was a small bathroom. It was times like this that Alex thought he could have done better by Margie. Gotten her a bigger house, for one thing. It was the same house where they had raised their kids, the babies sleeping in a crib here in the kitchen.

He sighed. No matter how hard he had worked, he seemed to stay in the same place. A poor place.

He went to the refrigerator and took out a half-gallon of milk, drank directly from the carton.

He put the carton back and watched the water drip into the bucket. It made him mad to see it. He had let the little house turn into a shack since he retired, and there was no real excuse for it. Surely, he wasn't that tired. It was a wonder Margie didn't complain more.

Well, there was nothing to do about it tonight. But he vowed that when dry weather came, he wouldn't forget about it this time. He'd get up there and fix that damn leak.

Quietly, he rummaged a pan from under the cabinet. He'd have to empty the bucket now if he didn't want it to run over before morning. He ran a little water into the pan before substituting it for the bucket so the drops wouldn't sound so loud.

He opened the front door, went out on the porch, carrying the bucket. He looked out at his mud-pie yard and his old, red wrecker, his white logo on the side of the door faded with time: ALEX BROOKS WRECKING AND MECHANIC SERVICE.

Tonight, looking at the old warhorse, he felt sadder than ever. He missed using it the way it was meant to be used. For work. Now it was nothing more than transportation. Before he retired, his tools and hands made a living. Now nothing. Picking up a Social Security check was all that was left.

Leaning over the edge of the porch, he poured the water into the bare and empty flower bed. When he lifted his head and looked at his yard again, and beyond Highway 59, he saw a light. Headlights, actually, looking fuzzy in the rain, like filmed-over amber eyes. They were way out there on the highway, coming from the South, winding their way toward him, moving fast.

Alex thought that whoever was driving that crate was crazy. Cruising like that on bone-dry highways with plenty of sunshine would have been dangerous, but in this weather, they were asking for a crackup.

As the car neared, he could see it was long, black and strangely shaped. He'd never seen anything like it, and he knew cars fairly well. This didn't look like something off the assembly line from Detroit. It had to be foreign.

Miraculously, the car slowed without so much as a quiver or a screech of brakes and tires. In fact, Alex could not even hear its motor, just the faint whispering of rubber on wet cement.

The car came even of the house just as lightning flashed, and in that instant, Alex got a good look at the driver, or at least the shape of the driver outlined in the flash, and he saw that it was a man with a cigar in his mouth and a bowler hat on his head. And the head was turning toward the house.

The lightning flash died, and now there was only the dark shape of the car and the red tip of the cigar jutting at the house. Alex felt stalactites of ice dripping down from the roof of his skull, extended through his body and out the soles of his feet.

The driver hit down on his horn; three sharp blasts that pricked at Alex's mind.

Honk. (visions of blooming roses, withering going black)

Honk. (funerals remembered, loved ones in boxes, going down)

Honk. (worms crawling through rotten flesh)

Then came a silence louder than the horn blasts. The car picked up speed again. Alex watched as its taillights winked away in the blackness. The chill became less chill. The stalactites in his brain and mind melted away.

But as he stood there, Margie's words of earlier that evening came at him in a rush: "Seen Death once . . . buggy slowed down out front . . . cracked his whip *three times* . . . man looked at the house, snapped his fingers *three times* . . . found dead a moment later . . ."

Alex's throat felt as if a pine knot had lodged there. The bucket slipped from his fingers, clattered on the porch and rolled into the flowerbed. He turned into the house and walked briskly toward the bedroom,

(*Can't be, just a wive's tale*)

his hands vibrating with fear,

(*Just a crazy coincidence*)

his stomach churning.

Margie wasn't snoring.

Alex grabbed her shoulder, shook her.

Nothing.

He rolled her on her back and screamed her name.

Nothing.

"Oh, baby. No."

He felt for her pulse.

None.

He put an ear to her chest, listening for a heartbeat (the other half of his life bongos), and there was none.

Quiet. Perfectly quiet.

"You can't . . ." Alex said. "You can't . . . we're supposed to go together . . . got to be that way."

And then it came to him. He had *seen* Death drive by, had *seen* him heading on down the highway.

He came to his feet, snatched his coat from the back of the chair, raced toward the front door. "You won't have her," he said aloud. "You won't."

Grabbing the wrecker keys from the nail beside the door, he leaped to the porch and dashed out into the cold and the rain.

A moment later he was heading down the highway, driving fast and crazy in pursuit of the strange car.

The wrecker was old and not built for speed, but since he kept it well tuned and it had new tires, it ran well over the wet highway. Alex kept pushing the pedal gradually until it met the floor. Faster and faster and faster.

After an hour, he saw Death.

Not the man himself but the license plate. Personalized and clear in his headlights. It read: DEATH / EXEMPT.

The wrecker and the strange black car were the only ones on the road. Alex closed in on him, honked his horn. Death tootled back (not the same horn sound he had given in front of Alex's house), stuck his arm out the window and waved the wrecker around.

Alex went, and when he was alongside the car, he turned his head to look at Death. He could still not see him clearly, but he could make out the shape of his bowler, and when Death turned to look at him, he could see the glowing tip of the cigar, like a bloody bullet wound.

Alex whipped hard right into the car, and Death swerved to the right, then back onto the road. Alex rammed again. The black car's tires hit roadside gravel and Alex swung closer, preventing it from returning to the highway. He rammed yet another time, and the car went into the grass alongside the road, skidded and went sailing down an embankment and into a tree.

Alex braked carefully, backed off the road and got out of the wrecker. He reached a small pipe wrench and a big crescent wrench out from under the seat, slipped the pipe wrench into his coat pocket for insurance, then went charging down the embankment waving the crescent.

Death opened his door and stepped out. The rain had subsided and the moon was peeking through the clouds like a shy child through gossamer curtains. Its light hit Death's round, pink face and made it look like a waxed pomegranate. His cigar hung from his mouth by a tobacco strand.

Glancing up the embankment, he saw an old, but strong-looking black man brandishing a wrench and wearing bunny slippers, charging down at him.

Spitting out the ruined cigar, Death stepped forward, grabbed Alex's wrist and forearm, twisted. The old man went up and over, the wrench went flying from his hand. Alex came down hard on his back, the breath bursting out of him in spurts.

Death leaned over Alex. Up close, Alex could see that the pink face was slightly pocked and that some of the pinkness was due to makeup. That was rich. Death was vain about his appearance. He was wearing a black T-shirt, pants and sneakers, and of course his derby, which had neither been stirred by the wreck or by the ju-jitsu maneuver.

"What's with you, man?" Death asked.

Alex wheezed, tried to catch his breath. "You . . . can't . . . have . . . her."

"Who? What are you talking about?"

"Don't play . . . dumb with me." Alex raised up on one elbow, his wind returning. "You're Death and you took my Margie's soul."

Death straightened. "So you know who I am. All right. But what of it? I'm only doing my job."

"It ain't her time."

"My list says it is, and my list is never wrong."

Alex felt something hard pressing against his hip, realized

what it was. The pipe wrench. Even the throw Death had put on him had not hurled it from his coat pocket. It had lodged there and the pocket had shifted beneath his hip, making his old bones hurt all the worse.

Alex made as to roll over, freed the pocket beneath him, shot his hand inside and produced the pipe wrench. He hurled it at Death, struck him just below the brim of the bowler and sent him stumbling back. This time the bowler fell off. Death's forehead was bleeding.

Before Death could collect himself, Alex was up and rushing. He used his head as a battering ram and struck Death in the stomach, knocking him to the ground. He put both knees on Death's arms, pinning them, clenched his throat with his strong, old hands.

"I ain't never hurt nobody before," Alex said. "Don't want to now. I didn't want to hit you with that wrench, but you give Margie back."

Death's eyes showed no expression at first, but slowly a light seemed to go on behind them. He easily pulled his arms out from under Alex's knees, reached up, took hold of the old man's wrist and pulled the hands away from his throat.

"You old rascal," Death said. "You outsmarted me."

Death flopped Alex over on his side, then stood up to once more lord over the man. Grinning, he turned, stooped to recover his bowler, but he never laid a hand on it.

Alex moved like a crab, scissored his legs and caught Death above and behind the knees, twisted, brought him down on his face.

Death raised up on his palms and crawled from behind Alex's legs like a snake, effortlessly. This time he grabbed the hat and put it on his head and stood up. He watched Alex carefully.

"I don't frighten you much, do I?" Death asked.

Alex noted that the wound on Death's forehead had vanished. There wasn't even a drop of blood. "No," Alex said. "You don't frighten me much. I just want my Margie back."

"All right," Death said.

Alex sat bolt upright.

"What?"

"I said, all right. For a time. Not many have outsmarted me, pinned me to the ground. I give you credit, and you've got courage. I like that. I'll give her back. For a time. Come here."

Death walked over to the car that was not from Detroit. Alex got to his feet and followed. Death took the keys out of the igni-

tion, moved to the trunk, worked the key in the lock. It popped
up with a hiss.

Inside were stacks and stacks of match boxes. Death moved his
hand over them, like a careful man selecting a special vegetable
at the supermarket. His fingers came to rest on a matchbox that
looked to Alex no different than the others.

Death handed Alex the matchbox. "Her soul's in here, old man.
You stand over her bed, open the box. Okay?"

"That's it?"

"That's it. Now get out of here before I change my mind. And
remember, I'm giving her back to you. But just for a while."

Alex started away, holding the matchbox carefully. As he
walked past Death's car, he saw the dents he had knocked in the
side with his wrecker were popping out. He turned to look at
Death, who was closing the trunk.

'Don't suppose you'll need a tow out of here?"

Death smiled thinly. "Not hardly."

Alex stood over their bed; the bed where they had loved, slept,
talked and dreamed. He stood there with the matchbox in his
hand, his eyes on Margie's cold face. He ever so gently eased the
box open. A small flash of blue light, like Peter Pan's friend Tinker
Bell, rushed out of it and hit Margie's lips. She made a sharp inhal-
ing sound and her chest rose. Her eyes came open. She turned
and looked at Alex and smiled.

"My lands, Alex. What are you doing there, and half-dressed?
What you been up to . . . is that a matchbox?"

Alex tried to speak, but he found he could not. All he could do
was grin.

"Have you gone nuts?" she asked.

"Maybe a little." He sat down on the bed and took her hand. "I
love you Margie."

"And I love you . . . you been drinking?"

"No."

Then came the overwhelming sound of Death's horn. One
harsh blast that shook the house, and the headbeams shone
brightly through the window and the cracks and lit up the shack
like a cheap nightclub act.

"Who in the world?" Margie asked.

"Him. But he said . . . stay here."

Alex got his shotgun out of the closet. He went out on the
porch. Death's car was pointed toward the house, and the headbeams seemed to hold Alex, like a fly in butter.

Death was standing on the bottom porch step, waiting.

Alex pointed the shotgun at him. "You git. You gave her back. You gave your word."

"And I kept it. But I said for a while."

"That wasn't any time at all."

"It was all I could give. My present."

"Short time like that's worse than no time at all."

"Be good about it, Alex. Let her go. I got records and they have to be kept. I'm going to take her anyway, you understand that?"

"Not tonight, you ain't." Alex pulled back the hammers on the shotgun. "Not tomorrow night neither. Not anytime soon."

"That gun won't do you any good, Alex. You know that. You can't stop Death. I can stand here and snap my fingers three times, or click my tongue, or go back to the car and honk my horn, and she's as good as mine. But I'm trying to reason with you, Alex. You're a brave man. I did you a favor because you bested me. I didn't want to just take her back without telling you. That's why I came here to talk. But she's got to go. Now."

Alex lowered the shotgun. "Can't . . . can't you take me in her place? You can do that can't you?"

"I . . . I don't know. It's highly irregular."

"Yeah, you can do that. Take me. Leave Margie."

"Well, I suppose."

The screen door creaked open and Margie stood there in her housecoat. "You're forgetting, Alex, I don't want to be left alone."

"Go in the house, Margie," Alex said.

"I know who this is. I heard you talking, Mr. Death, I don't want you taking my Alex. I'm the one you came for, I ought to have the right to go."

There was a pause, no one speaking. Then Alex said, "Take both of us. You can do that, can't you? I know I'm on that list of yours, and pretty high up. Man my age couldn't have too many years left. You can take me a little before my time, can't you? Well, can't you?"

Margie and Alex sat in their rocking chairs, their shawls over their knees. There was no fire in the fireplace. Behind them the bucket collected water and outside the wind whistled. They held hands. Death stood in front of them. He was holding a King Edward cigar box.

"You're sure of this?" Death asked. "You don't both have to go."

Alex looked at Margie, then back at Death.

"We're sure," he said. "Do it."

Death nodded. He opened the cigar box and held it out on one palm. He used his free hand to snap his fingers.

Once. (*the wind picked up, howled*)

Twice. (*the rain beat like drumsticks on the roof*)

Three times. (*lightning ripped and thunder roared*)

"And in you go," Death said.

A little blue light came out of the couple's mouths and jetted into the cigar box with a thump, and Death closed the lid.

The bodies of Alex and Margie slumped and their heads fell together between the rocking chairs. Their fingers were still entwined.

Death put the box under his arm and went out to the car. The rain beat on his derby hat and the wind sawed at his bare arms and T-shirt. He didn't seem to mind.

Opening the trunk, he started to put the box inside, then hesitated.

He closed the trunk.

"Damn," he said, "if I'm not getting to be a sentimental old fool."

He opened the box. Two blue lights rose out of it, elongated, touched ground. They took on the shape of Alex and Margie. They glowed against the night.

"Want to ride up front?" Death asked.

"That would be nice," Margie said.

"Yes, nice," Alex said.

Death opened the door and Alex and Margie slid inside. Death climbed in behind the wheel. He checked the clipboard dangling from the dash. There was a woman in a Tyler hospital, dying of brain damage. That would be his next stop.

He put the clipboard down and started the car that was not from Detroit.

"Sounds well-tuned," Alex said.

"I try to keep it that way," Death said.

They drove out of there then, and as they went, Death broke into song. "Row, row row your boat, gently down the stream," and Margie and Alex chimed in with, "Merrily, merrily, merrily, life is but a dream."

Off they went down the highway, the taillights fading, the song dying, the black metal of the car melting into the fabric of night, and then there was only the whispery sound of good tires on wet cement and finally not even that. Just the blowing sound of the wind and the rain.

A gaming company decided to produce a hard-boiled anthology to go with one of their games, and they asked me if I'd like to do a story. I decided to do something really dark and nutty. They liked it, but wanted the word "cunt" taken out of it. Since the story is filled with pretty nasty stuff I wondered why. On rereading I saw that the cunt hair in question belonged to the Virgin Mary.

So that was it. I guess the Virgin Mary was all smooth down there; maybe she was an early proponent of waxing.

Oh well, it didn't bother me. I've returned the cunt hair to its rightful place. Should I have said pubic hair? Maybe that's what they replaced it with. I don't remember. I could have said pussy hair. Or snatch hair, but I didn't. I could have said all kinds of things, but I didn't, I said cunt hair.

Funny, the stuff you remember about some stories.

The idea for the story came from reading about Nazi theft during and after World War II, and how some Allied soldiers decided to steal from the thieves. Among the items supposedly missing was some sort of icon that contained a hair from the Virgin Mary. If this hair was from her head, or another part of her anatomy, it was not determined. I, of course, made my own determination.

BOOTY AND THE BEAST

"WHERE DO YOU KEEP THE SUGAR?" MULROY said, as he pulled open cabinet doors and scrounged about.

"Go to hell," Standers said.

"That's no way to talk," Mulroy said. "I'm a guest in your house. A guest isn't supposed to be treated that way. All I asked was where's the sugar?"

"And I said go to hell. And you're not a guest."

Mulroy, who was standing in the kitchen part of the mobile home, stopped and stared at Standers in the living room. He had tied Standers's hands together and stretched them out so he could loop the remainder of the lamp cord around a doorknob. He had removed Standers's boots and tied his feet with a sheet, wrapped them several times. The door Standers was bound to was the front door of the trailer and it was open. Standers was tied so that he was sitting with his back against the door, his arms stretched and strained above him. Mulroy thought he ought to have done it a little neater, a little less painful, then he got to thinking about what he was going to do and decided it didn't matter, and if it did, tough.

"You got any syrup or honey?"

This time Standers didn't answer at all.

Mulroy neatly closed the cabinet doors and checked the refrigerator. He found a large plastic see-through bear nearly full of syrup. He squeezed the bear and shot some of the syrup on his finger and tasted it. Maple.

"This'll do. You know, I had time, I'd fix me up some pancakes and use this. I taste this, it makes me think pancakes. They got like an I-Hop in town?"

Standers didn't answer.

Mulroy strolled over to Standers and set the plastic bear on the floor and took off his cowboy hat and nice Western jacket. He tossed the hat on the couch and carefully hung his jacket on the back of a chair. The pistol in the holster under his arm dangled like a malignancy.

Mulroy took a moment to look out the open door at the sunparched grass and the fire ant hills in the yard. Here was a bad place for a mobile home. For a house. For anything. No neighbors. No trees, just lots of land with stumps. Mulroy figured the trees had been cut down for pulp money. Mulroy knew that's what he'd have done.

Because there were no trees, the mobile home was hot, even with the air conditioner going. And having the front door open didn't help much, way it was sucking out what cool air there was.

Mulroy watched as a mockingbird lit in the grass. It appeared on the verge of heat stroke. It made one sad sound, then went silent. Way, way out, Mulroy could hear cars on the highway, beyond the thin line of pine trees.

Mulroy reached down and unbuckled Standers's pants. He tugged down the pants and underwear, exposing Standers. He got hold of the bear and squeezed some of the syrup onto Standers's privates.

Standers said, "Whatcha doin', fixin' breakfast?"

"Oh ho," Mulroy said. "I am cut to the quick. Listen here. No use talkin' tough. This isn't personal. It's business. I'm going to do what I got to do, so you might as well not take it personal. I don't have anything against you."

"Yeah, well, great. I feel a hell of a lot better."

Mulroy eased down to Standers's feet, where his toes were exposed. He put the syrup on Standers's toes. He squirted some on Standers's head.

Mulroy went outside then. The mockingbird flew away. Mulroy walked around and looked at the fire ant hills. Fire ants were a bitch. They were tenacious bastards, and when they stung you, it was some kind of sting. There were some people so allergic to the little critters, one bite would make them go toes up. And if there were enough of them, and they were biting on you, it could be Goodbye City no matter if you were allergic or not. It was nasty poison.

Mulroy reached in his back pocket, pulled out a half-used sack of Red Man, opened it, pinched some out and put it in his mouth. He chewed a while, then spit on one of the ant hills. Agitated ants boiled out of the hill and spread in his direction. He walked off a ways and used the toe of his boot to stir up another hill, then another. He squirted syrup from the bear on one of the hills and ran a thin, dribbling stream of syrup back to the mobile home, up the steps, across the floor and directed the stream across Standers's thigh and onto his love apples. He said, "A fire ant hurts worse than a regular ant, but it isn't any different when it comes to sweets. He likes them. They like them. There're thousands of ants out there. Maybe millions. Who the hell knows. I mean, how you gonna count mad ants, way they're running around?"

For the first time since Mulroy first surprised Standers — pretending to be a Bible salesman, then giving him an overhand right, followed by a left uppercut to the chin — he saw true concern on Standers's face.

Mulroy said, "They hurt they bite you on the arm, leg, foot, something like that. But they get on your general, crawl between your toes, where it's soft, or nip your face around the lips, eyes and nose, it's some kind of painful. Or so I figure. You can tell me in a minute."

Suddenly, Mulroy cocked his head. He heard a car coming along the long road that wound up to the trailer. He went and looked out the door, came back, sat down on the couch and chewed his tobacco.

A few moments later the car parked behind Mulroy's car. A door slammed, a young slim woman in a short tight dress with hair the color of fire ants came through the door and looked first at Mulroy, then Standers. She pivoted on her high heels and waved her little handbag at Standers, said, "Hey, honey. What's that on your schlong?"

"Syrup," Mulroy said, got up, pushed past the woman and spat a stream of tobacco into the yard.

"Bitch," Standers said.

"The biggest," she said. Then to Mulroy: "Syrup on his tallywhacker?"

Mulroy stood in the doorway and nodded toward the yard. "The ants."

The woman looked outside, said, "I get it. Very imaginative." She eye'd the plastic bear where Mulroy had placed it on the arm of the couch. "Oh, that little bear is the cutest."

"You like it," Mulroy said. "Take it with you." Then to Standers he said, "You think maybe now you want to talk to us?"

Standers considered, decided either way he was screwed. He didn't tell, he was going to suffer, then die. Maybe he told what they wanted, he'd just die. He could make that part of the deal, and hope they kept their side of the bargain. Not that there was any reason they should. Still, Mulroy, he might do it. As for Babe, he couldn't trust her any kind of way.

Nonetheless, looking at her now, she was certainly beautiful. And his worms-eye view right up her dress was exceptional, considering Babe didn't wear panties and was a natural redhead.

"I was you," Mulroy said, "I'd start talking. Where's the loot?"

Standers took a deep breath. If he'd only kept his mouth shut, hadn't tried to impress Babe, he wouldn't be in this mess.

During World War II his dad had been assigned to guard Nazi treasure in Germany. His dad had confiscated a portion of the treasure, millions of dollars worth, and shipped it home to East Texas. A number of religious icons had been included in the theft, like a decorated box that was supposed to contain a hair from the Virgin Mary's head.

Standers's father had seen all this as spoils of war, not theft. When he returned home, much of the treasure was split up between relatives or sold. After the war the Germans had raised a stink and the U.S. government ended up making Standers's dad return what was left. The Germans offered to pay his father a price for it to keep things mellow. A flat million, a fraction of what it was worth.

Divided among family members, that million was long gone. But there was something else. Standers's Dad hadn't given up all the treasure. There were still a few unreturned items; gold bars and the so-called hair of the Virgin Mary.

Early last year the Germans raised yet another stink about items still missing. It had been in the papers and Standers's family had been named, and since he was the last of his family line, it was assumed he might know where this treasure was. Reporters came out. He told them he didn't know anything about any treasure. He laughed about how if he had treasure he wouldn't be living in a trailer in a cow pasture. The reporters believed him, or so it seemed from the way it read in the papers.

A month later he met Babe, in a store parking lot. She was changing a tire and just couldn't handle it, and would he help her. He had, and while he did the work he got to look up the line of her leg and find out she wore nothing underneath the short dresses she preferred. And she knew how to talk him up and lead him on. She was a silver-tongued, long-legged slut with heaven between her legs. He should have known better.

One night, after making love, Babe mentioned the stuff in the papers, and Standers, still high on flesh friction, feeling like a big man, admitted he had a large share of the money socked away in a foreign bank, and the rest, some gold bars, and the box containing the hair from the Virgin Mary, hidden away here in East Texas.

The relationship continued, but Standers began to worry when Babe kept coming back to the booty. She wanted to know where it was. She didn't ask straight out; she danced around matters; he didn't talk. He'd been stupid enough, no use compounding the matter. She was after the money, and not him, and he felt like a jackass. He doubled up on the sex for a while, then sent her away.

This morning, posing as a Bible salesman, Mulroy had shown up, clocked him, tied him up, introduced himself and tried to get him to tell the whereabouts of the loot. When Babe came through the door, it all clicked in place.

"I got a question," Standers said.

"So do we," Mulroy said. "Where's the spoils? We don't even want the money you got in a foreign bank. . . . Well, we want it, but that might be too much trouble. We'll settle for the other. What did you tell Babe it was? Gold bars and a cunt hair off the Virgin Mary?"

"I just want to know," Standers continued, "were you and Babe working together from the start?"

Mulroy laughed. "She was on her own, but when she couldn't get what she wanted from you, she needed someone to provide some muscle."

"So you're just another one she's conned," Standers said.

"No," Mulroy said, "you were conned. I'm a business partner. I'm not up for being conned. You wouldn't do that to me, would you, Babe?"

Babe smiled.

"Yeah, well, I guess you would," Mulroy said. "But I ain't gonna let you. You see, I know she's on the con. Knew it from the start. You didn't. Conning the marks is what I do for a living."

"It was all bullshit," Standers said. "I just told her that to sound big. She gets you in bed, she makes your dick think it's the president. I was tryin' to keep that pussy comin', is all. I had money, you think I'd be living like this?"

"If you were smart, you would," Mulroy said.

"I'm not smart," Standers said. "I sell cars. And that's it."

"Man," Mulroy said, "you tell that so good I almost believe it. Almost. Shit, I bet you could sell me an old Ford with a flat tire and missing transmission. Almost . . . hey, let's do it like this. You give the location of the stuff, and we let you go, and we even send you a little of the money. You know, ten thousand dollars. Isn't much, but it beats what you might get. I think that's a pretty good deal, all things considered."

"Yeah, I'll wait at the mail box for the ten thousand," Standers said.

"That's a pretty hard one to believe, isn't it?" Mulroy said. "But you can't blame me for tryin'. Hell, I got to go to the can. Watch him, Babe."

When Mulroy left the room, Standers said, "Nice, deal, huh? You and him get the loot, split it fifty-fifty."

Babe didn't say anything. She went over and sat on the couch.

"I can do you a better deal than he can," Standers said. "Get rid of him, and I'll show you the loot and split it fifty-fifty."

"What's better about that?" Babe said.

"I know where it is," Standers said. "It'd go real easy."

"I got time to go less easy, I want to take it," she said.

"Yeah," Standers said. "But why take it? Sooner you get it, sooner we spend it."

Mulroy came back into the room. Babe picked the plastic bear off the couch arm and went over to the refrigerator and opened it. She put the bear inside and got out a soft drink and pulled the tab on the can. "Man, I'm hungry," she said, then swigged the drink.

"What?" Mulroy said.

"Hungry," Babe said. "You know. I'd like to eat. You hungry?"

"Yeah," Mulroy said. "I was thinking about pancakes, but I kinda got other things on my mind here. We finish this, we'll eat. Besides, there's food here."

"Yeah, you want to eat this slop?" Babe said. "Go get us a pizza."

"A pizza?" Mulroy said. "You want I should get a pizza? We're fixin' to torture a guy with fire ants, maybe cut him up a little, set him on fire, whatever comes to mind that's fun, and you want me to drive out and get a fuckin' pizza? Honey, you need to stop lettin' men dick you in the ear. It's startin' to mess up your brain. Drink your soda pop."

"Canadian bacon, and none of those little fishies," Babe said. "Lots of cheese, and get the thick chewy crust."

"You got to be out of your beautiful red head."

"It'll take a while anyway," Babe said. "I don't think a couple of ant bites'll make him cave. And I'd rather not get tacky with cuttin' and burnin', we can avoid it. Whatever we do, it'll take some time, and I don't want to do it on an empty stomach. I'm tellin' you, I'm seriously and grown-up hungry here."

"You don't know fire ants, Baby," Mulroy said. "It ain't gonna take long at all."

"It's like, what, fifteen minutes into town?" Babe said, sipping her drink. "I could use a pizza. That's what I want. What's the big deal?"

Mulroy scratched the back of his neck, looked out the doorway. The ants were at the steps, following the trail of syrup.

"They'll be on him before I get back," he said.

"So," Babe said, "I've heard a grown man scream before. He tells me somethin', you get back, we'll go, eat the pizza on the way."

Mulroy used a finger to clear the tobacco out of his cheek. He flipped it into the yard. He said, "All right. I guess I could eat." Mulroy put on his coat and hat and smiled at Babe and went out.

When Mulroy's car was way out on the drive, near the highway, Babe opened her purse and took out a small .38 and pointed it at Standers. "I figure this will make you a more balanced kind of partner. You remember that. You mess with me, I'll shoot your dick off."

"All right," Standers said.

Babe put the revolver in her other hand, got a flick blade knife out of her purse, used it to cut the sheets around Standers's ankles. She cut the lamp cord off his wrist.

Standers stood, and without pulling his pants up, hopped to the sink. He got the hand towel off the rack and wet it and used it to clean the syrup off his privates, his feet and head. He pulled up his pants, got his socks, sat on the couch and put his boots back on.

"We got to hurry," Babe said. "Mulroy, he's got a temper. I seen him shoot a dog once for peeing on one of his hub caps."

"Let me get my car keys," Standers said.

"We'll take my car," she said. "You'll drive."

They went outside and she gave him the keys and they drove off.

As they drove onto the highway, Mulroy, who was parked behind a swathe of trees, poked a new wad of tobacco into his mouth and massaged it with his teeth.

Babe had sold out immediately, like he thought she would. Doing it this way, having them lead him to the treasure was a hell of a lot better than sitting around in a hot trailer watching fire ants crawl on a man's balls. And this way he didn't have to watch his back all the time. That Babe, what a kidder. She was so greedy, she thought he'd fall for that lame pizza gag. She'd been winning too long; she wasn't thinking enough moves ahead anymore.

Mulroy rode well back of them, putting his car behind other cars when he could. He figured his other advantage was they weren't expecting him. He thought about the treasure and what he could do with it while he drove.

Until Babe came along, he had been a private detective, doing nickel and dime divorces out of Tyler; taking pictures of people doing the naked horizontal mambo. It wasn't a lot of fun. And the little cons he pulled on the side, clever as they were, were bullshit money, hand to mouth.

He made the score he wanted from all this, he'd go down to Mexico, buy him a place with a pool, rent some women. One for each day of the week, and each one with a different sexual skill, and maybe a couple who could cook. He was damn sure tired of his own cooking. He wanted to eat a lot and get fat and lay around and poke the señoritas. This all fell through, he thought he might try and be an evangelist or some kind of politician or a lawman with a regular check.

Standers drove for a couple of hours, through three or four towns, and Mulroy followed. Eventually, Standers pulled off the highway, onto a blacktop. Mulroy gave him time to get ahead, then took the road too. With no cars to put between them and himself, Mulroy cruised along careful like. Finally he saw Standers way up ahead on a straight stretch. Standers veered off the road and into the woods.

Mulroy pulled to the side of the road and waited a minute, then followed. The road in the woods was a narrow dirt one, and Mulroy had only gone a little ways when he stopped his car and got out and started walking. He had a hunch the road was a short one, and he didn't want to surprise them too early.

Standers drove down the road until it dead-ended at some woods and a load of trash someone had dumped. He got out and Babe got out. Babe was still holding her gun.

"You're tellin' me it's hidden under the trash?" she said. "You better not be jackin' with me, honey."

"It's not under the trash. Come on."

They went into the woods and walked along awhile, came to an old white house with a bad roof. It was surrounded by vines and trees and the porch was falling down.

"You keep a treasure here?" she said.

Standers went up on the porch, got a key out of his pocket and unlocked the door. Inside, pigeons fluttered and went out holes in the windows and the roof. A snake darted into a hole in the floor. There were spiders and spider webs everywhere. The floor was dotted with rat turds.

Standers went carefully across the floor and into a bedroom. Babe followed, holding her revolver at the ready. The room was better kept than the rest of the house. She could see where boards had been replaced in the floor. The ceiling was good here. There were no windows, just plyboard over the spots where they ought to be. There was a dust-covered desk, a bed with ratty covers, and an armchair covered in a faded flower print.

Standers got down on his hands and knees, reached under the bed and tugged diligently at a large suitcase.

"It's under the bed?" Babe said.

Standers opened the suitcase. There was a crowbar in it. He got the crowbar out. Babe said, "Watch yourself. I don't want you should try and hit me. It could mess up my makeup."

Standers carried the crowbar to the closet, opened it. The closet was sound. There was a groove in the floor. Standers fitted the end of the crowbar into the groove and lifted. The flooring came up. Standers pulled the trap door out of the closet and put it on the floor.

Babe came over for a look, careful to keep an eye on Standers and a tight grip on the gun. Where the floor had been was a large metal-lined box. Standers opened the box so she could see what was inside.

What she saw inside made her breath snap out. Gold bars and a shiny wooden box about the size of a box of cigars.

"That's what's got the hair in it?" she asked.

"That's what they say. Inside is another box with some glass in it. You can look through the glass and see the hair. Box was made by the Catholic Church to hold the hair. For all I know it's an armpit hair off one of the Popes. Who's to say? But it's worth money."

"How much money?"

"It depends on who you're dealing with. A milllon. Two to three million. Twenty-five million."

"Let's deal with that last guy."

"The fence won't give money like that. We could sell the gold bars, use that to finance a trip to Germany. There're people there would pay plenty for the box."

"A goddamn hair," Babe said. "Can you picture that?"

"Yeah, I can picture that." Babe and Standers turned as Mulroy spoke, stepped into the room cocking his revolver with one hand, pushing his hat back with the other.

Mulroy said, "Put the gun down, Babe, or I part your hair about two inches above your nose."

Babe smiled at him, lowered her gun. "See," she said. "I got him to take me here, no trouble. Now we can take the treasure."

Mulroy smiled. "You are some kind of kidder. I never thought you'd let me have fifty percent anyway. I was gonna do you in from the start. Same as you were with me. Drop the gun, Babe."

Babe dropped the revolver. "You got me all wrong," she said.

"No I don't," Mulroy said.

"I guess you didn't go for pizza," Standers said.

"No, but I tell you what," Mulroy said. "I'm pretty hungry right now, so let's get this over with. I'll make it short and sweet. A bullet through the head for you, Standers. A couple more just to make sure you aren't gonna be some kind of living cabbage. As for you, Babe. There's a bed here, and I figure I might as well get all the treasure I can get. Look at it this way. It's the last nice thing you can do for anybody, so you might as well make it nice. If nothing else, be selfish and enjoy it."

"Well," Standers said, looking down at Babe's revolver on the floor. "You might as well take the gun."

Standers stepped out from behind Babe and kicked her gun toward Mulroy, and no sooner had he done that, than he threw the crowbar.

Mulroy looked down at the revolver sliding his way, then looked up. As he did, the crowbar hit him directly on the bridge of the nose and dropped him. He fell unconscious with his back against the wall.

Soon as Mulroy fell, Babe reached for her revolver. Standers kicked her legs out from under her, but she scuttled like a crab and got hold of it and shot in Standers's direction. The shot missed, but it stopped Standers.

Babe got up, pulled her dress down and smiled. "Looks like I'm ahead."

She turned suddenly and shot the unconscious Mulroy behind the ear. Mulroy's hat, which had maintained its position on his head, came off as he nodded forward. A wad of tobacco rolled over his lip and landed in his lap. Blood ran down his cheek and onto his nice Western coat.

Babe smiled again, spoke to Standers. "Now I just got you. And I need you to carry those bars out of here."

Standers said. "Why should I help?"

"Cause I'll let you go."

Standers snorted.

"All right then, because I'll shoot you in the knees and leave you here if you don't. That way, you go slow. Help me, I'll make it quick."

"Damn, that's a tough choice."

"Let's you and me finish up in a way you don't have to suffer, babycakes."

Standers nodded, said, "You promise to make it quick?"

"Honey, it'll happen so fast you won't know it happened."

"I can't take the strain," Standers said. He pointed to the room adjacent to the bedroom. "There's a wheelbarrow in there. It's the way I haul stuff out. I get that, we can make a few trips, get it over with. I don't like to think about dying for a long time. Let's just get it done."

"Fine with me," Babe said.

Standers started toward the other room. Babe said, "Hold on."

She bent down and got Mulroy's gun. Now she had one in either hand. She waved Standers back against the wall and peeked in the room he had indicated. There was a wheelbarrow in there.

"All right, let's do it," she said.

Standers stepped quickly inside, and as Babe started to enter the room, he said sharply, "Don't step there!"

Babe held her foot in mid-air, and Standers slapped her closest gun arm down and grabbed it, slid behind her and pinned her other arm. He slid his hands down and took the guns from her. He used his knee to shove her forward. She stumbled and the floor cracked and she went through and spun and there was another crack, but it wasn't the floor. She screamed and moaned something awful. After a moment, she stopped bellowing and turned to Standers, she opened her mouth to speak, but nothing came out.

Standers said, "What's the matter? Kind of run out of lies? There ain't nothing you can say would interest me. It's just a shame to have to kill a good-lookin' piece like you."

"Please," she said, but Standers shot her in the face with Mulroy's gun and she fell backwards, her broken leg still in the gap in the floor. Her other leg flew up and came down and her heel hit the floor with a slap. Her dress hiked up and exposed her privates.

"Not a bad way to remember you," Standers said. "It's the only part of you that wasn't a cheat."

Standers took the box containing the hair out of the closet, put the closet back in shape, got the wheelbarrow and used it to haul Babe, her purse, and the guns out of there and through the woods to a pond his relatives had built fifty years ago.

He dumped Babe beside the pond, went back for Mulroy and dumped him beside her. He got Mulroy's car keys out of his pocket and Babe's keys out of her purse.

Standers walked back to Babe's car and drove it to the edge of the pond, rolled down the windows a little, put her and Mulroy in the back seat with her purse and the guns, then he put the car in neutral. He pushed it off in the water. It was a deep, dirty pond. The car went down quick.

Standers waited at the shack until almost dark, then took the box containing the hair, walked back, found Mulroy's car and drove it out of there. He stopped the car beside a dirt road about a mile from his house and wiped it clean with a handkerchief he found in the front seat. He got the box out of the car and walked back to his trailer.

It was dark when he got there. The door was still open. He went inside, locked up and set the box with the hair on the counter beside the sink. He opened the box and took out the smaller box and studied the hair through the smeary glass.

He thought to himself: What if this is the Virgin Mary's hair? It could even be an ass hair, but if it's the Virgin Mary's . . . well, it's the Virgin Mary's. And what if it's a dog hair? It'll still sell for the same. It was time to get rid of it. He would book a flight to Germany tomorrow, search out the right people, sell it, sock what he got from it away in his foreign bank account, come back and fence the gold bars and sell all his land, except for the chunk with the house and pond on it. He'd fill the pond in himself with a rented backhoe and dozer, plant some trees on top of it, let it set while he lived abroad.

Simple, but a good plan, he thought.

Standers drank a glass of water and took the box and lay down on the couch snuggling it. He was exhausted. Fear of death did that to a fella. He closed his eyes and went to sleep immediately.

A short time later he awoke in pain. His whole body ached. He leaped up, dropping the box. He began to slap at his legs and chest, tear at his clothes.

Jesus. The fire ants! His entire body was covered with the bastards.

Standers felt queezy. My God, he thought. I'm having a reaction. I'm allergic to the little shits.

He got his pants and underwear peeled down to his ankles, but he couldn't get them over his boots. He began to hop about the room. He hit the light switch and saw the ants all over the place. They had followed the stream of syrup, and then they had found him on the couch and gone after him.

Standers screamed and slapped, hopped over and grabbed the box from the floor and jerked open the front door. He held the box in one hand and tugged at his pants with the other, but as he was going down the steps, he tripped, fell forward and landed on his head and lay there with his head and knees holding him up. He tried to stand, but couldn't. He realized he had broken his neck, and from the waist down he was paralyzed.

Oh God, he thought. The ants. Then he thought. Well, at least I can't feel them, but he found he could feel them on his face. His face still had sensation.

It's temporary, the paralysis will pass, he told himself, but it didn't. The ants began to climb into his hair and swarm over his lips. He batted at them with his eyelashes and blew at them with his mouth, but it didn't do any good. They swarmed him. He tried to scream, but with his neck bent the way it was, his throat constricted somewhat, he couldn't make a good noise. And when he opened his mouth the furious little ants swarmed in and bit his tongue, which swelled instantly.

Oh Jesus, he thought. Jesus and the Virgin Mary.

But Jesus wasn't listening. Neither was the Virgin Mary.

The night grew darker and the ants grew more intense, but Standers was dead long before morning.

*   *   *

About ten A.M. a car drove up in Standers's drive and a fat man in a cheap blue suit wlth a suitcase full of bibles got out; a real bible salesman with a craving for drink.

The bible salesman, whose name was Bill Longstreet, had his mind on business. He needed to sell a couple of moderate-priced bibles so he could get a drink. He'd spent his last money in Beaumont, Texas on a double, and now he needed another.

Longstreet strolled around his car, whistling, trying to put up a happy Christian front. Then he saw Standers in the front yard supported by his head and knees, his ass exposed, his entire body swarming with ants. The corpse was swollen up and spotted with bites. Standers's neck was twisted so that Longstreet could see the right side of his face, and his right eye was nothing more than an ant cavern, and the lips were eaten away and the nostrils were a tunnel for the ants. They were coming in one side, and going out the other.

Longstreet dropped his sample case, staggered back to his car, climbed on the hood and just sat there and looked for a long time.

Finally, he got over it. He looked about and saw no one other than the dead man. The door to the trailer was open. Longstreet got off the car. Watching for ants, he went as close as he had courage and yelled toward the open door a few times.

No one came out.

Longstreet licked his lips, eased over to Standers and moving quickly, stomping his feet, he reached in Standers's back pocket and pulled out his wallet.

Longstreet rushed back to his car and got up on the hood. He looked in the wallet. There were two ten dollar bills and a couple of ones. He took the money, folded it neatly and put it in his coat pocket. He tossed the wallet back at Standers, got down off the car and got his case and put it on the back seat. He got behind the wheel, was about to drive off, when he saw the little box near Standers's swollen hand.

Longstreet sat for a moment, then got out, ran over, grabbed the box, and ran back to the car, beating the ants off as he went. He got behind the wheel, opened the box and found another box with a little crude glass window fashioned into it. There was something small and dark and squiggly behind the glass. He wondered what it was.

He knew a junk store bought stuff like this. He might get a couple bucks from the lady who ran it. He tossed it in the back seat, cranked up the car and drove into town and had a drink. He had two drinks. Then three. It was nearly dark by the time he came out of the bar and wobbled out to his car. He started it up and drove out onto the highway right in front of a speeding semi.

The truck hit Longstreet's car and turned it into a horseshoe and sent it spinning across the road, into a telephone pole. The car ricocheted off the pole, back onto the road and the semi, which was slamming hard on its brakes, clipped it again. This time Longstreet and his car went through a barbed wire fence and spun about in a pasture and stopped near a startled bull.

The bull looked in the open car window and sniffed and went away. The semi driver parked and got out and ran over and looked in the window himself.

Longstreet's brains were all over the car and his face had lost a lot of definition. His mouth was dripping bloody teeth. He had fallen with his head against an open bible. Later, when he was hauled off, the bible had to go with him. Blood had plastered it to the side of his head, and when the ambulance arrived, the blood had clotted and the bible was even better attached; way it was on there, you would have thought it was some kind of bizarre growth Longstreet had been born with. Doctors at the hospital wouldn't mess with it. What was the point. Fucker was dead and they didn't know him.

At the funeral home they hosed his head down with warm water and yanked the bible off his face and threw it away.

Later on, well after the funeral, Longstreet's widow inherited what was left of Longstreet's car, which she gave to the junkyard. She burned the bibles and all of Longstreet's clothes. The box with the little box in it she opened and examined. She couldn't figure what was behind the glass. She used a screwdriver to get the glass off, tweezers to pinch out the hair.

She held the hair in the light, twisted it this way and that. She couldn't make out what it was. A bug leg, maybe. She tossed the hair in the commode and flushed it. She put the little box in the big box and threw it in the trash.

Later yet, she collected quite a bit of insurance money from Longstreet's death. She bought herself a new car and some see-through panties and used the rest to finance her lover's plans to open a used car lot in downtown Beaumont, but it didn't work out. He used the money to finance himself and she never saw him again.

This is one of my favorites of my own work. It's based on a number of true incidents, stories I heard, and damn lies. Certain kinds of stupidity amaze me, and I can't help but feel these types deserve exploring. I think the happily stupid, those people who are that way because they choose to be, or are too lazy or uninspired to be otherwise, are among the scariest people in the world. They are also, if you squint slightly, and can deal with a lot of sadness, pretty funny.

What amazes me about folks like this is the fact they can repeat the same bad mistakes time after time after time. Or if they avoid the repetition of a mistake, they have an amazing knack for choosing something just as, or even more stupid than their last choice. That really takes effort of a sort, don't you think? Or, maybe it doesn't.

Anyway, stupidity and adolescence, which, unfortunately, often go hand in hand, welded together with a rush of hormones often result in some of the most outlandish behaviors. This story is an example of all those elements at work.

STEPPIN' OUT, SUMMER, '68

BUDDY DRANK ANOTHER SWIG OF BEER AND when he brought the bottle down he said to Jake and Wilson, "I could sure use some pussy."

"We could all use some," Wilson said, "problem is we don't never get any."

"That's the way I see it too," Jake said.

"You don't get any," Buddy said. "I get plenty, you can count on that."

"Uh huh," Wilson said. "You talk pussy plenty good, but I don't ever see you with a date. I ain't never even seen you walking a dog, let alone a girl. You don't even have a car, so how you gonna get with a girl?"

"That's the way I see it too," Jake said.

"You see what you want," Buddy said. "I'm gonna be getting me a Chevy soon. I got my eye on one."

"Yeah?" Wilson said. "What one?"

"Drew Carrington's old crate."

"Shit," Wilson said, "that motherfucker caught on fire at a streetlight and he run it off in the creek."

"They got it out," Buddy said.

"They say them flames jumped twenty feet out from under the hood before he run it off in there," Jake said.

"Water put the fire out," Buddy said.

"Uh huh," Wilson said, "after the motor blowed up through the hood. They found that motherfucker in a tree out back of old Maud Page's place. One of the pistons fell out of it and hit her on the head while she was picking up apples. She was in the hospital three days."

"Yeah," Jake said. "And I hear Carrington's in Dallas now, never got better from the accident. Near drowned and some of the engine blew back into the car and hit him in the nuts, castrated him, fucked up his legs. He can't walk. He's on a wheeled board or something, got some retard that pulls him around."

"Them's just stories," Buddy said. "Motor's still in the car. Carrington got him a job in Dallas as a mechanic. He didn't get hurt at all. Old Woman Page didn't get hit by no piston either. It missed her by a foot. Scared her so bad she had a little stroke. That's why she was in the hospital."

"You seen the motor?" Wilson asked. "Tell me you've seen it."

"No," Buddy said, "but I've heard about it from good sources, and they say it can be fixed."

"Jack it up and drive another car under it," Wilson said, "it'll be all right."

"That's the way I see it too," Jake said.

"Listen to you two," Buddy said. "You know it all. You're real operators. I'll tell you morons one thing, I line up a little of the hole that winks and stinks, like I'm doing tonight, you won't get none of it."

Wilson and Jake shuffled and eyed each other. An unspoken, but clear message passed between them. They had never known Buddy to actually get any, or anyone else to know of him getting any, but he had a couple of years on them, and he might have gotten some, way he talked about it, and they damn sure knew they weren't getting any, and if there was a chance of it, things had to be patched up.

"Car like that," Wilson said, "if you worked hard enough, you might get it to run. Some new pistons or something . . . what you got lined up for tonight?"

Buddy's face put on some importance. "I know a gal likes to do the circle, you know what I mean?"

Wilson hated to admit it, but he didn't. "The circle?"

"Pull the train," Buddy said. "Do the team. You know, fuck a bunch a guys, one after the other."

"Oh," Wilson said.

"I knew that," Jake said.

"Yeah," Wilson said. "Yeah sure you did." Then to Buddy:
"When you gonna see this gal?"

Buddy, still important, took a swig of beer and pursed his lips
and studied the afternoon sky. "Figured I'd walk on over there
little after dark. It's a mile or so."

"Say she likes to do more than one guy?" Wilson asked.

"Way I hear it," Buddy said, "she'll do 'em till they ain't able to
do. My cousin, Butch, he told me about her."

Butch. The magic word. Wilson and Jake eyed each other
again. There could be something in this after all. Butch was
twenty, had a fast car, could play a little bit on the harmonica,
bought his own beer, cussed in front of adults, and most impor-
tantly, he had been seen with women.

Buddy continued. "Her name's Sally. Butch said she cost five
dollars. He's done her a few times. Got her name off a bathroom
wall."

"She costs?" Wilson asked.

"Think some gal's going to do us all without some money for
it?" Buddy said.

Again, an unspoken signal passed between Wilson and Jake.
There could be truth in that.

"Butch gave me her address, said her pimp sits on the front
porch and you go right up and negotiate with him. Says you talk
right, he might take four."

"I don't know," Wilson said. "I ain't never paid for it."

"Me neither," said Jake.

"Ain't neither one of you ever had any at all, let alone paid for
it," Buddy said.

Once more, Wilson and Jake were struck with the hard and
painful facts.

Buddy looked at their faces and smiled. He took another sip
of beer. "Well, you bring your five dollars, and I reckon you can
tag along with me. Come by the house about dark and we'll walk
over together."

"Yeah, well, all right," Wilson said. "I wish we had a car."

"Keep wishing," Buddy said. "You boys hang with me, we'll all
be riding in Carrington's old Chevy before long. I've got some
prospects."

It was just about dark when Wilson and Jake got over to
Buddy's neighborhood, which was a long street with four houses
on it widely spaced. Buddy's house was the ugliest of the four. It
looked ready to nod off its concrete blocks at any moment and go
crashing into the unkempt yard and die in a heap of rotting

lumber and squeaking nails. Great strips of graying Sherwin Williams flat-white paint hung from it in patches, giving it the appearance of having a skin disease. The roof was tin and loved the sun and pulled it in and held it so that the interior basked in a sort of slow simmer until well after sundown. Even now, late in the day, a rush of heat came off the roof and rippled down the street like the last results of a nuclear wind.

Wilson and Jake came up on the house from the side, not wanting to go to the door. Buddy's mother was a grumpy old bitch in a brown bathrobe and bunny rabbit slippers with an ear missing on the left foot. No one had ever seen her wearing anything else, except now and then she added a shower cap to her uniform, and no one had ever seen her, with or without the shower cap, except through the screen-wire door. She wasn't thought to leave the house. She played radio contests and had to be near the radio at strategic times throughout the day so she could phone if she knew the answer to something. She claimed to be listening for household tips, but no one had ever seen her apply any. She also watched her daughter's soap operas, though she never owned up to it. She always pretended to be reading, kept a *Reader's Digest* cracked so she could look over it and see the TV.

She wasn't friendly either. Times Wilson and Jake had come over before, she'd met them at the screen door and wouldn't let them in. She wouldn't even talk to them. She'd call back to Buddy inside, "Hey, those hoodlum friends of yours are here."

Neither Wilson or Jake could see any sort of relationship developing between them and Buddy's mother, and they had stopped trying. They hung around outside the house under the open windows until Buddy came out. There were always interesting things to hear while they waited. Wilson told Jake it was educational.

This time, as before, they sidled up close to the house where they could hear. The television was on. A laugh track drifted out to them. That meant Buddy's sister LuWanda was in there watching. If it wasn't on, it meant she was asleep. Like her mother, she was drawing a check. Back problems plagued the family. Except for Buddy's pa. His back was good. He was in prison for sticking up a liquor store. What little check he was getting for making license plates probably didn't amount to much.

Now they could hear Buddy's mother. Her voice had a quality that made you think of someone trying to talk while fatally injured; like she was lying under an overturned refrigerator, or had been thrown free of a car and had hit a tree.

"LuWanda, turn that thing down. You know I got bad feet."

"You don't listen none with your feet, Mama," LuWanda said. Her voice was kind of slow and lazy, faintly squeaky, as if hoisted from her throat by a hand-over pulley.

"No," Buddy's mother said. "But I got to get up on my old tired feet and come in here and tell you to turn it down."

"I can hear you yelling from the bedroom good enough when your radio ain't too high."

"But you still don't turn it down."

"I turn it down anymore, I won't be able to hear it."

"Your old tired mother, she ought to get some respect."

"You get about half my check," LuWanda said, "ain't that enough? I'm gonna get out of here when I have the baby."

"Yeah, and I bet that's some baby, way you lay up with anything's got pants."

"I hardly never leave the house to get the chance," LuWanda said. "It was pa done it before he tried to knock over that liquor store."

"Watch your mouth, young lady. I know you let them in through the windows. I'll be glad to see you go, way you lie around here an' watch that old TV. You ought to do something educational. Read the *Reader's Digest* like I do. There's tips for living in those, and you could sure profit some."

"Could be something to that all right," LuWanda said. "Pa read the *Reader's Digest* and he's over in Huntsville. I bet he likes there better than here. I bet he has a better time come night."

"Don't you start that again, young lady."

"Way he told me," LuWanda said, "I was always better with him than you was."

"I'm putting my hands right over my ears at those lies. I won't hear them."

"He sure had him a thrust, didn't he Mama?"

"Ooooh, you . . . you little shit, if I should say such a thing. You'll get yours in hell, sister."

"I been getting plenty of hell here."

Wilson leaned against the house under the window and whispered to Jake. "Where the hell's Buddy?"

This was answered by Buddy's mother's shrill voice. "Buddy, you are *not* going out of this house wearing them nigger shoes."

"Oh, Mama," Buddy said, "these ain't nigger shoes. I bought these over at K-Woolens."

"That's right where the niggers buy their things," she said.

"Ah, Mama," Buddy said.

"Don't you Mama me. You march right back in there and take

off them shoes and put on something else. And get you a pair of pants that don't fit so tight people can tell which side it's on."

A moment later, a window down from Wilson and Jake went up slowly. A hand holding a pair of shoes stuck out. The hand dropped the shoes and disappeared.

Then the screen door slammed and Wilson and Jake edged around to the corner of the house for a peek. It was Buddy coming out, and his mother's voice came after him, "Don't you come back to this house with a disease, you hear?"

"Ah, Mama," Buddy said.

Buddy was dressed in a long-sleeved paisley shirt with the sleeves rolled up so tight over his biceps they bulged as if actually full of muscle. He had on a pair of striped bell-bottoms and tennis shoes. His hair was combed high and hard and it lifted up on one side; it looked as if an oily squirrel were clinging precariously to the side of his head.

When Buddy saw Wilson and Jake peeking around the corner of the house, his chest got full and he walked off the porch with a cool step. His mother yelled from inside the house, "And don't walk like you got a corncob up you."

That cramped Buddy's style a little, but he sneered and went around the corner of the house trying to look like a man who knew things.

"Guess you boys are ready to stretch a little meat," Buddy said. He paused to locate an almost flat half-pack of Camels in his back pocket. He pulled a cigarette out and got a match from his shirt pocket and grinned and held his hand by his cheek and popped the match with his thumb. It sparked and he lit the cigarette and puffed. "Those things with filters, they're for sissies."

"Give us one of those," Wilson said.

"Yeah, well, all right, but this is it," Buddy said. "Only pack I got till I collect some money owed me."

Wilson and Jake stuck smokes in their faces and Buddy snapped another match and lit them up. Wilson and Jake coughed some smoke clouds.

"Sshhhh," Buddy said. "The old lady'll hear you."

They went around to the back window where Buddy had dropped the shoes and Buddy picked them up and took off the ones he had on and slipped on the others. They were smooth and dark and made of alligator hide. Their toes were pointed. Buddy wet his thumb and removed a speck of dirt from one of them. He put his tennis shoes under the house, brought a fruit jar of clear liquid out from there.

"Hooch," Buddy said, and winked. "Bought it off Old Man Hoyt."

"Hoyt?" Wilson said. "He sells hooch?"

"Makes it himself," Buddy said. "Get you a quart for five dollars. Got five dollars and he'll sell to bottle babies."

Buddy saw Wilson eyeing his shoes appreciatively.

"Mama don't like me wearing these," he said. "I have to sneak them out."

"They're cool," Jake said. "I wish I had me a pair like 'em."

"You got to know where to shop," Buddy said.

As they walked, the night became rich and cool and the moon went up and it was bright with a fuzzy ring around it. Crickets chirped. The streets they came to were little more than clay, but there were more houses than in Buddy's neighborhood, and they were in better shape. Some of the yards were mowed. The lights were on in the houses along the street, and the three of them could hear televisions talking from inside houses as they walked.

They finished off the street and turned onto another that was bordered by deep woods. They crossed a narrow wooden bridge that went over Mud Creek. They stopped and leaned on the bridge railing and watched the dark water in the moonlight. Wilson remembered when he was ten and out shooting birds with a BB gun, he had seen a dead squirrel in the water, floating out from under the bridge, face down, as if it were snorkeling. He had watched it sail on down the creek and out of sight. He had popped at it and all around it with his BB gun for as long as the gun had the distance. The memory made him nostalgic for his youth and he tried to remember what he had done with his old Daisy air rifle. Then it came to him that his dad had probably pawned it. He did that sort of thing now and then, when he fell off the wagon. Suddenly a lot of missing items over the years began to come together. He'd have to get him some kind of trunk with a lock on it and nail it to the floor or something. It wasn't nailed down, it and everything in it might end up at the pawn shop for strangers to paw over.

They walked on and finally came to a long street with houses at the end of it, and the lights there seemed less bright and the windows the lights came out of much smaller.

"That last house before the street crosses," Buddy said, "that's the one we want."

Wilson and Jake looked where Buddy was pointing. The house was dark except for a smudgy porch light and a sick yellow glow

that shone from behind a thick curtain. Someone was sitting on
the front porch doing something with their hands. They couldn't
tell anything about the person or about what the person was
doing. From that distance the figure could have been whittling or
masturbating.

"Ain't that nigger town on the other side of the street?" Jake
said. "This gal we're after, she a nigger? I don't know I'm ready to
fuck a nigger. I heard my old man say to a friend of his that
Mammy Clewson will give a hand job for a dollar and a half. I
might go that from a nigger, but I don't know about putting it in
one."

"House we want is on this side of the street, before nigger
town," Buddy said. "That's a full four foot difference. She ain't a
nigger. She's white trash."

"Well . . . all right," Jake said. "That's different."

"Everybody take a drink," Buddy said, and he unscrewed the
lid on the fruit jar and took a jolt. "Wheee. Straight from the
horse."

Buddy passed the jar to Wilson, and Wilson drank and nearly
threw it up. "Goddamn," he said. "Goddamn. He must run that
stuff through a radiator hose or something."

Jake took a turn, shivered as if in the early throes of an epileptic fit. He gave the jar back to Buddy. Buddy screwed the lid on
and they walked on down the street, stopped opposite the house
they wanted and looked at the man on the front porch, for they
could clearly see now it was a man. He was old and toothless and
he was shelling peas from a big paper sack into a little white wash
pan.

"That's the pimp," Buddy whispered. He opened up the jar
and took a sip and closed it and gave it to Wilson to hold. "Give
me your money."

They gave him their five dollars.

"I'll go across and make the arrangements," Buddy said. "When
I signal, come on over. The pimp might prefer we go in the house
one at a time. Maybe you can sit on the porch. I don't know yet."

The three smiled at each other. The passion was building.

Buddy straightened his shoulders, pulled his pants up, and
went across the street. He called a howdy to the man on the
porch.

"Who the hell are you?" the old man said. It sounded as if his
tongue got in the way of his words.

Buddy went boldly up to the house and stood at the porch
steps. Wilson and Jake could hear him from where they stood,

shuffling their feet and sipping from the jar. He said, "We come to buy a little pussy. I hear you're the man to supply it."

"What's that?" the old man said, and he stood up. When he did, it was obvious he had a problem with his balls. The right side of his pants looked to have a baby's head in it.

"I was him," Jake whispered to Wilson, "I'd save up my share of that pussy money and get me a truss."

"What is that now?" the old man was going on. "What is that you're saying, you little shit?"

"Well now," Buddy said, cocking a foot on the bottom step of the porch like someone who meant business, "I'm not asking for free. I've got fifteen dollars here. It's five a piece, ain't it? We're not asking for anything fancy. We just want to lay a little pipe."

A pale light went on inside the house and a plump, blond girl appeared at the screen door. She didn't open it. She stood there looking out.

"Boy, what in hell are you talking about?" the old man said. "You got the wrong house."

"No one here named Sally?" Buddy asked.

The old man turned his head toward the screen and looked at the plump girl.

"I don't know him, Papa," she said. "Honest."

"You sonofabitch," the old man said to Buddy, and he waddled down the step and swung an upward blow that hit Buddy under the chin and flicked his squirrel-looking hair-do out of shape, sent him hurtling into the front yard. The old man got a palm under his oversized balls and went after Buddy, walking like he had something heavy tied to one leg. Buddy twisted around to run and the old man kicked out and caught him one in the seat of the pants, knocked him stumbling into the street.

"You little bastard," the old man yelled, "don't you come sniffing around here after my daughter again, or I'll cut your nuts off."

Then the old man saw Wilson and Jake across the street. Jake, unable to stop himself, nervously lifted a hand and waved.

"Git on out of here, or I'll let Blackie out," the old man said. "He'll tear your asses up."

Buddy came on across the street, trying to step casually, but moving briskly just the same. "I'm gonna get that fucking Butch," he said.

The old man found a rock in the yard and threw it at them. It whizzed by Buddy's ear and he and Jake and Wilson stepped away lively.

Behind them they heard a screen door slam and the plump girl whined something and there was a whapping sound, like a fan belt come loose on a big truck, then they heard the plump girl yelling for mercy and the old man cried "Slut" once, and they were out of there, across the street, into the black side of town.

They walked along a while, then Jake said, "I guess we could find Mammy Clewson."

"Oh, shut up," Buddy said. "Here's your five dollars back. Here's both your five dollars back. The both of you can get her to do it for you till your money runs out."

"I was just kidding," Jake said.

"Well don't," Buddy said. "That Butch, I catch him, right in the kisser, man. I don't care how big and mean he is. Right in the kisser."

They walked along the street and turned left up another. "Let's get out of boogie town," Buddy said. "All these niggers around here, it makes me nervous."

When they were well up the street and there were no houses, they turned down a short dirt street with a bridge in the middle of it that went over the Sabine river. It wasn't a big bridge because the river was narrow there. Off to the right was a wide pasture. To the left a church. They crossed into the church back yard. There were a couple of wooden pews setting out there under an oak. Buddy went over to one and sat down.

"I thought you wanted to get away from the boogies?" Wilson said.

"Naw," Buddy said. "This is all right. This is fine. I'd like for a nigger to start something. I would. That old man back there hadn't been so old and had his balls fucked up like that, I'd have kicked his ass."

"We wondered what was holding you back," Wilson said.

Buddy looked at Wilson, didn't see any signs of sarcasm.

"Yeah, well, that was it. Give me the jar. There's some other women I know about. We might try something later on, we feel like it."

But a cloud of unspoken resignation, as far as pussy was concerned, had passed over them, and they labored beneath its darkness with their fruit jar of hooch. They sat and passed the jar around and the night got better and brighter. Behind them, off in the woods, they could hear the Sabine river running along. Now and then a car would go down or up the street, cross over the bridge with a rumble, and pass out of sight beyond the church, or if heading in the other direction, out of sight behind trees.

Buddy began to see the night's fiasco as funny. He mellowed. "That Butch, he's something, ain't he? Some joke, huh?"

"It was pretty funny," Jake said, "seeing that old man and his balls coming down the porch after you. That thing was any more ruptured, he'd need a wheelbarrow to get from room to room. Shit, I bet he couldn't have turned no dog on us. He'd had one in there, it'd have barked."

"Maybe he calls Sally Blackie," Wilson said. "Man, we're better off she didn't take money. You see that face. She could scare crows."

"Shit," Buddy said, sniffing at the jar of hooch. "I think Hoyt puts hair oil in this. Don't that smell like Vitalis to you?"

He held it under Wilson's nose, then Jake's.

"It does," Wilson said. "Right now, I wouldn't care if it smelled like sewer. Give me another swig."

"No," Buddy said, standing up, wobbling, holding the partially-filled jar in front of him. "Could be we've discovered a hair tonic we could sell. Buy it from Hoyt for five, sell it to guys to put on their heads for ten. We could go into business with Old Man Hoyt. Make a fortune."

Buddy poured some hooch into his palm and rubbed it into his hair, fanning his struggling squirrel-do into greater disarray. He gave the jar to Jake, got out his comb and sculptured his hair with it. Hooch ran down from his hairline and along his nose and cheeks. "See that," he said, holding out his arms as if he were styling. "Shit holds like glue."

Buddy seemed an incredible wit suddenly. They all laughed. Buddy got his cigarettes and shook one out for each of them. They lipped them. They smiled at one another. They were great friends. This was a magnificent and important moment in their lives. This night would live in memory forever.

Buddy produced a match, held it close to his cheek like always, smiled and flicked it with his thumb. The flaming head of the match jumped into his hair and lit the alcohol Buddy had combed into it. His hair flared up, and a circle of fire, like a halo for the devil, wound its way around his scalp and licked at his face and caught the hooch there on fire. Buddy screamed and bolted berserkly into a pew, tumbled over it and came up running. He looked like the Human Torch on a mission.

Wilson and Jake were stunned. They watched him run a goodly distance, circle, run back, hit the turned-over pew again and go down.

Wilson yelled, "Put his head out!"

Jake reflexively tossed the contents of the fruit jar at Buddy's head, realizing his mistake a moment too late. But it was like when he waved at Sally's pa. He couldn't help himself.

Buddy did a short tumble, came up still burning; in fact, he appeared to be more on fire than before. He ran straight at Wilson and Jake, his tongue out and flapping flames.

Wilson and Jake stepped aside and Buddy went between them, sprinted across the church yard toward the street.

"Throw dirt on his head!" Wilson said. Jake threw down the jar and they went after him, watching for dirt they could toss.

Buddy was fast for someone on fire. He reached the street well ahead of Wilson and Jake and any discovery of available dirt. But he didn't cross the street fast enough to beat the dump truck. Its headlights hit him first, then the left side of the bumper clipped him on the leg and he did a high complete flip, his blazing head resembling some sort of wheeled fireworks display. He landed on the bridge railing on the far side of the street with a crack of bone and a barking noise. With a burst of flames around his head, he fell off the bridge and into the water below.

The dump truck locked up its brakes and skidded.

Wilson and Jake stopped running. They stood looking at the spot where Buddy had gone over, paralyzed with disbelief.

The dump truck driver, a slim white man in overalls and a cap, got out of the truck and stopped at the rear of it, looked at where Buddy had gone over, looked up and down the street. He didn't seem to notice Wilson and Jake. He walked briskly back to the truck, got in, gunned the motor. The truck went away fast, took a right on the next street hard enough that the tires protested like a cat with its tail in a crack. It backfired once, then there was only the distant sound of the motor and gears being rapidly shifted.

"Sonofabitch!" Wilson yelled.

He and Jake ran to the street, paused, looked both ways in case of more dump trucks, and crossed. They glanced over the railing.

Buddy lay with his lower body on the bank. His left leg was twisted so that his shoe pointed in the wrong direction. His dark, crisp head was in the water. He was straining his neck to lift his blackened, eyeless face out of the water; white wisps of smoke swirled up from it and carried with it the smell of barbecued meat. His body shifted. He let out a groan.

"Goddamn," Wilson said. "He's alive. Let's get him."

But at that moment there was splashing in the water. A log came sailing down the river, directly at Buddy's head. The log opened its mouth and grabbed Buddy by the head and jerked him off the shore. A noise like walnuts being cracked and a muffled scream drifted up to Wilson and Jake.

"An alligator," Jake said, and noted vaguely how closely its skin and Buddy's shoes matched.

Wilson darted around the railing, slid down the incline to the water's edge. Jake followed. They ran alongside the bank.

The water turned extremely shallow, and they could see the shadowy shape of the gator as it waddled forward, following the path of the river, still holding Buddy by the head. Buddy stuck out of the side of its mouth like a curmudgeon's cigar. His arms were flapping and so was his good leg.

Wilson and Jake paused running and tried to get their breath. After some deep inhalations, Wilson said, "Gets in the deep water, it's all over." He grabbed up an old fence post that had washed onto the bank and began running again, yelling at the gator as he went. Jake looked about, but didn't see anything to hit with. He ran after Wilson.

The gator, panicked by the noisy pursuit, crawled out of the shallows and went into the high grass of a connecting pasture, ducking under the bottom strand of a barbwire fence. The wire caught one of Buddy's flailing arms and ripped a flap of flesh from it six inches long. Once on the other side of the wire his good leg kicked up and the fine shine on his alligator shoes flashed once in the moonlight and fell down.

Wilson went through the barbwire and after the gator with his fence post. The gator was making good time, pushing Buddy before it, leaving a trail of mashed grass behind it. Wilson could see its tail weaving in the moonlight. Its stink trailed behind it like fumes from a busted muffler.

Wilson put the fence post on his shoulder and ran as hard as he could, managed to close in. Behind him came Jake, huffing and puffing.

Wilson got alongside the gator and hit him in the tail with the fence post. The gator's tail whipped out and caught Wilson's ankles and knocked his feet from under him. He came down hard on his butt and lost the fence post.

Jake grabbed up the post and broke right as the gator turned in that direction. He caught the beast sideways and brought the post down on its head, and when it hit, Buddy's blood jumped out of the gator's mouth and landed in the grass and on Jake's shoes. In the moonlight it was the color of cough syrup.

Jake went wild. He began to hit the gator brutally, running

alongside it, following its every twist and turn. He swung the fence post mechanically, slamming the gator in the head. Behind him Wilson was saying, "You're hurting Buddy, you're hurting Buddy," but Jake couldn't stop, the frenzy was on him. Gator blood was flying, bursting out of the top of the reptile's head. Still, it held to Buddy, not giving up an inch of head. Buddy wasn't thrashing or kicking anymore. His legs slithered along in the grass as the gator ran; he looked like one of those dummies they throw off cliffs in old cowboy movies.

Wilson caught up, started kicking the gator in the side. The gator started rolling and thrashing, and Jake and Wilson hopped like rabbits and yelled. Finally the gator quit rolling. It quit crawling. Its sides heaved.

Jake continued to pound it with the post and Wilson continued to kick it. Eventually its sides quit swelling. Jake kept hitting it with the post until he staggered back and fell down in the grass exhausted. He sat there looking at the gator and Buddy. The gator trembled suddenly and spewed gator shit into the grass. It didn't move again.

After a few minutes, Wilson said, "I don't think Buddy's alive."

Just then, Buddy's body twitched.

"Hey, hey, you see that?" Jake said.

Wilson was touched with wisdom. "He's alive, the gator might be too."

Wilson got on his knees about six feet from the gator's mouth and bent over to see if he could see Buddy in there. All he could see were the gator's rubbery lips and the sides of its teeth and a little of Buddy's head shredded between them, like gray cheese on a grater. He could smell both the sour smell of the gator and the stink of burnt meat.

"I don't know if he's alive or not," Wilson said. "Maybe if we could get him out of its mouth, we could tell more."

Jake tried to wedge the fence post into the gator's mouth, but that didn't work. It was as if the great jaw was locked with a key.

They watched carefully, but Buddy didn't show any more signs of life.

"I know," Wilson said. "We'll carry him and the gator up to the road, find a house and get some help."

The gator was long and heavy. The best they could do was get hold of its tail and pull it and Buddy along. Jake managed this with the fence post under his arm. He didn't trust the gator and wouldn't give it up.

They went across an acre of grass and came to a barbwire fence that bordered the street where Buddy had been hit by the dump truck. The bridge was in sight.

They let go of the gator and climbed through the wire. Jake used the fence post to lift up the bottom strand, and Wilson got hold of the gator's tail and tugged the beast under, along with Buddy.

Pulling the gator and Buddy alongside the road, they watched for house lights. They went past the church on the opposite side of the road and turned left where the dump truck had turned right and backfired. They went alongside the street there, occasionally allowing the gator and Buddy to weave over into the street itself. It was hard work steering a gator and its lunch.

They finally came to a row of houses. The first one had an old Ford pickup parked out beside it and lots of junk piled in the yard. Lawn mowers, oily rope, overturned freezers, wheels, fishing reels and line, bicycle parts, and a busted commode. A tarp had been pulled half-heartedly over a tall stack of old shop creepers. There was a light on behind one window. The rest of the houses were dark.

Jake and Wilson let go of the gator in the front yard, and Wilson went up on the porch, knocked on the door, stepped off the porch and waited.

Briefly thereafter, the door opened a crack and a man called out, "Who's out there? Don't you know it's bedtime?"

"We seen your light on," Wilson said.

"I was in the shitter. You trying to sell me a brush or a book or something this time of night, I won't be in no good temper about it. I'm not through shitting either."

"We got a man hurt here," Wilson said. "A gator bit him."

There was a long moment of quiet. "What you want me to do? I don't know nothin' about no gator bites. I don't even know who you are. You might be with the Ku Kluxers."

"He's . . . he's kind of hung up with the gator," Wilson said.

"Just a minute," said the voice.

Moments later a short, fat black man came out. He was shirtless and barefooted, wearing overalls with the straps off his shoulders, dangling at his waist. He had a ball bat in his hand. He came down the steps and looked at Wilson and Jake carefully, as if expecting them to spring. "You stand away from me with that fence post, hear?" he said. Jake took a step back and this seemed to satisfy the man. He took a look at the gator and Buddy.

He went back up the porch and reached inside the door and

turned on the porch light. A child's face stuck through the crack in the door, said, "What's out there, papa?"

"You get your ass in that house, or I'll kick it," the black man said. The face disappeared.

The black man came off the porch again, looked at the gator and Buddy again, walked around them a couple of times, poked the gator with the ball bat, poked Buddy too.

He looked at Jake and Wilson. "Shit," he said. "You pecker-woods is crazy. That motherfucker's dead. He's dead enough for two men. He's deader than I ever seen anybody."

"He caught on fire," Jake offered suddenly, "and we tried to put his head out, and he got hit by a truck, knocked in the river, and the gator got him . . . We seen him twitch a little a while back . . . The fella, Buddy, not the gator, I mean."

"Them's nerves," the black man said. "You better dig a hole for this man-jack, skin that ole gator out and sell his hide. They bring a right smart price sometimes. You could probably get something for them shoes too, if'n they clean up good."

"We need you to help us load him up into your pickup and take him home," Jake said.

"You ain't putting that motherfucker in my pickup," the black man said. "I don't want no doings with you honkey motherfuckers. They'll be claiming I sicked that gator on him."

"That's silly," Wilson said. "You're acting like a fool."

"Uh-huh," said the black man, "and I'm gonna go on acting like one here in my house."

He went briskly up the porch steps, closed the door and turned out the light. A latch was thrown.

Wilson began to yell. He used the word nigger indiscrim-inately. He ran up on the porch and pounded on the door. He cussed a lot.

Doors of houses down the way opened up and people moved onto their front porches like shadows, looked at where the noise was coming from.

Jake, standing there in the yard with his fence post, looked like a man with a gun. The gator and Buddy could have been the body of their neighbor. The shadows watched Jake and listened to Wilson yell a moment, then went back inside.

"Goddamn you," Wilson yelled. "Come on out of there so I can whip your ass, you hear me? I'll whip your black ass."

"You come on in here, cocksucker," came the black man's voice from the other side of the door. "Come on in, you think you can. You do, you'll be trying to shit you some twelve gauge shot, that's what you'll be trying to do."

At mention of the twelve gauge, Wilson felt a certain calm descend on him. He began to acquire perspective. "We're leaving," he said to the door. "Right now." He backed off the porch. He spoke softly so only Jake could hear: "Boogie motherfucker."

"What we gonna do now?" Jake said. He sounded tired. All the juice had gone out of him.

"I reckon," Wilson said, "we got to get Buddy and the gator on over to his house."

"I don't think we can carry him that far," Jake said. "My back is hurting already."

Wilson looked at the junk beside the house. "Wait a minute." He went over to the junk pile and got three shop creepers out from under the tarp and found some hanks of rope. He used the rope to tie the creepers together, end to end. When he looked up, Jake was standing beside him, still holding the fence post. "You go on and stay by Buddy," Wilson said. "Turn your back too long, them niggers will be all over them shoes."

Jake went back to his former position.

Wilson collected several short pieces of rope and a twist of wire and tied them together and hooked the results to one of the creepers and used it as a handle. He pulled his contraption around front by Buddy and the gator. "Help me put 'em on there," he said.

They lifted the gator onto the creepers. He fit with only his tail overlapping. Buddy hung to the side, off the creepers, causing them to tilt.

"That won't work," Jake said.

"Well, here now," Wilson said, and he got Buddy by the legs and turned him. The head and neck were real flexible, like they were made of chewing gum. He was able to lay Buddy straight out in front of the gator. "Now we can pull the gator down a bit, drag all of its tail. That way we got 'em both on there."

When they got the gator and Buddy arranged, Wilson doubled the rope and began pulling. At first it was slow going, but after a moment they got out in the road and the creepers gained momentum and squeaked right along. Jake used his fence post to punch at the edges of the creepers when they swung out of line.

An ancient, one-eyed Cocker Spaniel with a foot missing came out and sat at the edge of the road and watched them pass. He barked once when the alligator's tail dragged by in the dirt behind the creepers, then he went and got under a porch.

They squeaked on until they passed the house where Sally lived. They stopped across from it for a breather and to listen. They didn't hear anyone screaming and they didn't hear any beatings going on.

They started up again, kept at it until they came to Buddy's street. It was deadly quiet, and the moon had been lost behind a cloud and everything was dark.

At Buddy's house, the silver light of the TV strobed behind the living room curtains. Wilson and Jake stopped on the far side of the street and squatted beside the creepers and considered their situation.

Wilson got in Buddy's back pocket and pulled the smokes out and found that though the package was damp from the water, a couple of cigarettes were dry enough to smoke. He gave one to Jake and took the other for himself. He got a match from Buddy's shirt pocket and struck it on a creeper, but it was too damp to light.

"Here," Jake said, and produced a lighter. "I stole this from my old man in case I ever got any cigarettes. It works most of the time." Jake clicked it repeatedly and finally it sparked well enough to light. They lit up.

"We knock on the door, his mom is gonna be mad," Jake said. "Us bringing home Buddy and an alligator, and Buddy wearing them shoes."

"Yeah," Wilson said. "You know, she don't know he went off with us. We could put him in the yard. Maybe she'll think the gator attacked him there."

"What for," Jake said, "them shoes? He recognized his aunt or something?" He began laughing at his own joke, but if Wilson got it he didn't give a sign. He seemed to be thinking. Jake quit laughing, scratched his head and looked off down the street. He tried to smoke his cigarette in a manful manner.

"Gators come up in yards and eat dogs now and then," Wilson said after a long silence. "We could leave him, and if his Mama don't believe a gator jumped him, that'll be all right. The figuring of it will be a town mystery. Nobody would ever know what happened. Those niggers won't be talking. And if they do, they don't know us from anybody else anyway. We all look alike to them."

"I was Buddy," Jake said, "that's the way I'd want it if I had a couple friends involved."

"Yeah, well," Wilson said, "I don't know I really liked him so much."

Jake thought about that. "He was all right. I bet he wasn't going to get that Chevy though."

"If he did," Wilson said, "there wouldn't have been no motor in it, I can promise you that. And I bet he never got any pussy neither."

They pulled the creepers across the road and tipped gator and Buddy onto the ground in front of the porch steps.

"That'll have to do," Wilson whispered.

Wilson crept up on the porch and over to the window, looked through a crack in the curtain and into the living room. Buddy's sister lay on the couch asleep, her mouth open, her huge belly bobbing up and down as she breathed. A half-destroyed bag of Cheetos lay beside the couch. The TV light flickered over her like saintly fire.

Jake came up on the porch and took a look.

"Maybe if she lost some pounds and fixed her hair different," he said.

"Maybe if she was somebody else," Wilson said.

They sat on the porch steps in the dark and finished smoking their cigarettes, watching the faint glow of the television through the curtain, listening to the tinny sound of a late night talk show.

When Jake finished his smoke, he pulled the alligator shoes off Buddy and checked them against the soles of his own shoes. "I think these dudes will fit me. We can't leave 'em on him. His Mama sees them, she might not consent to bury him."

He and Wilson left out of there then, pulling the creepers after them.

Not far down the road, they pushed the creepers off in a ditch and continued, Jake carrying the shoes under his arm. "These are all right," he said. "I might can get some pussy wearing these kind of shoes. My Mama don't care if I wear things like this."

"Hell, she don't care if you cut your head off," Wilson said.

"That's the way I see it," Jake said.

When I wrote this I was trying to write a good solid story that worked. This is not to say I'm not ambitious, but I am a professional writer, and sometimes you commit to something, and then you have to follow through, and for some reason you feel like your brain is stuffed with cotton. Every word is a chore.

I consider myself enough of a pro that I can do a good, competent story any day of the week. I prefer, of course, to always write a masterpiece, but, unfortunately, you can't make that choice. You can only choose to write as well as you can. Even if you have to wade through cotton.

When I was doing this one, I felt I was doing a solid job, and nothing more, but I gave it everything I had. When I reread it in print I liked it much better. It may not be a masterpiece, but it's been picked up for a best of the year volume, optioned twice for film, and I meet people all the time who think it's one of my best. Go figure.

I guess the motto of this story is simple. Listen to your gut. Write the best you can every time out. You never know what you'll come up with. And even if it's just a good professional story, that's nothing to be ashamed of.

INCIDENT ON AND OFF
A MOUNTAIN ROAD

WHEN ELLEN CAME TO THE MOONLIT MOUN-
tain curve, her thoughts, which had been adrift with
her problems, grounded, and she was suddenly aware
that she was driving much too fast. The sign said
CURVE: 30 MPH, and she was doing fifty.

She knew too that slamming on the brakes was the wrong
move, so she optioned to keep her speed and fight the curve and
make it, and she thought she could.

The moonlight was strong, so visibility was high, and she knew
her Chevy was in good shape, easy to handle, and she was a good
driver.

But as she negotiated the curve a blue Buick seemed to grow
out of the ground in front of her. It was parked on the shoulder
of the road, at the peak of the curve, its nose sticking out a foot
too far, its rear end against the moon-wet, silver railing that
separated the curve from a mountainous plunge.

Had she been going an appropriate speed, missing the Buick
wouldn't have been a problem, but at her speed she was swinging
too far right, directly in line with it, and was forced, after all, to
use her brakes. When she did, the back wheels slid and the brakes
groaned and the front of the Chevy hit the Buick, and there was

a sound like an explosion and then for a dizzy instant she felt as if she were in the tumblers of a dryer.

Through the windshield came: Moonlight. Blackness. Moonlight.

One high bounce and a tight roll, and the Chevy came to rest upright with the engine dead, the right side flush against the railing. Another inch of jump or greater impact against the rail, and the Chevy would have gone over.

Ellen felt a sharp pain in her leg and reached down to discover that during the tumble she had banged it against something, probably the gear shift, and had ripped her stocking and her flesh. Blood was trickling into her shoe. Probing her leg cautiously with the tips of her fingers, she determined the wound wasn't bad and that all other body parts were operative.

She unfastened her seat belt, and as a matter of habit, located her purse and slipped its strap over her shoulder. She got out of the Chevy feeling wobbly, eased around front of it and saw the hood and bumper and roof were crumpled. A wisp of radiator steam hissed from beneath the wadded hood, rose into the moonlight and dissolved.

She turned her attentions to the Buick. Its tail end was now turned to her, and as she edged alongside it, she saw the front left side had been badly damaged. Fearful of what she might see, she glanced inside.

The moonlight shone through the rear windshield bright as a spotlight and revealed no one, but the back seat was slick with something dark and wet and there was plenty of it. A foul scent seeped out of a partially rolled down back window. It was a hot coppery smell that gnawed at her nostrils and ached her stomach.

God, someone had been hurt. Maybe thrown free of the car, or perhaps they had gotten out and crawled off. But when? She and the Chevy had been airborne for only a moment, and she had gotten out of the vehicle instants after it ceased to roll. Surely she would have seen someone get out of the Buick, and if they had been thrown free by the collision, wouldn't at least one of the Buick's doors be open? If it had whipped back and closed, it seemed unlikely that it would be locked, and all the doors of the Buick were locked, and all the glass was intact, and only on her side was it rolled down, and only a crack. Enough for the smell of the blood to escape, not enough for a person to slip through unless they were thin and flexible as a feather.

On the other side of the Buick, on the ground, between the back door and the railing, there were drag marks and a thick swath of blood, and another swath on the top of the railing; it glowed there in the moonlight as if it were molasses laced with radio-activity.

Ellen moved cautiously to the railing and peered over.

No one lay mangled and bleeding and oozing their guts. The ground was not as precarious there as she expected it. It was pebbly and sloped out gradually and there was a trail going down it. The trail twisted slightly and as it deepened the foliage grew denser on either side of it. Finally it curlicued its way into the dark thicket of a forest below, and from the forest, hot on the wind, came the strong turpentine tang of pines and something less fresh and not as easily identifiable.

Now she saw someone moving down there, floating up from the forest like an apparition; a white face split by silver—braces, perhaps. She could tell from the way this someone moved that it was a man. She watched as he climbed the trail and came within examination range. He seemed to be surveying her as carefully as she was surveying him.

Could this be the driver of the Buick?

As he came nearer Ellen discovered she could not identify the expression he wore. It was neither joy or anger or fear or exhaustion or pain. It was somehow all and none of these.

When he was ten feet away, still looking up, that same odd expression on his face, she could hear him breathing. He was breathing with exertion, but not to the extent she thought him tired or injured. It was the sound of someone who had been about busy work.

She yelled down, "Are you injured?"

He turned his head quizzically, like a dog trying to make sense of a command, and it occurred to Ellen that he might be knocked about in the head enough to be disoriented.

"I'm the one who ran into your car," she said. "Are you all right?"

His expression changed then, and it was most certainly identifiable this time. He was surprised and angry. He came up the trail quickly, took hold of the top railing, his fingers going into the blood there, and vaulted over and onto the gravel.

Ellen stepped back out of his way and watched him from a distance. The guy made her nervous. Even close up, he looked like some kind of spook.

He eyed her briefly, glanced at the Chevy, turned to look at the Buick.

"It was my fault," Ellen said.

He didn't reply, but returned his attention to her and continued to cock his head in that curious dog sort of way.

Ellen noticed that one of his shirt sleeves was stained with blood, and that there was blood on the knees of his pants, but he didn't act as if he were hurt in any way. He reached into his pants pocket and pulled out something and made a move with his wrist. Out flicked a lock-blade knife. The thin edge of it sucked up the moonlight and spat it out in a silver spray that fanned wide when he held it before him and jiggled it like a man working a stubborn key into a lock. He advanced toward her, and as he came, his lips split and pulled back at the corners, exposing, not braces, but metal-capped teeth that matched the sparkle of his blade.

It occurred to her that she could bolt for the Chevy, but in the same mental flash of lightning, it occurred to her she wouldn't make it.

Ellen threw herself over the railing, and as she leapt, she saw out of the corner of her eye, the knife slashing the place she had occupied, catching moonbeams and throwing them away. Then the blade was out of her view and she hit on her stomach and skidded onto the narrow trail, slid downward, feet first. The gravel and roots tore at the front of her dress and ripped through her nylons and gouged her flesh. She cried out in pain and her sliding gained speed. Lifting her chin, she saw that the man was climbing over the railing and coming after her at a stumbling run, the knife held before him like a wand.

Her sliding stopped, and she pushed off with her hands to make it start again, not knowing if this was the thing to do or not, since the trail inclined sharply on her right side, and should she skid only slightly in that direction, she could hurtle off into blackness. But somehow she kept slithering along the trail and even spun around a corner and stopped with her head facing downward, her purse practically in her teeth.

She got up then, without looking back, and began to run into the woods, the purse beating at her side. She moved as far away from the trail as she could, fighting limbs that conspired to hit her across the face or hold her, vines and bushes that tried to tie her feet or trip her.

Behind her, she could hear the man coming after her, breathing heavily now, not really winded, but hurrying. For the first time in months, she was grateful for Bruce and his survivalist insanity. His passion to be in shape and for her to be in shape with him was paying off. All that jogging had given her the lungs of an ox and

strengthened her legs and ankles. A line from one of Bruce's survivalist books came to her: *Do the unexpected.*

She found a trail amongst the pines, and followed it, then,
abruptly broke from it and went back into the thicket. It was
harder going, but she assumed her pursuer would expect her to
follow a trail.

The pines became so thick she got down on her hands and
knees and began to crawl. It was easier to get through that way.
After a moment, she stopped scuttling and eased her back against
one of the pines and sat and listened. She felt reasonably well hidden, as the boughs of the pines grew low and drooped to the
ground. She took several deep breaths, holding each for a long
moment. Gradually, she began breathing normally. Above her,
from the direction of the trail, she could hear the man running,
coming nearer. She held her breath.

The running paused a couple of times, and she could imagine
the man, his strange, pale face turning from side to side, as he
tried to determine what had happened to her. The sound of running started again and the man moved on down the trail.

Ellen considered easing out and starting back up the trail, making her way to her car and driving off. Damaged as it was, she felt
it would still run, but she was reluctant to leave her hiding place
and step into the moonlight. Still, it seemed a better plan than
waiting. If she didn't do something, the man could always go back
topside himself and wait for her. The woods, covering acres and
acres of land below and beyond, would take her days to get
through, and without food and water and knowledge of the
geography, she might never make it, could end up going in circles
for days.

Bruce and his survivalist credos came back to her. She remembered something he had said to one of his self-defense classes, a
bunch of rednecks hoping and praying for a commie take-over so
they could show their stuff. He had told them: "Utilize what's at
hand. Size up what you have with you and how it can be put to
use."

All right, she thought. All right, Brucey, you sonofabitch. I'll
see what's at hand.

One thing she knew she had for sure was a little flashlight. It
wasn't much, but it would serve for her to check out the contents
of her purse. She located it easily, and without withdrawing it
from her purse, turned it on and held the open purse close to her
face to see what was inside. Before she actually found it, she

thought of her nail file kit. Besides the little bottle of nail polish remover, there was an emery board and two metal files. The files were the ticket. They might serve as weapons; they weren't much, but they were something.

She also carried a very small pair of nail scissors, independent of the kit, the points of the scissors being less than a quarter inch. That wouldn't be worth much, but she took note of it and mentally catalogued it.

She found the nail kit, turned off the flash and removed one of the files and returned the rest of the kit to her purse. She held the file tightly, made a little jabbing motion with it. It seemed so light and thin and insignificant.

She had been absently carrying her purse on one shoulder, and now to make sure she didn't lose it, she placed the strap over her neck and slid her arm through.

Clenching the nail file, she moved on hands and knees beneath the pine boughs and poked her head out into the clearing of the trail. She glanced down it first, and there, not ten yards from her, looking up the trail, holding his knife by his side, was the man. The moonlight lay cold on his face and the shadows of the wind-blown boughs fell across him and wavered. It seemed as if she were leaning over a pool and staring down into the water and seeing him at the bottom of it, or perhaps his reflection on the face of the pool.

She realized instantly that he had gone down the trail a ways, became suspicious of her ability to disappear so quickly, and had turned to judge where she might have gone. And, as if in answer to the question, she had poked her head into view.

They remained frozen for a moment, then the man took a step up the trail, and just as he began to run, Ellen went backwards into the pines on her hands and knees.

She had gone less than ten feet when she ran up against a thick limb that lay close to the ground and was preventing her passage. She got down on her belly and squirmed beneath it, and as she was pulling her head under, she saw Moon Face crawling into the thicket, making good time; time made better, when he lunged suddenly and covered half the space between them, the knife missing her by fractions.

Ellen jerked back and felt her feet falling away from her. She let go of the file and grabbed out for the limb and it bent way back and down with her weight. It lowered her enough for her feet to touch ground. Relieved, she realized she had fallen into a wash made by erosion, not off the edge of the mountain.

Above her, gathered in shadows and stray strands of moonlight that showed through the pine boughs, was the man. His metal-tipped teeth caught a moonbeam and twinkled. He placed a hand on the limb she held, as if to lower himself, and she let go of it.

The limb whispered away from her and hit him full in the face and knocked him back.

Ellen didn't bother to scrutinize the damage. Turning, she saw that the wash ended in a slope and that the slope was thick with trees growing out like great, feathered spears thrown into the side of the mountain.

She started down, letting the slant carry her, grasping limbs and tree trunks to slow her descent and keep her balance. She could hear the man climbing down and pursuing her, but she didn't bother to turn and look. Below she could see the incline was becoming steeper, and if she continued, it would be almost straight up and down with nothing but the trees for support, and to move from one to the other, she would have to drop, chimpanzee-like, from limb to limb. Not a pleasant thought.

Her only consolation was that the trees to her right, veering back up the mountain, were thick as cancer cells. She took off in that direction, going wide, and began plodding upwards again, trying to regain the concealment of the forest.

She chanced a look behind her before entering the pines, and saw that the man, who she had come to think of as Moon Face, was some distance away.

Weaving through a mass of trees, she integrated herself into the forest, and as she went the limbs began to grow closer to the ground and the trees became so thick they twisted together like pipe cleaners. She got down on her hands and knees and crawled between limbs and around tree trunks and tried to lose herself among them.

To follow her, Moon Face had to do the same thing, and at first she heard him behind her, but after a while, there were only the sounds she was making.

She paused and listened.

Nothing.

Glancing the way she had come, she saw the intertwining limbs she had crawled under mixed with penetrating moonbeams, heard the short bursts of her breath and the beating of her heart, but detected no evidence of Moon Face. She decided the head start she had, all the weaving she had done, the cover of the pines, had confused him, at least temporarily.

It occurred to her that if she had stopped to listen, he might have done the same, and she wondered if he could hear the pounding of her heart. She took a deep breath and held it and let it out slowly through her nose, did it again. She was breathing more normally now, and her heart, though still hammering furiously, felt as if it were back inside her chest where it belonged.

Easing her back against a tree trunk, she sat and listened, watching for that strange face, fearing it might abruptly burst through the limbs and brush, grinning its horrible teeth, or worse, that he might come up behind her, reach around the tree trunk with his knife and finish her in a bloody instant.

She checked and saw that she still had her purse. She opened it and got hold of the file kit by feel and removed the last file, determined to make better use of it than the first. She had no qualms about using it, knew she would, but what good would it do? The man was obviously stronger than she, and crazy as the pattern in a scratch quilt.

Once again, she thought of Bruce. What would he have done in this situation? He would certainly have been the man for the job. He would have relished it. Would probably have challenged old Moon Face to a one on one at the edge of the mountain, and even with a nail file, would have been confident that he could take him.

Ellen thought about how much she hated Bruce, and even now, shed of him, that hatred burned bright. How had she gotten mixed up with that dumb, macho bastard in the first place? He had seemed enticing at first. So powerful. Confident. Capable. The survivalist stuff had always seemed a little nutty, but at first no more nutty than an obsession with golf or a strong belief in astrology. Perhaps had she known how serious he was about it, she wouldn't have been attracted to him in the first place.

No. It wouldn't have mattered. She had been captivated by him, by his looks and build and power. She had nothing but her own libido and stupidity to blame. And worse yet, when things turned sour, she had stayed and let them sour even more. There had been good moments, but they were quickly eclipsed by Bruce's determination to be ready for the Big Day, as he referred to it. He knew it was coming, if he was somewhat vague on who was bringing it. But someone would start a war of some sort, a nuclear war, a war in the streets, and only the rugged individualist, well-armed and well-trained and strong of body and will, would survive beyond the initial attack. Those survivors would then carry out guerrilla warfare, hit and run operations, and eventually win back the country from . . . whoever. And if not win it back, at least have some kind of life free of dictatorship.

It was silly. It was every little boy's fantasy. Living by your wits with gun and knife. And owning a woman. She had been the woman. At first Bruce had been kind enough, treated her with respect. He was obviously on the male chauvinist side, but originally it had seemed harmless enough, kind of Old World charming. But when he moved them to the mountains, that charm had turned to domination, and the small crack in his mental state widened until it was a deep, dark gulf.

She was there to keep house and to warm his bed, and any opinions she had contrary to his own were stupid. He read survivalist books constantly and quoted passages to her and suggested she look the books over, be ready to stand tall against the oncoming aggressors.

By the time he had gone completely over the edge, living like a mountain man, ordering her about, his eyes roving from side to side, suspicious of her every move, expecting to hear on his shortwave at any moment World War Three had started, or that race riots were overrunning the U.S., or that a shiny probe packed with extraterrestrial invaders brandishing ray guns had landed on the White House lawn, she was trapped in his cabin in the mountains, with him holding the keys to her Chevy and his jeep.

For a time she feared he would become paranoid enough to imagine she was one of the "bad guys" and put a .357 round through her chest. But now she was free of him, escaped from all that . . . only to be threatened by another man; a moon-faced, silver-toothed monster with a knife.

She returned once again to the question, what would Bruce do, outside of challenging Moon Face in hand to hand combat? Sneaking past him would be the best bet, making it back to the Chevy. To do that Bruce would have used guerrilla techniques. "Take advantage of what's at hand," he always said.

Well, she had looked to see what was at hand, and that turned out to be a couple of fingernail files, one of them lost up the mountain.

Then maybe she wasn't thinking about this in the right way. She might not be able to outfight Moon Face, but perhaps she could outthink him. She had outthought Bruce, and he had considered himself a master of strategy and preparation.

She tried to put herself in Moon Face's head. What was he thinking? For the moment he saw her as his prey, a frightened animal on the run. He might be more cautious because of that trick with the limb, but he'd most likely chalk that one up to accident—which it was for the most part . . . but what if the prey turned on him?

There was a sudden cracking sound, and Ellen crawled a few feet in the direction of the noise, gently moved aside a limb. Some distance away, discerned faintly through a tangle of limbs, she saw light and detected movement, and knew it was Moon Face. The cracking sound must have been him stepping on a limb.

He was standing with his head bent, looking at the ground, flashing a little pocket flashlight, obviously examining the drag path she had made with her hands and knees when she entered into the pine thicket.

She watched as his shape and the light bobbed and twisted through the limbs and tree trunks, coming nearer. She wanted to run, but didn't know where to.

"All right," she thought. "All right. Take it easy. Think."

She made a quick decision. Removed the scissors from her purse, took off her shoes and slipped off her panty hose and put her shoes on again.

She quickly snipped three long strips of nylon from her damaged panty hose and knotted them together, using the sailor knots Bruce had taught her. She cut more thin strips from the hose—all the while listening for Moon Face's approach—and used all but one of them to fasten her fingernail file, point out, securely to the tapered end of one of the small, flexible pine limbs, then she tied one end of the long nylon strip she had made around the limb, just below the file, and crawled backwards, pulling the limb with her, bending it deep. When she had it back as far as she could manage, she took a death grip on the nylon strip, and using it to keep the limb's position taut, crawled around the trunk of a small pine and curved the nylon strip about it and made a loop knot at the base of a sapling that crossed her knee-drag trail. She used her last strip of nylon to fasten to the loop of the knot, and carefully stretched the remaining length across the trail and tied it to another sapling. If it worked correctly, when he came crawling through the thicket, following her, his hands or knees would hit the strip, pull the loop free, and the limb would fly forward, the file stabbing him, in an eye if she were lucky.

Pausing to look through the boughs again, she saw that Moon Face was on his hands and knees, moving through the thick foliage toward her. Only moments were left.

She shoved pine needles over the strip and moved away on her belly, sliding under the cocked sapling, no longer concerned that she might make noise, in fact hoping noise would bring Moon Face quickly.

Following the upward slope of the hill, she crawled until the trees became thin again and she could stand. She cut two long strips of nylon from her hose with the scissors, and stretched them between two trees about ankle high.

That one would make him mad if it caught him, but the next one would be the corker.

She went up the path, used the rest of the nylon to tie between two saplings, then grabbed hold of a thin, short limb and yanked at it until it cracked, worked it free so there was a point made from the break. She snapped that over her knee to form a point at the opposite end. She made a quick mental measurement, jammed one end of the stick into the soft ground, leaving a point facing up.

At that moment came evidence her first snare had worked—a loud swishing sound as the limb popped forward and a cry of pain. This was followed by a howl as Moon Face crawled out of the thicket and onto the trail. He stood slowly, one hand to his face. He glared up at her, removed his hand. The file had struck him in the cheek; it was covered with blood. Moon Face pointed his blood-covered hand at her and let out an accusing shriek so horrible she retreated rapidly up the trail. Behind her, she could hear Moon Face running.

The trail curved upward and turned abruptly. She followed the curve a ways, looked back as Moon Face tripped over her first strip and hit the ground, came up madder, charged even more violently up the path. But the second strip got him and he fell forward, throwing his hands out. The spike in the trail hit him low in the throat.

She stood transfixed at the top of the trail as he did a pushup and came to one knee and put a hand to his throat. Even from a distance, and with only the moonlight to show it to her, she could see that the wound was dreadful.

Good.

Moon Face looked up, stabbed her with a look, started to rise. Ellen turned and ran. As she made the turns in the trail, the going improved and she theorized that she was rushing up the trail she had originally come down.

This hopeful notion was dispelled when the pines thinned and the trail dropped, then leveled off, then tapered into nothing. Before she could slow up, she discovered she was on a sort of peninsula that jutted out from the mountain and resembled an irregular-shaped diving board from which you could leap off into night-black eternity.

In place of the pines on the sides of the trail were numerous scarecrows on poles, and out on the very tip of the peninsula, somewhat dispelling the diving board image, was a shack made of sticks and mud and brambles.

After pausing to suck in some deep breaths, Ellen discovered on closer examination that it wasn't scarecrows bordering her path after all. It was people.

Dead people. She could smell them.

There were at least a dozen on either side, placed upright on poles, their feet touching the ground, their knees slightly bent. They were all fully clothed, and in various states of deterioration. Holes had been poked through the backs of their heads to correspond with the hollow sockets of their eyes, and the moonlight came through the holes and shined through the sockets, and Ellen noted, with a warm sort of horror, that one wore a white sun dress and pink, plastic shoes, and through its head she could see stars. On the corpse's finger was a wedding ring, and the finger had grown thin and withered and the ring was trapped there by knuckle bone alone.

The man next to her was fresher. He too was eyeless and holes had been drilled through the back of his skull, but he still wore glasses and was fleshy. There was a pen and pencil set in his coat pocket. He wore only one shoe.

There was a skeleton in overalls, a wilting cigar stuck between his teeth. A fresh UPS man with his cap at a jaunty angle, the moon through his head, and a clipboard tied to his hand with string. His legs had been positioned in such a way it seemed as if he was walking. A housewife with a crumpled, nearly disintegrated grocery bag under her arm, the contents having long fallen through the worn, wet bottom to heap at her feet in a mass of colorless boxes and broken glass. A withered corpse in a ballerina's tutu and slippers, rotting grapefruits tied to her chest with cord to simulate breasts, her legs arranged in such a way she seemed in mid-dance, up on her toes, about to leap or whirl.

The real horror was the children. One pathetic little boy's corpse, still full of flesh and with only his drilled eyes to show death, had been arranged in such a way that a teddy bear drooped from the crook of his elbow. A toy metal tractor and a plastic truck were at his feet.

There was a little girl wearing a red, rubber clown nose and a propeller beenie. A green plastic purse hung from her shoulder by a strap and a doll's legs had been taped to her palm with black electrician's tape. The doll hung upside down, holes drilled through its plastic head so that it matched its owner.

Things began to click. Ellen understood what Moon Face had been doing down here in the first place. He hadn't been in the Buick when she struck it. He was disposing of a body. He was a murderer who brought his victims here and set them up on either side of the pathway, parodying the way they were in life, cutting out their eyes and punching through the backs of their heads to let the world in.

Ellen realized numbly that time was slipping away, and Moon Face was coming, and she had to find the trail up to her car. But when she turned to run, she froze.

Thirty feet away, where the trail met the last of the pines, squatting dead center in it, arms on his knees, one hand loosely holding the knife, was Moon Face. He looked calm, almost happy, in spite of the fact a large swath of dried blood was on his cheek and the wound in his throat was making a faint whistling sound as air escaped it.

He appeared to be gloating, savoring the moment when he would set his knife to work on her eyes, the gray matter behind them, the bone of her skull.

A vision of her corpse propped up next to the child with the teddy bear, or perhaps the skeletal ballerina, came to mind; she could see herself hanging there, the light of the moon falling through her empty head, melting into the path.

Then she felt anger. It boiled inside her. She determined she was not going to allow Moon Face his prize easily. He'd earn it.

Another line from Bruce's books came to her.

Consider your alternatives.

She did, in a flash. And they were grim. She could try charging past Moon Face, or pretend to, then dart into the pines. But it seemed unlikely she could make the trees before he overtook her. She could try going over the side of the trail and climbing down, but it was much too steep there, and she'd fall immediately. She could make for the shack and try and find something she could fight with. The last idea struck her as the correct one, the one Bruce would have pursued. What was his quote? "If you can't effect an escape, fall back and fight with what's available to you."

She hurried to the hut, glancing behind her from time to time to check on Moon Face. He hadn't moved. He was observing her calmly, as if he had all the time in the world.

When she was about to go through the doorless entry way, she looked back at him one last time. He was in the same spot, watching, the knife held limply against his leg. She knew he thought he had her right where he wanted her, and that's exactly what she wanted him to think. A surprise attack was the only chance she had. She just hoped she could find something to surprise him with.

She hastened inside and let out an involuntary rasp of breath.

The place stank, and for good reason. In the center of the little hut was a folding card table and some chairs, and seated in one of the chairs was a woman, the flesh rotting and dripping off her skull like candle wax, her eyes empty and holes in the back of her head. Her arm was resting on the table and her hand was clamped around an open bottle of whiskey. Beside her, also without eyes, suspended in a standing position by wires connected to the roof, was a man. He was a fresh kill. Big, dressed in khaki pants and shirt and work shoes. In one hand a doubled belt was taped, and wires were attached in such a way that his arm was drawn back as if ready to strike. Wires were secured to his lips and pulled tight behind his head so that he was smiling in a ghoulish way. Foil gum wrappers were fixed to his teeth, and the moonlight gleaming through the opening at the top of the hut fell on them and made them resemble Moon Face's metal-tipped choppers.

Ellen felt queasy, but fought the sensation down. She had more to worry about than corpses. She had to prevent herself from becoming one.

She gave the place a quick pan. To her left was a rust-framed roll-away bed with a thin, dirty mattress, and against the far wall was a baby crib, and next to that a camper stove with a small frying pan on it.

She glanced quickly out the door of the hut and saw that Moon Face had moved onto the stretch of trail bordered by the bodies. He was walking very slowly, looking up now and then as if to appreciate the stars.

Her heart pumped another beat.

She moved about the hut, looking for a weapon.

The frying pan.

She grabbed it, and as she did, she saw what was in the crib.

What belonged there. A baby. But dead. A few months old. Its skin thin as plastic and stretched tight over pathetic, little rib bones. Eyes gone, holes through its head. Burnt match stubs between blackened toes. It wore a diaper and the stink of feces wafted from it and into her nostrils. A rattle lay at the foot of the crib.

A horrible realization rushed through her. The baby had been alive when taken by this mad man, and it had died here, starved and tortured. She gripped the frying pan with such intensity her hand cramped.

Her foot touched something.

She looked down. Large bones were heaped there—discarded Mommies and Daddies, for it now occurred to her that was who the corpses represented.

Something gleamed amongst the bones. A gold cigarette lighter.

Through the doorway of the hut she saw Moon Face was halfway down the trail. He had paused to nonchantly adjust the UPS man's clipboard. The geek had made his own community here, his own family, people he could deal with—dead people—and it was obvious he intended for her to be part of his creation.

Ellen considered attacking straight-on with the frying pan when Moon Face came through the doorway, but so far he had proven strong enough to take a file in the cheek and a stick in the throat, and despite the severity of the latter wound, he had kept on coming. Chances were he was strong enough to handle her and her frying pan.

A back-up plan was necessary. Another one of Bruce's pronouncements. She recalled a college friend, Carol, who used to use her bikini panties to launch projectiles at a teddy bear propped on a chair. This graduated to an apple on the bear's head. Eventually, Ellen and her dorm sisters got into the act. Fresh panties with tight elastic and marbles for ammunition were ever ready in a box by the door, the bear and an apple were in constant position. In time, Ellen became the best shot of all. But that was ten years ago. Expertise was long gone, even the occasional shot now and then was no longer taken . . . still . . .

Ellen replaced the frying pan on the stove, hiked up her dress and pulled her bikini panties down and stepped out of them and picked up the lighter.

She put the lighter in the crotch of the panties and stuck her fingers into the leg loops to form a fork and took hold of the lighter through the panties and pulled it back, assured herself the elastic was strong enough to launch the projectile.

All right. That was a start.

She removed her purse, so Moon Face couldn't grab it and snare her, and tossed it aside. She grabbed the whiskey bottle from the corpse's hand and turned and smashed the bottom of it against the cook stove. Whiskey and glass flew. The result was a jagged weapon she could lunge with. She placed the broken bottle on the stove next to the frying pan.

Outside, Moon Face was strolling toward the hut, like a shy teenager about to call on his date.

There were only moments left. She glanced around the room, hoping insanely at the last second she would find some escape route, but there was none.

Sweat dripped from her forehead and ran into her eye and she blinked it out and half-drew back the panty sling with its golden projectile. She knew her makeshift weapon wasn't powerful enough to do much damage, but it might give her a moment of distraction, a chance to attack him with the bottle. If she went at him straight on with it, she felt certain he would disarm her and make short work of her, but if she could get him off guard . . .

She lowered her arms, kept her makeshift slingshot in front of her, ready to be cocked and shot.

Moon Face came through the door, ducking as he did, a sour sweat smell entering with him. His neck wound whistled at her like a teapot about to boil. She saw then that he was bigger than she first thought. Tall and broad-shouldered and strong.

He looked at her and there was that peculiar expression again. The moonlight from the hole in the roof hit his eyes and teeth, and it was as if that light was his source of energy. He filled his chest with air and seemed to stand a full two inches taller. He looked at the woman's corpse in the chair, the man's corpse supported on wires, glanced at the playpen.

He smiled at Ellen, squeaked more than spoke, "Bubba's home, Sissie."

I'm not Sissie yet, thought Ellen. Not yet.

Moon Face started to move around the card table and Ellen let out a blood-curdling scream that caused him to bob his head high like a rabbit surprised by headlights. Ellen jerked up the panties and pulled them back and let loose the lighter. It shot out of the panties and fell to the center of the card table with a clunk.

Moon Face looked down at it.

Ellen was temporarily gripped with paralysis, then she stepped forward and kicked the card table as hard as she could. It went into Moon Face, hitting him waist high, startling, but not hurting him.

Now! thought Ellen, grabbing her weapons. Now!

She rushed him, the broken bottle in one hand, the frying pan in the other. She slashed out with the bottle and it struck him in the center of the face and he let out a scream and the glass fractured and a splash of blood burst from him and in that same instant Ellen saw that his nose was cut half in two and she felt a tremendous throb in her hand. The bottle had broken in her palm and cut her.

She ignored the pain and as Moon Face bellowed and lashed out with the knife, cutting the front of her dress but not her flesh, she brought the frying pan around and caught him on the elbow, and the knife went soaring across the room and behind the rollaway bed.

Moon Face froze, glanced in the direction the knife had taken. He seemed empty and confused without it.

Ellen swung the pan again. Moon Face caught her wrist and jerked her around and she lost the pan and was sent hurtling toward the bed, where she collapsed on the mattress. The bed slid down and smashed through the thin wall of sticks and a foot of the bed stuck out into blackness and the great drop below. The bed tottered slightly, and Ellen rolled off of it, directly into the legs of Moon Face. As his knees bent, and he reached for her, she rolled backwards and went under the bed and her hand came to rest on the knife. She grabbed it, rolled back toward Moon Face's feet, reached out quickly and brought the knife down on one of his shoes and drove it in as hard as she could.

A bellow from Moon Face. His foot leaped back and it took the knife with it. Moon Face screamed, "Sissie! You're hurting me!"

Moon Face reached down and pulled the knife out, and Ellen saw his foot come forward, and then he was grabbing the bed and effortlessly jerking it off of her and back, smashing it into the crib, causing the child to topple out of it and roll across the floor, the rattle clattering behind it. He grabbed Ellen by the back of her dress and jerked her up and spun her around to face him, clutched her throat in one hand and held the knife close to her face with the other, as if for inspection; the blade caught the moonlight and winked.

Beyond the knife, she saw his face, pathetic and pained and

white. His breath, sharp as the knife, practically wilted her. His neck wound whistled softly. The remnants of his nose dangled wet and red against his upper lip and cheek and his teeth grinned a moon-lit, metal good-bye.

It was all over, and she knew it, but then Bruce's words came back to her in a rush. "When it looks as if you're defeated, and there's nothing left, try anything."

She twisted and jabbed out at his eyes with her fingers and caught him solid enough that he thrust her away and stumbled backwards. But only for an instant. He bolted forward, and Ellen stooped and grabbed the dead child by the ankle and struck Moon Face with it as if it were a club. Once in the face, once in the mid-section. The rotting child burst into a spray of desiccated flesh and innards and she hurled the leg at Moon Face and then she was circling around the roll-away bed, trying to make the door. Moon Face, at the other end of the bed, saw this, and when she moved for the door, he lunged in that direction, causing her to jump back to the end of the bed. Smiling, he returned to his end, waited for her next attempt.

She lurched for the door again, and Moon Face deep-stepped that way, and when she jerked back, Moon Face jerked back too, but this time Ellen bent and grabbed the end of the bed and hurled herself against it. The bed hit Moon Face in the knees, and as he fell, the bed rolled over him and he let go of the knife and tried to put out his hands to stop the bed's momentum. The impetus of the roll-away carried him across the short length of the dirt floor and his head hit the far wall and the sticks cracked and hurtled out into blackness, and Moon Face followed and the bed followed him, then caught on the edge of the drop and the wheels buried up in the dirt and hung there.

Ellen had shoved so hard she fell face down, and when she looked up, she saw the bed was dangling, shaking, the mattress slipping loose, about to glide off into nothingness.

Moon Face's hands flicked into sight, clawing at the sides of the bed's frame. Ellen gasped. He was going to make it up. The bed's wheels were going to hold.

She pulled a knee under her, cocking herself, then sprang forward, thrusting both palms savagely against the bed. The wheels popped free and the roll-away shot out into the dark emptiness.

Ellen scooted forward on her knees and looked over the edge. There was blackness, a glimpse of the mattress falling free, and a pale object, like a white-washed planet with a great vein of silver in it, jetting through the cold expanse of space. Then the mattress and the face were gone and there was just the darkness and a distant sound like a water balloon exploding.

Ellen sat back and took a breather. When she felt strong again and felt certain her heart wouldn't tear through her chest, she stood up and looked around the room. She thought a long time about what she saw.

She found her purse and panties, went out of the hut and up the trail, and after a few wrong turns, she found the proper trail that wound its way up the mountain side to where her car was parked. When she climbed over the railing, she was exhausted.

Everything was as it was. She wondered if anyone had seen the cars, if anyone had stopped, then decided it didn't matter. There was no one here now, and that's what was important.

She took the keys from her purse and tried the engine. It turned over. That was a relief.

She killed the engine, got out and went around and opened the trunk of the Chevy and looked down at Bruce's body. His face looked like one big bruise, his lips were as large as sausages. It made her happy to look at him.

A new energy came to her. She got him under the arms and pulled him out and managed him over to the rail and grabbed his legs and flipped him over the railing and onto the trail. She got one of his hands and started pulling him down the path, letting the momentum help her. She felt good. She felt strong. First Bruce had tried to dominate her, had threatened her, had thought she was weak because she was a woman, and one night, after slapping her, after raping her, while he slept a drunken sleep, she had pulled the blankets up tight around him and looped rope over and under the bed and used the knots he had taught her, and secured him.

Then she took a stick of stove wood and had beat him until she was so weak she fell to her knees. She hadn't meant to kill him, just punish him for slapping her around, but when she got started she couldn't stop until she was too worn out to go on, and when she was finished, she discovered he was dead.

That didn't disturb her much. The thing then was to get rid of the body somewhere, drive on back to the city and say he had abandoned her and not come back. It was weak, but all she had. Until now.

After several stops for breath, a chance to lie on her back and look up at the stars, Ellen managed Bruce to the hut and got her arms under his and got him seated in one of the empty chairs. She straightened things up as best as she could. She put the larger pieces of the baby back in the crib. She picked Moon Face's knife up off the floor and looked at it and looked at Bruce, his eyes wide open, the moonlight from the roof striking them, showing them to be dull as scratched glass.

Bending over his face, she went to work on his eyes. When she finished with them, she pushed his head forward and used the blade like a drill. She worked until the holes satisfied her. Now if the police found the Buick up there and came down the trail to investigate, and found the trail leading here, saw what was in the shack, Bruce would fit in with the rest of Moon Face's victims. The police would probably conclude Moon Face, sleeping here with his "family," had put his bed too close to the cliff and it had broken through the thin wall and he had tumbled to his death.

She liked it.

She held Bruce's chin, lifted it, examined her work.

"You can be Uncle Brucey," she said, and gave Bruce a pat on the shoulder. "Thanks for all your advice and help, Uncle Brucey. It's what got me through." She gave him another pat.

She found a shirt—possibly Moon Face's, possibly a victim's—on the opposite side of the shack, next to a little box of Harlequin Romances, and she used it to wipe the knife, pan, all she had touched, clean of her prints, then she went out of there, back up to her car.

This little short-short is one of my more popular stories. In one way it's amusing, but like most stories of this sort, its roots are not amusing. When you think about what it's really about, it's pretty damn depressing. But there's humor in horror. Robert Bloch, one of the greatest writers the field has ever known, proved that time after time. He was a great influence on me. I consider this a kind of Robert Bloch story. Or maybe Fred Brown, another of my favorites.

Voice wise, however, it's all me.

It first appeared in a small magazine, was then photocopied by readers to share with friends, told aloud, and talked about for some years before it was reprinted again. It was even read on Welsh radio.

It was inspired by eating too much popcorn, which always gives me bad dreams. There was a time in my career when popcorn and its influences were of great importance to me. I'd eat it before bed and it would give me a stomachache and bad dreams. Next morning those dreams would become a story or stories. My record of sales for stories based on gorging popcorn was remarkable. These days, the types of stories I write are not popcorn inspired; in fact, I don't eat a fraction of what I used to eat. My stomach can't take it. I like to think what I do now is just as good, or better. But there certainly was a type of story that seemed to come out of this habit, and I don't write that sort anymore. Occasionally I miss them and turn my head to the cabinet where the popcorn resides.

I always end up eating a proper amount however.

But who knows. Maybe a good gorging is just around the corner.

MY DEAD DOG, BOBBY

MY DEAD DOG, BOBBY, DOESN'T DO TRICKS ANY-more. In fact, to look that sucker in the eye I either have to get down on my knees and put my head to the ground or prop him up with a stick.

I've thought of nailing his head to the shed out back, that way maybe the ants won't be so bad. But as my Old Man says, "ants can climb." So, maybe that isn't such a good idea after all.

He was such a good dog, though, and I hate to see him rot away. But I'm also tired of carrying him around with me in a sack, lugging him into the freezer morning and night.

One thing though. Getting killed broke him from chasing cars, which is how he got mashed in the first place. Now, to get him to play with cars, I have to go out to the edge of the Interstate and throw him and his sack at them, and when he gets caught under the tires and bounced up, I have to use my foot to push on one end of him to make the other end fill up with guts again. I get so I really kind of hate to look in the sack at the end of the day, and I have to admit giving him his good night kiss on the lips is not nearly as fun as it used to be. He has a smell and the teeth that have been smashed through his snout are sharp and stick out every which way and sometimes cut my face.

I'm going to take Bobby down to the lake again tomorrow. If you tie him to a blowed-up inner tube he floats. It's not a bad way to cool off from a hot day, and it also drowns the ants and maggots and such.

I know it does. We kept my little brother in pretty good shape for six months that way. It wasn't until we started nailing him to the shed out back that he got to looking ragged. It wasn't the ants crawling up there and getting him, it was the damn nails. We ran out of good places to drive them after his ears came off, and we had to use longer and longer nails to put through his head and neck and the like. Pulling the nails out everyday with the hammer claw didn't do him any good either.

My Old Man said that if he had it do over, he wouldn't have hit my brother so hard with that chair. But he said that about my little sister too when he kicked her head in. She didn't keep long, by the way. We didn't know as many tricks then as we do now.

Well, I hope I can get Bobby back in this sack. He's starting to swell and come apart on me. I'm sort of ready to get him packed away so I can get home and see Mom. I always look at her for a few minutes before I put Bobby in the freezer with her.

This is considered atypical of me. Maybe it is. I think the truth is most readers remember the stories you do that they like, and the ones they like most often fit into one niche. Those outside of it they discard from their memory.

I think this one actually fits comfortably into a larger niche of my work than some realize. If I'm anything, it's varied.

I have always loved science fiction, and it was my original plan to write it. Problem was, I didn't know much science. I was more of the Bradbury school. Still, there were plenty of science fiction stories that didn't use real science, and I always presumed this would be where I ended up: a full-time science fiction writer. It wasn't.

I began to write crime and horror, which I also loved. And then other things: Westerns, etc. In fact, when I first started writing, I wrote non-fiction articles. Those took off and I lost interest in being a full-time science fiction writer.

I still love the genre, and now and then I like to dabble in it, but I have no regrets about how things turned out.

Anyway, my favorite kinds of science fiction, or science fantasy, or speculative fiction, if you prefer, were alternate universe, time travel, and apocalyptic. This is one of the former.

I love the Old West and it's no surprise to me that when I sat down to write an alternate universe story I used the West as the background. I knew what I was talking about for one, and knew I could tweak it in different directions if I so chose to make it interesting, and yet, maintain some resemblance to real history.

This story first appeared in a literary magazine, and has been reprinted numerous times. Funny thing, I've had some believe it's true history. Where were they during American History class? Smoking a joint in the bathroom?

On the other end of the spectrum, I had one reader dislike it because the history was wrong.

Bill Hickok wasn't a clerk. William Cody wasn't a diplomat.

Say they weren't?

Lack of imagination amazes me.

Not even a general idea of the events of American History amazes me.

I'm not talking dates and figures here, even names. But the broad knowledge that we really weren't colonized on the West coast by the Japanese and that the Europeans and the Japanese didn't really war with one another in North America until they joined hands to fight Native Americans.

That, my friends, is the part that didn't happen.

On the other hand, if you believe in alternate universes, maybe everything here did happen. Somewhere.

TRAINS NOT TAKEN

DAPPLED SUNLIGHT DANCED ON THE EASTERN side of the train. The boughs of the great cherry trees reached out along the tracks and almost touched the cars, but not quite; they had purposely been trimmed to fall short of that.

James Butler Hickok wondered how far the rows of cherry trees went. He leaned against the window of the Pullman car and tried to look down the track. The speed of the train, the shadows of the trees and the illness of his eyesight did not make the attempt very successful. But the dark line that filled his vision went on and on and on.

Leaning back, he felt more than just a bit awed. He was actually seeing the famous Japanese cherry trees of the Western Plains; one of the Great Cherry Roads that stretched along the tracks from mid-continent to the Black Hills of the Dakotas.

Turning, he glanced at his wife. She was sleeping, her attractive, sharp-boned face marred by the pout of her mouth and the tight lines around her eyes. That look was a perpetual item she had cultivated in the last few years, and it stayed in place both awake or asleep. Once her face held nothing but laughter, vision and hope, but now it hurt him to look at her.

For a while he turned his atttention back to the trees, allowing the rhythmic beat of the tracks, the overhead hiss of the fire line and the shadows of the limbs to pleasantly massage his mind into white oblivion.

After a while, he opened his eyes, noted that his wife had left her seat. Gone back to the sleeping car, most likely. He did not hasten to join her. He took out his pocket watch and looked at it. He had been asleep just under an hour. Both he and Mary Jane had had their breakfast early, and had decided to sit in the parlor car and watch the people pass. But they had proved disinterested in their fellow passengers and in each other, and had both fallen asleep.

Well, he did not blame her for going back to bed, though she spent a lot of time there these days. He was, and had been all morning, sorry company.

A big man with blonde goatee and mustache came down the aisle, spotted the empty seat next to Hickok and sat down. He produced a pipe and a leather pouch of tobacco, held it hopefully. "Could I trouble you for a light, sir?"

Hickok found a lucifer and lit the pipe while the man puffed.

"Thank you," the man said. "Name's Cody. Bill Cody."

"Jim Hickok."

They shook hands.

"Your first trip to the Dakotas?" Cody asked.

Hickok nodded.

"Beautiful country, Jim, beautiful. The Japanese may have been a pain in the neck in their time, but they sure know how to make a garden spot of the world. White men couldn't have grown sagebrush or tree moss in the places they've beautified."

"Quite true," Hickok said. He got out the makings and rolled himself a smoke. He did this slowly, with precision, as if the anticipation and preparation were greater than the final event. When he had rolled the cigarette to his satisfaction, he put a lucifer to it and glanced out the window. A small, attractive stone shrine, nestled among the cherry trees, whizzed past his vision.

Glancing back at Cody, Hickok said, "I take it this is not your first trip?"

"Oh no, no. I'm in politics. Something of an ambassador, guess you'd say. Necessary that I make a lot of trips this way. Cementing relationships with the Japanese, you know. To pat myself on the back a bit, friend, I'm responsible for the cherry road being expanded into the area of the U.S. Sort of a diplomatic gesture I arranged with the Japanese."

"Do you believe there will be more war?"

"Uncertain. But with the Sioux and the Cheyenne forming up again, I figure the yellows and the whites are going to be pretty busy with the reds. Especially after last week."

"Last week?"

"You haven't heard?"

Hickok shook his head.

"The Sioux and some Cheyenne under Crazy Horse and Sitting Bull wiped out General Custer and the Japanese General Miyamoto Yoshii."

"The whole command?"

"To the man. U.S. Cavalry and Samurai alike."

"My God!"

"Terrible. But I think it's the last rise for the red man, and not to sound ghoulish, friend, but I believe this will further cement Japanese and American relationships. A good thing, considering a number of miners in Cherrywood, both white and yellow have found gold. In a case like that, it's good to have a common enemy."

"I didn't know that either."

"Soon the whole continent will know, and there will be a scrambling to Cherrywood the likes you've never seen."

Hickok rubbed his eyes. Blast the things. His sight was good in the dark or in shadowed areas, but direct sunlight stabbed them like needles.

At the moment Hickok uncovered his eyes and glanced toward the shadowed comfort of the aisle, a slightly overweight woman came down it tugging on the ear of a little boy in short pants. "John Luther Jones," she said, "I've told you time and again to leave the Engineer alone. Not to ask so many questions." She pulled the boy on.

Cody looked at Hickok, said softly: "I've never seen a little boy that loves trains as much as that one. He's always trying to go up front and his mother is on him all the time. She must have whipped his little butt three times yesterday. Actually, I don't think the Engineer minds the boy."

Hickok started to smile, but his attention was drawn to an attractive woman who was following not far behind mother and son. In Dime Novels she would have been classified "a vision." Health lived on her heart-shaped face as surely as ill-content lived on that of his wife. Her hair was wheat-ripe yellow and her eyes were as green as the leaves of a spring-fresh tree. She was sleek in blue and white calico with a thick, black Japanese cloth belt gathered about her slim waist. All the joy of the world was in her motion, and Hickok did not want to look at her and compare her to his wife, but he did not want to lose sight of her either, and it was with near embarrassment that he turned his head and watched her pass until the joyful swing of her hips waved him goodbye, passing out of sight into the next car of the train.

When Hickok settled back in his seat, feeling somewhat worn under the collar, he noted that Cody was smiling at him.

"Kind of catches the eye, does she not?" Cody said. "My wife, Louisa, noticed me noticing the young thing yesterday, and she has since developed the irritating habit of waving her new Japanese fan in front of my face 'accidently', when she passes."

"You've seen her a lot?"

"Believe she has a sleeping car above the next parlor car. I think about that sleeping car a bunch. Every man on this train that's seen her, probably thinks about that sleeping car a bunch."

"Probably so."

"You single?"

"No."

"Ah, something of a pain sometimes, is it not? Well, friend, must get back to the wife, least she think I'm chasing the sweet, young thing. And if the Old Woman were not on this trip, I just might be."

Cody got up, and with a handshake and a politician wave, strode up the aisle and was gone.

Hickok turned to look out the window again, squinting somewhat to comfort his eyes. He actually saw little. His vision was turned inward. He thought about the girl. He had been more than a bit infatuated with her looks. For the first time in his life, infidelity truly crossed his mind.

Not since he had married Mary Jane and become a clerk, had he actually thought of trespassing on their marriage agreement. But as of late the mere sight of her was like a wound with salt in it.

After rolling and smoking another cigarette, Hickok rose and walked back toward his sleeping car, imagining that it was not his pinch-faced wife he was returning to, but the blonde girl and her sexual heaven. He imagined that she was a young girl on her first solo outing. Going out West to meet the man of her dreams. Probably had a father who worked as a military officer at the fort outside of Cherrywood, and now that Japanese and American relations had solidified considerably, she had been called to join him. Perhaps the woman with the child was her mother and the boy her brother.

He carried on this pretty fantasy until he reached the sleeping car and found his cabin. When he went inside, he found that Mary Jane was still sleeping.

She lay tossed out on the bunk with her arm thrown across her eyes. Her sour, puckering lips had not lost their bitterness. They projected upwards like the mouth of an active volcano about to spew. She had taken off her clothes and laid them neatly over the back of a chair, and her somewhat angular body was visible because the sheet she had pulled over herself had fallen half off and lay draped only over her right leg and the edge of the bunk. Hickok noted that the glass decanter of whiskey on the little table was less than half full. As of this morning only a drink or two had been missing. She had taken more than enough to fall comfortably back to sleep again, another habit of near recent vintage.

He let his eyes roam over her, looking for something that would stir old feelings—not sexual but loving. Her dark hair curled around her neck. Her shoulders, sharp as Army sabres, were her next most obvious feature. The light through the windows made the little freckles on her alabaster skin look like some sort of pox. The waist and hips that used to excite him still looked wasp-thin, but the sensuality and lividness of her flesh had disappeared. She was just thin from not eating enough. Whiskey was now often her breakfast, lunch and supper.

A tinge of sadness crept into Hickok as he looked at this angry, alcoholic lady with a life and a husband that had not lived up to her romantic and wealthy dreams. In the last two years she had lost her hope and her heart, and the bottle had become her lifeblood. Her faith in him had died, along with the little-girl look in her once-bright eyes.

Well, he had had his dreams too. Some of them a bit wild perhaps, but they had dreamed him through the dullness of a Kansas clerkery that had paid the dues of the flesh but not of the mind.

Pouring himself a shot from the decanter, he sat on the wall bench and looked at his wife some more. When he got tired of that, he put his hand on the bench, but found a book instead of wood. He picked it up and looked at it. It was titled: *Down the Whiskey River Blue*, by Edward Zane Carroll Judson.

Hickok placed his drink beside him and thumbed through the book. It did not do much for him. As were all of Judson's novels, it was a sensitive and overly poetic portrayal of life in our times. It was in a word, boring. Or perhaps he did not like it because his wife liked it so much. Or because she made certain that he knew the Dime Novels he read by Sam Clemens and the verse by Walt Whitman were trash and doggerel. She was the sensitive one, she said. She stuck to Judson and poets like John Wallace Crawford and Cincinnatus Hiner.

Well, she could have them.

Hickok put the book down and glanced at his wife. This trip had not worked out. They had designed it to remold what had been lost, but no effort had been expended on her part that he could see. He tried to feel guilty, conclude that he too had not pushed the matter, but that simply was not true. She had turned him into bad company with her sourness. When they had started out he had mined for their old love like a frantic prospector looking for color in a vein he knew was long mined out.

Finishing his drink, and placing the book behind his head for a pillow, Hickok threw his feet up on the long bench and stretched out, long-fingered hands meshed over his eyes. He found the weight of his discontent was more able than Morpheus to bring sleep.

When he awoke, it was because his wife was running a finger along the edge of his cheek, tracing his jawbone with it. He looked up into her smiling face, and for a moment he thought he had dreamed all the bad times and that things were fine and as they should be; imagined that time had not put a weight on their marriage and that it was shortly after their wedding when they were very much on fire with each other. But the rumble of the train assured him that this was not the case, and that time had indeed passed. The moment of their marriage was far behind.

Mary Jane smiled at him, and for a moment the smile held all of her lost hopes and dreams. He smiled back at her. At that moment he wished deeply that they had had children. But it had never worked. One of them had a flaw and no children came from their couplings.

She bent to kiss him and it was a warm kiss that tingled him all over. In that moment he wanted nothing but their marriage and for it to be good. He even forgot the young girl he had seen while talking to Cody.

They did not make love, though he hoped they would. But she kissed him deeply several times and said that after bath and dinner they would go to bed. It would be like old times. When they often performed the ceremony of pleasure.

*   *   *

After the Cherokee porter had filled their tub with water, and after she had bathed and he had bathed in the dregs of her bath and they had toweled themselves dry, they laughed while they dressed. He kissed her and she kissed him back, their bodies pushed together in familiar ritual, but the ritual was not consummated. Mary Jane would have nothing of that. "After dinner," she said. "Like old times."

"Like old times," he said.

Arm in arm they went to the dining car, dressed to the hilt and smiling. They paid their dollar and were conducted to their table where they were offered a drink to begin the meal. As if to suggest hope for later, he denied one, but Mary Jane did not follow his lead. She had one, then another.

When she was on her third drink and dinner was in the process of being served, the blonde girl with the sunshine smile came in and sat not three tables down from them. She sat with the matronly woman and the little boy who loved trains. He found he could not take his eyes off the young lovely.

"Are you thinking about something?" Mary Jane asked.

"No, not really. Mind was wandering," he said. He smiled at her and saw that her eyes were a trifle shiny with drunkenness.

They ate in near silence and Mary Jane drank two more whiskies.

When they went back to the cabin, she was leaning on him and his heart had fallen. He knew the signs.

They went into their cabin and he hoped she was not as far along in drunkenness as he thought. She kissed him and made movements against his body with hers. He felt desire.

She went to the bed and undressed, and he undressed by the bench seat and placed his clothes there. He turned down the lamp and climbed into bed with her.

She had fallen asleep. Her breath came out in alcoholic snores. There would be no love-making tonight.

He lay there for a while and thought of nothing. Then he got up, dressed, went into the cars to look for some diversion, a poker game perhaps.

No poker game to be found and no face offered any friendly summons to him. He found a place to sit in the parlor car where the overhead lamp was turned down and there was no one sitting nearby. He got out the makings, rolled himself a smoke, and was putting a lucifer to it when Cody fell into the seat across from him. Cody had his pipe like before. "You'd think I'd have found some lucifers of my own by now, wouldn't you?"

Hickok thought just that, but he offered his still burning light to Cody. Cody bent forward and puffed flame into his packed pipe. When it was lit he sat back and said, "I thought you had turned in early. I saw you leave the dining car."

"I didn't see you."

"You were not looking in my direction. I was nearby."

Hickok understood what Cody was implying, but he did not acknowledge. He smoked his cigarette furiously.

"She is quite lovely," Cody said.

"I guess I made a fool out of myself looking at her. She is half my age."

"I meant your wife, but yes, the girl is a beauty. And she has a way with her eyes, don't you think?"

Hickok grunted agreement. He felt like a school boy who had been caught looking up the teacher's dress.

"I was looking too," Cody said cheerfully. "You see, I don't care for my wife much. You?"

"I want to, but she is not making it easy. We're like two trains on different tracks. We pass close enough to wave, but never close enough to touch."

"My God, friend, but you are a poet."

"I didn't mean to be."

"Well, mean to. I could use a bit of color and poetry in my life."

"An ambassador is more colorful than a clerk."

"An ambassador is little more than a clerk who travels. Maybe it's not so bad, but I just don't feel tailored to it."

"Then we are both cut from the wrong cloth, Cody."

Hickok finished his cigarette and looked out into the night. The shapes of the cherry trees flew by, looked like multi-armed men waving gentle goodbyes.

"It seems I have done nothing with my life," Hickok said after a while, and he did not look at Cody when he said it. He continued to watch the night and the trees. "Today when you told me about Custer and Yoshii, I did not feel sadness. Surprise, but not sadness. Now I know why. I envy them. Not their death, but their glory. A hundred years from now, probably more, they will be remembered. I will be forgotten a month after my passing—if it takes that long."

Cody reached over and opened a window. The wind felt cool

and comfortable. He tapped his pipe on the outside of the train. Sparks flew from it and blew down the length of the cars like fireflies in a blizzard. Cody left the window open, returned his pipe to his pocket.

"You know," Cody said, "I wanted to go out West during the Japanese Wars: the time the Japanese were trying to push down into Colorado on account of the gold we'd found there, and on account of we'd taken the place away from them back when it was part of New Japan. I was young then and I should have gone. I wanted to be a soldier. I might have been a great scout, or a buffalo hunter had my life gone different then."

"Do you sometimes wonder that your dreams are your real life, Cody? That if you hope for them enough they become solid? Maybe our dreams are our trains not taken."

"Come again."

"Our possible futures. The things we might have done had we just edged our lives another way."

"I hadn't thought much about it actually, but I like the sound of it."

"Will you laugh if I tell you my dream?"

"How could I? I've just told you mine."

"I dream that I'm a gunman—and with these light-sensitive eyes that's a joke. But that's what I am. One of those long-haired shootists like in the Dime Novels, or that real life fellow Wild Jack McCall. I even dream of lying face down on a card table, my pistol career ended by some skulking knave who didn't have the guts to face me and so shot me from behind. It's a good dream, even with the death, because I am remembered, like those soldiers who died at the Little Big Horn. It's such a strong dream I like to believe that it is actually happening somewhere, and that I am that man that I would rather be."

"I think I understand you, friend. I even envy Morse and these damn trains; him and his telegraph and *'pulsating energy.'* Those discoveries will make him live forever. Every time a message is flashed across the country or a train bullets along on the crackling power of its fire line, it's like thousands of people crying his name."

"Sometimes—a lot of the time—I just wish that for once I could live a dream."

They sat in silence. The night and the shadowed limbs of the cherry trees fled by, occasionally mixed with the staggered light of the moon and the stars.

Finally Cody said, "To bed. Cherrywood is an early stop." He opened his pocket watch and looked at it. "Less than four hours. The wife will awake and call out the Cavalry if I'm not there."

As Cody stood, Hickok said, "I have something for you." He handed Cody a handful of lucifers.

Cody smiled. "Next time we meet, friend, perhaps I will have my own." As he stepped into the aisle he said, "I've enjoyed our little talk."

"So have I," Hickok said. "I don't feel any happier, but I feel less lonesome."

"Maybe that's the best we can do."

Hickok went back to his cabin but did not try to be overly quiet. There was no need. Mary Jane, when drunk, slept like an anvil.

He slipped out of his clothes and crawled into bed. Lay there feeling the warmth of his wife's shoulder and hip; smelling the alcoholic aroma of her breath. He could remember a time when they could not crawl into bed together without touching and expressing their love. Now he did not want to touch her and he did not want to be touched by her. He could not remember the last time she had bothered to tell him she loved him, and he could not remember the last time he had said it and it was not partly a lie.

Earlier, before dinner, the old good times had been recalled and for a few moments he adored her. Now he lay beside her feeling anger. Anger because she would not try. Or could not try. Anger because he was always the one to try, the one to apologize, even when he felt he was not wrong. Trains on a different track going opposite directions, passing fast in the night, going nowhere really. That was them.

Closing his eyes, he fell asleep instantly and dreamed of the blonde lovely in blue and white calico with a thick black Japanese belt. He dreamed of her without the calico, lying here beside him white-skinned and soft and passionate and all the things his wife was not.

And when the dream ended, so did his sleep. He got up and dressed and went out to the parlor car. It was empty and dark. He sat and smoked a cigarette. When that was through he opened a window, felt and smelled the wind. It was a fine night. A lover's night.

Then he sensed the train was slowing.

Cherrywood already?

No, it was still too early for that. What gave here?

In the car down from the one in which he sat, a lamp was suddenly lit, and there appeared beside it the chiseled face of the Cherokee porter. Behind him, bags against their legs, were three people: the matronly lady, the boy who loved trains and the beautiful blonde woman.

The train continued to slow. Stopped.

By God, he thought, they are getting off.

Hickok got out his little, crumpled train schedule and pressed it out on his knee. He struck a lucifer and held it down behind the seat so that he could read. After that he got out his pocket watch and held it next to the flame. Two-fifteen. The time on his watch and that on the schedule matched. This was a scheduled stop — the little town and fort outside of Cherrywood. He had been right in his day dreaming. The girl was going here.

Hickok pushed the schedule into his pocket and dropped the dead lucifer on the floor. Even from where he sat, he could see the blonde girl. As always, she was smiling. The porter was enjoying the smile and he was giving her one back.

The train began to stop.

For a moment, Hickok imagined that he too was getting off here and that the blonde woman was his sweetheart or better yet, would be. They would meet in the railway station and strike up some talk, and she would be one of those new modern women who did not mind a man buying her a drink in public. But she would not be like his wife. She would drink for taste and not effect.

They would fall instantly in love, and on occasion they would walk in the moonlight down by these tracks, stand beneath the cherry trees and watch the trains run by. And afterwards they would lie down beneath the trees and make love with shadows and starlight as their canopy. When it was over, and they were tired of satisfaction, they would walk arm in arm back towards the town, or the fort, all depending.

The dream floated away as the blonde girl moved down the steps and out of the train. Hickok watched as the porter handed down their bags. He wished he could still see the young girl, but to do that he would have to put his head out the window, and he was old enough that he did not want to appear foolish.

Goodbye, Little Pretty, he thought. I will think and dream of you often.

Suddenly he realized that his cheeks were wet with tears. God, but he was unhappy and lonely. He wondered if behind her smiles the young girl might be lonely too.

He stood and walked toward the light even as the porter reached to turn it out.

"Excuse me," Hickok said to the man. "I'd like to get off here."

The porter blinked. "Yes sir, but the schedule only calls for three."

"I have a ticket for Cherrywood, but I've changed my mind, I'd like to get off here."

"As you wish, sir." The porter turned up the lamp. "Best hurry, the train's starting. Watch your step. Uh, any luggage?"

"None."

Briskly, Hickok stepped down the steps and into the night. The three he had followed were gone. He strained his eyes and saw between a path of cherry trees that they were walking toward the lights of the rail station.

He turned back to the train. The porter had turned out the light and was no longer visible. The train sang its song. On the roof he saw a ripple of blue-white fulmination jump along the metal fire line. Then the train made a sound like a boiling tea pot and began to move.

For a moment he thought of his wife lying there in their cabin. He thought of her waking in Cherrywood and not finding him there. He did not know what she would do, nor did he know what he would do.

Perhaps the blonde girl would have nothing to do with him. Or maybe, he thought suddenly, she is married or has a sweetheart already.

No matter. It was the ambition of her that had lifted him out of the old funeral pyre, and like a phoenix fresh from the flames, he intended to stretch his wings and soar.

The train gained momentum, lashed shadows by him. He turned his back on it and looked through the cherrywood path. The three had reached the rail station and had gone inside.

Straightening his collar and buttoning his jacket, he walked toward the station and the pretty blonde girl with a face like a hopeful heart.

John Maclay asked me to write a story for an anthology titled Nukes. Up until that point I was known as a pro who could turn out a good story in a short time. I had begun to accumulate a small following who watched for my name and read my stories, but no one was beating a path to my door. Nukes was an independent anthology, but it paid well, and I saw it as a financial break, I wanted to do as good a story as possible, and felt it would give me a chance to break away from the short-shorts I had been writing and do something with a little more meat on its bones.

At the time of being asked to write for Nukes I couldn't come up with a new idea, but there was an old one about carnivorous roses that was in my head. It had probably been inspired by The Day of the Triffids. I love both the book and the film — the book especially. Problem was, the idea I had in mind was too much like it, so I forgot it. But when I was asked to write a story for Nukes, my roses, like the world in my story, mutated and became something quite different from the triffids.

Writing the story was actually a depressing experience. At the time, I thought the story stunk, but realized later that I had gotten into this grim world all too well and it was working on me. When I was finished I sent it off with low expectations. The editor loved it, was published, and it was the first story of mine to get a lot of response from readers and to be reviewed as a story of importance. It, along with Dead in the West, and the Magic Wagon, as well as an anthology I edited of Western stories that year, all came together to change my life and finally put me on the map. A small map, I admit, but at least I was listed.

For those of you who look for science in this story, all I can say is, sorry. You'll hurt yourself. New species wouldn't pop up overnight, I know, but it was a conceit I enjoyed, and undoubtedly a throwback to all those old "after the bomb" science fiction movies I love.

Anyway, I used the after the bomb idea and the triffids for influence, tried to build characters and a truly frightening world and situation for the protagonist and went at it. Looking back on it, some years after its conception, I must admit I'm pretty damn happy with it.

TIGHT LITTLE STITCHES IN A DEAD MAN'S BACK

FROM THE JOURNAL OF PAUL MARDER

(Boom!)

THAT'S A LITTLE SCIENTIST JOKE, AND THE PROPER way to begin this. As for the purpose of this notebook, I'm uncertain. Perhaps to organize my thoughts and not go insane.

No. Probably so I can read it and feel as if I'm being spoken to. Maybe neither of those reasons. It doesn't matter. I just want to do it, and that is enough.

What's new?

Well, Mr. Journal, after all these years I've taken up martial arts again—or at least the forms and calisthenics of Tae Kwon Do. There is no one to spar with here in the lighthouse, so the forms have to do.

There is Mary, of course, but she keeps all her sparring verbal. And as of late, there is not even that. I long for her to call me a sonofabitch. Anything. Her hatred of me has cured to 100% perfection and she no longer finds it necessary to speak. The tight lines around her eyes and mouth, the emotional heat that radiates from her body like a dreadful cold sore looking for a place to lie down is voice enough for her. She lives only for the moment when she (the cold sore) can attach herself to me with her needles, ink and thread. She lives only for the design on my back.

That's all I live for as well. Mary adds to it nightly and I enjoy the pain. The tattoo is of a great, blue mushroom cloud, and in the cloud, etched ghost-like, is the face of our daughter, Rae. Her lips are drawn tight, eyes are closed and there are stitches deeply pulled to simulate the lashes. When I move fast and hard they rip slightly and Rae cries bloody tears.

That's one reason for the martial arts. The hard practice of them helps me to tear the stitches so my daughter can cry. Tears are the only thing I can give her.

Each night I bare my back eagerly to Mary and her needles. She pokes deep and I moan in pain as she moans in ecstasy and hatred. She adds more color to the design, works with brutal precision to bring Rae's face out in sharper relief. After ten minutes she tires and will work no more. She puts the tools away and I go to the full-length mirror on the wall. The lantern on the shelf flickers like a jack-o-lantern in a high wind, but there is enough light for me to look over my shoulder and examine the tattoo. And it is beautiful. Better each night as Rae's face becomes more and more defined.

Rae.

Rae. God, can you forgive me, sweetheart?

But the pain of the needles, wonderful and cleansing as they are, is not enough. So I go sliding, kicking and punching along the walkway around the lighthouse, feeling Rae's red tears running down my spine, gathering in the waistband of my much-stained canvas pants.

Winded, unable to punch and kick anymore, I walk over to the railing and call down into the dark, "Hungry?"

In response to my voice a chorus of moans rises up to greet me.

Later, I lie on my pallet, hands behind my head, examine the ceiling and try to think of something worthy to write in you, Mr. Journal. So seldom is there anything. Nothing seems truly worthwhile.

Bored of this, I roll on my side and look at the great light that once shone out to the ships, but is now forever snuffed. Then I turn the other direction and look at my wife sleeping on her bunk, her naked ass turned toward me. I try to remember what it was like to make love to her, but it is difficult. I only remember that I miss it. For a long moment I stare at my wife's ass as if it is a mean mouth about to open and reveal teeth. Then I roll on my back again, stare at the ceiling, and continue this routine until daybreak.

Mornings I greet the flowers, their bright red and yellow blooms bursting from the heads of long-dead bodies that will not rot. The flowers open wide to reveal their little black brains and their feathery feelers, and they lift their blooms upward and moan. I get a wild pleasure out of this. For one crazed moment I feel like a rock singer appearing before his starry-eyed audience.

When I tire of the game I get the binoculars, Mr. Journal, and examine the eastern plains with them, as if I expect a city to materialize there. The most interesting thing I have seen on those plains is a herd of large lizards thundering north. For a moment, I considered calling Mary to see them, but I didn't. The sound of my voice, the sight of my face, upsets her. She loves only the tattoo and is interested in nothing more.

When I finish looking at the plains, I walk to the other side. To the west, where the ocean was, there is now nothing but miles and miles of cracked, black sea bottom. Its only resemblances to a great body of water are the occasional dust storms that blow out of the west like dark tidal waves and wash the windows black at mid-day. And the creatures. Mostly mutated whales. Monstrously large, sluggish things. Abundant now where once they were near extinction. (Perhaps the whales should form some sort of GREEN-PEACE organization for humans now. What do you think, Mr. Journal? No need to answer. Just another one of those little scientist jokes.)

These whales crawl across the sea bottom near the lighthouse from time to time, and if the mood strikes them, they rise on their tails and push their heads near the tower and examine it. I keep expecting one to flop down on us, crushing us like bugs. But no such luck. For some unknown reason the whales never leave the cracked sea bed to venture onto what we formerly called the shore. It's as if they live in invisible water and are bound by it. A racial memory perhaps. Or maybe there's something in that cracked black soil they need. I don't know.

Besides the whales I suppose I should mention I saw a shark once. It was slithering along at a great distance and the tip of its fin was winking in the sunlight. I've also seen some strange, legged fish and some things I could not put a name to. I'll just call them whale food since I saw one of the whales dragging his bottom jaw along the ground one day, scooping up the creatures as they tried to beat a hasty retreat.

Exciting, huh? Well, that's how I spend my day, Mr. Journal. Roaming about the tower with my glasses, coming in to write in you, waiting anxiously for Mary to take hold of that kit and give me the signal. The mere thought of it excites me to erection. I suppose you could call that our sex act together.

And what was I doing the day they dropped The Big One?

Glad you asked that Mr. Journal, really I am.

I was doing the usual. Up at six, did the shit, shower and shave routine. Had breakfast. Got dressed. Tied my tie. I remember doing the latter, and not very well, in front of the bedroom mirror, and noticing that I had shaved poorly. A hunk of dark beard decorated my chin like a bruise.

Rushing to the bathroom to remedy that, I opened the door as Rae, naked as the day of her birth, was stepping from the tub.

Surprised, she turned to look at me. An arm went over her breasts, and a hand, like a dove settling into a fiery bush, covered her pubic area.

Embarrassed, I closed the door with an "excuse me" and went about my business—unshaved. It was an innocent thing. An accident. Nothing sexual. But when I think of her now, more often than not, that is the first image that comes to mind. I guess it was the moment I realized my baby had grown into a beautiful woman.

That was also the day she went off to her first day of college and got to see, ever so briefly, the end of the world.

And it was the day the triangle—Mary, Rae and myself—shattered.

If my first memory of Rae alone is that day, naked in the bathroom, my foremost memory of us as a family is when Rae was six. We used to go to the park and she would ride the merry-go-round, swing, teeter-totter, and finally my back. ("I want to piggy Daddy.") We would gallop about until my legs were rubber, then we would stop at the bench where Mary sat waiting. I would turn my back to the bench so Mary could take Rae down, but always before she did, she would reach around from behind, caressing Rae, pushing her tight against my back, and Mary's hands would touch my chest.

God, but if I could describe those hands. She still has hands like that, after all these years. I feel them fluttering against my back when she works. They are long and sleek and artistic. Naturally soft, like the belly of a baby rabbit. And when she held

Rae and me that way, I felt that no matter what happened in the world, we three could stand against it and conquer.

But now the triangle is broken and the geometry has gone away.

So the day Rae went off to college and was fucked into oblivion by the dark, pelvic thrust of the bomb, Mary drove me to work. Me, Paul Marder, big shot with The Crew. One of the finest, brightest young minds in the industry. Always teaching, inventing and improving on our nuclear threat, because, as we often joked, "We cared enough to send only the very best."

When we arrived at the guard booth, I had out my pass, but there was no one to take it. Beyond the chain-link gate there was a wild melee of people running, screaming, falling down.

I got out of the car and ran to the gate. I called out to a man I knew as he ran by. When he turned his eyes were wild and his lips were flecked with foam. "The missiles are flying," he said, then he was gone, running madly.

I jumped in the car, pushed Mary aside and stomped the gas. The Buick leaped into the fence, knocking it asunder. The car spun, slammed into the edge of a building and went dead. I grabbed Mary's hand, pulled her from the car and we ran toward the great elevators. We made one just in time. There were others running for it as the door closed, and the elevator went down. I still remember the echo of their fists on the metal just as it began to drop. It was like the rapid heartbeat of something dying.

And so the elevator took us to the world of Down Under and we locked it off. There we were in a five-mile layered city designed not only as a massive office and laboratory, but as an impenetrable shelter. It was our special reward for creating the poisons of war. There was food, water, medical supplies, films, books, you name it. Enough to last two thousand people for a hundred years. Of the two thousand it was designed for, perhaps eleven hundred made it. The others didn't run fast enough from the parking lot or the other buildings, or they were late for work, or maybe they had called in sick.

Perhaps they were the lucky ones. They might have died in their sleep. Or while they were having a morning quickie with the spouse. Or perhaps as they lingered over that last cup of coffee.

Because you see, Mr. Journal, Down Under was no paradise. Before long, suicides were epidemic. I considered it myself from time to time. People slashed their throats, drank acid, took pills. It was not unusual to come out of your cubicle in the morning and find people dangling from pipes and rafters like ripe fruit.

There were also the murders. Most of them performed by a crazed group who lived in the deeper recesses of the unit and called themselves the Shit Faces. From time to time they smeared dung on themselves and ran amok, clubbing men, women, and children born down under, to death. It was rumored they ate human flesh.

We had a police force of sorts, but it didn't do much. It didn't have much sense of authority. Worse, we all viewed ourselves as deserving victims. Except for Mary, we had all helped to blow up the world.

Mary came to hate me. She came to the conclusion I had killed Rae. It was a realization that grew in her like a drip growing and growing until it became a gushing flood of hate. She seldom talked to me. She tacked up a picture of Rae and looked at it most of the time.

Topside she had been an artist, and she took that up again. She rigged a kit of tools and inks and became a tattooist. Everyone came to her for a mark. And though each was different, they all seemed to indicate one thing: I fucked up. I blew up the world. Brand me.

Day in and day out she did her tattoos, having less and less to do with me, pushing herself more and more into this work until she was as skilled with skin and needles as she had been Topside with brush and canvas. And one night, as we lay on our separate pallets, feigning sleep, she said to me, "I just want you to know how much I hate you."

"I know," I said.

"You killed Rae."

"I know."

"You say you killed her, you bastard. Say it."

"I killed her," I said, and meant it.

Next day I asked for my tattoo. I told her of this dream that came to me nightly. There would be darkness, and out of this darkness would come a swirl of glowing clouds, and the clouds would meld into a mushroom shape, and out of that—torpedo-shaped, nose pointing skyward, striding on ridiculous cartoon legs—would step The Bomb.

There was a face painted on The Bomb, and it was my face. And suddenly the dream's point of view would change, and I would be looking out of the eyes of that painted face. Before me was my daughter. Naked. Lying on the ground. Her legs wide apart. Her sex glazed like a wet canyon.

And I/The Bomb, would dive into her, pulling those silly feet

after me, and she would scream. I could hear it echo as I plunged
through her belly, finally driving myself out of the top of her head,
then blowing to terminal orgasm. And the dream would end
where it began. A mushroom cloud. Darkness.

When I told Mary the dream and asked her to interpret it in
her art, she said, "Bare your back," and that's how the design
began. An inch of work at a time—a painful inch. She made sure
of that.

Never once did I complain. She'd send the needles home as
hard and deep as she could, and though I might moan or cry out,
I never asked her to stop. I could feel those fine hands touching
my back and I loved it. The needles. The hands. The needles. The
hands.

And if that was so much fun, you ask, why did I come Topside?

You ask such probing questions, Mr. Journal. Really you do,
and I'm glad you asked that. My telling you will be like a laxative,
I hope. Maybe if I just let the shit flow I'll wake up tomorrow and
feel a lot better about myself.

Sure. And it will be the dawning of a new Pepsi generation as
well. It will have all been a bad dream. The alarm clock will ring,
I'll get up, have my bowl of Rice Krispies and tie my tie.

Okay, Mr. Journal. The answer. Twenty years or so after we
went Down Under, a fistful of us decided it couldn't be any worse
Topside than it was below. We made plans to go see. Simple as
that. Mary and I even talked a little. We both entertained the
crazed belief Rae might have survived. She would be thirty-eight.
We might have been hiding below like vermin for no reason. It
could be a brave new world up there.

I remember thinking these things, Mr. Journal, and half-
believing them.

We outfitted two sixty-foot crafts that were used as part of our
transportation system Down Under, plugged in the half-remem-
bered codes that opened the elevators, and drove the vehicles
inside. The elevator lasers cut through the debris above them and
before long we were Topside. The doors opened to sunlight
muted by grey-green clouds and a desert-like landscape. Immediately I knew there was no brave new world over the horizon. It
had all gone to hell in a fiery handbasket, and all that was left of
man's millions of years of development were a few pathetic
humans living Down Under like worms, and a few others crawling
Topside like the same.

We cruised about a week and finally came to what had once

been the Pacific Ocean. Only there wasn't any water now, just that cracked blackness.

We drove along the shore for another week and finally saw life. A whale. Jacobs immediately got the idea to shoot one and taste its meat.

Using a high-powered rifle he killed it, and he and seven others cut slabs off it, brought the meat back to cook. They invited all of us to eat, but the meat looked greenish and there wasn't much blood and we warned him against it. But Jacobs and the others ate it anyway. As Jacobs said, "It's something to do."

A little later on Jacobs threw up blood and his intestines boiled out of his mouth, and not long after those who had shared the meat had the same thing happen to thern. They died crawling on their bellies like gutted dogs. There wasn't a thing we could do for them. We couldn't even bury them. The ground was too hard. We stacked them like cordwood along the shoreline and moved camp down a way, tried to remember how remorse felt.

And that night, while we slept as best we could, the roses came.

Now, let me admit, Mr. Journal, I do not actually know how the roses survive, but I have an idea. And since you've agreed to hear my story—and even if you haven't, you're going to anyway—I'm going to put logic and fantasy together and hope to arrive at the truth.

These roses lived in the ocean bed, underground, and at night they came out. Up until then they had survived as parasites of reptiles and animals, but a new food had arrived from Down Under. Humans. Their creators actually. Looking at it that way, you might say we were the gods who conceived them, and their partaking of our flesh and blood was but a new version of wine and wafer.

I can imagine the pulsating brains pushing up through the sea bottom on thick stalks, extending feathery feelers and tasting the air out there beneath the light of the moon—which through those odd clouds gave the impression of a pus-filled boil—and I can imagine them uprooting and dragging their vines across the ground toward the shore where the corpses lay.

Thick vines sprouted little, thorny vines, and these moved up the bank and touched the corpses. Then, with a lashing motion, the thorns tore into the flesh, and the vines, like snakes, slithered through the wounds and inside. Secreting a dissolving fluid that turned the innards to the consistency of watery oatmeal, they slurped up the mess, and the vines grew and grew at amazing speed, moved and coiled throughout the bodies, replacing nerves and shaping into the symmetry of the muscles they had devoured, and lastly they pushed up through the necks, into the skulls, ate tongues and eyeballs and sucked up the mouse-grey brains like soggy gruel. With an explosion of skull shrapnel, the roses bloomed, their tooth-hard petals expanding into beautiful red and yellow flowers, hunks of human heads dangling from them like shattered watermelon rinds.

In the center of these blooms a fresh, black brain pulsed and feathery feelers once again tasted air for food and breeding grounds. Energy waves from the floral brains shot through the miles and miles of vines that were knotted inside the bodies, and as they had replaced nerves, muscles and vital organs, they made the bodies stand. Then those corpses turned their flowered heads toward the tents where we slept, and the blooming corpses (another little scientist joke there if you're into English idiom, Mr. Journal) walked, eager to add the rest of us to their animated bouquet.

I saw my first rose-head while I was taking a leak.

I had left the tent and gone down by the shore line to relieve myself, when I caught sight of it out of the corner of my eye. Because of the bloom I first thought it was Susan Myers. She wore a thick, wooly Afro that surrounded her head like a lion's mane, and the shape of the thing struck me as her silhouette. But when I zipped and turned, it wasn't an Afro. It was a flower blooming out of Jacobs. I recognized him by his clothes and the hunk of his face that hung off one of the petals like a worn-out hat on a peg.

In the center of the blood-red flower was a pulsating sack, and all around it little wormy things squirmed. Directly below the brain was a thin proboscis. It extended toward me like an erect penis. At its tip, just inside the opening, were a number of large thorns.

A sound like a moan came out of that proboscis, and I stumbled back. Jacobs' body quivered briefly, as if he had been besieged by a sudden chill, and ripping through his flesh and clothes, from neck to foot, was a mass of thorny, wagging vines that shot out to five feet in length.

With an almost invisible motion, they waved from west to east, slashed my clothes, tore my hide, knocked my feet out from beneath me. It was like being hit by a cat-o-nine-tails.

Dazed, I rolled onto my hands and knees, bear-walked away

from it. The vines whipped against my back and butt, cut deep.

Every time I got to my feet, they tripped me. The thorns not only cut, they burned like hot ice picks. I finally twisted away from a net of vines, slammed through one last shoot, and made a break for it.

Without realizing it, I was running back to the tent. My body felt as if I had been lying on a bed of nails and razor blades. My forearm hurt something terrible where I had used it to lash the thorns away from me. I glanced down at it as I ran. It was covered in blood. A strand of vine about two feet in length was coiled around it like a garter snake. A thorn had torn a deep wound in my arm, and the vine was sliding an end into the wound.

Screaming, I held my forearm in front of me like I had just discovered it. The flesh, where the vine had entered, rippled and made a bulge that looked like a junkie's favorite vein. The pain was nauseating. I snatched at the vine, ripped it free. The thorns turned against me like fishhooks.

The pain was so much I fell to my knees, but I had the vine out of me. It squirmed in my hand, and I felt a thorn gouge my palm. I threw the vine into the dark. Then I was up and running for the tent again.

The roses must have been at work for quite some time before I saw Jacobs, because when I broke back into camp yelling, I saw Susan, Ralph, Casey and some others, and already their heads were blooming, skulls cracking away like broken model kits.

Jane Calloway was facing a rose-possessed corpse, and the dead body had its hands on her shoulders, and the vines were jetting out of the corpse, weaving around her like a web, tearing, sliding inside her, breaking off. The proboscis poked into her mouth and extended down her throat, forced her head back. The scream she started came out a gurgle.

I tried to help her, but when I got close, the vines whipped at me and I had to jump back. I looked for something to grab, to hit the damn thing with, but there was nothing. When next I looked at Jane, vines were stabbing out of her eyes and her tongue, now nothing more than lava-thick blood, was dripping out of her mouth onto her breasts, which like the rest of her body, were riddled with stabbing vines.

I ran away then. There was nothing I could do for Jane. I saw others embraced by corpse hands and tangles of vines, but now my only thought was Mary. Our tent was to the rear of the campsite, and I ran there as fast as I could.

She was lumbering out of our tent when I arrived. The sound of screams had awakened her. When she saw me running she froze. By the time I got to her, two vine-riddled corpses were coming up on the tent from the left side. Grabbing her hand I half pulled, half dragged her away from there. I got to one of the vehicles and pushed her inside.

I locked the doors just as Jacobs, Susan, Jane and others appeared at the windshield, leaning over the rocket-nose hood, the feelers around the brain sacks vibrating like streamers in a high wind. Hands slid greasily down the windshield. Vines flopped and scratched and cracked against it like thin bicycle chains.

I got the vehicle started, stomped the accelerator, and the rose-heads went flying. One of them, Jacobs, bounced over the hood and splattered into a spray of flesh, ichor and petals.

I had never driven the vehicle, so my maneuvering was rusty. But it didn't matter. There wasn't exactly a traffic rush to worry about.

After an hour or so, I turned to look at Mary. She was staring at me, her eyes like the twin barrels of a double-barreled shotgun. They seemed to say, "More of your doing," and in a way she was right. I drove on.

Daybreak we came to the lighthouse. I don't know how it survived. One of those quirks. Even the glass was unbroken. It looked like a great stone finger shooting us the bird.

The vehicle's tank was near empty, so I assumed here was as good a place to stop as any. At least there was shelter, something we could fortify. Going on until the vehicle was empty of fuel didn't make much sense. There wouldn't be any more fill-ups, and there might not be any more shelter like this.

Mary and I (in our usual silence) unloaded the supplies from the vehicle and put them in the lighthouse. There was enough food, water, chemicals for the chemical toilet, odds and ends, extra clothes, to last us a year. There were also some guns. A Colt .45 revolver, two twelve-gauge shotguns and a .38, and enough shells to fight a small war.

When everything was unloaded, I found some old furniture downstairs, and using tools from the vehicle, tried to barricade the bottom door and the one at the top of the stairs. When I finished, I thought of a line from a story I had once read, a line that always disturbed me. It went something like, "Now we're shut in for the night."

Days. Nights. All the same. Shut in with one another, our memories and the fine tattoo.

A few days later I spotted the roses. It was as if they had smelled us out. And maybe they had. From a distance, through the binoculars, they reminded me of old women in bright sun hats.

It took them the rest of the day to reach the lighthouse, and they immediately surrounded it, and when I appeared at the railing they would lift their heads and moan.

And that, Mr. Journal, brings us up to now.

I thought I had written myself out, Mr. Journal. Told the only part of my life story I would ever tell, but now I'm back. You can't keep a good world destroyer down.

I saw my daughter last night and she's been dead for years. But I saw her, I did, naked, smiling at me, calling to ride piggyback.

Here's what happened.

It was cold last night. Must be getting along winter. I had rolled off my pallet onto the cold floor. Maybe that's what brought me awake. The cold. Or maybe it was just gut instinct.

It had been a particularly wonderful night with the tattoo. The face had been made so clear it seemed to stand out from my back. It had finally become more defined than the mushroom cloud. The needles went in hard and deep, but I've had them in me so much now I barely feel the pain. After looking in the mirror at the beauty of the design, I went to bed happy, or as happy as I can get.

During the night the eyes ripped open. The stitches came out and I didn't know it until I tried to rise from the cold, stone floor and my back puckered against it where the blood had dried.

I pulled myself free and got up. It was dark, but we had a good moonspill that night and I went to the mirror to look. It was bright enough that I could see Rae's reflection clearly, the color of her face, the color of the cloud. The stitches had fallen away and now the wounds were spread wide, and inside the wounds were eyes. Oh God, Rae's blue eyes. Her mouth smiled at me and her teeth were very white.

Oh, I hear you, Mr. Journal. I hear what you're saying. And I thought of that. My first impression was that I was about six bricks shy a load, gone around the old bend. But I know better now. You see, I lit a candle and held it over my shoulder, and with the candle and the moonlight, I could see even more clearly. It was Rae all right, not just a tattoo.

I looked over at my wife on the bunk, her back to me, as always. She had not moved.

I turned back to the reflection. I could hardly see the outline of myself, just Rae's face smiling out of that cloud.

"Rae," I whispered, "is that you?"

"Come on, Daddy," said the mouth in the mirror, "that's a stupid question. Of course, it's me."

"But . . . you're . . . you're . . ."

"Dead?"

"Yes . . . did . . . did it hurt much?"

She cackled so loudly the mirror shook. I could feel the hairs on my neck rising. I thought for sure Mary would wake up, but she slept on.

"It was instantaneous, Daddy, and even then, it was the greatest pain imaginable. Let me show you how it hurt."

The candle blew out and I dropped it. I didn't need it anyway. The mirror grew bright and Rae's smile went from ear to ear—literally—and the flesh on her bones seemed like crepe paper before a powerful fan, and that fan blew the hair off her head, the skin off her skull and melted those beautiful, blue eyes and those shiny white teeth of hers to a putrescent goo the color and consistency of fresh bird shit. Then there was only the skull, and it heaved in half and flew backwards into the dark world of the mirror and there was no reflection now, only the hurtling fragments of a life that once was and was now nothing more than swirling cosmic dust.

I closed my eyes and looked away.

"Daddy?"

I opened them, looked over my shoulder into the mirror. There was Rae again, smiling out of my back.

"Darling," I said, "I'm so sorry."

"So are we," she said, and there were faces floating past her in the mirror. Teenagers, children, men and women, babies, little embryos swirling around her head like planets around the sun. I closed my eyes again, but I could not keep them closed. When I opened them the multitudes of swirling dead, and those who had never had a chance to live, were gone. Only Rae was there.

"Come close to the mirror, Daddy."

I backed up to it. I backed until the hot wounds that were Rae's eyes touched the cold glass and the wounds became hotter and hotter and Rae called out, "Ride me piggy, Daddy," and then I felt her weight on my back, not the weight of a six-year-old child or a teenage girl, but a great weight, like the world was on my shoulders and bearing down.

Leaping away from the mirror I went hopping and whooping

about the room, same as I used to in the park. Around and around I went, and as I did, I glanced in the mirror. Astride me was Rae, lithe and naked, her red hair fanning around her as I spun. And when I whirled by the mirror again, I saw that she was six years old. Another spin and there was a skeleton with red hair, one hand held high, the jaws open and yelling, "Ride 'em, cowboy."

"How?" I managed, still bucking and leaping, giving Rae the ride of her life. She bent to my ear and I could feel her warm breath. "You want to know how I'm here, Daddy-dear? I'm here because you created me. Once you laid between Mother's legs and thrust me into existence, the two of you, with all the love there was in you. This time you thrust me into existence with your guilt and Mother's hate. Her thrusting needles, your arching back. And now I've come back for one last ride, Daddy-o. Ride, you bastard, ride."

All the while I had been spinning, and now as I glimpsed the mirror, I saw wall to wall faces, weaving in, weaving out, like smiling stars, and all those smiles opened wide and words came out in chorus, "Where were you when they dropped The Big One?"

Each time I spun and saw the mirror again, it was a new scene. Great flaming winds scorching across the world, babies turning to fleshy jello, heaps of charred bones, brains boiling out of the heads of men and women like backed-up toilets overflowing, The Almighty, Glory Hallelujah, Ours Is Bigger Than Yours Bomb hurtling forward, the mirror going mushroom-white, then clear, and me, spinning, Rae pressed tight against my back, melting like butter on a griddle, evaporating into the eye wounds on my back, and finally me alone, collapsing to the floor beneath the weight of the world.

Mary never awoke.

The vines outsmarted me.

A single strand found a crack downstairs somewhere and wound up the steps and slipped beneath the door that led into the tower. Mary's bunk was not far from the door, and in the night, while I slept and later while I spun in front of the mirror and lay on the floor before it, it made its way to Mary's bunk, up between her legs, and entered her sex effortlessly.

I suppose I should give the vine credit for doing what I had not been able to do in years, Mr. Journal, and that's enter Mary. Oh God, that's a funny one, Mr. Journal. Real funny. Another little scientist joke. Let's make that a mad scientist joke, what say? Who but a madman would play with the lives of human beings by constantly trying to build the bigger and better boom machine?

So what of Rae, you ask?

I'll tell you. She is inside me. My back feels the weight. She twists in my guts like a corkscrew. I went to the mirror a moment ago, and the tattoo no longer looks like it did. The eyes have turned to crusty sores and the entire face looks like a scab. It's as if the bile that made up my soul, the unthinking, nearsightedness, the guilt that I am, has festered from inside and spoiled the picture with pustule bumps, knots and scabs.

To put it in layman's terms, Mr. Journal, my back is infected. Infected with what I am. A blind, senseless fool.

The wife?

Ah, the wife. God, how I loved that woman. I have not really touched her in years, merely felt those wonderful hands on my back as she jabbed the needles home, but I never stopped loving her. It was not a love that glowed anymore, but it was there, though hers for me was long gone and wasted.

This morning when I got up from the floor, the weight of Rae and the world on my back, I saw the vine coming up from beneath the door and stretching over to her. I yelled her name. She did not move. I ran to her and saw it was too late. Before I could put a hand on her, I saw her flesh ripple and bump up, like a den of mice were nesting under a quilt. The vines were at work. (Out goes the old guts, in goes the new vines.)

There was nothing I could do for her.

I made a torch out of a chair leg and an old quilt, set fire to it, burned the vine from between her legs, watched it retreat, smoking, under the door. Then I got a board, nailed it along the bottom, hoping it would keep others out for at least a little while. I got one of the twelve-gauges and loaded it. It's on the desk beside me, Mr. Journal, but even I know I'll never use it. It was just something to do, as Jacobs said when he killed and ate the whale. Something to do.

I can hardly write anymore. My back and shoulders hurt so bad. It's the weight of Rae and the world.

I've just come back from the mirror and there is very little left of the tattoo. Some blue and black ink, a touch of red that was Rae's hair. It looks like an abstract painting now. Collapsed design, running colors. It's real swollen. I look like the hunchback of Notre Dame.

What am I going to do, Mr. Journal?

Well, as always, I'm glad you asked that. You see, I've thought this out.

I could throw Mary's body over the railing before it blooms. I could do that. Then I could doctor my back. It might even heal, though I doubt it. Rae wouldn't let that happen, I can tell you now. And I don't blame her. I'm on her side. I'm just a walking dead man and have been for years.

I could put the shotgun under my chin and work the trigger with my toe, or maybe push it with the very pen I'm using to create you, Mr. Journal. Wouldn't that be neat? Blow my brains to the ceiling and sprinkle you with my blood.

But as I said, I loaded the gun because it was something to do. I'd never use it on myself or Mary.

You see, I want Mary. I want her to hold Rae and me one last time like she used to in the park. And she can. There's a way.

I've drawn all the curtains and made curtains out of blankets for those spots where there aren't any. It'll be sunup soon and I don't want that kind of light in here. I'm writing this by candlelight and it gives the entire room a warm glow. I wish I had wine. I want the atmosphere to be just right.

Over on Mary's bunk she's starting to twitch. Her neck is swollen where the vines have congested and are writhing toward their favorite morsel, the brain. Pretty soon the rose will bloom (I hope she's one of the bright yellow ones, yellow was her favorite color and she wore it well) and Mary will come for me.

When she does, I'll stand with my naked back to her. The vines will whip out and cut me before she reaches me, but I can stand it. I'm used to pain. I'll pretend the thorns are Mary's needles. I'll stand that way until she folds her dead arms around me and her body pushes up against the wound she made in my back, the wound that is our daughter Rae. She'll hold me so the vines and the proboscis can do their work. And while she holds me, I'll grab her fine hands and push them against my chest, and it will be we three again, standing against the world, and I'll close my eyes and delight in her soft, soft hands one last time.

Not much to tell here. I had a new baby in the house and a dog, and of course I worried about that. Kept them apart as much as I could because I had read of dogs, trusted pets, killing infants. We also had a cat. I'm not a fan of cats. This all came together and produced this little tale.

DOG, CAT, AND BABY

DOG DID NOT LIKE BABY. FOR THAT MATTER, Dog did not like Cat. But Cat had claws—sharp claws. Dog had always gotten attention. Pat on head. "Here, boy, here's a treat. Nice dog. Good dog. Shake hands. Speak! Sit. Nice dog."

Now there was Baby.

Cat had not been problem, really.

Cat was liked, not loved by family. They petted Cat sometimes. Fed her. Did not mistreat her. But they not love her. Not way they loved Dog—before Baby.

Damn little pink thing that cried.

Baby got "Oooohs and Ahhhs." When Dog tried to get close to Masters, they say, "Get back, boy. Not *now*."

When would be *now?*

Dog never see now. Always Baby get now. Dog get nothing. Sometimes they so busy with Baby it be all day before dog get fed. Dog never get treats anymore. Could not remember last pat on head or "Good Dog!"

Bad business. Dog not like it.

Dog decide to do something about it.

Kill Baby. Then there be Dog, Cat again. They not love Cat, so things be okay.

119

Dog thought that over. Wouldn't take much to rip little Baby apart. Baby soft, pink. Would bleed easy.

Baby often put in Jumper which hung between doorway when Master Lady hung wash. Baby be easy to get then.

So Dog waited.

One day Baby put in Jumper and Master Lady go outside to hang out wash. Dog looks at pink thing jumping, thinks about ripping to pieces. Thinks on it long and hard. Thought makes him so happy his mouth drips water. Dog starts toward Baby, making fine moment last.

Baby looks up, sees Dog coming toward it slowly, almost creeping. Baby starts to cry.

But before Dog can reach Baby, Cat jumps.

Cat been hiding behind couch.

Cat goes after Dog, tears Dog's face with teeth, with claws. Dog bleeds, tries to run. Cat goes after him.

Dog turns to bite.

Cat hangs claw in Dog's eye.

Dog yelps, runs.

Cat jumps on Dog's back, biting Dog on top of head.

Dog tries to turn corner into bedroom. Cat, tearing at him with claws, biting with teeth, makes Dog lose balance. Dog running very fast, fast as he can go, hits the edge of doorway, stumbles back, falls over.

Cat gets off Dog.

Dog lies still.

Dog not breathing.

Cat knows Dog is dead. Cat licks blood from claws, from teeth with rough tongue.

Cat has gotten rid of Dog.

Cat turns to look down hall where Baby is screaming.

Now for *other* one.

Cat begins to creep down hall.

This was my attempt to write a story of one of life's innocents besieged by a considerably less innocent world. Saying the main character is an innocent is not the same as saying he's a swell guy. He just doesn't have a clue.

Also, this story is based on a true incident. Our next door neighbors really did have a blind groundskeeper, at least for one day, and some of the incidents I've portrayed in the story are also true. Fortunately, I never had to suffer like the protagonist of my story, and in no way does the family in the story mirror my own. But the fact that a blind groundskeeper asked me to come over and help him find the spots he missed got this tale a whirlin'. The descriptions of the groundskeeper, and my first encounter with him are fact, not fantasy. From there on out, well, it's a story. A good one, I hope. And like most of the stories in this collection, a personal favorite.

These folks who lived next door to me were the inspiration, and I say inspiration, nothing more, for a few other stories I wrote. When they moved, other oddball activities in that neighborhood came along to fill their void. Finally, fed up with all the weirdness that went on there, we moved. I missed it for about a month. Whenever I needed a story idea. But, I got over it.

MISTER WEED-EATER

MR. JOB HAROLD WAS IN HIS LIVING ROOM WITH his feet on the couch watching *Wheel of Fortune* when his five-year-old son came inside covered with dirt. "Daddy," said the boy dripping dirt, "there's a man outside want to see you."

Mr. Harold got up and went outside, and there standing at the back of the house next to his wife's flower bed, which was full of dead roses and a desiccated frog, was, just like his boy had said, a man.

It was over a hundred degrees out there, and the man, a skinny sucker in white T-shirt and jeans with a face red as a baboon's ass, a waterfall of inky hair dripping over his forehead and dark glasses, stood with his head cocked like a spaniel listening for trouble. He had a bright-toothed smile that indicated everything he heard struck him as funny.

In his left hand was a new weed-eater, the cutting line coated in greasy green grass the texture of margarita vomit, the price tag dangling proudly from the handle.

In the other hand the man held a blind man's cane, the tip of which had speared an oak leaf. His white T-shirt, stained pollen-yellow under the arms, stuck wetly to his chest and little pot belly tight as plastic wrap on a fish head. He had on dirty white socks

122

with played-out elastic and they had fallen over the tops of his tennis shoes as if in need of rest.

The man was shifting his weight from one leg to the other. Mr. Harold figured he needed to pee and wanted to use the bathroom, and the idea of letting him into the house with a weed-eater and pointing him at the pot didn't appeal to Mr. Harold cause there wasn't any question in Mr. Harold's mind the man was blind as a peach pit, and Mr. Harold figured he got in the bathroom, he was gonna pee from one end of the place to the other trying to hit the commode, and then Mr. Harold knew he'd have to clean it up or explain to his wife when she got home from work how on his day off he let a blind man piss all over their bathroom. Just thinking about all that gave Mr. Harold a headache.

"What can I do for you?" Mr. Harold asked.

"Well, sir," said the blind man in a voice dry as Mrs. Harold's sexual equipment, "I heard your boy playin' over here, and I followed the sound. You see, I'm the groundskeeper next door, and I need a little help. I was wonderin' you could come over and show me if I've missed a few spots?"

Mr. Harold tried not to miss a beat. "You talking about the church over there?"

"Yes, sir. Just got hired. Wouldn't want to look bad on my first day."

Mr. Harold considered this. Cameras could be set in place somewhere. People in trees waiting for him to do something they could record for a TV show. He didn't want to go on record as not helping a blind man, but on the other hand, he didn't want to be caught up in no silliness either.

Finally, he decided it was better to look like a fool and a Samaritan than a cantankerous asshole who wouldn't help a poor blind man cut weeds.

"I reckon I can do that," Mr. Harold said. Then to his five-year-old who'd followed him outside and was sitting in the dirt playing with a plastic truck: "Son, you stay right here and don't go off."

"Okay, Daddy," the boy said.

The church across the street had been opened in a building about the size of an aircraft hanger. It had once been used as a liquor warehouse, and later it was called Community Storage, but items had a way of disappearing. It was a little too community for its renters, and it went out of business and Sonny Guy, who owned the place, had to pay some kind of fine and turn up with certain items deemed as missing.

This turn of events had depressed Mr. Guy, so he'd gotten religion and opened a church. God wasn't knocking them dead either, so to compensate, Sonny Guy started a Gospel Opry, and to advertise and indicate its location, beginning on their street and on up to the highway, there was a line of huge orange Day-Glo guitars that pointed from highway to Opry.

The guitars didn't pull a lot of people in though, bright as they were. Come Sunday the place was mostly vacant, and when the doors were open on the building back and front, you could hear wind whistling through there like it was blowing through a pipe. A special ticket you could cut out of the newspaper for five dollars off a fifteen dollar buffet of country sausages and sliced canta- loupe hadn't rolled them in either. Sonny and God most definitely needed a more exciting game plan. Something with titties.

Taking the blind man by the elbow, Mr. Harold led him across the little street and into the yard of the church. Well, actually, it was more than a yard. About four acres. On the front acre sat Sonny Guy's house, and out to the right of it was a little music studio he'd built, and over to the left was the metal building that served as the church. The metal was aluminum and very bright and you could feel the heat bouncing off of it like it was an oven with bread baking inside.

Behind the house were three more acres, most of it weeds, and at the back of it all was a chicken wire fence where a big black dog of undetermined breed liked to pace.

When Mr. Harold saw what the blind man had done, he let out his breath. The fella had been all over that four acres, and it wasn't just a patch of weeds now, but it wasn't manicured either. The poor bastard had tried to do the job of a lawn mower with a weed- eater, and he'd mostly succeeded in chopping down the few flow- ers that grew in the midst of brick-lined beds, and he'd chopped weeds and dried grass here and there, so that the whole place looked as if it were a head of hair mistreated by a drunk barber with an attitude.

At Mr. Harold's feet, he discovered a mole the blind man's shoe had dislodged from a narrow tunnel. The mole had been whipped to death by the weed-eater sling. It looked like a wad of dirty hair dipped in red paint. A lasso loop of guts had been knocked out of its mouth and ants were crawling on it. The blind had slain the blind.

"How's it look?"

"Well," Mr. Harold said, "you missed some spots."

"Yeah, well they hired me cause they wanted to help the handicapped, but I figure it was just as much cause they knew I'd do the job. They had 'em a crippled nigger used to come out and do it, but they said he charged too much and kept making a mess of things."

Mr. Harold had seen the black man mow. He might have been crippled, but he'd had a riding mower and he was fast. He didn't do such a bad job either. He always wore a straw hat pushed up on the back of his head, and when he got off the mower to get on his crutches, he did it with the style of a rodeo star dismounting a show horse. There hadn't been a thing wrong with the black man's work. Mr. Harold figured Sonny Guy wanted to cut a few corners. Switch a crippled nigger for a blind honkey.

"How'd you come to get this job?" Mr. Harold asked. He tried to make the question pleasant, as if he were asking him how his weekend had been.

"References," the blind man said.

"Of course," said Mr. Harold.

"Well, what do I need to touch up? I stayed me a line from the building there, tried to work straight, turn when I got to the fence and come back. I do it mostly straight?"

"You got off a mite. You've missed some pretty good-sized patches."

Mr. Harold, still holding the blind man's elbow, felt the blind man go a little limp with disappointment. "How bad is it?"

"Well . . ."

"Go on and tell me."

"A weed-eater ain't for this much place. You need a mower."

"I'm blind. You can't turn me loose out here with a mower. I'd cut my foot off."

"I'm just saying."

"Well, come on, how bad is it? It look worse than when the nigger did it?"

"I believe so."

"By much?"

"When he did it, you could look out here and tell the place had been mowed. Way it looks now, you might do better just to poison the weeds and hope the grass dies."

The blind man really slumped now, and Mr. Harold wished he'd chosen his words more carefully. It wasn't his intention to insult a blind man on his lawn skills in a hundred degree heat. He began to wish the fella had only wanted to wet on the walls of his bathroom.

"Can't even do a nigger's job," the blind man said.

"It ain't so bad if they're not too picky."

"Shit," said the blind man. "Shit, I didn't have no references. I didn't never have a job before, really. Well, I worked out at the chicken processing plant tossing chicken heads in a metal drum, but I kept missing and tossin' them on this lady worked by me. I just couldn't keep my mind on the drum's location. I think I might actually be more artistic than mechanical. I got one side of the brain works harder, you know?"

"You could just slip off and go home. Leave 'em a note."

"Naw, I can't do that. Besides, I ain't got no way home. They pick me up and brought me here. I come to church last week and they offered me the job, and then they come and got me and brought me here and I made a mess of it. They'll be back later and they won't like it. They ain't gonna give me my five dollars, I can see that and I can't see nothing."

"Hell, man," Mr. Harold said, "that black fella mowed this lawn, you can bet he got more than five dollars."

"You tryin' to say I ain't good as a nigger?"

"I'm not trying to say anything 'cept you're not being paid enough. A guy ought to get five dollars an hour just for standing around in this heat."

"People charge too much these days. Niggers especially will stick you when they can. It's that civil rights business. It's gone to their heads."

"It ain't got nothing to do with what color you are."

"By the hour, I reckon I'm making 'bout what I got processing chicken heads," the blind man said. "Course, they had a damn fine company picnic this time each year."

"Listen here. We'll do what we were gonna do. Check the spots you've missed. I'll lead you around to bad places, and you chop 'em."

"That sounds all right, but I don't want to share my five dollars. I was gonna get me something with that. Little check I get from the government just covers my necessities, you know?"

"You don't owe me anything."

Mr. Harold took the blind man by the elbow and led him around to where the grass was missed or whacked high, which was just about everywhere you looked. After about fifteen minutes, the blind man said he was tired. They went over to the house and leaned on a tree in the front yard. The blind man said, "You seen them shows about those crop circles, in England, I think it is?"

"No," said Mr. Harold.

"Well, they found these circles in the wheat. Just appeared out there. They think it's aliens."

"Oh yeah, I seen about those," Mr. Harold said, suddenly recalling what it was the man was talking about. "There ain't no mystery to that. It's some guys with a stick and a cord. We used to do that in tall weed patches when we were kids. There's nothing to it. Someone's just making jackasses out of folks."

The blind man took a defiant posture. "Not everything like that is a bunch of kids with a string."

"I wasn't saying that."

"For all I know, what's wrong with that patch there's got nothing to do with me and my work. It could have been alien involvement."

"Aliens with weed-eaters?"

"It could be what happened when they landed, their saucers messin' it up like that."

"If they landed, why didn't they land on you? You was out there with the weed-eater. How come nobody saw or heard them?"

"They could have messed up the yard while I was coming to get you."

"Kind of a short visit, wasn't it?"

"You don't know everything, Mister-I-Got-Eyeballs. Those that talk the loudest know less than anybody."

"And them that believe every damn thing they hear are pretty stupid, Mister Weed-Eater. I know what's wrong with you now. You're lazy. It's hot out there and you don't want to be here, so you're trying to make me feel sorry for you and do the job myself, and it ain't gonna work. I don't feel sorry for you cause you're blind. I ain't gonna feel sorry at all. I think you're an asshole."

Mr. Harold went across the road and back to the house and called his son inside. He sat down in front of the TV. *Wheel of Fortune* wasn't on anymore. Hell, it was a rerun anyway. He changed the channel looking for something worth watching but all that was on was midget wrestling, so he watched a few minutes of that.

Those little guys were fast and entertaining and it was cool inside with the air-conditioner cranked up, so after a couple minutes Mr. Harold got comfortable watching the midgets sling each other around, tumble up together and tie themselves in knots.

However, time eroded Mr. Harold's contentment. He couldn't stop thinking about the blind man out there in the heat. He called to his son and told him to go outside and see if the blind man was still there.

The boy came back a minute later. He said, "He's out there, Daddy. He said you better come on out and help him. He said he ain't gonna talk about crop circles no more."

Mr. Harold thought a moment. You were supposed to help the blind, the hot and the stupid. Besides, the old boy might need someone to pour gas in that weed-eater. He did it himself he was liable to pour it all over his shoes and later get around someone who smoked and wanted to toss a match. An accident might be in the making.

Mr. Harold switched the channel to cartoons and pointed them out to his son. The boy sat down immediately and started watching. Mr. Harold got the boy a glass of Kool-Aid and a stack of chocolate cookies. He went outside to find the blind man.

The blind man was in Mr. Harold's yard. He had the weed-eater on and was holding it above his head whacking at the leaves on Mr. Harold's red-bud tree; his wife's favorite tree.

"Hey, now stop that," Mr. Harold said. "Ain't no call to be malicious."

The blind man cut the weed-eater and cocked his head and listened. "That you, Mister-I-Know-There-Ain't-No-Aliens?"

"Now come on. I want to help you. My son said you said you wasn't gonna get into that again."

"Come on over here," said the blind man.

Mr. Harold went over, cautiously. When he was just outside of weed-eater range, he said, "What you want?"

"Do I look all right to you? Besides being blind?"

"Yeah. I guess so. I don't see nothing wrong with you. You found the leaves on that tree good enough."

"Come and look closer."

"Naw, I ain't gonna do it. You just want to get me in range. Hit me with that weed-eater. I'll stay right here. You come at me, I'll move off. You won't be able to find me."

"You saying I can't find you cause I'm blind?"

"Come after me, I'll put stuff in front of you so you trip."

The blind man leaned the weed-eater against his leg. His cane was on a loop over his other hand, and he took hold of it and tapped it against his tennis shoe.

"Yeah, well you could do that," the blind man said, "and I bet you would too. You're like a guy would do things to the handicapped. I'll tell you now, sir, they take roll in heaven, you ain't gonna be on it."

"Listen here. You want some help over there, I'll give it, but I ain't gonna stand here in this heat and take insults. Midget wrestling's on TV and it's cool inside and I might just go back to it."

The blind man's posture straightened with interest. "Midget wrestling? Hell, that's right. It's Saturday. Was it Little Bronco Bill and Low Dozer McGuirk?"

"I think it was. They look alike to me. I don't know one midget from another, though one was a little fatter and had a haircut like he'd got out of the barber chair too soon."

"That's Dozer. He trains on beer and doughnuts. I heard him talk about it on the TV."

"You watch TV?"

"You tryin' to hurt my feelings?"

"No. I mean, it's just, well, you're blind."

"What? I am? I'll be damned! I didn't know that. Glad you was here to tell me."

"I didn't mean no harm."

"Look here, I got ears. I listen to them thumping on that floor and I listen to the announcer. I listen so good I can imagine, kinda, what's goin' on. I 'specially like them little scudders, the midgets. I think maybe on a day I've had enough to eat, I had on some pants weren't too tight, I'd like to get in a ring with one of 'em."

"You always been blind? I mean, was you born that way?"

"Naw. Got bleach in my eyes. My mama told me a nigger done it to me when I was a baby, but it was my daddy. I know that now. Mama had a bad eye herself, then the cancer got her good one. She says she sees out of her bad eye way you'd see if you seen something through a Coke bottle with dirt on the bottom."

Mr. Harold didn't really want to hear about the blind man's family history. He groped for a fresh conversation handle. Before he could get hold of one, the blind man said, "Let's go to your place and watch some of that wrestlin' and cool off, then you can come out with me and show me them places I missed."

Mr. Harold didn't like the direction this conversation was taking. "I don't know," he said. "Won't the preacher be back in a bit and want his yard cut?"

"You want to know the truth?" the blind man said, "I don't care. You're right. Five dollars ain't any wages. Them little things I wanted with that five dollars I couldn't get no how."

Mr. Harold's mind raced. "Yeah, but five dollars is five dollars, and you could put it toward something. You know, save it up till you got some more. They're planning on making you a permanent groundskeeper, aren't they? A little time, a raise could be in order."

"This here's kinda a trial run. They can always get the crippled nigger back."

Mr. Harold checked his watch. There probably wasn't more than twenty minutes left of the wrestling program, so he took a flyer. "Well, all right. We'll finish up the wrestling show, then come back and do the work. You ain't gonna hit me with that weed-eater if I try to guide you into the house, are you?"

"Naw, I ain't mad no more. I get like that sometimes. It's just my way."

Mr. Harold led him into the house and onto the couch and talked the boy out of the cartoons, which wasn't hard; it was some kind of stuff the boy hated. The blind man had him crank the audio on the TV up a notch and sat sideways on the couch with his weed-eater and cane, taking up all the room and leaving Mr. Harold nowhere to sit. Dirt and chopped grass dripped off of the blind man's shoes and onto the couch.

Mr. Harold finally sat on the floor beside his boy and tried to get the boy to give him a cookie, but his son didn't play that way. Mr. Harold had to get his own Kool-Aid and cookies, and he got the blind man some too.

The blind man took the Kool-Aid and cookies and didn't say thanks or kiss my ass. Just stretched out there on the couch listening, shaking from side to side, cheering the wrestlers on. He was obviously on Low Dozer McGuirk's side, and Mr. Harold figured it was primarily because he'd heard Dozer trained on beer and doughnuts. That struck Mr. Harold as a thing the blind man would latch onto and love. That and crop circles and flying saucers.

When the blind man finished up his cookies and Kool-Aid, he put Mr. Harold to work getting more, and when Mr. Harold came back with them, his son and the blind man were chatting about the wrestling match. The blind man was giving the boy some insights into the wrestling game and was trying to get the boy to try a hold on him so he could show how easily he could work out of it.

Mr. Harold nixed that plan, and the blind man ate his next plate of cookies and Kool-Aid, and somehow the wrestling show moved into an after show talk session on wrestling. When Mr. Harold looked at his watch nearly an hour had passed.

"We ought to get back over there and finish up," Mr. Harold said.

"Naw," said the blind man, "not just yet. This talk show stuff is good. This is where I get most of my tips."

"Well, all right, but when this is over, we're out of here."

But they weren't. The talk show wrapped up, the *Beverly Hillbillies* came on, then *Green Acres*, then *Gilligan's Island*. The blind man and Mr. Harold's son laughed their way through the first two, and damn near killed themselves with humor when *Gilligan's* was on.

Mr. Harold learned the Professor and Ginger were the blind man's favorites on *Gilligan's*, and he liked the pig, Arnold, on *Green Acres*. No one was a particular favorite on the *Beverly Hillbillies*, however.

"Ain't this stuff good?" the blind man said. "They don't make 'em like this anymore."

"I prefer educational programming myself," Mr. Harold said, though the last educational program he'd watched was a PBS special on lobsters. He'd watched it because he was sick as a dog and lying on the couch and his wife had put the remote across the room and he didn't feel good enough to get up and get hold of it.

In his feverish delirium he remembered the lobster special as pretty good cause it had come across a little like a science fiction movie. But that lobster special, as viewed through feverish eyes, had been the closest Mr. Harold had ever gotten to educational TV.

The sickness, the remote lying across the room, had caused him to miss what he'd really wanted to see that day, and even now, on occasion, he thought of what he had missed with a certain pang of regret; a special on how young women were chosen to wear swim suits in special issues of sports magazines. He kept hoping it was a show that would play in rerun.

"My back's hurtin' from sitting on the floor," Mr. Harold said, but the blind man didn't move his feet so Mr. Harold could have a place on the couch. He offered a pointer, though.

"Sit on the floor, you got to hold your back straight, just like you was in a wooden chair, otherwise you'll really tighten them muscles up close to your butt."

When *Gilligan's* was wrapped up, Mr. Harold impulsively cut the television and got hold of the blind man and started pulling him up. "We got to go to work now. I'm gonna help you, it has to be now. I got plans for the rest of the day."

"Ah, Daddy, he was gonna show me a couple wrestling holds," the boy said.

"Not today," Mr. Harold said, tugging on the blind man, and

suddenly the blind man moved and was behind him and had him wrestled to the floor. Mr. Harold tried to move, but couldn't. His arm was twisted behind his back and he was lying face down and the blind man was on top of him pressing a knee into his spine.

"Wow!" said the boy. "Neat!"

"Not bad for a blind fella," said the blind man. "I told you I get my tips from that show."

"All right, all right, let me go," said Mr. Harold.

"Squeal like a pig for me," said the blind man.

"Now wait just a goddamned minute," Mr. Harold said.

The blind man pressed his knee harder into Mr. Harold's spine. "Squeal like a pig for me. Come on."

Mr. Harold made a squeaking noise.

"That ain't no squeal," said the blind man. "Squeal!"

The boy got down by Mr. Harold's face. "Come on, Dad," he said. "Squeal."

"Big pig squeal," said the blind man. "Big pig! Big pig! Big pig!"

Mr. Harold squealed. The blind man didn't let go.

"Say calf rope," said the blind man.

"All right, all right. Calf rope! Calf rope! Now let me up."

The blind man eased his knee off Mr. Harold's spine and let go of the arm lock. He stood up and said to the boy, "It's mostly in the hips."

"Wow!" said the boy, "You made Dad squeal like a pig."

Mr. Harold, red faced, got up. He said, "Come on, right now."

"I need my weed-eater," said the blind man.

The boy got both the weed-eater and the cane for the blind man. The blind man said to the boy as they went outside, "Remember, it's in the hips."

Mr. Harold and the blind man went over to the church property and started in on some spots with the weed-eater. In spite of the fact Mr. Harold found himself doing most of the weed-eating, the blind man just clinging to this elbow and being pulled around like he was a side car, it wasn't five minutes before the blind man wanted some shade and a drink of water.

Mr. Harold was trying to talk him out of it when Sonny Guy and his family drove up in a club cab Dodge pickup.

The pickup was black and shiny and looked as if it had just come off the showroom floor. Mr. Harold knew Sonny Guy's money for such things had come from Mrs. Guy's insurance before she was Mrs. Guy. Her first husband had gotten kicked to death by a maniac escaped from the nut-house; kicked until they couldn't tell if he was a man or a jelly doughnut that had gotten run over by a truck.

When that insurance money came due, Sonny Guy, a man who had antennas for such things, showed up and began to woo her. They were married pretty quick, and the money from the insurance settlement had bought the house, the aircraft hanger church, the Day-Glo guitar signs, and the pickup. Mr. Harold wondered if there was any money left. He figured they might be pretty well run through it by now.

"Is that the Guys?" the blind man asked as the pickup engine was cut.

"Yeah," said Mr. Harold.

"Maybe we ought to look busy."

"I don't reckon it matters now."

Sonny got out of the pickup and waddled over to the edge of the property and looked at the mauled grass and weeds. He walked over to the aircraft hanger church and took it all in from that angle with his hands on his ample hips. He stuck his fingers under his overall straps and walked alongside the fence with the big black dog running behind it, barking, grabbing at the chicken wire with his teeth.

The minister's wife stood by the pickup. She had a bun of colorless hair stacked on her head. The stack had the general shape of some kind of tropical ant-hill that might house millions of angry ants. Way she was built, that hair and all, it looked as if the hill had been precariously built on top of a small round rock supported by an irregular-shaped one, the bottom rock wearing a print dress and a pair of black flat-heeled shoes.

The two dumpling kids, one boy, and one girl, leaned against the truck's bumper as if they had just felt the effect of some relaxing drug. They both wore jeans, tennis shoes and Disney T-shirts with the Magic Kingdom in the background. Mr. Harold couldn't help but note the whole family had upturned noses, like pigs. It wasn't something that could be ignored.

Sonny Guy shook his head and walked across the lot and over to the blind man. "You sure messed this up. It's gonna cost me more'n I'd have paid you to get it fixed. That crippled nigger never done nothing like this. He run over a sprinkler head once, but that was it. And he paid for it." Sonny turned his attention to Mr. Harold. "You have anything to do with this?"

"I was just tryin' to help," Mr. Harold said.

"I was doin' all right until he come over," said the blind man.

"He started tellin' me how I was messin' up and all and got me nervous, and sure enough, I began to lose my place and my concentration. You can see the results."

"You'd have minded your own business," Sonny said to Mr. Harold, "the man woulda done all right, but you're one of those thinks a handicap can't do some jobs."

"The man's blind," said Mr. Harold. "He can't see to cut grass. Not four acres with a weed-eater. Any moron can see that."

The Reverend Sonny Guy had a pretty fast right hand for a fat man. He caught Mr. Harold a good one over the left eye and staggered him.

The blind man stepped aside so they'd have plenty of room, and Sonny set to punching Mr. Harold quite regularly. It seemed like something the two of them were made for. Sonny to throw punches and Mr. Harold to absorb them.

When Mr. Harold woke up, he was lying on his back in the grass and the shadow of the blind man lay like a slat across him.

"Where is he?" asked Mr. Harold, feeling hot and sick to his stomach.

"When he knocked you down and you didn't get up, he went in the house with his wife," said the blind man. "I think he was thirsty. He told me he wasn't giving me no five dollars. Actually, he said he wasn't giving me jackshit. And him a minister. The kids are still out here though, they're looking at their watches, I think. They had a bet on how long it'd be before you got up. I heard them talking."

Mr. Harold sat up and glanced toward the Dodge club cab. The blind man was right. The kids were still leaning against the truck. When Mr. Harold looked at them, the boy, who was glancing at his watch, lifted one eye and raised his hand quickly and pulled it down, said, "Yesss!" The little girl looked pouty. The little boy said, "This time you blow me."

They went in the house. Mr. Harold stood up. The blind man gave him the weed-eater for support. He said, "Sonny says the crippled nigger will be back next week. I can't believe it. Scooped by a nigger. A crippled nigger."

Mr. Harold pursed his lips and tried to recall a couple of calming Bible verses. When he felt somewhat relaxed, he said, "Why'd you tell him it was my fault?"

"I figured you could handle yourself," the blind man said.

Mr. Harold rubbed one of the knots Sonny had knocked on his head. He considered homicide, but knew there wasn't any future in it. He said, "Tell you what. I'll give you a ride home."

"We could watch some more TV?"

"Nope," said Mr. Harold, probing a split in his lip. "I've got other plans."

Mr. Harold got his son and the three of them drove over to where the blind man said he lived. It was a lot on the far side of town, outside the city limits. It was bordered on either side by trees. It was a trailer lot, scraped down to the red clay. There were a few anemic grass patches here and there and it had a couple of lawn ornaments out front. A cow and a pig with tails that hooked up to hoses and spun around and around and worked as lawn sprinklers.

Behind the sprinklers a heap of wood and metal smoked pleasantly in the sunlight.

They got out of the car and Mr. Harold's son said, "Holy shit."

"Let me ask you something," said Mr. Harold to the blind man. "Your place got a cow and a pig lawn ornament? Kind that sprinkles the yard?"

The blind man appeared nervous. He sniffed the air. He said, "Is the cow one of those spotted kind?"

"A Holstein?" asked Mr. Harold. "My guess is the pig is a Yorkshire."

"That's them."

"Well, I reckon we're at your place all right, but it's burned down."

"Oh, shit," said the blind man. "I left the beans on."

"They're done now," said the boy.

The blind man sat down in the dirt and began to cry. It was a serious cry. A cat walking along the edge of the woods behind the remains of the trailer stopped to watch in amazement. The cat seemed surprised that any one thing could make such noise.

"Was they pinto beans?" the boy asked.

The blind man sputtered and sobbed and his chest heaved. Mr. Harold went and got the pig sprinkler and turned it on so that the water from its tail splattered on the pile of smoking rubble. When he felt that was going good, he got the cow working. He thought about calling the fire department, but that seemed kind of silly. About all they could do was come out and stir what was left with a stick.

"Is it all gone?" asked the blind man.

"The cow's all right," said Mr. Harold, "but the pig was a little too close to the fire, there's a little paint bubbled up on one of his legs."

Now the blind man really began to cry. "I damn near had it

paid for. It wasn't no double-wide, but it was mine."

They stayed that way momentarily, the blind man crying, the water hissing onto the trailer's remains, then the blind man said, "Did the dogs get out?"

Mr. Harold gave the question some deep consideration. "My guess would be no."

"Then I don't guess there's any hope for the parakeet neither," said the blind man.

Reluctantly, Mr. Harold loaded the blind man back in the car with his son, and started home.

It wasn't the way Mr. Harold had hoped the day would turn out. He had been trying to do nothing more than a good deed, and now he couldn't get rid of the blind man. He wondered if this kind of shit ever happened to Jesus. He was always doing good stuff in the Bible. Mr. Harold wondered if he'd ever had an incident misfire on him, something that hadn't been reported in the Testaments.

Once, when Mr. Harold was about eleven, he'd experienced a similar incident, only he hadn't been trying to be a good Samaritan. Still, it was one of those times where you go in with one thing certain and it turns on you.

During recess he'd gotten in a fight with a little kid he thought would be easy to take. He punched the kid when he wasn't looking, and that little dude dropped and got hold of his knee with his arms and wrapped both his legs around him, positioned himself so that his bottom was on Mr. Harold's shoe.

Mr. Harold couldn't shake him. He dragged him across the school yard and even walked him into a puddle of water, but the kid stuck. Mr. Harold got a pretty good sized stick and hit the kid over the head with it, but that hadn't changed conditions. A dog tick couldn't have been fastened any tighter. He had to go back to class with the kid on his leg, pulling that little rascal after him wherever he went, like he had an anvil tied to his foot.

The teacher couldn't get the kid to let go either. They finally had to go to the principal's office and get the principal and the football coach to pry him off, and even they had to work at it. The coach said he'd once wrestled a madman with a butcher knife, and he'd rather do that again than try and get that kid off someone's leg.

The blind man was kind of like that kid. You couldn't lose the sonofabitch.

Near the house, Mr. Harold glanced at his watch and noted it was time for his wife to be home. He was overcome with deep concerns. He'd just thought the blind man pissing on his bathroom wall would be a problem, now he had greater worries. He actually had the gentleman in tow, bringing him to the house at supper time. Mr. Harold pulled over at a station and got some gas and bought the boy and the blind man a Coke. The blind man seemed to have gotten over the loss of his trailer. Sadness for its contents, the dogs and the parakeet, failed to plague him.

While the boy and the blind man sat on the curb, Mr. Harold went around to a pay booth and called home. On the third ring his wife answered.

"Where in the world are you?" she said.

"I'm out here at a filling station. I got someone with me."

"You better have Marvin with you."

"I do, but I ain't talking about the boy. I got a blind man with me."

"You mean he can't see?"

"Not a lick. He's got a weed-eater. He's the groundskeeper next door. I tried to take him home but his trailer burned up with his dogs and bird in it, and I ain't got no place to take him but home for supper."

A moment of silence passed as Mrs. Harold considered. "Ain't there some kinda home you can put him in?"

"I can't think of any. I suppose I could tie a sign around his neck said 'Blind Man' and leave him on someone's step with his weed-eater."

"Well, that wouldn't be fair to whoever lived in that house, just pushing problems on someone else."

Mr. Harold was nervous. Mrs. Harold seemed awfully polite. Usually she got mad over the littlest thing. He was trying to figure if it was a trap when he realized that something about all this was bound to appeal to her religious nature. She went to church a lot. She read the *Baptist Standard* and watched a couple of Sunday afternoon TV shows with preaching in them. Blind people were loved by Baptists. Them and cripples. They got mentioned in the Bible a lot. Jesus had a special affection for them. Well, he liked lepers too, but Mr. Harold figured that was where even Mrs. Harold's dedicated Baptist beliefs might falter.

A loophole presented itself to Mr. Harold. He said, "I figure it's our Christian charity to take this fella in, honey. He can't see and he's lost his job and his trailer burned down with his pets in it."

"Well, I reckon you ought to bring him on over then. We'll feed him and I'll call around and see what my ladies' charities can do. It'll be my project. Wendy Lee is goin' around gettin' folks to pick up trash on a section of the highway, but I figure helping out a blind man would be Christian. Jesus helped blind people, but I don't never remember him picking up any trash."

When Mr. Harold loaded his son and the blind man back into the car, he was a happier man. He wasn't in trouble. Mrs. Harold thought taking in the blind man was her idea. He figured he could put up with the bastard another couple hours, then he'd find him a place to stay. Some homeless shelter with a cot and some hot soup if he wanted it. Maybe some preaching and breakfast before he had to hit the road.

At the house, Mrs. Harold met them at the door. Her little round body practically bounced. She found the blind man's hand and shook it. She told him how sorry she was, and he dropped his head and looked sad and thanked her. When they were inside, he said, "Is that cornbread I smell?"

"Yes it is," Mrs. Harold said, "and it won't be no time till it's ready. And we're having pinto beans with it. The beans were cooked yesterday and just need heating. They taste best when they've set a night."

"That's what burned his trailer down," the boy said. "He was cooking some pinto beans and forget 'em."

"Oh my," said Mrs. Harold, "I hope the beans won't bring back sad memories."

"No ma'am, them was limas I was cookin'."

"There was dogs in there and a parakeet," said the boy. "They got burned up too. There wasn't nothing left but some burnt wood and a piece of a couch and an old bird cage."

"I have some insurance papers in a deposit box downtown," the blind man said. "I could probably get me a couple of double-wides and have enough left over for a vacation with the money I'll get. I could get me some dogs and a bird easy enough too. I could even name them the same names as the ones burned up."

They sat and visited for a while in the living room while the cornbread cooked and the beans warmed up. The blind man and Mrs. Harold talked about religion. The blind man knew her favorite gospel tunes and sang a couple of them. Not too good, Mr. Harold thought, but Mrs. Harold seemed almost swoony.

The blind man knew her Sunday preaching programs too, and they talked about a few highlighted TV sermons. They debated the parables in the Bible and ended up discussing important and obscure points in the scripture, discovered the two of them saw things a lot alike when it came to interpretation. They had found dire warnings in Deuteronomy that scholars had overlooked.

Mrs. Harold got so lathered up with enthusiasm, she went into the kitchen and started throwing an apple pie together. Mr. Harold became nervous as soon as the pie pans began to rattle. This wasn't like her. She only cooked a pie to take to relatives after someone died or if it was Christmas or Thanksgiving and more than ten people were coming.

While she cooked, the blind man discussed wrestling holds with Mr. Harold's son. When dinner was ready, the blind man was positioned in Mr. Harold's chair, next to Mrs. Harold. They ate, and the blind man and Mrs. Harold further discussed scripture, and from time to time, the blind man would stop the religious talk long enough to give the boy a synopsis of some wrestling match or another. He had a way of cleverly turning the conversation without seeming to. He wasn't nearly as clever about passing the beans or the cornbread. The apple pie remained strategically guarded by his elbow.

After a while, the topic switched from the Bible and wrestling to the blind man's aches and miseries. He was overcome with them. There wasn't a thing that could be wrong with a person he didn't have.

Mrs. Harold used this conversational opportunity to complain about hip problems, hypoglycemia, overactive thyroids, and out-of-control sweat glands.

The blind man had a tip or two on how to make living with each of Mrs. Harold's complaints more congenial. Mrs. Harold said, "Well, sir, there's just not a thing you don't know something about. From wrestling to medicine."

The blind man nodded. "I try to keep up. I read a lot of braille and listen to the TV and the radio. They criticize the TV, but they shouldn't. I get lots of my education there. I can learn from just about anything or anyone but a nigger."

Mrs. Harold, much to Mr. Harold's chagrin, agreed. This was a side of his wife he had never known. She had opinions and he hadn't known that. Stupid opinions, but opinions.

When Mr. Harold finally left the table, pieless, to hide out in the bathroom, the blind man and Mrs. Harold were discussing a plan for getting all the black folk back to Africa. Something to do with the number of boats necessary and the amount of proper hygiene needed.

And speaking of hygiene, Mr. Harold stood up as his bottom became wet. He had been sitting on the lid of the toilet and dampness had soaked through his pants. The blind man had been in the bathroom last and he'd pissed all over the lowered lid and splattered the wall.

Mr. Harold changed clothes and cleaned up the piss and washed his hands and splashed his face and looked at himself in the mirror. It was still him in there and he was awake.

About ten P.M. Mrs. Harold and the blind man put the boy to bed and the blind man sang the kid a rockabilly song, told him a couple of nigger jokes and one kike joke, and tucked him in.

Mr. Harold went in to see the boy, but he was asleep. The blind man and Mrs. Harold sat on the couch and talked about chicken and dumpling recipes and how to clean squirrels properly for frying. Mr. Harold sat in a chair and listened, hoping for some opening in the conversation into which he could spring. None presented itself.

Finally Mrs. Harold got the blind man some bedclothes and folded out the couch and told him a pleasant good night, touching the blind man's arm as she did. Mr. Harold noted she left her hand there quite a while.

In bed, Mr. Harold, hoping to prove to himself he was still man of the house, rolled over and put his arm around Mrs. Harold's hip. She had gotten dressed and gotten into bed in record time while he was taking a leak, and now she was feigning sleep, but Mr. Harold decided he wasn't going to go for it. He rubbed her ass and tried to work his hand between her legs from behind. He touched what he wanted, but it was as dry as a ditch in the Sahara.

Mrs. Harold pretended to wake up. She was mad. She said he ought to let a woman sleep, and didn't he think about anything else? Mr. Harold admitted that sex was a foremost thought of his, but he knew now nothing he said would matter. Neither humor nor flattery would work. He would not only go pieless this night, he would go assless as well.

Mrs. Harold began to explain how one of her mysterious headaches with back pain had descended on her. Arthritis might be the culprit, she said, though sometimes she suspicioned something more mysterious and deadly. Perhaps something incurable that would eventually involve large leaking sores and a deep coma.

Mr. Harold, frustrated, closed his eyes and tried to go to sleep with a hard-on. He couldn't understand, having had so much experience now, why it was so difficult for him to just forget his boner and go to bed, but it was, as always, a trial.

Finally, after making a trip to the bathroom to work his pistol and plunk its stringy wet bullet into the toilet water, he was able to go back to bed and drift off into an unhappy sleep.

A few hours later he awoke. He heard a noise like girlish laughter. He lay in bed and listened. It was in fact, laughter, and it was coming from the living room. The blind man must have the TV on. But then he recognized the laughter. It hadn't come to him right away, because it had been ages since he had heard it. He reached for Mrs. Harold and she was gone.

He got out of bed and opened the bedroom door and crept quietly down the hall. There was a soft light on in the living room; it was the lamp on the TV muted by a white towel.

On the couch-bed was the blind man, wearing only his underwear and dark glasses. Mrs. Harold was on the bed too. She was wearing her nightie. The blind man was on top of her and they were pressed close. Mrs. Harold's hand sneaked over the blind's man's back and slid into his underwear and cupped his ass.

Mr. Harold let out his breath, and Mrs. Harold turned her head and saw him. She gave a little cry and rolled out from under the blind man. She laughed hysterically. "Why, honey, you're up."

The blind man explained immediately. They had been practicing a wrestling hold, one of the more complicated, and not entirely legal ones, that involved grabbing the back of an opponent's tights. Mrs. Harold admitted, that as of tonight, she had been overcome with a passion for wrestling and was going to watch all the wrestling programs from now on. She thanked the blind man for the wrestling lesson and shook his hand and went past Mr. Harold and back to bed.

Mr. Harold stood looking at the blind man. He was on the couch on all fours looking in Mr. Harold's direction. The muted light from the towel-covered lamp hit the blind man's dark glasses and made them shine like the eyes of a wolf. His bared teeth completed the image.

Mr. Harold went back to bed. Mrs. Harold snuggled close. She wanted to be friendly. She ran her hand over his chest and down his belly and held his equipment, but he was as soft as a sock. She worked him a little and finally he got hard in spite of himself. They rolled together and did what he wanted to do earlier. For the first time in years, Mrs. Harold got off. She came with a squeak and thrust of her hips, and Mr. Harold knew that behind her closed eyes she saw a pale face and dark glasses, not him.

Later, he lay in bed and stared at the ceiling. Mrs. Harold's pussy had been as wet as a fish farm after her encounter with the blind man, wetter than he remembered it in years. What was it about the blind man that excited her? He was a racist cracker asshole who really knew nothing. He didn't have a job. He couldn't even work a weed-eater that good.

Mr. Harold felt fear. What he had here at home wasn't all that good, but he realized now he might lose it, and it was probably the best he could do. Even if his wife's conversation was as dull as the Republican convention and his son was as interesting as needlework, his home life took on a new and desperate importance. Something had to be done.

Next day, Mr. Harold got a break. The blind man made a comment about his love for snow cones. It was made while they were sitting alone in the kitchen. Mrs. Harold was in the shower and the boy was playing Nintendo in the living room. The blind man was rattling on like always. Last night rang no guilty bells for him.

"You know," said Mr. Harold, "I like a good snow cone myself. One of those blue ones."

"Oh yeah, that's coconut," said the blind man.

"What you say you and me go get one?"

"Ain't it gonna be lunch soon? I don't want to spoil my appetite."

"A cone won't spoil nothing. Come on, my treat."

The blind man was a little uncertain, but Mr. Harold could tell the idea of a free snow cone was strong within him. He let Mr. Harold lead him out to the car. Mr. Harold began to tremble with anticipation. He drove toward town, but when he got there, he drove on through.

"I thought you said the stand was close?" said the blind man. "Ain't we been driving a while?"

"Well, it's Sunday, and that one I was thinking of was closed. I know one cross the way stays open seven days a week during the summer."

Mr. Harold drove out into the country. He drove off the main highway and down a red clay road and pulled over to the side near a gap where irresponsibles dumped their garbage. He got out and went around to the blind man's side and took the blind man's arm and led him away from the car toward a pile of garbage. Flies hummed operative notes in the late morning air.

"We're in luck," Mr. Harold said. "Ain't no one here but us."

"Yeah, well it don't smell so good around here. Somethin' dead somewheres?"

"There's a cat hit out there on the highway."

"I'm kinda losin' my appetite for a cone."

"It'll come back soon as you put that cone in your mouth. Besides, we'll eat in the car."

Mr. Harold placed the blind man directly in front of a bag of household garbage. "You stand right here. Tell me what you want and I'll get it."

"I like a strawberry. Double on the juice."

"Strawberry it is."

Mr. Harold walked briskly back to his car, cranked it, and drove by the blind man who cocked his head as the automobile passed. Mr. Harold drove down a ways, turned around and drove back the way he had come. The blind man still stood by the garbage heap, his cane looped over his wrist, only now he was facing the road.

Mr. Harold honked the horn as he drove past.

Just before reaching the city limits, a big black pickup began to make ominous manueuvers. The pickup was behind him and was riding his bumper. Mr. Harold tried to speed up, but that didn't work. He tried slowing down, but the truck nearly ran up his ass. He decided to pull to the side, but the truck wouldn't pass.

Eventually, Mr. Harold coasted to the emergency lane and stopped, but the truck pulled up behind him and two burly men got out. They looked as if the last bath they'd had was during the last rain, probably caught out in it while pulp wooding someone's posted land.

Mr. Harold assumed it was all some dreadful mistake. He got out of the car so they could see he wasn't who they thought he must be. The biggest one walked up to him and grabbed him behind the head with one hand and hit him with the other. The smaller man, smaller because his head seemed undersized, took his turn and hit Mr. Harold. The two men began to work on him. He couldn't fall down because the car held him up, and for some reason he couldn't pass out. These guys weren't as fast as Sonny Guy, and they weren't knocking him out, but they certainly hurt more.

"What kinda fella are you that would leave a blind man beside the road?" said the bigger man just before he busted Mr. Harold a good one in the nose.

Mr. Harold finally hit the ground. The small-headed man kicked him in the balls and the bigger man kicked him in the mouth, knocking out what was left of his front teeth; the man's fist had already stolen the others. When Mr. Harold was close to passing out, the small-headed man bent down and got hold of Mr.

Harold's hair and looked him in the eye and said, "We hadn't been throwing out an old stray dog down that road, that fella might have got lost or hurt."

"He's much more resourceful than you think," Mr. Harold said, realizing who they meant, and then the small-headed man hit him a short chopping blow.

"I'm glad we seen him," said the bigger man, "and I'm glad we caught up with you. You just think you've took a beating. We're just getting started."

But at that moment the blind man appeared above Mr. Harold. He had found his way from the truck to the car, directed by the sound of the beating most likely. "No, boys," said the blind man, "that's good enough. I ain't the kind holds a grudge, even 'gainst a man would do what he did. I've had some theology training and done a little Baptist ministering. Holding a grudge ain't my way."

"Well, you're a good one," said the bigger man. "I ain't like that at all. I was blind and I was told I was gonna get a snow cone and a fella put me out at a garbage dump, I'd want that fella dead, or crippled up at the least."

"I understand," said the blind man. "It's hard to believe there's people like this in the world. But if you'll just drive me home, that'll be enough. I'd like to get on the way if it's no inconvenience. I have a little Bible lesson in braille I'd like to study."

They went away and left Mr. Harold lying on the highway beside his car. As they drove by, the pickup tires tossed gravel on him and the exhaust enveloped him like a foul cotton sack.

Mr. Harold got up after five minutes and got inside his car and fell across the seat and lay there. He couldn't move. He spat out a tooth. His balls hurt. His face hurt. For that matter, his kneecaps where they'd kicked him didn't feel all that good either.

After an hour or so, Mr. Harold began to come around. An intense hatred for the blind man boiled up in his stomach. He sat up and started the car and headed home.

When he turned on his road, he was nearly sideswiped by a yellow moving van. It came at him so hard and fast he swerved into a ditch filled with sand and got his right rear tire stuck. He couldn't drive the car out. More he worked at it, the deeper the back tire spun in the sand. He got his jack out of the trunk and cranked up the rear end and put debris under the tire. Bad as he felt, it was quite a job. He finally drove out of there, and off the jack, leaving it lying in the dirt.

When he got to his house, certain in his heart the blind man was inside, he parked next to Mrs. Harold's station wagon. The station wagon was stuffed to the gills with boxes and sacks. He wondered what that was all about, but he didn't wonder too hard. He looked around the yard for a weapon. Out by the side of the house was the blind man's weed-eater. That would do. He figured he caught the blind man a couple of licks with that, he could get him down on the ground and finish him, stun him before the sonofabitch applied a wrestling hold.

He went in the house by the back door with the weed-eater cocked, and was astonished to find the room was empty. The kitchen table and chairs were gone. The cabinet doors were open and all the canned goods were missing. Where the stove had set was a greasy spot. Where the refrigerator had set was a wet spot. A couple of roaches, feeling brave and free to roam, scuttled across the kitchen floor as merry as kids on skates.

The living room was empty too. Not only of people, but furniture and roaches. The rest of the house was the same. Dust motes spun in the light. The front door was open.

Outside, Mr. Harold heard a car door slam. He limped out the front door and saw the station wagon. His wife was behind the wheel, and sitting next to her was the boy, and beside him the blind man, his arm hanging out the open window.

Mr. Harold beckoned to them by waving the weed-eater, but they ignored him. Mrs. Harold backed out of the drive quickly. Mr. Harold could hear the blind man talking to the boy about something or another and the boy was laughing. The station wagon turned onto the road and the car picked up speed. Mr. Harold went slack and leaned on the weed-eater for support.

At the moment before the station wagon passed in front of a line of high shurbs, the blind man turned to look out the window, and Mr. Harold saw his own reflection in the blind man's glasses.

This story was the namesake of my first collection. The title for the story came first. I had either heard something about someone having bizarre hands, or it just came to me out of the blue, I'm uncertain, but the story developed from the title. I just felt my way into it. When I was a kid, there were bums who went to houses, knocked on doors, and asked for food, or asked for work they could do to pay for food. Often, they claimed to be preachers. I guess, in their minds, this gave them more identity than a bum.

My mother was a sucker for this sort of thing, and she often fed them, no work involved. I think she did this because she enjoyed their stories. We were poor, but these folks were worse off than we were, and maybe there was a certain joy in that. That business about, "I may be bad off, but this poor sonofabitch has it worse." It makes your position look better.

When my father heard about these folks coming by (he heard them from me because I always blabbed), he insisted my mother watch herself. In fact, he wanted her to leave them alone. Not because he was heartless, but because he feared who they might be, though fear of serial killers, robbers, and the conventional murderer was not as high as now. Knowing my mother, however, he insisted if she had to feed them, she give them something to go or let them eat on the porch.

This didn't make much difference, but sometimes my mother would hand them food, then lock the screen door and talk to them. They generally had stories of woe, and my mother always felt sorry for them and sometimes even gave them money. Considering we had very little ourselves, this shows how generous she was, and I loved her for it.

Still, most of these guys were just assholes who didn't want to work. And as I said, many of them claimed to be preachers. What they were doing mostly, or so it seemed to me, were hiding behind religion. When the title "By Bizarre Hands" began to grow in my mind, and a story gradually began to sprout from it, these wandering preacher bums came to mind, the bit of fear and tension they produced was remembered, and gradually this story developed.

Oh, I liked the idea of the lady of the house referring to mass murderers as "mash" murderers. I once heard an older woman use this term, having misunderstood what someone was saying on a newscast. I guess she was relating it to someone who killed their victims by mashing, or perhaps she just thought that was a broad term for these kinds of murderers.

Anyway, this story has also been adapted to play form. As a play, I found the old ending didn't work as well. Not because there was anything wrong with it, but because I couldn't make it play as well as I wanted. The play was supposed to be for a series of plays in the Grand Guignol tradition, and therefore it needed a kicker ending. It reads pretty good, but I still prefer this version.

BY BIZARRE HANDS

WHEN THE TRAVELING PREACHER HEARD about the Widow Case and her retarded girl, he set out in his black Dodge to get over there before Halloween night.

Preacher Judd, as he called himself—though his name was really Billy Fred Williams—had this thing for retarded girls, due to the fact that his sister had been simple-headed, and his mama always said it was a shame she was probably going to burn in hell like a pan of biscuits forgot in the oven, just on account of not having a full set of brains.

This was a thing he had thought on considerable, and this considerable thinking made it so he couldn't pass up the idea of baptizing and giving some God-training to female retards. It was something he wanted to do in the worst way, though he had to admit there wasn't any burning desire in him to do the same for boys or men or women that were half-wits, but due to his sister having been one, he certainly had this thing for girl simples.

And he had this thing for Halloween, because that was the night the Lord took his sister to hell, and he might have taken her to glory had she had any bible-learning or God-sense. But she didn't have a drop, and it was partly his own fault, because he knew about God and could sing some hymns pretty good. But he'd never turned a word of benediction or gospel music in her direction. Not one word. Nor had his mama, and his papa wasn't around to do squat.

The old man ran off with a bucktoothed laundry woman that used to go house to house taking in wash and bringing it back the next day, but when she took in their wash, she took in Papa too, and she never brought either of them back. And if that wasn't bad enough, the laundry contained everything they had in the way of decent clothes, including a couple of pairs of nice dress pants and some pin-striped shirts like niggers wear to funerals. This left him with one old pair of faded overalls that he used to wear to slop the hogs before the critters killed and ate Granny, and they had to get rid of them because they didn't want to eat nothing that had eaten somebody they knew. So, it wasn't bad enough Papa ran off with a beaver-toothed wash woman and his sister was a drooling retard, he now had only the one pair of ugly, old overalls to wear to school, and this gave the other kids three things to tease him about, and they never missed a chance to do it. Well, four things. He was kind of ugly too.

It got tiresome.

Preacher Judd could remember nights waking up with his sister crawled up in the bed alongside him, lying on her back, eyes wide open, her face bathed in cool moonlight, picking her nose and eating what she found, while he rested on one elbow and tried to figure out why she was that way.

He finally gave up figuring, decided that she ought to have some fun, and he could have some fun too. Come Halloween, he got him a bar of soap for marking up windows and a few rocks for knocking out some, and he made his sister and himself ghost-suits out of old sheets in which he cut mouth and eye holes.

This was her fifteenth year and she had never been trick-or-treating. He had designs that she should go this time, and they did, and later after they'd done it, he walked her back home, and later yet, they found her out back of the house in her ghost-suit, only the sheet had turned red because her head was bashed in with something and she had bled out like an ankle-hung hog. And someone had turned her trick-or-treat sack—the handle of which was still clutched in her fat grip—inside out and taken every bit of candy she'd gotten from the neighbors.

The sheriff came out, pulled up the sheet and saw that she was naked under it, and he looked her over and said that she looked raped to him, and that she had been killed by bizarre hands.

Bizarre hands never did make sense to Preacher Judd, but he loved the sound of it, and never did let it slip away, and when he would tell about his poor sister, naked under the sheets, her brains smashed out and her trick-or-treat bag turned inside out, he'd never miss ending the story with the sheriff's line about her having died by bizarre hands.

It had a kind of ring to it.

He parked his Dodge by the roadside, got out and walked up to the Widow Case's, sipping on a Frosty Root Beer. But even though it was late October, the Southern sun was as hot as Satan's ass and the root beer was anything but frosty.

Preacher Judd was decked out in his black suit, white shirt and black loafers with black and white checked socks, and he had on his black hat, which was short-brimmed and made him look, he thought, exactly like a traveling preacher ought to look.

Widow Case was out at the well, cranking a bucket of water, and nearby, running hell out of a hill of ants with a stick she was waggling, was the retarded girl, and Preacher Judd thought she looked remarkably like his sister.

He came up, took off his hat and held it over his chest as though he were pressing his heart into proper place, and smiled at the widow with all his gold-backed teeth.

Widow Case put one hand on a bony hip, used the other to prop the bucket of water on the well-curbing. She looked like a shaved weasel, Preacher Judd thought, though her ankles weren't shaved a bit and were perfectly weasel-like. The hair there was thick and black enough to be mistaken for thin socks at a distance.

"Reckon you've come far enough," she said. "You look like one of them Jehovah Witnesses or such. Or one of them kind that run around with snakes in their teeth and hop to nigger music."

"No ma'am, I don't hop to nothing, and last snake I seen I run over with my car."

"You here to take up money for missionaries to give to them starving African niggers? If you are, forget it. I don't give to the niggers around here, sure ain't giving to no hungry foreign niggers that can't even speak English."

"Ain't collecting money for nobody. Not even myself."

"Well, I ain't seen you around here before, and I don't know you from white rice. You might be one of them mash murderers for all I know."

"No ma'am, I ain't a mash murderer, and I ain't from around here. I'm from East Texas."

She gave him a hard look. "Lots of niggers there."

"Place is rotten with them. Can't throw a dog tick without you've hit a burr-head in the noggin'. That's one of the reasons I'm traveling through here, so I can talk to white folks about God. Talking to niggers is like," and he lifted a hand to point, "talking to that well-curbing there, only that well-curbing is smarter and a lot less likely to sass, since it ain't expecting no civil rights or a chance to crowd up with our young'ns in schools. It knows its place and it stays there, and that's something for that well-curbing, if it ain't nothing for niggers."

"Amen."

Preacher Judd was feeling pretty good now. He could see she was starting to eat out of his hand. He put on his hat and looked at the girl. She was on her elbows now, her head down and her butt up. The dress she was wearing was way too short and had broken open in back from her having outgrown it. Her panties were dirt-stained and there was gravel, like little BBs hanging off of them. He thought she had legs that looked strong enough to wrap around an alligator's neck and choke it to death.

"Cindereller there," the widow said, noticing he was watching, "ain't gonna have to worry about going to school with niggers. She ain't got the sense of a nigger. She ain't got no sense at all. A dead rabbit knows more than she knows. All she does is play around all day, eat bugs and such and drool. In case you haven't noticed, she's simple."

"Yes ma'am, I noticed. Had a sister the same way. She got killed on a Halloween night, was raped and murdered and had her trick-or-treat candy stolen, and it was done, the sheriff said, by bizarre hands."

"No kiddin'?"

Preacher Judd held up a hand. "No kiddin'. She went on to hell, I reckon, cause she didn't have any God-talk in her. And retard or not, she deserved some so she wouldn't have to cook for eternity. I mean, think on it. How hot it must be down there, her boiling in her own sweat, and she didn't do nothing, and it's mostly my fault cause I didn't teach her a thing about The Lord Jesus and his daddy, God."

Widow Case thought that over. "Took her Halloween candy too, huh?"

"Whole kitandkaboodle. Rape, murder and candy theft, one fatal swoop. That's why I hate to see a young'n like yours who might not have no Word of God in her . . . is she without training?"

"She ain't even toilet trained. You couldn't perch her on the outdoor convenience if she was sick and her manage to hit the hole. She can't do nothing that don't make a mess. You can't teach her a thing. Half the time she don't even know her name." As if to prove this, Widow Case called, "Cindereller."

Cinderella had one eye against the ant hill now and was trying to look down the hole. Her butt was way up and she was rocking forward on her knees.

"See," said Widow Case, throwing up her hands. "She's worse than any little ole baby, and it ain't no easy row to hoe with her here and me not having a man around to do the heavy work."

"I can't see that . . . by the way, call me Preacher Judd . . . and can I help you tote that bucket up to the house there?"

"Well now," said Widow Case, looking all the more like a weasel, "I'd appreciate that kindly."

He got the bucket and they walked up to the house. Cinderella followed, and pretty soon she was circling around him like she was a shark closing in for the kill, the circles each time getting a mite smaller. She did this by running with her back bent and her knuckles almost touching the ground. Ropes of saliva dripped out of her mouth.

Watching her, Preacher Judd got a sort of warm feeling all over. She certainly reminded him of his sister. Only she had liked to scoop up dirt, dog mess and stuff as she ran, and toss it at him. It wasn't a thing he thought he'd missed until just that moment, but now the truth was out and he felt a little teary-eyed. He half-hoped Cinderella would pick up something and throw it on him.

The house was a big, drafty thing circled by a wide flower bed that didn't look to have been worked in years. A narrow porch ran half-way around it, and the front porch had man-tall windows on either side of the door.

Inside, Preacher Judd hung his hat on one of the foil-wrapped rabbit ears perched on top of an old Sylvania TV set, and followed the widow and her child into the kitchen.

The kitchen had big iron frying pans hanging on wall pegs, and there was a framed embroidery that read GOD WATCHES OVER THIS HOUSE. It had been faded by sunlight coming through the window over the sink.

Preacher Judd sat the bucket on the ice box—the old sort that used real ice—then they all went back to the living room. Widow Case told him to sit down and asked him if he'd like some ice tea.

"Yes, this bottle of Frosty ain't so good." He took the bottle out of his coat pocket and gave it to her.

Widow Case held it up and squinted at the little line of liquid in the bottom. "You gonna want this?"

"No ma'am, just pour what's left out and you can have the deposit." He took his Bible from his other pocket and opened it. "You don't mind if I try and read a verse or two to your Cindy, do you?"

"You make an effort on that while I fix us some tea. And I'll bring some things for ham sandwiches, too."

"That would be right nice. I could use a bite."

Widow Case went to the kitchen and Preacher Judd smiled at Cinderella. "You know tonight's Halloween, Cindy?"

Cinderella pulled up her dress, picked a stray ant off her knee and ate it.

"Halloween is my favorite time of the year," he continued. "That may be strange for a preacher to say, considering it's a devil thing, but I've always loved it. It just does something to my blood. It's like a tonic for me, you know?"

She didn't know. Cinderella went over to the TV and turned it on.

Preacher Judd got up, turned it off. "Let's don't run the Sylvania right now, baby child," he said. "Let's you and me talk about God."

Cinderella squatted down in front of the set, not seeming to notice it had been cut off. She watched the dark screen like the White Rabbit considering a plunge down the rabbit hole.

Glancing out the window, Preacher Judd saw that the sun looked like a dropped cherry snow cone melting into the clay road that led out to Highway 80, and already the tumble bug of night was rolling in blue-black and heavy. A feeling of frustration went over him, because he knew he was losing time and he knew what he had to do.

Opening his Bible, he read a verse and Cinderella didn't so much as look up until he finished and said a prayer and ended it with "Amen."

"Uhman," she said suddenly.

Preacher Judd jumped with surprise, slammed the Bible shut and dunked it in his pocket. "Well, well now," he said with delight, "that does it. She's got some Bible training."

Widow Case came in with the tray of fixings. "What's that?"

"She said some of a prayer," Preacher Judd said. "That cinches it. God don't expect much from retards, and that ought to do for keeping her from burning in hell." He practically skipped over to the woman and her tray, stuck two fingers in a glass of tea, whirled and sprinkled the drops on Cinderella's head. Cinderella held out a hand as if checking for rain.

Preacher Judd bellowed out, "I pronounce you baptized. In the name of God, The Son, and The Holy Ghost. Amen."

"Well, I'll swan," the widow said. "That there tea works for baptizing?" She sat the tray on the coffee table.

"It ain't the tea water, it's what's said and who says it that makes it take . . . consider that gal legal baptized . . . now, she ought to have some fun too, don't you think? Not having a full head of brains don't mean she shouldn't have some fun."

"She likes what she does with them ants," Widow Case said.

"I know, but I'm talking about something special. It's Halloween. Time for young folks to have fun, even if they are retards. In fact, retards like it better than anyone else. They love this stuff . . . a thing my sister enjoyed was dressing up like a ghost."

"Ghost?" Widow Case was seated on the couch, making the sandwiches. She had a big butcher knife and she was using it to spread mustard on bread and cut ham slices.

"We took this old sheet, you see, cut some mouth and eye holes in it, then we wore them and went trick-or-treating."

"I don't know that I've got an old sheet. And there ain't a house close enough for trick-or-treatin' at."

"I could take her around in my car. That would be fun, I think. I'd like to see her have fun, wouldn't you? She'd be real scary too under that sheet, big as she is and liking to run stooped down with her knuckles dragging."

To make his point, he bent forward, humped his back, let his hands dangle and made a face he thought was an imitation of Cinderella.

"She would be scary, I admit that," Widow Case said. "Though that sheet over her head would take some away from it. Sometimes she scares me when I don't got my mind on her, you know? Like if I'm napping in there on the bed, and I sorta open my eyes, *and there she is*, looking at me like she looks at them ants. I declare, she looks like she'd like to take a stick and whirl it around on me."

"You need a sheet, a white one, for a ghost-suit."

"Now maybe it would be nice for Cindereller to go out and have some fun." She finished making the sandwiches and stood up. "I'll see what I can find."

"Good, good," Preacher Judd said, rubbing his hands together.

"You can let me make the outfit. I'm real good at it."

While Widow Case went to look for a sheet, Preacher Judd ate one of the sandwiches, took one and handed it down to Cinderella. Cinderella promptly took the bread off of it, ate the meat, and laid the mustard sides down on her knees.

When the meat was chewed, she took to the mustard bread, cramming it into her mouth and smacking her lips loudly.

"Is that good, sugar?" Preacher Judd asked.

Cinderella smiled some mustard bread at him, and he couldn't help but think the mustard looked a lot like baby shit, and he had to turn his head away.

"This do?" Widow Case said, coming into the room with a slightly yellowed sheet and a pair of scissors.

"That's the thing," Preacher Judd said, taking a swig from his ice tea. He set the tea down and called to Cinderella.

"Come on, sugar, let's you and me go in the bedroom there and get you fixed up and surprise your mama."

It took a bit of coaxing, but he finally got her up and took her into the bedroom with the sheet and scissors. He half-closed the bedroom door and called out to the widow, "You're going to like this."

After a moment, Widow Case heard the scissors snipping away and Cinderella grunting like a hog to trough. When the scissor sound stopped, she heard Preacher Judd talking in a low voice, trying to coach Cinderella on something, but as she wanted it to be a surprise, she quit trying to hear. She went over to the couch and fiddled with a sandwich, but she didn't eat it. As soon as she'd gotten out of eyesight of Preacher Judd, she'd upended the last of his root beer and it was as bad as he said. It sort of made her stomach sick and didn't encourage her to add any food to it.

Suddenly the bedroom door was knocked back, and Cinderella, having a big time of it, charged into the room with her arms held out in front of her yelling, "Woooo, woooo, goats."

Widow Case let out a laugh. Cinderella ran around the room yelling, "Woooo, woooo, goats," until she tripped over the coffee table and sent the sandwich makings and herself flying.

Preacher Judd, who'd followed her in after a second, went over and helped her up. The Widow Case, who had curled up on the couch in natural defense against the flying food and retarded girl, now uncurled when she saw something dangling on Preacher Judd's arm. She knew what it was, but she asked anyway. "What's that?"

"One of your piller cases. For a trick-or-treat sack."

"Oh," Widow Case said stiffly, and she went to straightening up the coffee table and picking the ham and makings off the floor.

Preacher Judd saw that the sun was no longer visible. He walked over to a window and looked out. The tumble bug of night was even more blue-black now and the moon was out, big as a dinner plate, and looking like it had gravy stains on it.

"I think we've got to go now," he said. "We'll be back in a few hours, just long enough to run the houses around here."

"Whoa, whoa," Widow Case said. "Trick-or-treatin' I can go for, but I can't let my daughter go off with no strange man."

"I ain't strange. I'm a preacher."

"You strike me as an all right fella that wants to do things right, but I still can't let you take my daughter off without me going. People would talk."

Preacher Judd started to sweat. "I'll pay you some money to let me take her on."

Widow Case stared at him. She had moved up close now and he could smell root beer on her breath. Right then he knew what she'd done and he didn't like it any. It wasn't that he'd wanted it, but somehow it seemed dishonest to him that she swigged it without asking him. He thought she was going to pour it out. He started to say as much when she spoke up.

"I don't like the sound of that none, you offering me money."

"I just want her for the night," he said, pulling Cinderella close to him. "She'd have fun."

"I don't like the sound of that no better. Maybe you ain't as right thinking as I thought."

Widow Case took a step back and reached the butcher knife off the table and pushed it at him. "I reckon you better just let go of her and run on out to that car of yours and take your ownself trick-or-treatin'. And without my piller case."

"No ma'am, can't do that. I've come for Cindy and that's the thing God expects of me, and I'm going to do it. I got to do it. I didn't do my sister right and she's burning in hell. I'm doing Cindy right. She said some of a prayer and she's baptized. Anything happened to her, wouldn't be on my conscience."

Widow Case trembled a bit. Cinderella lifted up her ghost-suit with her free hand to look at herself, and Widow Case saw that she was naked as a jay-bird underneath.

"You let go of her arm right now, you pervert. And drop that piller case . . . toss it on the couch would be better. It's clean."

He didn't do either.

Widow Case's teeth went together like a bear trap and made about as much noise, and she slashed at him with the knife.

He stepped back out of the way and let go of Cinderella, who suddenly let out a screech, broke and ran, started around the room yelling, "Wooooo, wooooo, goats."

Preacher Judd hadn't moved quick enough, and the knife had cut through the pillow case, his coat and shirt sleeve, but hadn't broke the skin.

When Widow Case saw her slashed pillow case fall to the floor, a fire went through her. The same fire that went through Preacher Judd when he realized his J.C. Penney's suit coat which had cost him, with the pants, $39.95 on sale, was ruined.

They started circling one another, arms outstretched like wrestlers ready for the run-together, and Widow Case had the advantage on account of having the knife.

But she fell for Preacher Judd holding up his left hand and wiggling two fingers like mule ears, and while she was looking at that, he hit her with a right cross and floored her. Her head hit the coffee table and the ham and fixings flew up again.

Preacher Judd jumped on top of her and held her knife hand down with one of his, while he picked up the ham with the other and hit her in the face with it, but the ham was so greasy it kept sliding off and he couldn't get a good blow in.

Finally he tossed the ham down and started wrestling the knife away from her with both hands while she chewed on one of his forearms until he screamed.

Cinderella was still running about, going, "Wooooo, wooooo, goats," and when she ran by the Sylvania, her arm hit the foil-wrapped rabbit ears and sent them flying.

Preacher Judd finally got the knife away from Widow Case, cutting his hand slightly in the process, and that made him mad. He stabbed her in the back as she rolled out from under him and tried to run off on all fours. He got on top of her again, knocking her flat, and he tried to pull the knife out. He pulled and tugged, but it wouldn't come free. She was as strong as a cow and was crawling across the floor and pulling him along as he hung tight to the thick, wooden butcher knife handle. Blood was boiling all over the place.

Out of the corner of his eye, Preacher Judd saw that his retard was going wild, flapping around in her ghost-suit like a fat dove, bouncing off walls and tumbling over furniture. She wasn't making the ghost sounds now. She knew something was up and she didn't like it.

"Now, now," he called to her as Widow Case dragged him across the floor, yelling all the while, "Bloody murder, I'm being kilt, bloody murder, bloody murder!"

"Shut up, goddamnit!" he yelled. Then, reflecting on his words, he turned his face heavenward. "Forgive me my language, God." Then he said sweetly to Cinderella, who was in complete bouncing distress, "Take it easy, honey. Ain't nothing wrong, not a thing."

"Oh Lordy mercy, I'm being kilt!" Widow Case yelled.

"Die, you stupid old cow."

But she didn't die. He couldn't believe it, but she was starting to stand. The knife he was clinging to pulled him to his feet, and when she was up, she whipped an elbow around, whacked him in the ribs and sent him flying.

About that time, Cinderella broke through a window, tumbled onto the porch, over the edge and into the empty flower bed.

Preacher Judd got up and ran at Widow Case, hitting her just above the knees and knocking her down, cracking her head a loud one on the Sylvania, but it still didn't send her out. She was strong enough to grab him by the throat with both hands and throttle him.

As she did, he turned his head slightly away from her digging fingers, and through the broken window he could see his retarded ghost. She was doing a kind of two step, first to the left, then to the right, going, "Unhhh, unhhhh," and it reminded Preacher Judd of one of them dances sinners do in them places with lots of blinking lights and girls up on pedestals doing lashes with their hips.

He made a fist and hit the widow a couple of times, and she let go of him and rolled away. She got up, staggered a second, then started running toward the kitchen, the knife still in her back, only deeper from having fallen on it.

He ran after her and she staggered into the wall, her hands hitting out and knocking one of the big iron frying pans off its peg and down on her head. It made a loud BONG, and Widow Case went down.

Preacher Judd let out a sigh. He was glad for that. He was tired. He grabbed up the pan and whammed her a few times, then, still carrying the pan, he found his hat in the living room and went out on the porch to look for Cinderella.

She wasn't in sight.

He ran out in the front yard calling her, and saw her making the rear corner of the house, running wildly, hands close to the ground, her butt flashing in the moonlight every time the sheet popped up. She was heading for the woods out back.

He ran after her, but she made the woods well ahead of him. He followed in, but didn't see her. "Cindy," he called. "It's me. Ole Preacher Judd. I come to read you some Bible verses. You'd like that wouldn't you?" Then he commenced to coo like he was talking to a baby, but still Cinderella did not appear.

He trucked around through the woods with his frying pan for half an hour, but didn't see a sign of her. For a half-wit, she was a good hider.

Preacher Judd was covered in sweat and the night was growing slightly cool and the old Halloween moon was climbing to the stars. He felt like just giving up. He sat down on the ground and started to cry.

Nothing ever seemed to work out right. That night he'd taken his sister out hadn't gone fully right. They'd gotten the candy and he'd brought her home, but later, when he tried to get her in bed with him for a little bit of the thing animals do without sin, she wouldn't go for it, and she always had before. Now she was uppity over having a ghost-suit and going trick-or-treating. Worse yet, her wearing that sheet with nothing under it did something for him. He didn't know what it was, but the idea of it made him kind of crazy.

But he couldn't talk or bribe her into a thing. She ran out back and he ran after her and tackled her, and when he started doing to her what he wanted to do, out beneath the Halloween moon, underneath the apple tree, she started screaming. She could scream real loud, and he'd had to choke her some and beat her in the head with a rock. After that, he felt he should make like some kind of theft was at the bottom of it all, so he took all her Halloween candy.

He was sick thinking back on that night. Her dying without no God-training made him feel lousy. And he couldn't get those Tootsie Rolls out of his mind. There must have been three dozen of them. Later he got so sick from eating them all in one sitting that to this day he couldn't stand the smell of chocolate.

He was thinking on these misfortunes, when he saw through the limbs and brush a white sheet go by.

Preacher Judd poked his head up and saw Cinderella running down a little path going, "Wooooo, wooooo, goats."

She had already forgotten about him and had the ghost thing on her mind.

He got up and crept after her with his frying pan. Pretty soon she disappeared over a dip in the trail and he followed her down.

She was sitting at the bottom of the trail between two pines, and ahead of her was a clear lake with the moon shining its face in the water. Across the water the trees thinned, and he could see the glow of lights from a house. She was looking at those lights and the big moon in the water and was saying over and over, "Oh, priddy, priddy."

He walked up behind her and said, "It sure is, sugar," and he hit her in the head with the pan. It gave a real solid ring, kind of like the clap of a sweet church bell. He figured that one shot to the bean was sufficient, since it was a good overhand lick, but she was still sitting up and he didn't want to be no slacker about things, so he hit her a couple more times, and by the second time, her head didn't give a ring, just sort of a dull thump, like he was hitting a thick, rubber bag full of mud.

She fell over on what was left of her head and her butt cocked up in the air, exposed as the sheet fell down her back. He took a long look at it, but found he wasn't interested in doing what animals do without sin anymore. All that hitting on the Widow Case and Cinderella had tuckered him out.

He pulled his arm way back, tossed the frying pan with all his might toward the lake. It went in with a soft splash. He turned back toward the house and his car, and when he got out to the road, he cranked up the Dodge and drove away noticing that the Halloween sky was looking blacker. It was because the moon had slipped behind some dark clouds. He thought it looked like a suffering face behind a veil, and as he drove away from the Case's, he stuck his head out the window for a better look. By the time he made the hill that dipped down toward Highway 80, the clouds had passed along, and he'd come to see it more as a happy jack-o'-lantern than a sad face, and he took that as a sign that he had done well.

I don't really know where this came from. It just sort of jumped out of the blue. Or seemed to. I suppose nothing really comes out of thin air, but for the life of me I can't remember the roots of it. It's one of my absolute favorites, and to the best of my memory it has never been reprinted outside of the collection it first appeared in, and that collection — By Bizarre Hands — is long out of print.

Well, as I write this it occurred to me that there were a couple sources for this. Ideas that must have spurred it, but the content of it . . . well, I can't begin to guess. The first source is the fact that I used to see, and still occasionally see, roadside attractions. You know, stop and see the three-legged calf, the giant rats of Sumatra. Snake farm. That kind of thing. Usually, it's a pretty pathetic sight. There was even one that I heard about that had the world's largest gopher. Which was true. Only the gopher was a statue. It was the world's largest all right, but it wasn't alive. It was just a come-on to get your money, and I suppose it worked. I once stopped to see the giant rats of Sumatra to be greeted by the sight of shaved possums. Sheessshhhh.

THE FAT MAN AND
THE ELEPHANT

THE SIGNS WERE SET IN RELAY AND WENT ON FOR miles. The closer you got to the place the bigger they became. They were so enthusiastic in size and brightness of paint it might be thought you were driving to heaven and God had posted a sure route so you wouldn't miss it. They read:

WORLD'S LARGEST GOPHER!
ODDITIES!
SEE THE SNAKES! SEE THE ELEPHANT!
SOUVENIRS!
BUTCH'S HIGHWAY MUSEUM AND EMPORIUM!

But Sonny knew he wasn't driving to heaven. Butch's was far from heaven and he didn't want to see anything but the elephant. He had been to the Museum and Emporium many times, and the first time was enough for the sights—because there weren't any.

The World's Largest Gopher was six feet tall and inside a fenced-in enclosure. It cost you two dollars on top of the dollar admission fee to get in there and have a peek at it and feel like a jackass. The gopher was a statue, and it wasn't even a good statue. It looked more like a dog standing on its haunches than a gopher. It had a strained, constipated look on its homely face, and one of its two front teeth had been chipped off by a disappointed visitor with a rock.

The snake show wasn't any better. Couple of dead, stuffed rattlers with the rib bones sticking through their taxidermied hides, and one live, but about to go, cottonmouth who didn't have any fangs and looked a lot like a deflated bicycle tire when it was coiled and asleep. Which was most of the time. You couldn't wake the sonofabitch if you beat on the glass with a rubber hose and yelled FIRE!

There were two main souvenirs. One was the armadillo purses, and the other was a miniature statue of the gopher with a little plaque on it that read: I SAW THE WORLD'S LARGEST GOPHER AT BUTCH'S HIGHWAY MUSEUM AND EMPORIUM OFF HIGHWAY 59. And the letters were so crowded on there you had to draw mental slashes between the words. They sold for a dollar fifty apiece and they moved right smart. In fact, Butch made more money on those (75¢ profit per statue) than he did on anything else, except the cold drinks which he marked up a quarter. When you were hot from a long drive and irritated about actually seeing the World's Largest Gopher, you tended to spend money foolishly on soda waters and gopher statues.

Or armadillo purses. The armadillos came from Hank's Armadillo Farm and Hank was the one that killed them and scooped their guts out and made purses from them. He lacquered the bodies and painted them gold and tossed glitter in the paint before it dried. The 'dillos were quite bright and had little zippers fixed into their bellies and a rope handle attached to their necks and tails so you could carry them upside down with their sad, little feet pointing skyward.

Butch's wife had owned several of the purses. One Fourth of July she and the week's receipts had turned up missing along with one of her 'dillo bags. She and the purse and the receipts were never seen again. Elrod down at the Gull station disappeared too. Astute observers said there was a connection.

But Sonny came to see the elephant, not buy souvenirs or look at dead snakes and statues. The elephant was different from the rest of Butch's stuff. It was special.

It wasn't that it was beautiful, because it wasn't. It was in bad shape. It could hardly even stand up. But the first time Sonny had seen it, he had fallen in love with it. Not in the romantic sense, but in the sense of two great souls encountering one another. Sonny came back time after time to see it when he needed inspiration, which of late, with the money dwindling and his preaching services not bringing in the kind of offerings he thought they should, was quite often.

Sonny wheeled his red Chevy pickup with the GOD LOVES EVEN FOOLS LIKE ME sticker on the back windshield through the gate of Butch's and paid his dollar for admission, plus two dollars to see the elephant.

Butch was sitting at the window of the little ticket house as usual. He was toothless and also wore a greasy, black work cap, though Sonny couldn't figure where the grease came from. He had never known Butch to do any kind of work, let alone something greasy—unless you counted the serious eating of fried chicken. Butch just sat there in the window of the little house in his zip-up coveralls (summer or winter) and let Levis Garrett snuff drip down his chin while he played with a pencil or watched a fly dive bomb a jelly doughnut. He seldom talked, unless it was to argue about money. He didn't even like to tell you how much admission was. It was like it was some secret you were supposed to know, and when he did finally reveal it, was as if he had given up part of his heart.

Sonny drove his pickup over to the big barn where the elephant stayed, got out and went inside.

Candy, the ancient clean-up nigger, was shoving some dirt around with a push broom, stirring up dust mostly. When Candy saw Sonny wobble in, his eyes lit up.

"Hello there, Mr. Sonny. You done come to see your elephant, ain't you?"

"Yeah, I have," Sonny said.

"That's good, that's good." Candy looked over Sonny's shoulder at the entrance, then glanced at the back of the barn. "That's good, and you right on time too, like you always is."

Candy held out his hand.

Sonny slipped a five into it and Candy folded it carefully and put it in the front pocket of his faded khakis, gave it a pat like a good dog, then swept up the length of the barn. When he got to the open door, he stood there watching, waiting for Mr. Butch to go to lunch, like he did every day at eleven-thirty sharp.

And sure enough, there he went in his black Ford pickup out the gate of Butch's Museum and Emporium. Then came the sound of the truck stopping and the gate being locked. Butch closed the whole thing down every day for lunch rather than leave it open for the nigger to tend. Anyone inside the Emporium at that time was just shit out of luck. They were trapped there until Butch came back from lunch thirty minutes later, unless they wanted to go over the top or ram the gate with their vehicle.

It wasn't a real problem however. Customers seldom showed up mid-day, dead of summer. They didn't seem to want to see the World's Largest Gopher at lunch time.

Which was why Sonny liked to come when he did. He and Candy had an arrangement.

When Candy heard Butch's truck clattering up the highway, he dropped the broom, came back and led Sonny over to the elephant stall.

"He in this one today, Mr. Sonny."

Candy took out a key and unlocked the chainlink gate that led inside the stall and Sonny stepped inside and Candy said what he always said. "I ain't supposed to do this now. You supposed to do all your looking through this gate." Then, without waiting for a reply he closed the gate behind Sonny and leaned on it.

The elephant was lying on its knees and it stirred slightly. Its skin creaked like tight shoes and its breathing was heavy.

"You wants the usual, Mr. Sonny?"

"Does it have to be so hot this time? Ain't it hot enough in here already?"

"It can be anyway you wants it, Mr. Sonny, but if you wants to do it right, it's got to be hot. You know I'm telling the truth now, don't you?"

"Yeah . . . but it's so hot."

"Don't do no good if it ain't, Mr. Sonny. Now we got to get these things done before Mr. Butch comes back. He ain't one for spir'tual things. That Mr. Butch ain't like you and me. He just wants that dollar. You get that stool and sit yourself down, and I'll be back dreckly, Mr. Sonny."

Sonny sat the stool upright and perched his ample butt on it, smelled the elephant shit and studied the old pachyderm. The critter didn't look as if it had a lot of time left, and Sonny wanted to get all the wisdom from it he could.

The elephant's skin was mottled grey and more wrinkled than a bloodhound's. Its tusks had been cut off short years before and they had turned a ripe lemon yellow, except for the jagged tips, and they were the color of dung. Its eyes were skummy and it seldom stood anymore, not even to shit. Therefore, its flanks were caked with it. Flies had collected in the mess like raisins spread thickly on rank chocolate icing. When the old boy made a feeble attempt to slap at them with his tail, they rose up en masse like bad omens.

Candy changed the hay the elephant lay on now and then, but

not often enough to rid the stall of the stink. With the heat like it was, and the barn being made of tin and old oak, it clung to the structure and the elephant even when the bedding was fresh and the beast had been hosed down. But that was all right with Sonny. He had come to associate the stench with God.

The elephant was God's special animal—shit smell and all. God had created the creature in the same way he had created everything else—with a wave of his majestic hand (Sonny always imagined the hand bejeweled with rings). But God had given the elephant something special—which seemed fair to Sonny, since he had put the poor creature in the land of crocodiles and nig-gers—and that special something was wisdom.

Sonny had learned of this from Candy. He figured since Candy was born of niggers who came from Africa, he knew about elephants. Sonny reasoned that elephant love was just the sort of information niggers would pass down to one another over the years. They probably passed along other stuff that wasn't of importance too, like the best bones for your nose and how to make wooden dishes you could put inside your lips so you could flap them like Donald Duck. But the stuff on the elephants would be the good stuff.

He was even more certain of this when Candy told him on his first visit to see the elephant that the critter was most likely his totem. Candy had taken one look at him and said that. It surprised Sonny a bit that Candy would even consider such things. He seemed like a plain old clean-up nigger to him. In fact, he had hired Candy to work for him before. The sort of work you wanted a nigger to do, hot and dirty. He'd found Candy to be slow and lazy and at the end of the day he had almost denied him the two dollars he'd promised. He could hardly see that he'd earned it. In fact, he'd gotten the distinct impression that Candy was getting uppity in his old age and thought he deserved a white man's wages.

But, lazy or not, Candy did have wisdom—least when it came to elephants. When Candy told him he thought the elephant was his totem, Sonny asked how he had come by that, and Candy said, "You big and the elephant is big, and you both tough-hided and just wise as Old Methus'la. And you can attract them gals just like an ole bull elephant can attract them elephant females, now can't you? Don't lie to Candy now, you know you can."

This was true. All of it. And the only way Candy could have known about it was to know he was like the elephant and the elephant was his totem. And the last thing about attracting the women, well, that was the thing above all that convinced him that the nigger knew his business.

Course, even though he had this ability to attract the women, he had never put it to bad use. That wouldn't be God's way. Some preachers, men of God or not, would have taken advantage of such a gift, but not him. That wouldn't be right.

It did make him wonder about Louise though. Since the Lord had seen fit to give him this gift, why in the world had he ended up with her? What was God's master plan there? She was a right nice Christian woman on the inside, but the outside looked like a four car pileup. She could use some work.

He couldn't remember what it was that had attracted him to her in the first place. He had even gone so far as to look at old pictures of them together to see if she had gotten ugly slowly. But no, she'd always been that way. He finally had to blame his choice on being a drinking man in them days and a sinner. But now, having lost his liquor store business, and having sobered to God's will and gotten a little money (though that was dwindling), he could see her for what she was.

Fat and ugly.

There, he'd thought it clearly. But he did like her. He knew that. There was something so wonderfully Christian about her. She could recite from heart dozens of Bible verses, and he'd heard her give good argument against them that thought white man came from monkey, and a better argument that the nigger did. But he wished God had packaged her a little better. Like in the body of his next-door neighbor's wife for instance. Now there was a Godly piece of work.

It seemed to him, a man like himself, destined for great things in God's arena, ought to at least have a wife who could turn heads toward her instead of away from her. A woman like that could help a man go far.

There wasn't any denying that Louise had been a big help. When he married her she had all that insurance money, most of which they'd used to buy their place and build a church on it. But the settlement was almost run through now, and thinking on it, he couldn't help but think Louise had gotten cheated.

Seemed to him that if your first husband got kicked to death by a wild lunatic that the nut house let out that very afternoon calling him cured, they ought to have to fork up enough money to take care of the man's widow for the rest of her life. And anyone she might remarry, especially if that person had some medical problems, like a trick back, and couldn't get regular work anymore.

Still, they had managed what she had well; had gotten some real mileage out of the four hundred thousand. There was the land and the house and the church and the four hundred red-jacketed, leatherette Bibles that read in gold, gilt letters on the front: THE MASTER'S OWN BAPTIST MINISTRIES INC., SONNY GUY OFFICIATING. And there were some little odds and ends here and there he couldn't quite recall. But he felt certain not a penny had been wasted. Well, maybe those seven thousand bumper stickers they bought that said GO JESUS on them was a mistake. They should have made certain that the people who made them were going to put glue on the backs so they'd stick to something. Most folks just wouldn't go to the trouble to tape them on the bumpers and back glasses of their automobiles, and therefore weren't willing to put out four-fifty per sticker.

But that was all right. Mistakes were to be expected in a big enterprise. Even if it was for God, The Holy Ghost, and The Lord Jesus Crucified.

Yet things weren't going right, least not until he started visiting the elephant. Now he had him some guidance and there was this feeling he had that told him it was all going to pay off. That through this creature of the Lord he was about to learn God's *grand-doise plan* for his future. And when he did learn it, he was going to start seeing those offering plates (a bunch of used hubcaps bought cheap from the wrecking yard) fill up with some serious jack.

Candy came back with the electric heater, extension cord and tarp. He had a paper bag in one back pocket, his harmonica in the other. He looked toward the entrance, just in case Butch should decide for the first time in his life to come back early.

But no Butch.

Candy smiled and opened the stall's gate.

"Here we go, Mr. Sonny, you ready to get right with God and the elephant?"

Sonny took hold of the tarp and pulled it over his head and Candy came in and found places to attach all four corners to the fence near the ground and draped it over the old elephant who squeaked its skin and turned its head ever so slightly and rolled its goo-filled eyes.

"Now you just keep you seat, Mr. Bull Elephant," Candy said, "and we all gonna be happy and ain't none of us gonna get trampled."

Candy stooped back past Sonny on his stool and crawled out from under the tarp and let it fall down Sonny's back to the ground. He got the electric heater and pushed it under the tarp next to Sonny's stool, then he took the extension cord and went around and plugged it into one of the barn's deadly-looking wall sockets. He went back to the tarp and lifted it up and said to Sonny, "You can turn it on now, Mr. Sonny. It's all set up."

Sonny sighed and turned the heater on. The grill work went pink, then red, and the fan in the machine began to whirl, blowing the heat at him.

Candy, who still had his face under the tarp, said. "You got to lean over it now to get the full effects, Mr. Sonny. Get that heat on you good. Get just as hot as a nigger field hand."

"I know," Sonny said. "I remember how to do it."

"I knows you do, Mr. Sonny. You great for remembering, like an elephant. It heating up in there good?"

"Yeah."

"Real hot?"

"Yeah."

"That's good. Make you wonder how anyone wouldn't want to do good and stay out of hell, don't it, Mr. Sonny? I mean it's hotter under here than when I used to work out in that hot sun for folks like you, and I bet when I drop this here tarp it just gonna get hotter, and then that heat and that stink gonna build up in there and things gonna get right for you . . . here's you paper bag."

Candy took the bag out of his back pocket and gave it to Sonny. "Remember now," Candy said, "when you get good and full of that shit-smell and that heat, you put this bag over you face and you start blowing like you trying to push a grapefruit through a straw. That gonna get you right for the ole elephant spirit to get inside you and do some talking at you cause it's gonna be hot as Africa and you gonna be out of breath just like niggers dancing to drums, and that's how it's got to be."

"Ain't I done this enough to know, Candy?"

"Yes suh, you have. Just like to earns my five dollars and see a good man get right with God."

Candy's head disappeared from beneath the tarp and when the tarp hit the ground it went dark in there except for the little red lines of the heater grate, and for a moment all Sonny could see was the lumpy shape of the elephant and the smaller lumps of his own knees. He could hear the elephant's labored breathing and his own labored breathing. Outside, Candy began to play nigger music on the harmonica. It filtered into the hot tent and the notes were fire ants crawling over his skin and under his overalls. The sweat rolled down him like goat berries.

After a moment, Candy began to punctuate the harmonica notes with singing. "Sho gonna hate it when the elephant dies. Hot in here, worse than outside, and I'm sho gonna hate it when the elephant dies." A few notes on the harmonica. "Yes suh, gonna be bad when the pachyderm's dead, ain't gonna have five dollars to buy Coalie's bed." More notes. "Come on brother can you feel the heat. I'm calling to you Jesus, cross my street."

Sonny put the bag over his face and began to blow viciously. He was blowing so hard he thought he would knock the bottom out of the bag, but that didn't happen. He grew dizzy, very dizzy, felt stranger than the times before. The harmonica notes and singing were far away and he felt like a huge hunk of ice cream melting on a hot stone. Then he didn't feel the heat anymore. He was flying. Below him the ribs of the heater were little rivers of molten lava and he was falling toward them from a great height. Then the rivers were gone. There was only darkness and the smell of elephant shit, and finally that went away and he sat on his stool on a sunny landscape covered in tall grass. But he and his stool were taller than the grass, tall as an elephant itself. He could see scrubby trees in the distance and mountains and to the left of him was a blue-green line of jungle from which came the constant and numerous sounds of animals. Birds soared overhead in a sky bluer than a jay's feathers. The air was as fresh as a baby's first breath.

There was a dot in the direction of the mountains and the dot grew and became silver-grey and there was a wink of white on either side of it. The dot became an elephant and the closer it came the more magnificent it looked, its skin tight and grey and its tusks huge and long and porcelain-white. A fire sprang up before the elephant and the grass blazed in a long, hot line from the beast to the stool where Sonny sat. The elephant didn't slow. It kept coming. The fire didn't bother it. The blaze wrapped around its massive legs and licked at its belly like a lover's tongue. Then the elephant stood before him and they were eye to eye; the tusks extended over Sonny's shoulders. The trunk reached out and touched his cheek; it was as soft as a woman's lips.

The smell of elephant shit filled the air and the light went dark and another smell intruded, the smell of burning flesh. Sonny felt pain. He let out a whoop. He had fallen off the stool on top of the heater and the heater had burned his chest above the bib of his overalls.

There was light again. Candy had ripped off the tarp and was pulling him up and sitting him on the stool and righting the electric heater. "Now there, Mr. Sonny, you ain't on fire no more. You get home you get you some shaving cream and put on them burns, that'll make you feel right smart again. Did you have a good trip?"

"Africa again, Candy," Sonny said, the hot day air feeling cool to him after the rancid heat beneath the tarp. "And this time I saw the whole thing. It was all clearer than before and the elephant came all the way up to me."

"Say he did?" Candy said, looking toward the barn door.

"Yeah, and I had a revelation."

"That's good you did, Mr. Sonny. I was afraid you wasn't gonna have it before Mr. Butch come back. You gonna have to get out of here now. You know how Mr. Butch is, 'specially since his wife done run off with that ole 'diller purse and the money that time. Ain't been a fit man to take a shit next to since."

Candy helped Sonny to his feet and guided him out of the stall and leaned him against it.

"A firewalking elephant," Sonny said. "Soon as I seen it, it come to me what it all meant."

"I'm sho glad of that, Mr. Sonny."

Candy looked toward the open door to watch for Butch. He then stepped quickly into the stall, jammed the paper bag in his back pocket and folded up the tarp and put it under his arm and picked the heater up by the handle and carried it out, the cord dragging behind it. He sat the tarp and the heater down and closed the gate and locked it. He looked at the elephant. Except for a slight nodding of its head it looked dead.

Candy got hold of the tarp and the heater again and put them in their place. He had no more than finished when he heard Butch's truck pulling up to the gate. He went over to Sonny and took him by the arm and smiled at him and said, "It sho been a pleasure having you, and the elephant done went and gave you one of them rav'lations too. And the best one yet, you say?"

"It was a sign from God," Sonny said.

"God's big on them signs. He's always sending someone a sign or a bush on fire or a flood or some such thing, ain't he, Mr. Sonny?"

"He's given me a dream to figure on, and in that dream he's done told me some other things he ain't never told any them other preachers."

"That's nice of him, Mr. Sonny. He don't talk to just everyone. It's the elephant connection does it."

Butch drove through the open gate and parked his truck in the usual spot and started for the ticket booth. He had the same forward trudge he always had, like he was pushing against a great wind and not thinking it was worth it.

"The Lord has told me to expand the minds of Baptists," Sonny said.

"That's a job he's given you, Mr. Sonny."

"There is another path from the one we've been taking. Oh, some of the Baptist talk is all right, but God had shown me that firewalking is the correct way to get right with the holy spirit."

"Like walking on coals and stuff?"

"That's what I mean."

"You gonna walk on coals, Mr. Sonny?"

"I am."

"I'd sho like to see that, Mr. Sonny, I really would."

Candy led Sonny out to the pickup and Sonny opened the door and climbed in, visions of firewalking Baptists trucking through his head.

"You gonna do this with no shoes on?" Candy asked, closing the pickup door for Sonny.

"It wouldn't be right to wear shoes. That would be cheating. It wouldn't have a purpose."

"Do you feet a mite better."

Sonny wasn't listening. He found the keys in his overalls and touched the red furrows on his chest that the heater had made. He was proud of them. They were a sign from God. They were like the trenches of fire he would build for his Baptists. He would teach them to walk the trenches and open their hearts and souls and trust their feet to Jesus. And not mind putting a little something extra in the offering plate. People would get so excited he could move those red leatherette Bibles.

"Lord be praised," Sonny said.

"Ain't that the truth," Candy said.

Sonny backed the truck around and drove out of the gate onto the highway. He felt like Moses must have felt when he was chosen to lead the Jews out of the wilderness. But he had been chosen instead to lead the Baptists into a new way of Salvation by forming a firewalking branch of the Baptist church. He smiled and leaned over the steering wheel, letting it touch the hot wounds on his chest. Rows of rich converts somewhere beyond the horizon of his mind stepped briskly through trenches of hot coals, smiling.

This one was based on a true incident. A woman very much like the one described in this story arrived at my house on a day very much like the one described in the story, and then the events, up to a point, occurred as they do in the story.

Obviously, the woman and the events were only the catalyst, as the protagonist of this story has a kind of, well, uh, adventure with the Phone Woman that certainly didn't occur. Least not at my house. Not with me. I just write crazy stories. I try not to perform them.

THE PHONE WOMAN

Journal Entries

A WEEK TO REMEMBER ...
After this, my little white page friend, you shall have greater security, kept under not only lock and key, but you will have a hiding place. If I were truly as smart as I sometimes think I am, I wouldn't write this down. I know better. But, I am compelled.

Compulsion. It comes out of nowhere and owns us all. We put a suit and tie and hat on the primitive part of our brain and call it manners and civilization, but ultimately, it's just a suit and tie and a hat. The primitive brain is still primitive, and it compels, pulses to the same dark beat that made our less civilized ancestors and the primordial ooze before them throb to simple, savage rhythms of sex, death and destruction.

Our nerves call out to us to touch and taste life, and without our suits of civilization, we can do that immediately. Take what we need if we've muscle enough. Will enough. But all dressed up in the trappings of civilization, we're forced to find our thrills vicariously. And eventually, that is not enough. Controlling our impulses that way is like having someone eat your food for you. No taste. No texture. No nourishment. Pitiful business.

Without catering to the needs of our primitive brains, without feeding impulses, trying instead to get what we need through books and films and the lives of the more adventurous, we cease to live. We wither. We bore ourselves and others. We die. And are glad of it.

Whatcha gonna do, huh?

*　　*　　*

Saturday morning, June 10th through Saturday 17th:

I haven't written in a while, so I'll cover a few days, beginning with a week ago today.

It was one of those mornings when I woke up on the wrong side of the bed, feeling a little out of sorts, mad at the wife over something I've forgotten and she probably hasn't forgotten, and we grumbled down the hall, into the kitchen, and there's our dog, a Siberian Husky—my wife always refers to him as a Suburban Husky because of his pampered lifestyle, though any resemblance to where we live and suburbia requires a great deal of faith—and he's smiling at us, and then we see why he's smiling. Two reasons: (1) He's happy to see us. (2) He feels a little guilty.

He has reason to feel guilty. Not far behind him, next to the kitchen table, was a pile of shit. I'm not talking your casual little whoopsie-doo, and I'm not talking your inconvenient pile, and I'm not talking six to eight turds the size of large bananas. I'm talking a certified, pure-dee, goddamn prize-winning SHIT. There were enough dog turds there to shovel out in a pickup truck and dump on the lawn and let dry so you could use them to build an adobe hut big enough to keep your tools in and have room to house your cat in the winter.

And, right beside this sterling deposit, was a lake of piss wide enough and deep enough to go rowing on.

I had visions of a Siberian Husky hat and slippers, or possibly a nice throw rug for the bedroom, a necklace of dog claws and teeth; maybe cut that smile right out of his face and frame it.

But the dog-lover in me took over, and I put him outside in his pen where he cooled his dewclaws for a while. Then I spent about a half-hour cleaning up dog shit while my wife spent the same amount of time keeping our two-year-old son, Kevin, known to me as Fruit of My Loins, out of the shit.

Yep, Oh Great White Page of a Diary, he was up now. It always works that way. In times of greatest stress, in times of greatest need for contemplation or privacy, like when you're trying to get that morning piece off the Old Lady, the kid shows up, and suddenly it's as if you've been deposited inside an ant farm and the ants are crawling and stinging. By the time I finished cleaning up the mess, it was time for breakfast, and I got to tell you, I didn't want anything that looked like link sausage that morning.

So Janet and I ate, hoping that what we smelled while eating was the aroma of disinfectant and not the stench of shit wearing a coat of disinfectant, and we watched the kid spill his milk eighty-lebben times and throw food and drop stuff on the floor, and me and the wife we're fussing at each other more and more, about whatever it was we were mad about that morning—a little item intensified by our dog's deposits—and by the time we're through eating our meal, and Janet leaves me with Fruit of My Loins and his View Master and goes out to the laundry room to do what the room is named for—probably went out there to beat the laundry clean with rocks or bricks, pretending shirts and pants were my head—I'm beginning to think things couldn't get worse. About that time the earth passes through the tail of a comet or something, some kind of dimensional gate is opened, and the world goes weird.

There's a knock at the door.

At first I thought it was a bird pecking on the glass, it was that soft. Then it came again and I went to the front door and opened it, and there stood a woman about five feet tall wearing a long, wool coat, and untied, flared-at-the-ankles shoes, and a ski cap decorated with a silver pin. The wool ski cap was pulled down so tight over her ears, her face was pale. Keep in mind that it was probably eighty degrees that morning, and the temperature was rising steadily, and she was dressed like she was on her way to plant the flag at the summit of Everest. Her age was hard to guess. Had that kind of face. She could have been twenty-two or forty-two.

She said, "Can I use your phone, mister? I got an important call to make."

Well, I didn't see any ready-to-leap companions hiding in the shrubbery, and I figured if she got out of line I could handle her, so I said, "Yeah, sure. Be my guest," and let her in.

The phone was in the kitchen, on the wall, and I pointed it out to her, and me and Fruit of My Loins went back to doing what we were doing, which was looking at the View Master. We switched from Goofy to Winnie the Pooh, the one about Tigger in the tree, and it was my turn to look at it, and I couldn't help but hear my guest's conversation with her mother was becoming stressful—I knew it was her mother because she addressed her by that title—and suddenly Fruit of My Loins yelled, "Wook, Daddy wook."

I turned and "wooked," and what do I see but what appears to be some rare tribal dance, possibly something having originated in higher altitudes where the lack of oxygen to the brain causes wilder abandon with the dance steps. This gal was all over the place. Fred Astaire with a hot coat hanger up his ass couldn't have been any brisker. I've never seen anything like it. Then, in mid-dossey-do, she did a leap like cheerleaders do, one of those things where they kick their legs out to the side, open up like a nut-cracker and kick the palms of their hands, then she hit the floor on her ass, spun, and wheeled as if on a swivel into the hallway and went out of sight. Then there came a sound from in there like someone on speed beating the bongos. She hadn't dropped the phone either. The wire was stretched tight around the corner and was vibrating like a big fish was on the line.

I dashed over there and saw she was lying crosswise in the hallway, bamming her head against the wall, clutching at the phone with one hand and pulling her dress up over her waist with the other, and she was making horrible sounds and rolling her eyes, and I immediately thought: this is it, she's gonna die. Then I saw she wasn't dying, just thrashing, and I decided it was an epileptic fit.

I got down and took the phone away from her, took hold of her jaw, got her tongue straight without getting bit, stretched her out on the floor away from the wall, picked up the phone and told her mama, who was still fussing about something or another, that things weren't so good, hung up on her in mid-sentence and called the ambulance.

I ran out to the laundry room, told Janet a strange woman was in our hallway pulling her dress over her head and that an ambulance was coming. Janet, bless her heart, has become quite accustomed to weird events following me around, and she went outside to direct the ambulance, like one of those people at the airport with light sticks.

I went back to the woman and watched her thrash a while, trying to make sure she didn't choke to death, or injure herself, and Fruit of My Loins kept clutching my leg and asking me what was wrong. I didn't know what to tell him.

After what seemed a couple of months and a long holiday, the ambulance showed up with a whoop of siren, and I finally decided the lady was doing as good as she was going to do, so I went outside. On either side of my walk were all these people. It's like Bradbury's story "The Crowd." The one where when there's an accident all these strange people show up out of nowhere and stand around and watch.

I'd never seen but two of these people before in my life, and I've been living in this neighborhood for years.

One lady immediately wanted to go inside and pray for the woman, who she somehow knew, but Janet whispered to me there wasn't enough room for our guest in there, let alone this other woman and her buddy, God, so I didn't let her in.

All the other folks are just a jabbering, and about all sorts of things. One woman said to another, "Mildred, how you been?"

"I been good. They took my kids away from me this morning, though. I hate that. How you been?"

"Them hogs breeding yet?" one man says to another, and the other goes into not only that they're breeding, but he tells how much fun they're having at it.

Then here comes the ambulance boys with a stretcher. One of the guys knew me somehow, and he stopped and said, "You're that writer, aren't you?"

I admitted it.

"I always wanted to write. I got some ideas that'd make a good book and a movie. I'll tell you about 'em. I got good ideas, I just can't write them down. I could tell them to you and you could write them up and we could split the money."

"Could we talk about this later?" I said. "There's a lady in there thrashing in my hallway."

So they went in with the stretcher, and after a few minutes the guy I talked to came out and said, "We can't get her out of there and turned through the door. We may have to take your back door out."

That made no sense to me at all. They brought the stretcher through and now they were telling me they couldn't carry it out. But I was too addled to argue and told them to do what they had to do.

Well, they managed her out of the back door without having to remodel our home after all, and when they came around the edge of the house I heard the guy I'd talked to go, "Ahhh, damn, I'd known it was her I wouldn't have come."

I thought they were going to set her and the stretcher down right there, but they went on out to the ambulance and jerked open the door and tossed her and the stretcher inside like they were tossing a dead body over a cliff. You could hear the stretcher strike the back of the ambulance and bounce forward and slide back again.

I had to ask: "You know her?"

"Dark enough in the house there, I couldn't tell at first. But when we got outside, I seen who it was. She does this all the time, but not over on this side of town in a while. She don't take her medicine on purpose so she'll have fits when she gets stressed, or she fakes them, like this time. Way she gets attention. Sometimes she hangs herself, cuts off her air. Likes the way it feels. Sexual or something. She's damn near died half-dozen times. Between you and me, wish she'd go on and do it and save me some trips."

And the ambulance driver and his assistant were out of there. No lights. No siren.

Well, the two people standing in the yard that we knew were still there when I turned around, but the others, like mythical creatures, were gone, turned to smoke, dissolved, become one with the universe, whatever. The two people we knew, elderly neighbors, said they knew the woman, who by this time, I had come to think of as the Phone Woman.

"She goes around doing that," the old man said. "She stays with her mamma who lives on the other side of town, but they get in fights on account of the girl likes to hang herself sometimes for entertainment. Never quite makes it over the ridge, you know, but gets her mother worked up. They say her mother used to do that too, hang herself, when she was a little girl. She outgrowed it. I guess the girl there . . . you know I don't even know her name . . . must have seen her mamma do that when she was little, and it kind of caught on. She has that 'lepsy stuff too, you know, thrashing around and all, biting on her tongue?"

I said I knew and had seen a demonstration of it this morning.

"Anyway," he continued, "they get in fights and she comes over here and tries to stay with some relatives that live up the street there, but they don't cotton much to her hanging herself to things. She broke down their clothesline post last year. Good thing it was old, or she'd been dead. Wasn't nobody home that time. I hear tell they sometimes go off and leave her there and leave rope and wire and stuff laying around, sort of hoping, you know. But except for that time with the clothesline, she usually does her hanging when someone's around. Or she goes in to use the phone at houses and does what she did here."

"She's nutty as a fruitcake," said the old woman. "She goes back on behind here to where that little trailer park is, knocks on doors where the wetbacks live, about twenty to a can, and they ain't got no phone, and she knows it. She's gotten raped couple times doing that, and it ain't just them Mex's that have got to her. White folks, niggers. She tries to pick who she thinks will do what she wants. She wants to be raped. It's like the hanging. She gets some kind of attention out of it, some kind of loving. Course, I ain't saying she chose you cause you're that kind of person."

I assured her I understood.

The old couple went home then, and another lady came up, and sure enough, I hadn't seen her before either, and she said, "Did that crazy ole girl come over here and ask to use the phone, then fall down on you and flop?"

"Yes, ma'am."

"Does that all the time."

Then this woman went around the corner of the house and was gone, and I never saw her again. In fact, with the exception of the elderly neighbors and the Phone Woman, I never saw any of those people again and never knew where they came from. Next day there was a soft knock on the door. It was the Phone Woman again. She asked to use the phone.

I told her we'd had it taken out.

She went away and I saw her several times that day. She'd come up our street about once every half hour, wearing that same coat and hat and those sad shoes, and I guess it must have been a hundred and ten out there. I watched her from the window. In fact, I couldn't get any writing done because I was watching for her. Thinking about her lying there on the floor, pulling her dress up, flopping. I thought too of her hanging herself now and then, like she was some kind of suit on a hanger.

Anyway, the day passed and I tried to forget about her, then the other night, Monday probably, I went out on the porch to smoke one of my rare cigars (about four to six a year), and I saw someone coming down the dark street, and from the way that someone walked, I knew it was her, the Phone Woman.

She went on by the house and stopped down the road a piece and looked up and I looked where she was looking, and through the trees I could see what she saw. The moon.

We both looked at it a while, and she finally walked on, slow, with her head down, and I put my cigar out well before it was finished and went inside and brushed my teeth and took off my clothes, and tried to go to sleep. Instead, I lay there for a long time and thought about her, walking those dark streets, maybe thinking about her mom, or a lost love, or a phone, or sex in the form of rape because it was some kind of human connection, about hanging herself because it was attention and it gave her a sexual high . . . and then again, maybe I'm full of shit and she wasn't thinking about any of those things.

Then it struck me suddenly, as I lay there in bed beside my wife, in my quiet house, my son sleeping with his teddy bear in the room across the way, that maybe she was the one in touch with the world, with life, and that I was the one gone stale from civilization. Perhaps life had been civilized right out of me.

The times I had truly felt alive, in touch with my nerve centers, were in times of violence or extreme stress.

Where I had grown up, in Mud Creek, violence simmered underneath everyday life like lava cooking beneath a thin crust of earth, ready at any time to explode and spew. I had been in fights, been cut by knives. I once had a job bouncing drunks. I had been a bodyguard in my earlier years, had illegally carried a .38. On one occasion, due to a dispute the day before while protecting my employer, who sometimes dealt with a bad crowd, a man I had insulted and hit with my fists pulled a gun on me, and I had been forced to pull mine. The both of us ended up with guns in our faces, looking into each other's eyes, knowing full well our lives hung by a thread and the snap of a trigger.

I had killed no one, and had avoided being shot. The Mexican stand-off ended with us both backing away and running off, but there had been that moment when I knew it could all be over in a flash. Out of the picture in a blaze of glory. No old folks home for me. No drool running down my chin and some young nurse wiping my ass, thinking how repulsive and old I was, wishing for quitting time so she could roll up with some young stud some place sweet and cozy, open her legs to him with a smile and a sigh, and later a passionate scream, while in the meantime, back at the old folks ranch, I lay in the bed with a dead dick and an oxygen mask strapped to my face.

Something about the Phone Woman had clicked with me. I understood her suddenly. I understood then that the lava that had boiled beneath the civilized facade of my brain was no longer boiling. It might be bubbling way down low, but it wasn't boiling, and the realization of that went all over me and I felt sad, very, very sad. I had dug a grave and crawled into it and was slowly pulling the dirt in after me. I had a home. I had a wife. I had a son. Dirt clods all. Dirt clods filling in my grave while life simmered somewhere down deep and useless within me.

I lay there for a long time with tears on my cheeks before exhaustion took over and I slept in a dark world of dormant passion.

Couple days went by, and one night after Fruit of My Loins and Janet were in bed, I went out on the front porch to sit and look at the stars and think about what I'm working on—a novella that isn't going well—and what do I see but the Phone Woman, coming down the road again, walking past the house, stopping once more to look at the moon.

I didn't go in this time, but sat there waiting, and she went on up the street and turned right and went out of sight. I walked across the yard and went out to the center of the street and watched her back going away from me, mixing into the shadows of the trees and houses along the street, and I followed.

I don't know what I wanted to see, but I wanted to see something, and I found for some reason that I was thinking of her lying there on the floor in my hallway, her dress up, the mound of her sex, as they say in porno novels, pushing up at me. The thought gave me an erection, and I was conscious of how silly this was, how unattractive this woman was to me, how odd she looked, and then another thought came to me: I was a snob. I didn't want to feel sexual towards anyone ugly or smelly in a winter coat in the dead of summer.

But the night was cool and the shadows were thick, and they made me feel all right, romantic maybe, or so I told myself.

I moved through a neighbor's backyard where a dog barked at me a couple of times and shut up. I reached the street across the way and looked for the Phone Woman, but didn't see her.

I took a flyer, and walked on down the street toward the trailer park where those poor illegal aliens were stuffed in like sardines by their unscrupulous employers, and I saw a shadow move among shadows, and then there was a split in the trees that provided the shadows, and I saw her, the Phone Woman. She was standing in a yard under a great oak, and not far from her was a trailer. A pathetic air conditioner hummed in one of its windows.

She stopped and looked up through that split in the trees

above, and I knew she was trying to find the moon again, that she had staked out spots that she traveled to at night; spots where she stood and looked at the moon or the stars or the pure and sweet black eternity between them.

Like the time before, I looked up too, took in the moon, and it was beautiful, as gold as if it were a great glob of honey. The wind moved my hair, and it seemed solid and purposeful, like a lover's soft touch, like the beginning of foreplay. I breathed deep and tasted the fragrance of the night, and my lungs felt full and strong and young.

I looked back at the woman and saw she was reaching out her hands to the moon. No, a low limb. She touched it with her fingertips. She raised her other hand, and in it was a short, thick rope. She tossed the rope over the limb and made a loop and pulled it taut to the limb. Then she tied a loop to the other end, quickly expertly, and put that around her neck.

Of course, I knew what she was going to do. But I didn't move. I could have stopped her, I knew, but what was the point? Death was the siren she had called on many a time, and finally, she had heard it sing.

She jumped and pulled her legs under her and the limb took her jump and held her. Her head twisted to the left and she spun about on the rope and the moonlight caught the silver pin on her ski cap and it threw out a cool beacon of silver light, and as she spun, it hit me once, twice, three times.

On the third spin her mouth went wide and her tongue went out and her legs dropped down and hit the ground and she dangled there, unconscious.

I unrooted my feet and walked over there, looking about as I went.

I didn't see anyone. No lights went on in the trailer.

I moved up close to her. Her eyes were open. Her tongue was out. She was swinging a little, her knees were bent and the toes and tops of her silly shoes dragged the ground. I walked around and around her, an erection pushing at my pants. I observed her closely, trying to see what death looked like.

She coughed. A little choking cough. Her eyes shifted toward me. Her chest heaved. She was beginning to breathe. She made a feeble effort to get her feet under her, to raise her hands to the rope around her neck.

She was back from the dead.

I went to her. I took her hands, gently pulled them from her throat, let them go. I looked into her eyes. I saw the moon there. She shifted so that her legs held her weight better. Her hands went to her dress. She pulled it up to her waist. She wore no panties. Her bush was like a nest built between the boughs of a snow-white elm.

I remembered the day she came into the house. Everything since then, leading up to this moment, seemed like a kind of perverse mating ritual. I put my hand to her throat. I took hold of the rope with my other hand and jerked it so that her knees straightened, then I eased behind her, put my forearm against the rope around her throat, and I began to tighten my hold until she made a soft noise, like a virgin taking a man for the first time. She didn't lift her hands. She continued to tug her dress up. She was trembling from lack of oxygen. I pressed myself against her buttocks, moved my hips rhythmically, my hard-on bound by my underwear and pants. I tightened the pressure on her throat.

And choked her.

And choked her.

She gave up what was left of her life with a shiver and a thrusting of her pelvis, and finally she jammed her buttocks back into me and I felt myself ejaculate, thick and hot and rich as shaving foam.

Her hands fell to her side. I loosened the pressure on her throat but clung to her for a while, getting my breath and my strength back. When I felt strong enough, I let her go. She swung out and around on the rope and her knees bent and her head cocked up to stare blindly at the gap in the trees above, at the honey-golden moon.

I left her there and went back to the house and slipped into the bedroom and took off my clothes. I removed my wet underwear carefully and wiped them out with toilet paper and flushed the paper down the toilet. I put the underwear in the clothes hamper. I put on fresh and climbed into bed and rubbed my hands over my wife's buttocks until she moaned and woke up. I rolled her on her stomach and mounted her and made love to her. Hard, violent love, my forearm around her throat, not squeezing, but thinking about the Phone Woman, the sound she had made when I choked her from behind, the way her buttocks had thrust back into me at the end. I closed my eyes until the sound that Janet made was the sound the Phone Woman made and I could visualize her there in the moonlight, swinging by the rope.

When it was over, I held Janet and she kissed me and joked about my arm around her throat, about how it seemed I had wanted to choke her. We laughed a little. She went to sleep. I let go of her and moved to my side of the bed and looked at the ceiling and thought about the Phone Woman. I tried to feel guilt. I could not. She had wanted it. She had tried for it many times. I had helped her do what she had never been able to manage. And I had felt alive again. Doing something on the edge. Taking a risk.

Well, journal, here's the question: Am I a sociopath?

No. I love my wife. I love my child. I even love my Suburban Husky. I have never hunted and fished, because I thought I didn't like to kill. But there are those who want to die. It is their one moment of life; to totter on the brink between light and darkness, to take the final, dark rush down a corridor of black, hot pain.

So, Oh Great White Pages, should I feel guilt, some inner torment, a fear that I am at heart a cold-blooded murderer?

I think not.

I gave the sweet gift of truly being alive to a woman who wanted someone to participate in her moment of joy. Death ended that, but without the threat of it, her moment would have been nothing. A stage rehearsal for a high-school play in street clothes.

Nor do I feel fear. The law will never suspect me. There's no reason to. The Phone Woman had a record of near suicides. It would never occur to anyone to think she had died by anyone's hand other than her own.

I felt content, in touch again with the lava beneath the primal crust. I have allowed it to boil up and burst through and flow, and now it has gone down once more. But it's no longer a distant memory. It throbs and rolls and laps just below ready to jump and give me life. Are there others out there like me? Or better yet, others for me, like the Phone Woman?

Most certainly.

And now I will recognize them. The Phone Woman has taught me that. She came into my life on a silly morning and brought me adventure, took me away from the grind, and then she brought me more, much, much more. She helped me recognize the fine but perfect line between desire and murder; let me know that there are happy victims and loving executioners.

I will know the happy victims now when I see them, know who needs to be satisfied. I will give them their desire, while they give me mine.

*   *   *

This last part with the Phone Woman happened last night and I am recording it now, while it is fresh, as Janet sleeps. I think of Janet in there and I have a hard time imagining her face. I want her, but I want her to be the Phone Woman, or someone like her.

I can feel the urge rising up in me again. The urge to give someone that tremendous double-edged surge of life and death.

It's like they say about sex. Once you get it, you got to have it on a regular basis. But it isn't sex I want. It's something like it, only sweeter.

I'll wrap this up. I'm tired. Thinking that I'll have to wake Janet and take the edge off my need, imagine that she and I are going to do more than fornicate; that she wants to take that special plunge and that she wants me to shove her.

But she doesn't want that. I'd know. I have to find that in my dreams, when I nestle down into the happy depths of the primitive brain.

At least until I find someone like the Phone Woman, again, that is. Someone with whom I can commit the finest of adultery.

And until that search proves fruitful and I have something special to report, dear diary, I say, good night.

I love science fiction, and I've always enjoyed alternate universe stories. I sat down one day with the intent to write one. And I did. It's based on a number of historical interests of mine, and I really enjoyed twisting history, and hopefully twisting the reader.

LETTER FROM THE SOUTH, TWO MOONS WEST OF NACOGDOCHES

EAR HAWK:

Your letter stating that you can't believe I'm not a Baptist, due to the fact my morals and yours are so similar, astonishes me. How can you think only Baptists are good people and lead happy lives? You've known me longer than that, even if most of our contact has been through letters and phone calls.

Well, I might ask you the same in reverse. How can you accept such a silly pagan religion? And if you must consider a religion, why not look back to your heritage, instead of taking on a Hebrew mythology.

And how in the world can you believe being a Baptist makes you happier than others?

I'm quite happy, thank you. I mean I have my ups and downs, but from your cards and letters, our occasional phone calls, so do you. Don't we all?

In answering your question about why I don't believe more fully, I might add that I've been a student, if not a scholar, of religions all my life, and I find nothing to recommend the Baptist over any other religion, no matter what the origin. Only the Aztec and their nasty custom of human sacrifice could be worse, and I'll

187

tell you, though it's off the subject, I think the old Chief of this country is crazy as hell to sell them the makings for a nuclear reactor. I don't care what sort of diplomatic gesture it was meant to be. Those heart-cutters get up here on us and it's the last pow-wow, buddy. With just sticks and stones, practically, they ran the Spaniards off, so I sure don't want to see them with the ability to make the big shitty boom machine, if you know what I mean? They're tougher than us, I admit it. I say let's let our technology be our muscle, and not let those mean pyramid builders have an equalizer, because with their attitude about war and sacrifice, they're going to be a whole hell of a lot more equal than we are.

But that's off the point, as usual.

On to why I'm not a Baptist. Well, first off, let's keep this simple. Consult history text if you don't believe me, though that won't keep you from twisting them around to suit you, or from picking just those that say what you want them to say (I remember our argument before on the civil war with the Japs, and I've got to add, though I shouldn't bring it up again, how you can side at all with those bastards after what they've done to our people on the West Coast is beyond me), so perhaps my asking you to examine historical text isn't sound advice on my part, and you're sure to take it as an insult.

But history does show, Hawk, that John the Baptist was not the only religious nut running around at that time, and it was only fate that gave him the honor (a dubious one in my book) of becoming the "Messiah." I mean a dramatic death like decapitation and having the head put on a silver (does the text actually say silver, I can't remember and am too lazy to check?) platter, and then the fact that the execution was performed at the bidding of a dance-hall floozy of the time, and the head presented to her as a gift, does have a certain element of showboating, and that's just the sort of thing people latch onto. High drama.

It always occurs to me that Jesus of Nazareth, mentioned briefly in your so-called "Holy Book," and I believe he was a cousin or something to John if memory serves me, was as likely a candidate for martyrdom as John. Except for fate, he might well have been the one your congregation worships.

He, however, in spite of his many similarities to John, had the misfortune to suffer less than a martyr's death. He was hit and killed by a runaway donkey cart and knocked up on the curbing with his, how was it put in the book. . . ? Can't remember, but something like "with his flanks exposed." Words to that effect.

I believe it was Jesus' inglorious death, more than anything else, that jockeyed him to a lowly position in the race toward Messiahism (did I make that word up?). He certainly had all the goods John did. Nice fanaticism, pie in the sky, promises of an afterlife, etc. But it seems to be in our natures to prefer bloody, dramatic demises such as decapitation, to a relatively minor death by a runaway donkey cart, the latter casualty being all the more jinxed by the fact that he ended up draped over some curb with his ass exposed, his little deep, brown eye winking at the world.

If we were more open-minded, a religion might have formed where Jesus was worshipped, and instead of the little bleeding-head-on-a-platter medallions many of your congregation wear, they might be adorning themselves with little buttocks with donkey cart tracks across them.

Just a thought. Don't get mad.

The other thing you mention is the Platter of Turin. And I admit to you that it is indeed mysterious and fascinating. But I've never seen nor read anything that convinces me that whatever is making itself manifest on the platter—and I also admit it does look like a head with a bleeding stump—is in fact, the likeness of John the Baptist. And even if it is his likeness, and somehow the trauma of his death caused it to be forever captured in the platter, that still does not mean he is the Messiah.

Consider the statue of Custer at the site of The Battle Of The Little Big Horn. Many have reported (and I believe it has been filmed) that it bleeds from the mouth, nose, ears and mouth from time to time. To some, this was interpreted to mean that Custer was a Saint and that the statue could cure illnesses. I know from our letters in the past that you hardly believe Custer a Saint, quite the contrary.

What I'm saying is this: there are many mysteries in the world, Hawk, and there are many interpretations. You need only choose a mystery and an interpretation to suit you.

Well, got to cut this short. Got to get dressed. There's a meeting tonight. They're having another public execution, and it's about time. Bunch of niggers are going to be crucified along Caddo Street and I don't want to miss that. Those stupid black bastards thinking they're good as us makes me ill. I've had my hood and robes starched special for the occasion, and I'm actually getting to light one of the pitch-covered niggers placed at the end to provide light. I also get to lead the local Scout troops in a song. I'm excited.

Oh, almost forgot. If you haven't read about it, we finally got that troublemaker Martin Luther King, and he's the main feature tonight. I know from your letters that you have a sort of begrudging respect for him, and I must admit his guerrilla activities conducted with only twenty-two men throughout the South have been brilliant for his kind. But after tonight he'll plague the South no more.

As I said, wish you could be here, but I know you've got a big pow-wow going up there and I wish I could see it. Like to see your tribe strip the skin off those White Eyes slow and easy. They're worse than our niggers, and I'm only glad the last of them (far as we know) have been eliminated down here.

Another thing just hit me about this Baptist business, and I'll go ahead and get it off my chest. Here we are getting rid of the whites and the niggers, and you and some others have adopted their silly religion. I admit that our own is pretty damned dumb (Great Heap Big Spirit, Ugh), but doesn't that kind of thing, accepting their religion, give the lowlifes a sort of existence through us? Think about it.

Guess while I'm bad mouthing them, might as well admit I'm against the trend that wants to drop all of their ways, as some of them would just be too difficult to adopt. This two moons and two suns bit is just ridiculous. With automobiles that method is no longer correct. What used to be a two day trip is now only a matter of hours. And this switch over from their language to ours, the use of Cherokee writing for all tribes, is going to be a pain. I mean we'll all be speaking our tribal languages, translating the writing to Cherokee and when we all get together how are we going to converse? Which language will we pick? Cherokee for writing, because of their good alphabet, makes sense, but which will be the superior tribal language, and how's it going to go down with folks when one is chosen over all the others?

Oh, to hell with it. This old gal is going to have to get to stepping or she isn't going to have time to get dressed and moving.

Best to you,

Running Fox

This was my attempt to write something quiet and sneaky and creepy. I wrote it specifically with Charlie Grant and the anthology series he edited in the 1980's, Shadows, in mind. I wanted to write a story that had the feel of the old Alfred Hitchcock TV series, and I think I did just that. It could be called a story of witchcraft. A ghost story. A story of psychological suspense. It sort of depends on the reader.

BY THE HAIR OF THE HEAD

THE LIGHTHOUSE WAS GREY AND BRUTALLY WEA-thered, kissed each morning by a cold, salt spray. Perched there among the rocks and sand, it seemed a last, weak sentinel against an encroaching sea; a relentless, pounding surf that had slowly swallowed up the shoreline and deposited it in the all-consuming belly of the ocean.

Once the lighthouse had been bright-colored, candy-striped like a barber's pole, with a high beacon light and a horn that honked out to the ships on the sea. No more. The lighthouse director, the last of a long line of sea watchers, had cashed in the job ten years back when the need died, but the lighthouse was now his and he lived there alone, bunked down nightly to the tune of the wind and the raging sea.

Below he had renovated the bottom of the tower and built rooms, and one of these he had locked away from all persons, from all eyes but his own.

I came there fresh from college to write my novel, dreams of being the new Norman Mailer dancing in my head. I rented in with him, as he needed a boarder to help him pay for the place, for he no longer worked and his pension was as meager as stale bread.

High up in the top was where we lived, a bamboo partition drawn between our cots each night, giving us some semblance of privacy, and dark curtains were pulled round the thick, foggy windows that traveled the tower completely around.

By day the curtains were drawn and the partition was pulled and I sat at my typewriter, and he, Howard Machen, sat with his book and his pipe, swelled the room full of grey smoke the thickness of his beard. Sometimes he rose and went below, but he was always quiet and never disturbed my work.

It was a pleasant life. Agreeable to both of us. Mornings we had coffee outside on the little railed walkway and had a word or two as well, then I went to my work and he to his book, and at dinner we had food and talk and brandies; sometimes one, sometimes two, depending on mood and the content of our chatter.

We sometimes spoke of the lighthouse and he told me of the old days, of how he had shone that light out many times on the sea. Out like a great, bright fishing line to snag the ships and guide them in; let them follow the light in the manner that Theseus followed Ariadne's thread.

"Was fine," he'd say. "That pretty old light flashing out there. Best job I had in all my born days. Just couldn't leave her when she shut down, so I bought her."

"It is beautiful up here, but lonely at times."

"I have my company."

I took that as a compliment, and we tossed off another brandy. Any idea of my writing later I cast aside. I had done four good pages and was content to spit the rest of the day away in talk and dreams.

"You say this was your best job," I said as a way of conversation. "What did you do before this?"

He lifted his head and looked at me over the briar and its smoke. His eyes squinted against the tinge of the tobacco. "A good many things. I was born in Wales. Moved to Ireland with my family, was brought up there, and went to work there. Learned the carpentry trade from my father. Later I was a tailor. I've also been a mason—note the rooms I built below with my own two hands—and I've been a boat builder and a ventriloquist in a magician's show."

"A ventriloquist?"

"Correct," he said, and his voice danced around me and seemed not to come from where he sat.

"Hey, that's good."

"Not so good really. I was never good, just sort of fell into it. I'm worse now. No practice, but I've no urge to take it up again."

"I've an interest in such things."

"Have you now?"

"Yes."

"Ever tried a bit of voice throwing?"

"No. But it interests me. The magic stuff interests me more. You said you worked in a magician's show?"

"That I did. I was the lead-up act."

"Learn any of the magic tricks, being an insider and all?"

"That I did, but that's not something I'm interested in," he said flatly.

"Was the magician you worked for good?"

"Damn good, m'boy. But his wife was better."

"His wife?"

"Marilyn was her name. A beautiful woman." He winked at me. "Claimed to be a witch."

"You don't say?"

"I do, I do. Said her father was a witch and she learned it and inherited it from him."

"Her father?"

"That's right. Not just women can be witches. Men too."

We poured ourselves another and exchanged sloppy grins, hooked elbows, and tossed it down.

"And another to meet the first," the old man said and poured. Then: "Here's to company." We tossed it off.

"She taught me the ventriloquism, you know," the old man said, relighting his pipe.

"Marilyn?"

"Right, Marilyn."

"She seems to have been a rather all-around lady."

"She was at that. And pretty as an Irish morning."

"I thought witches were all old crones, or young crones. Hook noses, warts . . ."

"Not Marilyn. She was a fine-looking woman. Fine bones, agate eyes that clouded in mystery, and hair the color of a fresh-robbed hive."

"Odd she didn't do the magic herself. I mean, if she was the better magician, why was her husband the star attraction?"

"Oh, but she did do magic. Or rather she helped McDonald to look better than he was, and he was some good. But Marilyn was better.

"Those days were different, m'boy. Women weren't the ones to take the initiative, least not openly. Kept to themselves. Was a sad thing. Back then it wasn't thought fittin' for a woman to be about such business. Wasn't ladylike. Oh, she could get sawed in half, or disappear in a wooden crate, priss and look pretty, but take the lead? Not on your life!"

I fumbled myself another brandy. "A pretty witch, huh?"

"Ummmm."

"Had the old pointed hat and broom passed down, so to speak?" My voice was becoming slightly slurred.

"It's not a laughin' matter, m'boy." Machen clenched the pipe in his teeth.

"I've touched a nerve, have I not? I apologize. Too much sauce."

Machen smiled. "Not at all. It's a silly thing, you're right. To hell with it."

"No, no. I'm the one who spoiled the fun. You were telling me she claimed to be the descendant of a long line of witches."

Machen smiled. It did not remind me of other smiles he had worn. This one seemed to come from a borrowed collection.

"Just some silly tattle is all. Don't really know much about it, just worked for her, m'boy." That was the end of that. Standing, he knocked out his pipe on the concrete floor and went to his cot.

For a moment I sat there, the last breath of Machen's pipe still in the air, the brandy still warm in my throat and stomach. I looked at the windows that surrounded the lighthouse, and everywhere I looked was my own ghostly reflection. It was like looking out through the compound eyes of an insect, seeing a multiple image.

I turned out the lights, pulled the curtains and drew the partition between our beds, wrapped myself in my blanket, and soon washed up on the distant shore of a recurring dream. A dream not quite in grasp, but heard like the far, fuzzy cry of a gull out from land.

It had been with me almost since moving into the tower. Sounds, voices . . .

A clunking noise like peg legs on stone . . .

. . . a voice, fading in, fading out . . . Machen's voice, the words not quite clear, but soft and coaxing . . . then solid and firm: "Then be a beast. Have your own way. Look away from me with your mother's eyes."

". . . your fault," came a child's voice, followed by other words that were chopped out by the howl of the sea wind, the roar of the waves.

". . . getting too loud. He'll hear . . ." came Machen's voice.

"Don't care . . . I . . ." lost voices now.

I tried to stir, but then the tube of sleep, nourished by the brandy, came unclogged, and I descended down into richer blackness.

Was a bright morning full of sun, and no fog for a change. Cool clear out there on the landing, and the sea even seemed to roll in soft and bounce against the rocks and lighthouse like puffy cotton balls blown on the wind.

I was out there with my morning coffee, holding the cup in one hand and grasping the railing with the other. It was a narrow area but safe enough, provided you didn't lean too far out or run along the walk when it was slick with rain. Machen told me of a man who had done just that and found himself plummeting over to be shattered like a dropped melon on the rocks below.

Machen came out with a cup of coffee in one hand, his unlit pipe in the other. He looked haggard this morning, as if a bit of old age had crept upon him in the night, fastened a straw to his face, and sucked out part of his substance.

"Morning," I said.

"Morning." He emptied his cup in one long draft. He balanced the cup on the metal railing and began to pack his pipe.

"Sleep bad?" I asked.

He looked at me, then at his pipe, finished his packing, and put the pouch away in his coat pocket. He took a long match from the same pocket, gave it fire with his thumbnail, lit the pipe. He puffed quite a while before he answered me. "Not too well. Not too well."

"We drank too much."

"We did at that."

I sipped my coffee and looked at the sky, watched a snowy gull dive down and peck at the foam, rise up with a wriggling fish in its beak. It climbed high in the sky, became a speck of froth on the crystal blue.

"I had funny dreams," I said. "I think I've had them all along, since I came here. But last night they were stronger than ever."

"Oh?"

"Thought I heard your voice speaking to someone. Thought I heard steps on the stairs, or more like the plunking of peg legs, like those old sea captains have."

"You don't say?"

"And another voice, a child's."

"That right? Well . . . maybe you did hear me speakin'. I wasn't entirely straight with you last night. I do have quite an interest in the voice throwing, and I practice it from time to time on my dummy. Last night must have been louder than usual, being drunk and all."

"Dummy?"

"My old dummy from the act. Keep it in the room below."

"Could I see it?"

He grimaced. "Maybe another time. It's kind of a private thing with me. Only bring her out when we're alone."

"Her?"

"Right. Name's Caroline, a right smart-looking girl dummy, rosy-cheeked with blonde pigtails."

"Well, maybe someday I can look at her."

"Maybe someday." He stood up, popped the contents of the pipe out over the railing, and started inside. Then he turned: "I talk too much. Pay no mind to an old, crazy man."

Then he was gone, and I was there with a hot cup of coffee, a bright, warm day, and an odd, unexplained chill at the base of my bones.

Two days later we got on witches again, and I guess it was my fault. We hit the brandy hard that night. I had sold a short story for a goodly sum — my largest check to date — and we were celebrating and talking and saying how my fame would be as high as the stars. We got pretty sicky there, and to hear Machen tell it, and to hear me agree — no matter he hadn't read the story — I was another Hemingway, Wolfe, and Fitzgerald all balled into one.

"If Marilyn were here," I said thoughtlessly, drunk, "why we could get her to consult her crystal and tell us my literary future."

"Why that's nonsense, she used no crystal."

"No crystal, broom, or pointed hat? No eerie evil deeds for her? A white magician no doubt?"

"Magic is magic, m'boy. And even good intentions can backfire."

"Whatever happened to her, Marilyn I mean?"

"Dead."

"Old age?"

"Died young and beautiful, m'boy. Grief killed her."

"I see," I said, as you'll do to show attentiveness.

Suddenly, it was if the memories were a balloon overloaded

with air, about to burst if pressure was not taken off. So, he let loose the pressure and began to talk.

"She took her a lover, Marilyn did. Taught him many a thing, about love, magic, what have you. Lost her husband on account of it, the magician, I mean. Lost respect for herself in time.

"You see, there was this little girl she had, by her lover. A fine-looking sprite, lived until she was three. Had no proper father. He had taken to the sea and had never much entertained the idea of marryin' Marilyn. Keep them stringing was his motto then, damn his eyes. So he left them to fend for themselves."

"What happened to the child?"

"She died. Some childhood disease."

"That's sad," I said, "a little girl gone and having only sipped at life."

"Gone? Oh, no. There's the soul, you know."

I wasn't much of a believer in the soul and I said so.

"Oh, but there is a soul. The body perishes but the soul lives on."

"I've seen no evidence of it."

"But I have," Machen said solemnly. "Marilyn was determined that the girl would live on, if not in her own form, then in another."

"Hogwash!"

Machen looked at me sternly. "Maybe. You see, there is a part of witchcraft that deals with the soul, a part that believes the soul can be trapped and held, kept from escaping this earth and into the beyond. That's why a lot of natives are superstitious about having their picture taken. They believe once their image is captured, through magic, their soul can be contained.

"Voodoo works much the same. It's nothing but another form of witchcraft. Practitioners of that art believe their souls can be held to this earth by means of someone collecting nail parin's or hair from them while they're still alive.

"That's what Marilyn had in mind. When she saw the girl was fadin', she snipped one of the girl's long pigtails and kept it to herself. Cast spells on it while the child lay dyin', and again after life had left the child."

"The soul was supposed to be contained within the hair?"

"That's right. It can be restored, in a sense, to some other object through the hair. It's like those voodoo dolls. A bit of hair or nail parin' is collected from the person you want to control, or if not control, maintain the presence of their soul, and it's sewn into those dolls. That way, when the pins are stuck into the doll, the living suffer, and when they die their soul is trapped in the doll for all eternity, or rather as long as the doll with its hair or nail parin's exists."

"So she preserved the hair so she could make a doll and have the little girl live on, in a sense?"

"Something like that."

"Sounds crazy."

"I suppose."

"And what of the little girl's father?"

"Ah, that sonofabitch! He came home to find the little girl dead and buried and the mother mad. But there was that little gold lock of hair, and knowing Marilyn, he figured her intentions."

"Machen," I said slowly. "It was you, was it not? You were the father?"

"I was."

"I'm sorry."

"Don't be. We were both foolish. I was the more foolish. She left her husband for me and I cast her aside. Ignored my own child. I was the fool, a great fool."

"Do you really believe in that stuff about the soul? About the hair and what Marilyn was doing?"

"Better I didn't. A soul once lost from the body would best prefer to be departed I think . . . but love is some times a brutal thing."

We just sat there after that. We drank more. Machen smoked his pipe, and about an hour later we went to bed.

There were sounds again, gnawing at the edge of my sleep. The sounds that had always been there, but now, since we had talked of Marilyn, I was less able to drift off into blissful slumber. I kept thinking of those crazy things Machen had said. I remembered, too, those voices I had heard, and the fact that Machen was a ventriloquist, and perhaps, not altogether stable.

But those sounds.

I sat up and opened my eyes. They were coming from below. Voices. Machen's first. ". . . not be the death of you, girl, not at all . . . my only reminder of Marilyn . . ."

And then to my horror. "Let me be, Papa. Let it end." The last had been a little girl's voice, but the words had been bitter and wise beyond the youngness of the tone.

I stepped out of bed and into my trousers, crept to the curtain, and looked on Machen's side.

Nothing, just a lonely cot. I wasn't dreaming. I had heard him all right, and the other voice . . . it had to be that Machen, grieved over what he had done in the past, over Marilyn's death, had taken to speaking to himself in the little girl's voice. All that stuff Marilyn had told him about the soul, it had gotten to him, cracked his stability.

I climbed down the cold metal stairs, listening. Below I heard the old, weathered door that led outside slam. Heard the thud of boots going down the outside steps.

I went back up, went to the windows, and pulling back the curtains section by section, finally saw the old man. He was carrying something wrapped in a black cloth and he had a shovel in his hand. I watched as, out there by the shore, he dug a shallow grave and placed the cloth-wrapped object within, placed a rock over it, and left it to the night and the incoming tide.

I pretended to be asleep when he returned, and later, when I felt certain he was well visited by Morpheus, I went downstairs and retrieved the shovel from the tool room. I went out to where I had seen him dig and went to work, first turning over the large stone and shoveling down into the pebbly dirt. Due to the freshness of the hole, it was easy digging.

I found the cloth and what was inside. It made me flinch at first, it looked so real. I thought it was a little rosy-cheeked girl buried alive, for it looked alive . . . but it was a dummy. A ventriloquist's dummy. It had aged badly, as if water had gotten to it. In some ways it looked as if it were rotting from the inside out. My finger went easily and deeply into the wood of one of the legs.

Out of some odd curiosity, I reached up and pushed back the wooden eyelids. There were no wooden painted eyes, just darkness, empty sockets that uncomfortably reminded me of looking down into the black hollows of a human skull. And the hair. On one side of the head was a yellow pigtail, but where the other should have been was a bare spot, as if the hair had been ripped away from the wooden skull.

With a trembling hand I closed the lids down over those empty eyes, put the dirt back in place, the rock, and returned to bed. But I did not sleep well. I dreamed of a grown man talking to a wooden doll and using another voice to answer back, pretending that the doll lived and loved him too.

But the water had gotten to it, and the sight of those rotting legs had snapped him back to reality, dashed his insane hopes of containing a soul by magic, shocked him brutally from foolish dreams. Dead is dead.

*   *   *

The next day, Machen was silent and had little to say. I suspected the events of last night weighed on his mind. Our conversation must have returned to him this morning in sober memory, and he, somewhat embarrassed, was reluctant to recall it. He kept to himself down below in the locked room, and I busied myself with my work.

It was night when he came up, and there was a smug look about him, as if he had accomplished some great deed. We spoke a bit, but not of witches, of past times and the sea. Then he pulled back the curtains and looked at the moon rise above the water like a cold fish eye.

"Machen," I said, "maybe I shouldn't say anything, but if you should ever have something bothering you, if you should ever want to talk about it . . . well, feel free to come to me."

We said little more and soon went to bed.

I slept sounder that night, but again I was rousted from my dreams by voices. Machen's voice again, and the poor man speaking in that little child's voice.

"It's a fine home for you," Machen said in his own voice.

"I want no home," came the little girl's voice. "I want to be free."

"You want to stay with me, with the living. You're just not thinking. There's only darkness beyond the veil."

The voices were very clear and loud. I sat up in bed and strained my ears.

"It's where I belong," the little girl's voice again, but it spoke not in a little girl manner. There was only the tone.

"Things have been bad lately," Machen said. "And you're not yourself."

Laughter, horrible little girl laughter.

"I haven't been myself for years."

"Now, Caroline . . . play your piano. You used to play it so well. Why, you haven't touched it in years."

"Play. Play. With these!"

"You're too loud."

"I don't care. Let him hear, let him . . ."

A door closed sharply and the sound died off to a mumble; a word caught here and there was scattered and confused by the throb of the sea.

Next morning Machen had nothing for me, not even a smile from his borrowed collection. Nothing but coldness, his back, and a frown.

I saw little of him after coffee, and once, from below—for he stayed down there the whole day through—I thought I heard him cry in a loud voice. "Have it your way, then," and then there was the sound of a slamming door and some other sort of commotion below.

After a while I looked out at the land and the sea, and down there, striding back and forth, hands behind his back, went Machen, like some great confused penguin contemplating the far shore.

I like to think there was something more than curiosity in what I did next. Like to think I was looking for the source of my friend's agony; looking for some way to help him find peace.

I went downstairs and pulled at the door he kept locked, hoping that, in his anguish, he had forgotten to lock it back. He had not forgotten.

I pressed my ear against the door and listened. Was that crying I heard?

No. I was being susceptible, caught up in Machen's fantasy. It was merely the wind whipping about the tower.

I went back upstairs, had coffee, and wrote not a line.

So day fell into night, and I could not sleep, but finally got the strange business out of my mind by reading a novel. A rollicking good sea story of daring men and bloody battles, great ships clashing in a merciless sea.

And then, from his side of the curtain, I heard Machen creak off his cot and take to the stairs. One flight below was the door that led to the railing round about the tower, and I heard that open and close.

I rose, folded a small piece of paper into my book for a marker, and pulled back one of the window curtains. I walked around pulling curtains and looking until I could see him below.

He stood with his hands behind his back, looking out at the sea like a stern father keeping an eye on his children. Then, calmly, he mounted the railing and leaped out into the air.

I ran. Not that it mattered, but I ran, out to the railing . . . and looked down. His body looked like a rag doll splayed on the rocks.

There was no question in my mind that he was dead, but slowly I wound my way down the steps . . . and was distracted by the room. The door stood wide open.

I don't know what compelled me to look in, but I was drawn to it. It was a small room with a desk and a lot of shelves filled with books, mostly occult and black magic. There were carpentry tools on the wall, and all manner of needles and devices that might be used by a tailor. The air was filled with an odd odor I could not place, and on Machen's desk, something that was definitely not tobacco smoldered away.

There was another room beyond the one in which I stood. The door to it was cracked open. I pushed it back and stepped inside. It was a little child's room filled thick with toys and such: jack-in-the-boxes, dolls, kid books, and a toy piano. All were covered in dust.

On the bed lay a teddy bear. It was ripped open and the stuffing was pulled out. There was one long strand of hair hanging out of that gutted belly, just one, as if it were the last morsel of a greater whole. It was the color of honey from a fresh-robbed hive. I knew what the smell in the ashtry was now.

I took the hair and put a match to it, just in case.

This little short-short was written for Razored Saddles, *and was supposed to be a kind of modern Western. It doesn't entirely fill the bill on that account, but I'm proud of it. A short film was made of it, and my son, Keith, and I even appear in the background of scenes. It wasn't bad, and is now on video and DVD. It was fun to watch your characters brought to life by actors, one of which was an Elvis impersonator out of Las Vegas. Instead of the older Elvis, they changed the part to fit a younger Elvis, because, well, they had a younger, thinner, Elvis impersonator.*

THE JOB

BOWER PULLED THE SUN VISOR DOWN AND looked in the mirror there and said, "You know, hadn't been for the travel, I'd have done alright. I could even shake my ass like him. I tell you, it drove the women wild. You should have seen 'em."

"Don't shake it for me," Kelly said. "I don't want to see it. Things I got to do are tough enough without having to see that."

Bower pushed the visor back. The light turned green. Kelly put the gas to the car and they went up and over a hill and turned right on Melroy.

"Guess maybe you do look like him," Kelly said. "During his fatter days, when he was on the drugs and the peanut butter."

"Yeah, but these pocks on my cheeks messes it up some. When I was on stage I had makeup on 'em. I looked okay then."

They stopped at a stop sign and Kelly got out a cigarette and pushed in the lighter.

"A nigger nearly tail-ended me here once," Kelly said. "Just come barreling down on me." He took the lighter and lit his smoke. "Scared the piss out of me. I got him out of his car and popped him some. I bet he was one careful nigger from then on." He pulled away from the stop sign and cruised.

205

"You done one like this before? I know you've done it, but like this?"

"Not just like this. But I done some things might surprise you. You getting nervous on me?"

"I'm alright. You know, thing made me quit the Elvis imitating was travel, cause one night on the road I was staying in this cheap motel, and it wasn't heated too good. I'd had those kind of rooms before, and I always carried couple of space heaters in the trunk of the car with the rest of my junk, you know. I got them plugged in, and I was still cold, so I pulled the mattress on the floor by the heaters. I woke up and was on fire. I had been so worn out I'd gone to sleep in my Elvis outfit. That was the end of my best white jumpsuit, you know, like he wore with the gold glitter and all. I must have been funny on fire like that, hopping around the room beating it out. When I got that suit off I was burned like the way you get when you been out in the sun too long."

"You gonna be able to do this?"

"Did I say I couldn't?"

"You're nervous. I can tell, way you talk."

"A little. I always got nervous before I went on stage too, but I always came through. Crowd came to see Elvis, by God, they got Elvis. I used to sign autographs with his name. People wanted it like that. They wanted to pretend, see."

"Women mostly?"

"Uh huh."

"What were they, say, fifty-five?"

"They were all ages. Some of them were pretty young."

"Ever fuck any of 'em?"

"Sure, I got plenty. Sing a little "Love Me Tender" to them in the bedroom and they'd do whatever I wanted."

"Was it the old ones you was fucking?"

"I didn't fuck no real old ones, no. Whose idea is it to do things this way anyhow?"

"Boss, of course. You think he lets me plan this stuff? He don't want them chinks muscling in on the shrimping and all."

"I don't know, we fought for these guys. It seems a little funny."

"Reason we lost the war over there is not being able to tell one chink from another and all of them being the way they are. I think we should have nuked the whole goddamned place. Went over there when it cooled down and stopped glowing, put in a fucking Disneyland or something."

They were moving out of the city now, picking up speed.

"I don't see why we don't just whack this guy outright and not do it this way," Bower said. "This seems kind of funny."

"No one's asking you. You come on a job, you do it. Boss wants the chink to suffer, so he's gonna suffer. Not like he didn't get some warnings or nothing. Boss wants him to take it hard."

"Maybe this isn't a smart thing on account of it may not bother chinks like it'd bother us. They're different about stuff like this, all the things they've seen."

"It'll bother him," Kelly said. "And if it don't, that ain't our problem. We got a job to do and we're gonna do it. Whatever comes after comes after. Boss wants us to do different next time, we do different. Whatever he wants we do it. He's the one paying."

They were out of the city now, and to the left of the highway they could see the glint of the sea through a line of scrubby trees.

"How're we gonna know?" Bower says. "One chink looks like another."

"I got a photograph. This one's got a burn on the face. Everything's timed. Boss has been planning this. He had some of the guys watch and take notes. It's all set up."

"Why us?"

"Me because I've done some things before. You because he wants to see what you're made of. I'm kind of here as your nursemaid."

"I don't need anybody to see that I do what I'm supposed to do."

They drove past a lot of boats pulled up to a dock. They drove into a small town called Wilborn. They turned a corner at Catlow Street.

"It's down here a ways," Kelly said. "You got your knife? You left your knife and brought your comb, I'm gonna whack you."

Bower got the knife out of his pocket. "Thing got a lot of blades, some utility stuff. Even a comb."

"Christ, you're gonna do it with a Boy Scout knife?"

"Utility knife. The blade I want is plenty sharp, you'll see. Why couldn't we use a gun? That wouldn't be as messy. A lot easier."

"Boss wants it messy. He wants the chink to think about it some. He wants all the chinks down here to think about it some. He wants them to pack their stuff on their boats and sail back to chink land. Either that, or they can pay their percentages like everyone else. He lets the chinks get away with things, everyone'll want to get away with things."

They pulled over to the curb. Down the street was a school. Kelly looked at his watch.

"Maybe if it was a nigger," Bower said.

"Chink, nigger, what's the difference?"

They could hear a bell ringing. After five minutes they saw kids going out to the curb to get on the buses parked there. A few kids came down the sidewalk toward them. One of them was a Vietnamese girl about eight years old. The left side of her face was scarred.

"Won't they remember me?" Bower said.

"Kids? Naw. Nobody knows you around here. Get rid of that Elvis look and you'll be okay."

"It don't seem right. In front of these kids and all. I think we ought to whack her father."

"No one's paying you to think, Elvis. Do what you're supposed to do. I have to do it and you'll wish you had."

Bower opened the utility knife and got out of the car. He held the knife by his leg and walked around front and leaned on the hood just as the Vietnamese girl came up. He said, "Hey, kid, come here a minute." His voice got thick. "Elvis wants to show you something."

I grew up on those old monster movies. You know, the ones with men in rubber suits. Though I still love horror and monster movies, I can't say that I continued to be a Godzilla fan. It didn't take long before these got pretty silly. But I still remember fondly how I first felt about the old boy, and all the other monsters. This is a kind of tribute to those feelings, though, I must admit, a slightly askew one.

GODZILLA'S TWELVE STEP PROGRAM

ONE: Honest Work

ODZILLA, ON HIS WAY TO WORK AT THE FOUN-dry, sees a large building that seems to be mostly made of shiny copper and dark, reflecting solar glass. He sees his image in the glass and thinks of the old days, wonders what it would be like to stomp on the building, to blow flames at it, kiss the windows black with his burning breath, then dance rapturously in the smoking debris.

One day at a time, he tells himself. One day at a time.

Godzilla makes himself look at the building hard. He passes it by. He goes to the foundry. He puts on his hard hat. He blows his fiery breath into the great vat full of used car parts, turns the car parts to molten metal. The metal runs through pipes and into new molds for new car parts. Doors. Roofs. Etc.

Godzilla feels some of the tension drain out.

TWO: Recreation

After work Godzilla stays away from downtown. He feels tense. To stop blowing flames after work is difficult. He goes over to the BIG MONSTER RECREATION CENTER.

Gorgo is there. Drunk from oily seawater, as usual. Gorgo talks about the old days. She's like that. Always the old days.

They go out back and use their breath on the debris that is deposited there daily for the center's use. Kong is out back. Drunk as a monkey. He's playing with Barbie dolls. He does that all the time. Finally, he puts the Barbies away in his coat pocket, takes hold of his walker and wobbles past Godzilla and Gorgo.

Gorgo says, "Since the fall he ain't been worth shit. And what's with him and the little plastic broads anyway? Don't he know there're real women in the world?"

Godzilla thinks Gorgo looks at Kong's departing walker-supported ass a little too wistfully. He's sure he sees wetness in Gorgo's eyes.

Godzilla blows some scrap to cinders for recreation, but it doesn't do much for him, as he's been blowing fire all day long and has, at best, merely taken the edge off his compulsions. This isn't even as satisfying as the foundry. He goes home.

THREE: Sex and Destruction

That night there's a monster movie on television. The usual one. Big beasts wrecking havoc on city after city. Crushing pedestrians under foot.

Godzilla examines the bottom of his right foot, looks at the scar there from stomping cars flat. He remembers how it was to have people squish between his toes. He thinks about all of that and changes the channel. He watches twenty minutes of *Mr. Ed*, turns off the TV, masturbates to the images of burning cities and squashing flesh.

Later, deep into the night, he awakens in a cold sweat. He goes to the bathroom and quickly carves crude human figures from bars of soap. He mashes the soap between his toes, closes his eyes and imagines. Tries to remember.

FOUR: Beach Trip and The Big Turtle

Saturday, Godzilla goes to the beach. A drunk monster that looks like a big turtle flies by and bumps Godzilla. The turtle calls Godzilla a name, looking for a fight. Godzilla remembers the turtle is called Gamera.

Gamera is always trouble. No one liked Gamera. The turtle was a real asshole.

Godzilla grits his teeth and holds back the flames. He turns his back and walks along the beach. He mutters a secret mantra given him by his sponsor. The giant turtle follows after, calling him names.

Godzilla packs up his beach stuff and goes home. At his back he hears the turtle, still cussing, still pushing. It's all he can do not to respond to the big dumb bastard. All he can do. He knows the turtle will be in the news tomorrow. He will have destroyed something, or will have been destroyed himself.

Godzilla thinks perhaps he should try and talk to the turtle, get him on the twelve step program. That's what you're supposed to do. Help others. Maybe the turtle could find some peace.

But then, again, you can only help those who help themselves. Godzilla realizes he can not save all the monsters of the world. They have to make these decisions for themselves. But he makes a mental note to go armed with leaflets about the twelve step program from now on.

Later, he calls in to his sponsor. Tells him he's had a bad day. That he wanted to burn buildings and fight the big turtle. Reptilicus tells him it's okay. He's had days like that. Will have days like that once again.

Once a monster, always a monster. But a recovering monster is where it's at. Take it one day at a time. It's the only way to be happy in the world. You can't burn and kill and chew up humans and their creations without paying the price of guilt and multiple artillery wounds.

Godzilla thanks Reptilicus and hangs up. He feels better for a while, but deep down he wonders just how much guilt he really harbors. He thinks maybe it's the artillery and the rocket-firing jets he really hates, not the guilt.

FIVE: Off The Wagon

It happens suddenly. He falls off the wagon. Coming back from work he sees a small doghouse with a sleeping dog sticking halfway out of a doorway. There's no one around. The dog looks old. It's on a chain. Probably miserable anyway. The water dish is empty. The dog is living a worthless life. Chained. Bored. No water.

Godzilla leaps and comes down on the doghouse and squashes dog in all directions. He burns what's left of the doghouse with a blast of his breath. He leaps and spins on tip-toe through the wreckage. Black cinders and cooked dog slip through his toes and remind him of the old days.

He gets away fast. No one has seen him. He feels giddy. He

can hardly walk he's so intoxicated. He calls Reptilicus, gets his answering machine. "I'm not in right now. I'm out doing good. But please leave a message, and I'll get right back to you."

The machine beeps. Godzilla says, "Help."

SIX: His Sponsor

The doghouse rolls around in his head all the next day. While at work he thinks of the dog and the way it burned. He thinks of the little house and the way it crumbled. He thinks of the dance he did in the ruins.

The day drags on forever. He thinks maybe when work is through he might find another doghouse, another dog.

On the way home he keeps an eye peeled, but no doghouses or dogs are seen.

When he gets home his answering machine light is blinking. It's a message from Reptilicus. Reptilicus's voice says, "Call me."

Godzilla does. He says, "Reptilicus. Forgive me, for I have sinned."

SEVEN: Disillusioned. Disappointed.

Reptilicus's talk doesn't help much. Godzilla shreds all the twelve step program leaflets. He wipes his butt on a couple and throws them out the window. He puts the scraps of the others in the sink and sets them on fire with his breath. He burns a coffee table and a chair, and when he's through, feels bad for it. He knows the landlady will expect him to replace them.

He turns on the radio and lies on the bed listening to an Oldies station. After a while, he falls asleep to Martha and the Vandellas singing "Heat Wave."

EIGHT: Unemployed

Godzilla dreams. In it God comes to him, all scaly and blowing fire. He tells Godzilla he's ashamed of him. He says he should do better. Godzilla awakes covered in sweat. No one is in the room.

Godzilla feels guilt. He has faint memories of waking up and going out to destroy part of the city. He really tied one on, but he can't remember everything he did. Maybe he'll read about it in the papers. He notices he smells like charred lumber and melted plastic. There's gooshy stuff between his toes, and something tells him it isn't soap.

He wants to kill himself. He goes to look for his gun, but he's too drunk to find it. He passes out on the floor. He dreams of the devil this time. He looks just like God except he has one eyebrow that goes over both eyes. The devil says he's come for Godzilla.

Godzilla moans and fights. He dreams he gets up and takes pokes at the devil, blows ineffective fire on him.

Godzilla rises late the next morning, hung over. He remembers the dream. He calls into work sick. Sleeps off most of the day. That evening, he reads about himself in the papers. He really did some damage. Smoked a large part of the city. There's a very clear picture of him biting the head off of a woman.

He gets a call from the plant manager that night. The manager's seen the paper. He tells Godzilla he's fired.

NINE: Enticement

Next day some humans show up. They're wearing black suits and white shirts and polished shoes and they've got badges. They've got guns, too. One of them says, "You're a problem. Our government wants to send you back to Japan."

"They hate me there," says Godzilla. "I burned Tokyo down."

"You haven't done so good here either. Lucky that was a colored section of town you burned, or we'd be on your ass. As it is, we've got a job proposition for you."

"What?" Godzilla asks.

"You scratch our back, we'll scratch yours." Then the men tell him what they have in mind.

TEN: Choosing

Godzilla sleeps badly that night. He gets up and plays the monster mash on his little record player. He dances around the room as if he's enjoying himself, but knows he's not. He goes over to the BIG MONSTER RECREATION CENTER. He sees Kong there, on a stool, undressing one of his Barbies, fingering the smooth spot between her legs. He sees that Kong has drawn a crack there, like a vagina. It appears to have been drawn with a blue ink pen. He's feathered the central line with ink-drawn pubic hair. Godzilla thinks he should have got someone to do the work for him. It doesn't look all that natural.

God, he doesn't want to end up like Kong. Completely spaced. Then again, maybe if he had some dolls he could melt, maybe that would serve to relax him.

No. After the real thing, what was a Barbie? Some kind of form of Near Beer. That's what the debris out back was. Near Beer. The foundry. The Twelve Step Program. All of it. Near Beer.

ELEVEN: Working for the Government

Godzilla calls the government assholes. "All right," he says. "I'll do it."

"Good," says the government man. "We thought you would. Check your mail box. The map and instructions are there."

Godzilla goes outside and looks in his box. There's a manila envelope there. Inside are instructions. They say: "Burn all the spots you see on the map. You finish those, we'll find others. No penalties. Just make sure no one escapes. Any rioting starts, you finish them. To the last man, woman and child."

Godzilla unfolds the map. On it are red marks. Above the red marks are listings: *Nigger Town. Chink Village. White Trash Enclave. A Clutch of Queers. Mostly Democrats.*

Godzilla thinks about what he can do now. Unbidden. He can burn without guilt. He can stomp without guilt. Not only that, they'll send him a check. He has been hired by his adopted country to clean out the bad spots as they see them.

TWELVE: The Final Step

Godzilla stops near the first place on the list: *Nigger Town.* He sees kids playing in the streets. Dogs. Humans looking up at him, wondering what the hell he's doing here.

Godzilla suddenly feels something move inside him. He knows he's being used. He turns around and walks away. He heads toward the government section of town. He starts with the governor's mansion. He goes wild. Artillery is brought out, but it's no use, he's rampaging. Like the old days.

Reptilicus shows up with a megaphone, tries to talk Godzilla down from the top of the Great Monument Building, but Godzilla doesn't listen. He's burning the top of the building off with his breath, moving down, burning some more, moving down, burning some more, all the way to the ground.

Kong shows up and cheers him on. Kong drops his walker and crawls along the road on his belly and reaches a building and pulls himself up and starts climbing. Bullets spark all around the big ape.

Godzilla watches as Kong reaches the summit of the building and clings by one hand and waves the other, which contains a Barbie doll.

Kong puts the Barbie doll between his teeth. He reaches in his coat and brings out a naked Ken doll. Godzilla can see that Kong has made Ken some kind of penis out of silly putty or something. The penis is as big as Ken's leg.

Kong is yelling, "Yeah, that's right. That's right. I'm AC/DC, you sonsofabitches."

Jets appear and swoop down on Kong. The big ape catches a load of rocket right in the teeth. Barbie, teeth and brains decorate the greying sky. Kong falls.

Gorgo comes out of the crowd and bends over the ape, takes him in her arms and cries. Kong's hand slowly opens, revealing Ken, his penis broken off.

The flying turtle shows up and starts trying to steal Godzilla's thunder, but Godzilla isn't having it. He tears the top off the building Kong had mounted and beats Gamera with it. Even the cops and the army cheer over this.

Godzilla beats and beats the turtle, splattering turtle meat all over the place, like an overheated poodle in a microwave. A few quick pedestrians gather up chunks of the turtle meat to take home and cook, cause the rumor is it tastes just like chicken.

Godzilla takes a triple shot of rockets in the chest, staggers, goes down. Tanks gather around him.

Godzilla opens his bloody mouth and laughs. He thinks: If I'd have gotten finished here, then I'd have done the black people too. I'd have gotten the yellow people and the white trash and the homosexuals. I'm an equal opportunity destroyer. To hell with the twelve step program. To hell with humanity.

Then Godzilla dies and makes a mess on the street. Military men tip-toe around the mess and hold their noses.

Later, Gorgo claims Kong's body and leaves.

Reptilicus, being interviewed by television reporters, says, "Zilla was almost there, man. Almost. If he could have completed the program, he'd have been all right. But the pressures of society were too much for him. You can't blame him for what society made of him."

On the way home, Reptilicus thinks about all the excitement. The burning buildings. The gunfire. Just like the old days when he and Zilla and Kong and that goon-ball turtle were young.

Reptilicus thinks of Kong's defiance, waving the Ken doll, the Barbie in his teeth. He thinks of Godzilla, laughing as he died.

Reptilicus finds a lot of old feelings resurfacing. They're hard to fight. He locates a lonesome spot and a dark house and urinates through an open window, then goes home.

This is the darkest story I've ever written. Thing about it is this: serial killers seem quite normal, and in many ways they are. These two guys are not exactly monsters in appearance or general attitude, but somewhere, in those little wet brain cells something isn't quite right. Environment? Genetics? Personal choice? All three? I have my feelings on the matter, but I've expressed those elsewhere. What I will say is that after writing this story, I felt I had gone about as far as I needed to go with this sort of thing. I had expressed the horror of it, the weirdness of it, about as much as I needed to. And in a horrible way, the whole damn thing is funny. Unless you happen to be a victim of creatures like this, then, it'll be easy to decide on which side of the coin of horror and humor you will come down. Still, humor is one way we deal with horror. Ask cops, social workers, and firefighters. Ask surviving victims how funny it is, and you might get another take.

DRIVE-IN DATE

THE LINE INTO THE STARLIGHT DRIVE-IN THAT night was short. Monday nights were like that. Dave and Merle paid their money at the ticket house and Dave drove the Ford to a spot up near the front where there were only a few cars. He parked in a space with no one directly on either side. On the left the first car was four speakers away, on the right, six speakers.

Dave said, "I like to be up close so it all looks bigger than life. You don't mind do you?"

"You ask me that every time," Merle said. "You don't never ask me that when we're driving in, you ask when we're parked."

"You don't like it, we can move."

"No. I like it. I'm just saying, you don't really care if I like it. You just ask."

"Politeness isn't a crime."

"No, but you ought to mean it."

"I said we can move."

"Hell no, stay where you are. I'm just saying when you ask me what I like, you could mean it."

"You're a testy motherfucker tonight. I thought coming to see a monster picture would cheer you up."

"You're the one likes 'em, and that's why you come. It wasn't for me, so don't talk like it was. I don't believe in monsters, so I can't enjoy what I'm seeing. I like something that's real. Cop movie. Things like that."

"I tell you, Merle, there's just no satisfying you, man. You'll feel better when they cut the lot lights and the movie starts. We can get our date then."

"I don't know that makes me feel better."

"You done quit liking pussy?"

"Watch your mouth. I didn't say that. You know I like pussy. I like pussy fine."

"Whoa. Aren't we fussy? Way you talk, you're trying to convince me. Maybe it's butt holes you like."

"Goddamnit, don't start on the butt holes."

Dave laughed and got out a cigarette and lipped it. "I know you did that one ole gal in the butt that night." Dave reached up and tapped the rearview mirror. "I seen you in the mirror here."

"You didn't see nothing," Merle said.

"I seen you get in her butt hole. I seen that much."

"What the hell you doing watching? It ain't good enough for you by yourself, so you got to watch someone else get theirs?"

"I don't mind watching."

"Yeah, well, I bet you don't. You're like one of those fucking perverts."

Dave snickered, popped his lighter and lit his cigarette. The lot lights went out. The big lights at the top of the drive-in screen went black. Dave rolled down the window and pulled the speaker in and fastened it to the door. He slapped at a mosquito on his neck.

"Won't be long now," Dave said.

"I don't know I feel up to it tonight."

"You don't like this first feature, the second's some kind of mystery. It might be like a cop show."

"I don't mean the movies."

"The girl?"

"Yeah. I'm in a funny mood."

Dave smoked for a moment. "Merle, this is kind of a touchy subject, but you been having trouble, you know, getting a bone to keep, I'll tell you, that happens. It's happened to me. Once."

"I'm not having trouble with my dick, okay?"

"If you are, it's no disgrace. It'll happen to a man from time to time."

"My tool is all right. It works. No problem."

"Then what's the beef?"

"I don't know. It's a mood. I feel like I'm going through a kind of, I don't know, mid-life crisis or something."

"Mood, huh? Let me tell you, when she's stretched out on that back seat, you'll be all right, crisis or no crisis. Hell, get her butt hole if you want it, I don't care."

"Don't start on me."

"Who's starting? I'm telling you, you want her butt hole, her ear, her goddamn nostril, that's your business. Me, I'll stick to the right hole, though."

"Think I don't know a snide remark when you make it?"

"I hope you do, or I wouldn't make it. You don't know I'm making one, what's the fun in making it?" Dave reached over and slapped Merle playfully on the arm. "Lighten up, boy. Let's see a movie, get some pussy. Hey, you feel better if I went and got us some corn and stuff . . . that'd do you better, wouldn't it?"

Merle hesitated. "I guess."

"Back in a jiffy."

Dave got out of the car.

Fifteen minutes and Dave was back. He had a cardboard box that held two bags of popcorn and some tall drinks. He set the box on top of the car, opened the door then got the box and slid inside. He put the box on the seat between them.

"How much I owe you?" Merle said.

"Not a thing. You get it next time . . . think how much more expensive this would be we had to pay for her to eat too."

"A couple or three dollars. So what? That gonna break us?"

"No, but it's beer money. You think about it."

Merle sat and thought about it.

The big white drive-in screen was turned whiter by the projector light, then there was a flicker and images moved on the screen: Ads for the concession. Coming attractions.

Dave got his popcorn, started eating. He said, "I'm getting kind of horny thinking about her. You see the legs on that bitch?"

"Course I seen the legs. You don't know from legs. A woman's got legs is all you care, and you might not care about that. Couple of stumps would be all the same to you."

"No, I don't care for any stumps. Got to be feet on one end, pussy on the other. That's legs enough. But this one, she's got some good ones. Hell, you're bound to've noticed how good they were."

"I noticed. You saying I'm queer or something? I noticed. I noticed she's got an ankle bracelet on the right leg and she wears about a size ten shoe. Biggest goddamn feet I've ever seen on a woman."

"Now, it comes out. You wanted to pick the date, not me?"

"I never did care for a woman with big feet. You got a good-looking woman all over and you get down to them feet and they look like something goes on either side of a water plane . . . well, it ruins things."

"She ain't ruined. Way she looks, big feet or not, she ain't ruined. Besides, you don't fuck the feet . . . well, maybe *you* do. Right after the butt hole."

"You gonna push one time too much, Dave. One time too much."

"I'm just kidding, man. Lighten up. You don't ever lighten up. Don't we deserve some fun after working like niggers all day?"

Merle sighed. "You got to use that nigger stuff? I don't like it. It makes you sound ignorant. Will, he's colored and I like him. He's done me all right. Man like that, he don't deserve to be called nigger."

"He's all right at the plant, but you go by his house and ask for a loan."

"I don't want to borrow nothing from him. I'm just saying people ought to get their due, no matter what color they are. Nigger is an ugly word."

"You like boogie better, Martin Luther? How about coon or shine? I was always kind of fond of burrhead or wooly myself."

"There's just no talking to you, is there?"

"Hell, you like niggers so much, next date we set up, we'll make it a nigger. Shit, I'd fuck a nigger. It's all pink on the inside, ain't that what you've heard?"

"You're a bigot is what you are."

"If that means I'm not wanting to buddy up to coons, then, yeah, that's what I am." Dave thumped his cigarette butt out the window. "You got to learn to lighten up, Merle. You don't, you'll die. My uncle, he couldn't never lighten up. Gave him a spastic colon, all that tension. He swelled up until he couldn't wear his pants. Had to get some stretch pants, one of those running suits, just so he could have on clothes. He eventually got so bad they had to go in and operate. You can bet he wishes he didn't do all that worrying now. It didn't get him a thing but sick. He didn't get a better life on account of that worry, now did he? Still lives over in that apartment where he's been living, on account of he got so sick from worry he couldn't work. They're about to throw him out of there, and him a grown man and sixty years old. Lost his good job, his wife — which he ought to know is a good thing — and now he's doing little odd shit here and there to make ends meet. Going down to catch the day work truck with the winos and niggers — excuse me. Afro-Americans, Colored Folks, whatever you prefer.

"Before he got to worrying over nothing, he had him some serious savings and was about ready to put some money down on a couple of acres and a good double wide."

"I was planning on buying me a double wide, that'd make me worry. Them old trailers ain't worth a shit. Comes a tornado, or just a good wind, and you can find those fuckers at the bottom of the Gulf of Mexico next to the regular trailers. Tornado will take a double wide easy as any of the others."

Dave shook his head. "You go from one thing to the other, don't you? I know what a tornado can do. It can take a house, too. Your house. That don't matter. I'm not talking about mobile homes here, Merle. I'm talking about living. It's a thing you better attend to. You're forty goddamn years old. Your life's half over . . . I know that's a cold thing to say, but there you have it. It's out of my mouth. I'm forty this next birthday, so I'm not just putting the doom on you. It's a thing ever man's got to face. Getting over the hill. Before I die, I'd like to think I did something fun with my life. It's the little things that count. I want to enjoy things, not worry them away. Hear what I'm saying, Merle?"

"Hard not to, being in the goddamn car with you."

"Look here, way we work, we deserve to lighten up a little. You haul your ashes first. That'll take some edge off."

"Well . . ."

"Naw, go on."

"All right . . . but, one thing . . ."

"What?"

"Don't do me no more butt hole jokes, okay? One friend to another, Dave, no more butt hole jokes."

"It bothers you that bad, okay. Deal."

Merle climbed over the seat and got on his knees in the floor-board. He took hold of the back seat and pulled. It was rigged with a hinge. It folded down. He got on top of the folded-down seat and bent and looked into the exposed trunk. The young woman's face was turned toward him, half of her cheek was hidden by the spare tire. There was a smudge of grease on her nose.

"We should have put a blanket back here," Merle said. "Wrapped her in that. I don't like 'em dirty."

"She's got pants on," Dave said. "You take them off, the part that counts won't be dirty."

"That part's always dirty. They pee and bleed out of it don't they? Hell, hot as it is back here, she's already starting to smell."

"Oh, bullshit." Dave turned and looked over the seat at Merle. "You can't get pleased, can you? She ain't stinking. She didn't even shit her pants when she checked out. And she ain't been dead long enough to smell, and you know it. Quit being so goddamn contrary." Dave turned back around and shook out a cigarette and lit it.

"Blow that out the window, damnit," Merle said. "You know that smoke works my allergies."

Dave shook his head and blew smoke out the window. He turned up the speaker. The ads and commercials were over. The movie was starting.

"And don't be looking back here at me neither," Merle said.

Merle rolled the woman out of the trunk, across the seat, onto the floorboard and up against him. He pushed the seat back into place and got hold of the woman and hoisted her onto the back seat. He pushed her T-shirt up over her breasts. He fondled her breasts. They were big and firm and rubbery-cold. He unfastened her shorts and pulled them over her shoes and ripped her panties apart at one side. He pushed one of her legs onto the floorboard and gripped her hips and pulled her ass down a little, got it cocked to a position he liked. He unfastened and pulled down his jeans and boxer shorts and got on her.

Dave roamed an eye to the rearview mirror, caught sight of Merle's butt bobbing. He grinned and puffed at his cigarette. After a while, he turned his attention to the movie.

When Merle was finished he looked at the woman's dead eyes. He couldn't see their color in the dark, but he guessed blue. Her hair he could tell was blond.

"How was it?" Dave asked.

"It was pussy. Hand me the flashlight."

Dave reached over and got the light out of the glove box and handed it over the seat. Merle took it. He put it close to the woman's face and turned it on.

"She's got blue eyes," Merle said.

"I noticed that right off when we grabbed her," Dave said. "I thought then you'd like that, being how you are about blue eyes."

Merle turned off the flashlight, handed it to Dave, pulled up his pants and climbed over the seat. On the screen a wormlike monster was coming out of the sand on a beach.

"This flick isn't half bad," Dave said. "It's kind of funny, really. You don't get too good a look at the monster though . . . that all the pussy you gonna get?"

"Maybe some later," Merle said.

"You feeling any better?"

"Some."

"Yeah, well, why don't you eat some popcorn while I get me a little. Want a cigarette? You like a cigarette after sex, don't you?"

"All right."

Dave gave Merle a cigarette, lit it. Merle sucked the smoke in deeply.

"Better?" Dave asked.

"Yeah, I guess."

"Good." Dave thumped his cigarette out the window. "I'm gonna take my turn now. Don't let nothing happen on the movie. Make it wait."

"Sure."

Dave climbed over the seat. Merle tried to watch the movie. After a moment, he quit. He turned and looked out his window. Six speakers down he could see a Chevy rocking.

"Got to be something more to life than this?" Merle said without turning to look at Dave.

"I been telling you," Dave said, "this is life, and you better start enjoying. Get you some orientation before it's too late and it's all over but the dirt in the face . . . talk to me later. Right now this is what I want out of life. Little later, I might want a drink."

Merle shook his head.

Dave lifted the woman's leg and hooked her ankle over the front seat. Merle looked at her foot, the ankle bracelet dangling from it. "I bet that damn foot's more a size eleven than a ten," Merle said. "Probably buys her shoes at the ski shop."

Dave hooked her other ankle over the back seat, on the package shelf. "Like I said, it's not the feet I'm interested in."

Merle shook his head again. He rolled down his window and thumped out some ash and turned his attention to the Chevy again. It was still rocking.

Dave shifted into position in the back seat. The Ford began to rock. The foot next to Merle vibrated, made little dead hops.

From the back seat Dave began to chant: "Give it to me, baby. Give it to me. Am I your Prince, baby? Am I your goddamn King? Take that anaconda, bitch. Take it!"

"For heaven's sake," Merle said.

Five minutes later Dave climbed into the front seat, said, "Damn. Damn good piece."

"You act like she had something to do with it," Merle said.

"Her pussy, ain't it?"

"We're doing all the work. We could cut a hole in the seat back there and get it that good."

"That ain't true. It ain't the hole does it, and it damn sure ain't the personality, it's how they look. That flesh under you. Young. Firm. Try coming in an ugly or fat woman and you'll see what I mean. You'll have some troubles. Or maybe you won't."

"I don't like 'em old or fat."

"Yeah, well, I don't see the live ones like either one of us all that much. The old ones or the fat ones. Face it, we've got no way with live women. And I don't like the courting. I like to know I see one I like, I can have her if I can catch her."

Merle reached over and shoved the woman's foot off the seat. It fell heavily into the floorboard. "I'm tired of looking at that slat. Feet like that, they ought to have paper bags over them."

When the second feature was over, they drove to Dave's house and parked out back next to the tall board fence. They killed the lights and sat there for a while, watching, listening.

No movement at the neighbors.

"You get the gate," Dave said, "I'll get the meat."

"We could just go on and dump her," Merle said. "We could call it a night."

"It's best to be careful. The law can look at sput now and know who it comes from. We got to clean her up some."

Merle got out and opened the gate and Dave got out and opened the trunk and pulled the woman out by the foot and let her fall on her face to the ground. He reached in and got her shorts and put them in the crook of his arm, then bent and ripped her torn panties the rest of the way off and stuffed them in a pocket of her shorts, and stuffed the shorts into the front of his pants. He got hold of her ankle and dragged her through the gate.

Merle closed the gate as Dave and the corpse came through. "You got to drag her on her face?" he said.

"She don't care," Dave said.

"I know, but I don't like her messed up."

"We're through with her."

"When we let her off, I want her to be, you know, okay."

"She ain't okay now, Merle. She's dead."

"I'm don't want her messed up."

Dave shrugged. He crossed her ankles and flipped her on her back and dragged her over next to the house and let go of her by the water hose. He uncoiled the hose and took the nozzle and inserted it up the woman with a sound like a boot being withdrawn from mud, and turned the water on low.

When he looked up from his work, Merle was coming out of the house with a six-pack of beer. He carried it over to the redwood picnic table and sat down. Dave joined him.

"Have a Lone Star," Merle said.

Dave twisted the top off one. "You're thinking on something, I can tell."

"I was thinking we ought to take them alive," Merle said.

Dave lit a cigarette and looked at him. "We been over this. We take one alive she might scream or get away. We could get caught easy enough."

"We could kill her when we're finished. Way we're doing, we could buy one of those blow-up dolls, put it in the glove box and bring it to the drive-in."

"I've never cottoned to something like that. Even jacking off bothers me. A man ought to have a woman."

"A dead woman?"

"That's the best kind. She's quiet. You haven't got to put up with clothes and makeup jabber, keeping up with the Jones' jabber, getting that promotion jabber. She's not gonna tell you no in the middle of the night. Ain't gonna complain about how you put it to her. One stroke's as good as the next to a dead bitch."

"I kind of like hearing 'em grunt, though. I like being kissed."

"Rape some girl, think she'll want to kiss you?"

"I can make her."

"Dead's better. You don't have to worry yourself about how happy she is. You don't pay for nothing. If you got a live woman, one you're married to even, you're still paying for pussy. If you don't pay in money, you'll pay in pain. They'll smile and coo for a time, but stay out late with the boys, have a little financial stress, they all revert to just what my mama was. A bitch. She drove my daddy into an early grave, way she nagged, and the old sow lived to be ninety. No wonder women live longer than men. They worry men to death.

"Like my uncle I was talking about. All that worry . . . hell, that was his wife put it on him. Wanting this and wanting that. When he got sick, had that operation and had to dip into his savings, she was out of there. They'd been married thirty years, but things got tough, you could see what those thirty years meant. He didn't even come out of that deal with a place to put his dick at night."

"Ain't all women that way."

"Yeah they are. They can't help it. I'm not blaming them. It's in them, like germs. In time, they all turn out just the same."

"I'm talking about raping them, though, not marrying them. Getting kissed."

"You're with the kissing again. You been reading Cosmo or something? What's this kiss stuff? You get hungry, you eat. You get thirsty, you drink. You get tired, you sleep. You get horny, you kill and fuck. You use them like a product, Merle, then when you get through with the product, you throw out the package. Get a new one when you need it. This way you always got the young ones, the tan ones, no matter how old or fat or ugly you get. You don't have to see a pretty woman get old, see that tan turn her face to leather. You can keep the world bright and fresh all the time. You listen to me, Merle. It's the best way."

Merle looked at the woman's body. Her head was turned toward him. Her eyes looked to have filled with milk. Water was running out of her and pooling on the grass and starting to spurt from between her legs. Merle looked away from her, said, "Guess I'm just looking for a little romance. I had me a taste of it, you know. It was all right. She could really kiss."

"Yeah, it was all right for a while, then she ran off with a sand nigger."

"Arab, Dave. She ran off with an Arab."

"He was here right now, you'd call him an Arab?"

"I'd kill him."

"There you are. Call him an Arab or a sand nigger, you'd kill him, right?"

Merle nodded.

"Listen," Dave said. "Don't think I don't understand what you're saying. Thing I like about you, Merle, is you aren't like those guys down at the plant, come in do your job, go home, watch a little TV, fall asleep in the chair dreaming about some magazine model cause the old lady won't give out, or you don't want to think about her giving out on account of the way she's got ugly. Thing is, Merle, you know you're dissatisfied. That's the first step to knowing there's more to life than the old grind. I appreciate that in you. It's a kind of sensitivity some men don't like to face. Think it makes them weak. It's a strength, is what it is, Merle. Something I wish I had more of."

"That's damn nice of you to say, Dave."

"It's true. Anybody knows you, knows you feel things deeply. And I don't want you to think that I don't appreciate romance, but you get our age, you got to look at things a little straighter. I can't see any romance with an old woman anyway, and a young one, she ain't gonna have me . . . unless it's the way we're doing it now."

Merle glanced at the corpse. Water was spewing up from between her legs like a whale blowing. Her stomach was a fat, white mound.

"We don't get that hose out of her," Merle said, "she's gonna blow the hell up."

"I'll get it," Dave said. He went over and turned off the water and pulled the hose out of her and put his foot on her stomach and began to pump his leg. Water gushed from her and her stomach began to flatten. "She was all right, wasn't she, Merle?"

" 'Cept for them feet, she was fine."

They drove out into the pines and pulled off to the side of a little dirt road and parked. They got out and went around to the trunk and Dave unlocked it. They looked at the young woman's body for a moment, then they each took a leg and jerked her from the trunk, and with her legs spread like a wishbone, they dragged her into the brush and dropped her on the edge of an incline coated in blackberry briars.

"Man," Dave said. "Taste that air. This is the prettiest night I can remember."

"It's nice," Merle said.

Dave put a boot to the woman and pushed, she went rolling down the incline in a white moon-licked haze and crashed into the brush at the bottom. Dave pulled her shorts from the front of his pants and tossed them after her.

"Time they find her, the worms will have had some pussy too," Dave said.

They got in the car and Dave started it up and eased down the road.

"Dave?"

"Yeah?"

"You're a good friend," Merle said. "The talk and all, it done me good. Really."

Dave smiled, clapped Merle's shoulder. "Hey, it's all right. I been seeing this coming in you for a time, since the girl before last . . . you're all right now, though. Right?"

"Well, I'm better."

"That's how you start."

They drove a piece. Merle said, "But I got to admit to you, I still miss being kissed."

Dave laughed. "You and the kiss. You're some piece of work buddy . . . I got your kiss. Kiss my ass."

Merle grinned. "Way I feel, your ass could kiss back, I just might."

Dave laughed again. They drove out of the woods and onto the highway. The moon was high and bright.

My wife, as a joke, bought a rubber blow-up Godzilla for me, or maybe it was just a dinosaur. I put a Mickey Mouse cap on its head, and suddenly, a story idea was born. I think I probably ate popcorn the night I got the dinosaur, thought about that hat, had a bellyache, and it all came together. It has certainly been one of my more popular stories.

BOB THE DINOSAUR GOES TO DISNEYLAND

OR A BIRTHDAY PRESENT, FRED'S WIFE, KAREN, bought him a plastic, inflatable dinosaur—a Tyrannosaurus Rex. It was in a cardboard box, and Fred thanked her and took the dinosaur downstairs to his study and took it out of the box and spent twenty minutes taking deep breaths and blowing air into it.

When the dinosaur was inflated, he sat it in front of his bookshelves, and as a joke, got a mouse ear hat he had bought at Disneyland three years before, and put it on the dinosaur's head and named it Bob.

Immediately, Bob wanted to go to Disneyland. There was no snuffing the ambition. He talked about it night and day, and it got so the study was no place to visit, because Bob would become most unpleasant on the matter. He scrounged around downstairs at night, pacing the floor, singing the Mouseketeer theme loud and long, waking up Fred and Karen, and when Fred would come downstairs to reason with Bob, Bob wouldn't listen. He wouldn't have a minute's worth of it. No sir, he by golly wanted to go to Disneyland.

Fred said to Karen, "You should have bought me a Brontosaurus, or maybe a Stegosaurus. I have a feeling they'd have been easier to reason with."

Bob kept it up night and day. "Disneyland, Disneyland, I want to go to Disneyland. I want to see Mickey. I want to see Donald." It was like some kind of mantra, Bob said it so much. He even found some old brochures on Disneyland that Fred had stored in his closet, and Bob spread them out on the floor and lay down near them and studied the pictures and wagged his great tail and looked wistful.

"Disneyland," he would whisper. "I want to go to Disneyland."

And when he wasn't talking about it, he was mooning. He'd come up to breakfast and sit in two chairs at the table and stare blankly into the syrup on his pancakes, possibly visualizing the Matterhorn ride or Sleeping Beauty's castle. It got so it was a painful thing to see. And Bob got mean. He chased the neighbor's dogs and tore open garbage sacks and fought with the kids on the bus and argued with his teachers and took up slovenly habits, like throwing his used Kleenex on the floor of the study. There was no living with that dinosaur.

Finally, Fred had had enough, and one morning at breakfast, while Bob was staring into his pancakes, moving his fork through them lazily, but not really trying to eat them (and Fred had noticed that Bob had lost weight and looked as if he needed air), Fred said, "Bob, we've decided that you may go to Disneyland."

"What?" Bob said, jerking his head up so fast his mouse hat flew off and his fork scraped across his plate with a sound like a fingernail on a blackboard. "Really?"

"Yes, but you must wait until school is out for the summer, and you really have to act better."

"Oh, I will, I will," Bob said.

Well now, Bob was one happy dinosaur. He quit throwing Kleenex down and bothering the dogs and the kids on the bus and his teachers, and in fact, he became a model citizen. His school grades even picked up.

Finally, the big day came, and Fred and Karen bought Bob a suit of clothes and a nice John Deere cap, but Bob would have nothing to do with the new duds. He wore his mouse ear hat and a sweatshirt he had bought at Goodwill with a faded picture of Mickey Mouse on it with the word Disneyland inscribed above it. He even insisted on carrying a battered Disney lunchbox he had picked up at the Salvation Army, but other than that, he was very cooperative.

Fred gave Bob plenty of money and Karen gave him some tips on how to eat a balanced meal daily, and then they drove him to the airport in the back of the pickup. Bob was so excited he could hardly sit still in the airport lounge, and when his seat section was called, he gave Fred and Karen quick kisses and pushed in front of an old lady and darted onto the plane.

As the plane lifted into the sky, heading for California and Disneyland, Karen said, "He's so happy. Do you think he'll be all right by himself?"

"He's very mature," Fred said. "He has his hotel arrangements, plenty of money, a snack in his lunchbox and lots of common sense. He'll be all right."

At the end of the week, when it was time for Bob to return, Fred and Karen were not available to pick him up at the airport. They made arrangements with their next-door neighbor, Sally, to do the job for them. When they got home, they could hear Bob playing the stereo in the study, and they went down to see him.

The music was loud and heavy metal and Bob had never listened to that sort of thing before. The room smelled of smoke, and not cigarettes. Bob was lying on the floor reading, and at first, Fred and Karen thought it was the Disney brochures, but then they saw those wadded up in the trashcan by the door.

Bob was looking at a girlie magazine and a reefer was hanging out of his mouth. Fred looked at Karen and Karen was clearly shaken.

"Bob?" Fred said.

"Yeah," Bob said without looking up from the foldout, and his tone was surly.

"Did you enjoy Disneyland?"

Bob carefully took the reefer out of his mouth and thumped ash on the carpet. There was the faintest impression of tears in his eyes. He stood up and tossed the reefer down and ground it into the carpet with his foot.

"Did . . . did you see Mickey Mouse?" Karen asked.

"Shit," Bob said, "there isn't any goddamn mouse. It's just some guy in a suit. The same with the duck." And with that, Bob stalked into the bathroom and slammed the door and they couldn't get him out of there for the rest of the day.

This is another of those stories that I thought was a good standard tale. I wrote it for a Valentine anthology, and the editor of the anthology accepted it, but the editor at the publishing house was upset with it. The dog business got her goat. Okay. But what about the human business? Folks are weird. Anyway, for a while it was certainly one of my more popular stories, and to be quite honest, I've grown pretty fond of it myself.

THE STEEL VALENTINE

EVEN BEFORE MORLEY TOLD HIM, DENNIS knew things were about to get ugly.

A man did not club you unconscious, bring you to his estate and tie you to a chair in an empty storage shed out back of the place if he merely intended to give you a valentine.

Morley had found out about him and Julie.

Dennis blinked his eyes several times as he came to, and each time he did, more of the dimly lit room came into view. It was the room where he and Julie had first made love. It was the only building on the estate that looked out of place: it was old, worn, and not even used for storage; it was a collector of dust, cobwebs, spiders and dessicated flies.

There was a table in front of Dennis, a kerosene lantern on it, and beyond, partially hidden in shadow, a man sitting in a chair smoking a cigarette. Dennis could see the red tip glowing in the dark, and the smoke from it drifted against the lantern light and hung in the air like thin, suspended wads of cotton.

The man leaned out of shadow, and as Dennis expected, it was Morley. His shaved, bullet-shaped head was sweaty and reflected the light. He was smiling with his fine, white teeth, and the high cheek bones were round, flushed circles that looked like clown rouge. The tightness of his skin, the few wrinkles, made him look younger than his fifty-one years.

And in most ways he was younger than his age. He was a man who took care of himself. Jogged eight miles every morning before breakfast, lifted weights three times a week and had only one bad habit—cigarettes. He smoked three packs a day. Dennis knew all that and he had only met the man twice. He had learned it from Julie, Morley's wife. She told him about Morley while they lay in bed. She liked to talk and she often talked about Morley; about how much she hated him.

"Good to see you," Morley said, and blew smoke across the table into Dennis's face. "Happy Valentine's Day, my good man. I was beginning to think I hit you too hard, put you in a coma."

"What is this, Morley?" Dennis found that the mere act of speaking sent nails of pain through his skull. Morley really had lowered the boom on him.

"Spare me the innocent act, lover boy. You've been laying the pipe to Julie, and I don't like it."

"This is silly, Morley. Let me loose."

"God, they do say stupid things like that in real life. It isn't just the movies . . . you think I brought you here just to let you go, lover boy?"

Dennis didn't answer. He tried to silently work the ropes loose that held his hands to the back of the chair. If he could get free, maybe he could grab the lantern, toss it in Morley's face. There would still be the strand holding his ankles to the chair, but maybe it wouldn't take too long to undo that. And even if it did, it was at least some kind of plan.

If he got the chance to go one on one with Morley, he might take him. He was twenty-five years younger and in good shape himself. Not as good as when he was playing pro basketball, but good shape nonetheless. He had height, reach, and he still had wind. He kept the latter with plenty of jogging and tossing the special-made, sixty-five pound medicine ball around with Raul at the gym.

Still, Morley was strong. Plenty strong. Dennis could testify to that. The pulsating knot on the side of his head was there to remind him.

He remembered the voice in the parking lot, turning toward it and seeing a fist. Nothing more, just a fist hurtling toward him like a comet. Next thing he knew, he was here, the outbuilding.

Last time he was here, circumstances were different, and

better. He was with Julie. He met her for the first time at the club where he worked out, and they had spoken, and ended up playing racquetball together. Eventually she brought him here and they made love on an old mattress in the corner; lay there afterward in the June heat of a Mexican summer, holding each other in a warm, sweaty embrace.

After that, there had been many other times. In the great house; in cars; hotels. Always careful to arrange a tryst when Morley was out of town. Or so they thought. But somehow he had found out.

"This is where you first had her," Morley said suddenly. "And don't look so wide-eyed. I'm not a mind reader. She told me all the other times and places too. She spat at me when I told her I knew, but I made her tell me every little detail, even when I knew them. I wanted it to come from her lips. She got so she couldn't wait to tell me. She was begging to tell me. She asked me to forgive her and take her back. She no longer wanted to leave Mexico and go back to the States with you. She just wanted to live."

"You bastard. If you've hurt her—"

"You'll what? Shit your pants? That's the best you can do, Dennis. You see, it's me that has *you* tied to the chair. Not the other way around."

Morley leaned back into the shadows again, and his hands came to rest on the table, the perfectly manicured fingertips steepling together, twitching ever so gently.

"I think it would have been inconsiderate of her to have gone back to the States with you, Dennis. Very inconsiderate. She knows I'm a wanted man there, that I can't go back. She thought she'd be rid of me. Start a new life with her ex-basketball player. That hurt my feelings, Dennis. Right to the bone." Morley smiled. "But she wouldn't have been rid of me, lover boy. Not by a long shot. I've got connections in my business. I could have followed her anywhere . . . in fact, the idea that she thought I couldn't offended my sense of pride."

"Where is she? What have you done with her, you bald-headed bastard?"

After a moment of silence, during which Morley examined Dennis's face, he said, "Let me put it this way. Do you remember her dogs?"

Of course he remembered the dogs. Seven Dobermans. Attack dogs. They always frightened him. They were big mothers, too. Except for her favorite, a reddish, undersized Doberman named

Chum. He was about sixty pounds, and vicious. "Light, but quick," Julie used to say. "Light, but quick."

Oh yeah, he remembered those goddamn dogs. Sometimes when they made love in an estate bedroom, the dogs would wander in, sit down around the bed and watch. Dennis felt they were considering the soft, rolling meat of his testicles, savoring the possibility. It made him feel like a mean kid teasing them with a treat he never intended to give. The idea of them taking that treat by force made his erection soften, and he finally convinced Julie, who found his nervousness hysterically funny, that the dogs should be banned from the bedroom, the door closed.

Except for Julie, those dogs hated everyone. Morley included. They obeyed him, but they did not like him. Julie felt that under the right circumstances, they might go nuts and tear him apart. Something she hoped for, but never happened.

"Sure," Morley continued. "You remember her little pets. Especially Chum, her favorite. He'd growl at me when I tried to touch her. Can you imagine that? All I had to do was touch her, and that damn beast would growl. He was crazy about his mistress, just crazy about her."

Dennis couldn't figure what Morley was leading up to, but he knew in some way he was being baited. And it was working. He was starting to sweat.

"Been what," Morley asked, "a week since you've seen your precious sweetheart? Am I right?"

Dennis did not answer, but Morley was right. A week. He had gone back to the States for a while to settle some matters, get part of his inheritance out of legal bondage so he could come back, get Julie, and take her to the States for good. He was tired of the Mexican heat and tired of Morley owning the woman he loved.

It was Julie who had arranged for him to meet Morley in the first place, and probably even then the old bastard had suspected. She told Morley a partial truth. That she had met Dennis at the club, that they had played racquetball together, and that since he was an American, and supposedly a mean hand at chess, she thought Morley might enjoy the company. This way Julie had a chance to be with her lover, and let Dennis see exactly what kind of man Morley was.

And from the first moment Dennis met him, he knew he had to get Julie away from him. Even if he hadn't loved her and wanted her, he would have helped her leave Morley.

It wasn't that Morley was openly abusive—in fact, he was the perfect host all the while Dennis was there—but there was an obvious undercurrent of connubial dominance and menace that revealed itself like a shark fin everytime he looked at Julie.

Still, in a strange way, Dennis found Morley interesting, if not likeable. He was a bright and intriguing talker, and a wizard at chess. But when they played and Morley took a piece, he smirked over it in such a way as to make you feel he had actually vanquished an opponent.

The second and last time Dennis visited the house was the night before he left for the States. Morley had wiped him out in chess, and when finally Julie walked him to the door and called the dogs in from the yard so he could leave without being eaten, she whispered, "I can't take him much longer."

"I know," he whispered back. "See you in about a week. And it'll be all over."

Dennis looked over his shoulder, back into the house, and there was Morley leaning against the fireplace mantle drinking a martini. He lifted the glass to Dennis as if in salute and smiled. Dennis smiled back, called goodbye to Morley and went out to his car feeling uneasy. The smile Morley had given him was exactly the same one he used when he took a chess piece from the board.

"Tonight. Valentine's Day," Morley said, "that's when you two planned to meet again, wasn't it? In the parking lot of your hotel. That's sweet. Really. Lovers planning to elope on Valentine's Day. It has a sort of poetry, don't you think?"

Morley held up a huge fist. "But what you met instead of your sweetheart was this . . . I beat a man to death with this once, lover boy. Enjoyed every second of it."

Morley moved swiftly around the table, came to stand behind Dennis. He put his hands on the sides of Dennis's face. "I could twist your head until your neck broke, lover boy. You believe that, don't you? Don't you? . . . Goddamnit, answer me."

"Yes," Dennis said, and the word was soft because his mouth was so dry.

"Good. That's good. Let me show you something, Dennis."

Morley picked up the chair from behind, carried Dennis effortlessly to the center of the room, then went back for the lantern and the other chair. He sat down across from Dennis and turned the wick of the lantern up. And even before Dennis saw the dog, he heard the growl.

The dog was straining at a large leather strap attached to the wall. He was muzzled and ragged looking. At his feet lay something red and white. "Chum," Morley said. "The light bothers him. You remember ole Chum, don't you? Julie's favorite pet . . . ah, but I see you're wondering what that is at his feet. That sort of surprises me, Dennis. Really. As intimate as you and Julie were, I'd think you'd know her. Even without her makeup."

Now that Dennis knew what he was looking at he could make out the white bone of her skull, a dark patch of matted hair still clinging to it. He also recognized what was left of the dress she had been wearing. It was a red and white tennis dress, the one she wore when they played racquetball. It was mostly red now. Her entire body had been gnawed savagely.

"Murderer!" Dennis rocked savagely in the chair, tried to pull free of his bonds. After a moment of useless struggle and useless epithets, he leaned forward and let the lava-hot gorge in his stomach pour out.

"Oh, Dennis," Morley said. "That's going to be stinky. Just awful. Will you look at your shoes? And calling me a murderer. Now, I ask you, Dennis, is that nice? I didn't murder anyone. Chum did the dirty work. After four days without food and water he was ravenous and thirsty. Wouldn't you be? And he was a little crazy too. I burned his feet some. Not as bad as I burned Julie's, but enough to really piss him off. And I sprayed her with this."

Morley reached into his coat pocket, produced an aerosol canister and waved it at Dennis.

"This was invented by some business associate of mine. It came out of some chemical warfare research I'm conducting. I'm in, shall we say . . . espionage? I work for the highest bidder. I have plants here for arms and chemical warfare . . . if it's profitable and ugly, I'm involved. I'm a real stinker sometimes. I certainly am."

Morley was still waving the canister, as if trying to hypnotize Dennis with it. "We came up with this to train attack dogs. We found we could spray a padded-up man with this and the dogs would go bonkers. Rip the pads right off of him. Sometimes the only way to stop the beggers was to shoot them. It was a failure, actually. It activated the dogs, but it drove them out of their minds and they couldn't be controlled at all. And after a short time the odor faded and the spray became quite the reverse. It made it so the dogs couldn't smell the spray at all. It made whoever was wearing it odorless. Still. I found a use for it. A very personal use.

"I let Chum go a few days without food and water while I worked on Julie . . . and she wasn't tough at all, Dennis. Not even a little bit. Spilled her guts. Now that isn't entirely correct. She didn't spill her guts until later, when Chum got hold of her . . . anyway, she told me what I wanted to know about you two, then I sprayed that delicate thirty-six, twenty-four, thirty-six figure of hers with this. And with Chum so hungry, and me having burned his feet and done some mean things to him, he was not in the best of humor when I gave him Julie.

"It was disgusting, Dennis. Really. I had to come back when it was over and shoot Chum with a tranquilizer dart, get him tied and muzzled for your arrival."

Morley leaned forward, sprayed Dennis from head to foot with the canister. Dennis turned his head and closed his eyes, tried not to breathe the foul-smelling mist.

"He's probably not all that hungry now," Morley said, "but this will still drive him wild."

Already Chum had gotten a whiff and was leaping at his leash. Foam burst from between his lips and frothed on the leather bands of the muzzle.

"I suppose it isn't polite to lecture a captive audience, Dennis, but I thought you might like to know a few things about dogs. No need to take notes. You won't be around for a quiz later.

"But here's some things to tuck in the back of your mind while you and Chum are alone. Dogs are very strong, Dennis. Very. They look small compared to a man, even a big dog like a Doberman, but they can exert a lot of pressure with their bite. I've seen dogs like Chum here, especially when they're exposed to my little spray, bite through the thicker end of a baseball bat. And they're quick. You'd have a better chance against a black belt in karate than an attack dog."

"Morley," Dennis said softly, "you can't do this."

"I can't?" Morley seemed to consider. "No, Dennis, I believe I can. I give myself permission. But hey, Dennis, I'm going to give you a chance. This is the good part now, so listen up. You're a sporting man. Basketball. Racquetball. Chess. Another man's woman. So you'll like this. This will appeal to your sense of competition.

"Julie didn't give Chum a fight at all. She just couldn't believe her Chummy-whummy wanted to eat her. Just wouldn't. She held out her hand, trying to soothe the old boy, and he just bit it right off. Right off. Got half the palm and the fingers in one bite. That's when I left them alone. I had a feeling her Chummy-whummy might start on me next, and I wouldn't have wanted that.

Oooohhh, those sharp teeth. Like nails being driven into you."

"Morley, listen—"

"Shut up! You, Mr. Cock Dog and Basketball Star, just might have a chance. Not much of one, but I know you'll fight. You're not a quitter. I can tell by the way you play chess. You still lose, but you're not a quitter. You hang in there to the bitter end."

Morley took a deep breath, stood in the chair and hung the lantern on a low rafter. There was something else up there too. A coiled chain. Morley pulled it down and it clattered to the floor. At the sound of it Chum leaped against his leash and flecks of saliva flew from his mouth and Dennis felt them fall lightly on his hands and face.

Morley lifted one end of the chain toward Dennis. There was a thin, open collar attached to it.

"Once this closes it locks and can only be opened with this." Morley reached into his coat pocket and produced a key, held it up briefly and returned it. "There's a collar for Chum on the other end. Both are made out of good leather over strong, steel chain. See what I'm getting at here, Dennis?"

Morley leaned forward and snapped the collar around Dennis's neck.

"Oh, Dennis," Morley said, standing back to observe his handiwork. "It's you. Really. Great fit. And considering the day, just call this my valentine to you."

"You bastard."

"The biggest."

Morley walked over to Chum. Chum lunged at him, but with the muzzle on he was relatively harmless. Still, his weight hit Morley's legs, almost knocked him down.

Turning to smile at Dennis, Morley said, "See how strong he is? Add teeth to this little engine, some maneuverability . . . it's going to be awesome, lover boy. Awesome."

Morley slipped the collar under Chum's leash and snapped it into place even as the dog rushed against him, nearly knocking him down. But it wasn't Morley he wanted. He was trying to get at the smell. At Dennis. Dennis felt as if the fluids in his body were running out of drains at the bottoms of his feet.

"Was a little poontang worth this, Dennis? I certainly hope you think so. I hope it was the best goddamn piece you ever got. Sincerely, I do. Because death by dog is slow and ugly, lover boy. They like the throat and balls. So, you watch those spots, hear?"

"Morley, for God's sake, don't do this!"

Morley pulled a revolver from his coat pocket and walked over to Dennis. "I'm going to untie you now, stud. I want you to be real good, or I'll shoot you. If I shoot you, I'll gut shoot you, then let the dog loose. You got no chance that way. At least my way you've got a sporting chance—slim to none."

He untied Dennis. "Now stand."

Dennis stood in front of the chair, his knees quivering. He was looking at Chum and Chum was looking at him, tugging wildly at the leash, which looked ready to snap. Saliva was thick as shaving cream over the front of Chum's muzzle.

Morley held the revolver on Dennis with one hand, and with the other he reproduced the aerosol can, sprayed Dennis once more. The stench made Dennis's head float.

"Last word of advice," Morley said. "He'll go straight for you."

"Morley . . ." Dennis started, but one look at the man and he knew he was better off saving the breath. He was going to need it.

Still holding the gun on Dennis, Morley eased behind the frantic dog, took hold of the muzzle with his free hand, and with a quick ripping motion, pulled it and the leash loose.

Chum sprang.

Dennis stepped back, caught the chair between his legs, lost his balance. Chum's leap carried him into Dennis's chest, and they both went flipping over the chair.

Chum kept rolling and the chain pulled across Dennis's face as the dog tumbled to its full length; the jerk of the sixty pound weight against Dennis's neck was like a blow.

The chain went slack, and Dennis knew Chum was coming. In that same instant he heard the door open, glimpsed a wedge of moonlight that came and went, heard the door lock and Morley laugh. Then he was rolling, coming to his knees, grabbing the chair, pointing it with the legs out.

And Chum hit him.

The chair took most of the impact, but it was like trying to block a cannonball. The chair's bottom cracked and a leg broke off, went skidding across the floor.

The truncated triangle of the Doberman's head appeared over the top of the chair, straining for Dennis's face. Dennis rammed the chair forward.

Chum dipped under it, grabbed Dennis's ankle. It was like stepping into a bear trap. The agony wasn't just in the ankle, it was a sizzling web of electricity that surged through his entire body.

The dog's teeth grated bone and Dennis let forth with a noise that was too wicked to be called a scream.

Blackness waved in and out, but the thought of Julie lying there in ragged display gave him new determination.

He brought the chair down on the dog's head with all his might.

Chum let out a yelp, and the dark head darted away.

Dennis stayed low, pulled his wounded leg back, attempted to keep the chair in front of him. But Chum was a black bullet. He shot under again, hit Dennis in the same leg, higher up this time. The impact slid Dennis back a foot. Still, he felt a certain relief. The dog's teeth had missed his balls by an inch.

Oddly, there was little pain this time. It was as if he were being encased in dark amber; floating in limbo. Must be like this when a shark hits, he thought. So hard and fast and clean you don't really feel it at first. Just go numb. Look down for your leg and it's gone.

The dark amber was penetrated by a bright stab of pain. But Dennis was grateful for it. It meant that his brain was working again. He swiped at Chum with the chair, broke him loose.

Swiveling on one knee, Dennis again used the chair as a shield. Chum launched forward, trying to go under it, but Dennis was ready this time and brought it down hard against the floor.

Chum hit the bottom of the chair with such an impact, his head broke through the thin slats. Teeth snapped in Dennis's face, but the dog couldn't squirm its shoulders completely through the hole and reach him.

Dennis let go of the chair with one hand, slugged the dog in the side of the head with the other. Chum twisted and the chair came loose from Dennis. The dog bounded away, leaping and whipping its body left and right, finally tossing off the wooden collar.

Grabbing the slack of the chain, Dennis used both hands to whip it into the dog's head, then swung it back and caught Chum's feet, knocking him on his side with a loud splat.

Even as Chum was scrambling to his feet, out of the corner of his eye Dennis spotted the leg that had broken off the chair. It was lying less than three feet away.

Chum rushed and Dennis dove for the leg, grabbed it, twisted and swatted at the Doberman. On the floor as he was, he couldn't get full power into the blow, but still it was a good one.

The dog skidded sideways on its belly and forelegs. When it

came to a halt, it tried to raise its head, but didn't completely make it.

Dennis scrambled forward on his hands and knees, chopped the chair leg down on the Doberman's head with every ounce of muscle he could muster. The strike was solid, caught the dog right between the pointed ears and drove his head to the floor.

The dog whimpered. Dennis hit him again. And again.

Chum lay still.

Dennis took a deep breath, watched the dog and held his club cocked.

Chum did not move. He lay on the floor with his legs spread wide, his tongue sticking out of his foam-wet mouth.

Dennis was breathing heavily, and his wounded leg felt as if it were melting. He tried to stretch it out, alleviate some of the pain, but nothing helped.

He checked the dog again.

Still not moving.

He took hold of the chain and jerked it. Chum's head came up and smacked back down against the floor.

The dog was dead. He could see that.

He relaxed, closed his eyes and tried to make the spinning stop. He knew he had to bandage his leg somehow, stop the flow of blood. But at the moment he could hardly think.

And Chum, who was not dead, but stunned, lifted his head, and at the same moment, Dennis opened his eyes.

The Doberman's recovery was remarkable. It came off the floor with only the slightest wobble and jumped.

Dennis couldn't get the chair leg around in time and it deflected off of the animal's smooth back and slipped from his grasp.

He got Chum around the throat and tried to strangle him, but the collar was in the way and the dog's neck was too damn big.

Trying to get better traction, Dennis got his bad leg under him and made an effort to stand, lifting the dog with him. He used his good leg to knee Chum sharply in the chest, but the injured leg wasn't good for holding him up for another move like that. He kept trying to ease his thumbs beneath the collar and lock them behind the dog's windpipe.

Chum's hind legs were off the floor and scrambling, the toenails tearing at Dennis's lower abdomen and crotch.

Dennis couldn't believe how strong the dog was. Sixty pounds of pure muscle and energy, made more deadly by Morley's spray and tortures.

Sixty pounds of muscle.

The thought went through Dennis's head again.

Sixty pounds.

The medicine ball he tossed at the gym weighed more. It didn't have teeth, muscle and determination, but it did weigh more.

And as the realization soaked in, as his grip weakened and Chum's rancid breath coated his face, Dennis lifted his eyes to a rafter just two feet above his head; considered there was another two feet of space between the rafter and the ceiling.

He quit trying to choke Chum, eased his left hand into the dog's collar, and grabbed a hind leg with his other. Slowly, he lifted Chum over his head. Teeth snapped at Dennis's hair, pulled loose a few tufts.

Dennis spread his legs slightly. The wounded leg wobbled like an old pipe cleaner, but held. The dog seemed to weigh a hundred pounds. Even the sweat on his face and the dense, hot air in the room seemed heavy.

Sixty pounds.

A basketball weighed little to nothing, and the dog weighed less than the huge medicine ball in the gym. Somewhere between the two was a happy medium; he had the strength to lift the dog, the skill to make the shot—the most important of his life.

Grunting, cocking the wiggling dog into position, he prepared to shoot. Chum nearly twisted free, but Dennis gritted his teeth, and with a wild scream, launched the dog into space.

Chum didn't go up straight, but he did go up. He hit the top of the rafter with his back, tried to twist in the direction he had come, couldn't, and went over the other side.

Dennis grabbed the chain as high up as possible, bracing as Chum's weight came down on the other side so violently it pulled him onto his toes.

The dog made a gurgling sound, spun on the end of the chain, legs thrashing.

It took a long fifteen minutes for Chum to strangle.

When Chum was dead, Dennis tried to pull him over the rafter. The dog's weight, Dennis's bad leg, and his now aching arms and back, made it a greater chore than he had anticipated. Chum's head kept slamming against the rafter. Dennis got hold of the unbroken chair, and used it as a stepladder. He managed the Doberman over, and Chum fell to the floor, his neck flopping loosely.

Dennis sat down on the floor beside the dog and patted it on the head. "Sorry," he said.

He took off his shirt, tore it into rags and bound his bad leg with it. It was still bleeding steadily, but not gushing; no major artery had been torn. His ankle wasn't bleeding as much, but in the dim lantern light he could see that Chum had bitten him to the bone. He used most of the shirt to wrap and strengthen the ankle.

When he finished, he managed to stand. The shirt binding had stopped the bleeding and the short rest had slightly rejuvenated him.

He found his eyes drawn to the mess in the corner that was Julie, and his first though was to cover her, but there wasn't anything in the room sufficient for the job.

He closed his eyes and tried to remember how it had been before. When she was whole and the room had a mattress and they had made love all the long, sweet, Mexican afternoon. But the right images would not come. Even with his eyes closed, he could see her mauled body on the floor.

Ducking his head made some of the dizziness go away, and he was able to get Julie out of his mind by thinking of Morley. He wondered when he would come back. If he was waiting outside.

But no, that wouldn't be Morley's way. He wouldn't be anxious. He was cocksure of himself, he would go back to the estate for a drink and maybe play a game of chess against himself, gloat a long, sweet while before coming back to check on his handiwork. It would never occur to Morley to think he had survived. That would not cross his mind. Morley saw himself as Life's best chess master, and he did not make wrong moves; things went according to plan. Most likely, he wouldn't even check until morning.

The more Dennis thought about it, the madder he got and the stronger he felt. He moved the chair beneath the rafter where the lantern was hung, climbed up and got it down. He inspected the windows and doors. The door had a sound lock, but the windows were merely boarded. Barrier enough when he was busy with the dog, but not now.

He put the lantern on the floor, turned it up, found the chair leg he had used against Chum, and substituted it for a pry bar. It was hard work and by the time he had worked the boards off the window his hands were bleeding and full of splinters. His face looked demonic.

Pulling Chum to him, he tossed him out the window, climbed

after him clutching the chair leg. He took up the chain's slack and hitched it around his forearm. He wondered about the other Dobermans. Wondered if Morley had killed them too, or if he was keeping them around. As he recalled, the Dobermans were usually loose on the yard at night. The rest of the time they had free run of the house, except Morley's study, his sanctuary. And hadn't Morley said that later on the spray killed a man's scent? That was worth something; it could be the edge he needed.

But it didn't really matter. Nothing mattered anymore. Six dogs. Six war elephants. He was going after Morley.

He began dragging the floppy-necked Chum toward the estate.

Morley was sitting at his desk playing a game of chess with himself, and both sides were doing quite well, he thought. He had a glass of brandy at his elbow, and from time to time he would drink from it, cock his head and consider his next move.

Outside the study door, in the hall, he could hear Julie's dogs padding nervously. They wanted out and in the past they would have been on the yard long before now. But tonight he hadn't bothered. He hated those bastards, and just maybe he'd get rid of them. Shoot them and install a burglar alarm. Alarms didn't have to eat or be let out to shit, and they wouldn't turn on you. And he wouldn't have to listen to the sound of dog toenails clicking on the tile outside of his study door.

He considered letting the Dobermans out, but hesitated. Instead, he opened a box of special Cuban cigars, took one, rolled it between his fingers near his ear so he could hear the fresh crackle of good tobacco. He clipped the end off the cigar with a silver clipper, put it in his mouth and lit it with a desk lighter without actually putting the flame to it. He drew in a deep lungful of smoke and relished it, let it out with a soft, contented sigh.

At the same moment he heard a sound, like something being dragged across the gravel drive. He sat motionless a moment, not batting an eye. It couldn't be lover boy, he thought. No way.

He walked across the room, pulled the curtain back from the huge glass door, unlocked it and slid it open.

A cool wind had come along and it was shaking the trees in the yard, but nothing else was moving. Morley searched the tree shadows for some tell-tale sign, but saw nothing.

Still, he was not one for imagination. He *had* heard something. He went back to the desk chair where his coat hung, reached the revolver from his pocket, turned.

And there was Dennis. Shirtless, one pants leg mostly ripped away. There were blood-stained bandages on his thigh and ankle. He had the chain partially coiled around one arm and Chum, quite dead, was lying on the floor beside him. In his right hand Dennis held a chair leg, and at the same moment Morley noted this and raised the revolver, Dennis threw it.

The leg hit Morley squarely between the eyes, knocked him against his desk and as he tried to right himself, Dennis took hold of the chain and used it to swing the dead dog. Chum struck Morley on the ankles and took him down like a scythe cutting fresh wheat. Morley's head slammed into the edge of the desk and blood dribbled into his eyes; everything seemed to be in a mix-master, whirling so fast nothing was identifiable.

When the world came to rest, he saw Dennis standing over him with the revolver. Morley could not believe the man's appearance. His lips were split in a thin grin that barely showed his teeth. His face was drawn and his eyes were strange and savage. It was apparent he had found the key in the coat, because the collar was gone.

Out in the hall, bouncing against the door, Morley could hear Julie's dogs. They sensed the intruder and wanted at him. He wished now he had left the study door open, or put them out on the yard.

"I've got money," Morley said.

"Fuck your money," Dennis screamed. "I'm not selling anything here. Get up and get over here."

Morley followed the wave of the revolver to the front of his desk. Dennis swept the chess set and stuff aside with a swipe of his arm and bent Morley backwards over the desk. He put one of the collars around Morley's neck, pulled the chain around the desk a few times, pushed it under and fastened the other collar over Morley's ankles.

Tucking the revolver into the waistband of his pants, Dennis picked up Chum and tenderly placed him on the desk chair, half-curled. He tried to poke the dog's tongue back into his mouth, but that didn't work. He patted Chum on the head, said, "There, now."

Dennis went around and stood in front of Morley and looked at him, as if memorizing the moment.

At his back the Dobermans rattled the door.

"We can make a deal," Morley said. "I can give you a lot of money, and you can go away. We'll call it even."

Dennis unfastened Morley's pants, pulled them down to his knees. He pulled the underwear down. He went around and got the spray can out of Morley's coat and came back.

"This isn't sporting, Dennis. At least I gave you a fighting chance."

"I'm not a sport," Dennis said.

He sprayed Morley's testicles with the chemical. When he finished he tossed the canister aside, walked over to the door and listened to the Dobermans scuttling on the other side.

"Dennis!"

Dennis took hold of the doorknob.

"Screw you then," Morley said. "I'm not afraid. I won't scream. I won't give you the pleasure."

"You didn't even love her," Dennis said, and opened the door.

The Dobermans went straight for the stench of the spray, straight for Morley's testicles.

Dennis walked calmly out the back way, closed the glass door. And as he limped down the drive, making for the gate, he began to laugh.

Morley had lied. He did too scream. In fact, he was still screaming.

I suppose this is my signature story. It wasn't the first story of mine to get some real attention—that would be "Tight Little Stitches in a Dead Man's Back," but it was the one that really got the ball rolling faster. I read it at a World Fantasy Convention in Nashville just before the book containing it came out, and when I first started reading, the audience went stone quiet, then someone snickered, letting folks realize it was okay to laugh. Then everyone was laughing. This was okay. But there was a point when I felt everyone should cease to laugh, and when I came to that point, they did. I could feel the audience with me all the way. I knew I had done good. And I must admit, to this day, this is my favorite of all my short stories. I felt I had turned a big corner when I wrote it. This was made all the better with the experience of the reading, and then it came out in Silver Scream, my pick for the best horror anthology of the eighties, and it got a lot of attention, and is periodically reprinted here or abroad.

That said, it seems the perfect story to close out this collection.

NIGHT THEY MISSED THE HORROR SHOW

IF THEY'D GONE TO THE DRIVE-IN LIKE THEY'D planned, none of this would have happened. But Leonard didn't like drive-ins when he didn't have a date, and he'd heard about *Night Of The Living Dead*, and he knew a nigger starred in it. He didn't want to see no movie with a nigger star. Niggers chopped cotton, fixed flats, and pimped nigger girls, but he'd never heard of one that killed zombies. And he'd heard too that there was a white girl in the movie that let the nigger touch her, and that peeved him. Any white gal that would let a nigger touch her must be the lowest trash in the world. Probably from Hollywood, New York, or Waco, some godforsaken place like that.

Now Steve McQueen would have been all right for zombie killing and girl handling. He would have been the ticket. But a nigger? No sir.

Boy, that Steve McQueen was one cool head. Way he said stuff in them pictures was so good you couldn't help but think someone had written it down for him. He could sure think fast on his feet to come up with the things he said, and he had that real cool, mean look.

Leonard wished he could be Steve McQueen, or Paul Newman even. Someone like that always knew what to say, and he figured they got plenty of bush too. Certainly they didn't get as bored as he did. He was so bored he felt as if he were going to die from it before the night was out. Bored, bored, bored. Just wasn't nothing exciting about being in the Dairy Queen parking lot, leaning on the front of his '64 Impala looking out at the highway. He figured maybe old crazy Harry who janitored at the high school might be right about them flying saucers. Harry was always seeing something. Bigfoot, six-legged weasels, all manner of things. But maybe he was right about the saucers. He'd said he'd seen one a couple nights back hovering over Mud Creek and it was shooting down these rays that looked like wet peppermint sticks. Leonard figured if Harry really had seen the saucers and the rays, then those rays were boredom rays. It would be a way for space critters to get at Earth folks, boring them to death. Getting melted down by heat rays would have been better. That was at least quick, but being bored to death was sort of like being nibbled to death by ducks.

Leonard continued looking at the highway, trying to imagine flying saucers and boredom rays, but he couldn't keep his mind on it. He finally focused on something in the highway. A dead dog.

Not just a dead dog. But a DEAD DOG. The mutt had been hit by a semi at least, maybe several. It looked as if it had rained dog. There were pieces of that pooch all over the concrete and one leg was lying on the curbing on the opposite side, stuck up in such a way that it seemed to be waving hello. Doctor Frankenstein with a grant from Johns Hopkins and assistance from NASA couldn't have put that sucker together again.

Leonard leaned over to his faithful, drunk companion, Billy— known among the gang as Farto, because he was fart-lighting champion of Mud Creek—and said, "See that dog there?"

Farto looked where Leonard was pointing. He hadn't noticed the dog before, and he wasn't nearly as casual about it as Leonard. The puzzle-piece hound brought back memories. It reminded him of a dog he'd had when he was thirteen. A big, fine German shepherd that loved him better than his Mama.

Sonofabitch dog tangled its chain through and over a barbed wire fence somehow and hung itself. When Farto found the dog its tongue looked like a stuffed, black sock and he could see where its claws had just been able to scrape the ground, but not quite enough to get a toe hold. It looked as if the dog had been scratching out some sort of coded message in the dirt. When Farto told his old man about it later, crying as he did, his old man laughed and said, "Probably a goddamn suicide note."

Now, as he looked out at the highway, and his whiskey-laced Coke collected warmly in his gut, he felt a tear form in his eyes. Last time he'd felt that sappy was when he'd won the fart-lighting championship with a four-inch burner that singed the hairs of his ass, and the gang awarded him with a pair of colored boxing shorts. Brown and yellow ones so he could wear them without having to change them too often.

So there they were, Leonard and Farto, parked outside the DQ, leaning on the hood of Leonard's Impala, sipping Coke and whiskey, feeling bored and blue and horny, looking at a dead dog and having nothing to do but go to a show with a nigger starring in it. Which, to be up front, wouldn't have been so bad if they'd had dates. Dates could make up for a lot of sins, or help make a few good ones, depending on one's outlook.

But the night was criminal. Dates they didn't have. Worse yet, wasn't a girl in the entire high school would date them. Not even Marylou Flowers, and she had some kind of disease.

All this nagged Leonard something awful. He could see what the problem was with Farto. He was ugly. Had the kind of face that attracted flies. And though being fart-lighting champion of Mud Creek had a certain prestige among the gang, it lacked a certain something when it came to charming the gals.

But for the life of him, Leonard couldn't figure his own problem. He was handsome, had some good clothes, and his car ran good when he didn't buy that old cheap gas. He even had a few bucks in his jeans from breaking into washaterias. Yet his right arm had damn near grown to the size of his thigh from all the whacking off he did. Last time he'd been out with a girl had been a month ago, and as he'd been out with her along with nine other guys, he wasn't rightly sure he could call that a date. He wondered about it so much, he'd asked Farto if he thought it qualified as a date. Farto, who had been fifth in line, said he didn't think so, but if Leonard wanted to call it one, wasn't no skin off his dick.

But Leonard didn't want to call it a date. It just didn't have the feel of one, lacked that something special. There was no romance to it.

True, Big Red had called him Honey when he put the mule in the barn, but she called everyone Honey—except Stoney. Stoney was Possum sweets, and he was the one who talked her into wearing the grocery bag with the mouth and eye holes. Stoney was like that. He could sweet talk the camel out from under a sand nigger. When he got through chatting Big Red down, she was plumb proud to wear that bag.

When finally it came his turn to do Big Red, Leonard had let her take the bag off as a gesture of good will. That was a mistake. He just hadn't known a good thing when he had it. Stoney had had the right idea. The bag coming off spoiled everything. With it on, it was sort of like balling the Lone Hippo or some such thing, but with the bag off, you were absolutely certain what you were getting, and it wasn't pretty.

Even closing his eyes hadn't helped. He found that the ugliness of that face had branded itself on the back of his eyeballs. He couldn't even imagine the sack back over her head. All he could think about was that puffy, too-painted face with the sort of bad complexion that began at the bone.

He'd gotten so disappointed, he'd had to fake an orgasm and get off before his hooter shriveled up and his Trojan fell off and was lost in the vacuum.

Thinking back on it, Leonard sighed. It would certainly be nice for a change to go with a girl that didn't pull the train or had a hole between her legs that looked like a manhole cover ought to be on it. Sometimes he wished he could be like Farto, who was as happy as if he had good sense. Anything thrilled him. Give him a can of Wolf Brand Chili, a big moon pie, Coke and whiskey and he could spend the rest of his life fucking Big Red and lighting the gas out of his asshole.

God, but this was no way to live. No women and no fun. Bored, bored, bored. Leonard found himself looking overhead for space ships and peppermint-colored boredom rays, but he saw only a few moths fluttering drunkenly through the beams of the DQ's lights.

Lowering his eyes back to the highway and the dog, Leonard had a sudden flash. "Why don't we get the chain out of the back and hook it up to Rex there? Take him for a ride."

"You mean drag his dead ass around?" Farto asked.

Leonard nodded.

"Beats stepping on a tack," Farto said.

They drove the Impala into the middle of the highway at a safe moment and got out for a look. Up close the mutt was a lot worse. Its innards had been mashed out of its mouth and asshole and it stunk something awful. The dog was wearing a thick, metal-studded collar and they fastened one end of their fifteen foot chain to that and the other to the rear bumper.

Bob, the Dairy Queen manager, noticed them through the window, came outside and yelled, "What are you fucking morons doing?"

"Taking this doggie to the vet," Leonard said. "We think this sumbitch looks a might peaked. He may have been hit by a car."

"That's so fucking funny I'm about to piss myself," Bob said.

"Old folks have that problem," Leonard said.

Leonard got behind the wheel and Farto climbed in on the passenger side. They manuvered the car and dog around and out of the path of a tractor-trailer truck just in time. As they drove off, Bob screamed after them, "I hope you two no-dicks wrap that Chevy piece of shit around a goddamn pole."

As they roared along, parts of the dog, like crumbs from a flaky loaf of bread, came off. A tooth here. Some hair there. A string of guts. A dew claw. And some unidentifiable pink stuff. The metal-studded collar and chain threw up sparks now and then like fiery crickets. Finally they hit seventy-five and the dog was swinging wider and wider on the chain, like it was looking for an opportunity to pass.

Farto poured him and Leonard Cokes and whiskey as they drove along. He handed Leonard his paper cup and Leonard knocked it back, a lot happier now than he had been a moment ago. Maybe this night wasn't going to turn out so bad after all.

They drove by a crowd at the side of the road, a tan station wagon and a wreck of a Ford up on a jack. At a glance they could see that there was a nigger in the middle of the crowd and he wasn't witnessing to the white boys. He was hopping around like a pig with a hotshot up his ass, trying to find a break in the white boys so he could make a run for it. But there wasn't any break to be found and there were too many to fight. Nine white boys were knocking him around like he was a pinball and they were a malicious machine.

"Ain't that one of our niggers?" Farto asked. "And ain't that some of them White Tree football players that's trying to kill him?"

"Scott," Leonard said, and the name was dogshit in his mouth. It had been Scott who had outdone him for the position of quarterback on the team. That damn jig could put together a play more tangled than a can of fishing worms, but it damn near always worked. And he could run like a spotted-ass ape.

As they passed, Fatto said, "We'll read about him tomorrow in the papers."

But Leonard drove only a short way before slamming on the brakes and whipping the Impala around. Rex swung way out and clipped off some tall, dried sunflowers at the edge of the road like a scythe.

"We gonna go back and watch?" Farto said. "I don't think them White Tree boys would bother us none if that's all we was gonna do, watch."

"He may be a nigger," Leonard said, not liking himself, "but he's our nigger and we can't let them do that. They kill him, they'll beat us in football."

Farto saw the truth of this immediately. "Damn right. They can't do that to our nigger."

Leonard crossed the road again and went straight for the White Tree boys, hit down hard on the horn. The White Tree boys abandoned beating their prey and jumped in all directions. Bullfrogs couldn't have done any better.

Scott stood startled and weak where he was, his knees bent in and touching one another, his eyes big as pizza pans. He had never noticed how big grillwork was. It looked like teeth there in the night and the headlights looked like eyes. He felt like a stupid fish about to be eaten by a shark.

Leonard braked hard, but off the highway in the dirt it wasn't enough to keep from bumping Scott, sending him flying over the hood and against the glass where his face mashed to it then rolled away, his shirt snagging one of the windshield wipers and pulling it off.

Leonard opened the car door and called to Scott who lay on the ground. "It's now or never."

A White Tree boy made for the car, and Leonard pulled the taped hammer handle out from beneath the seat and stepped out of the car and hit him with it. The White Tree boy went down to his knees and said something that sounded like French but wasn't. Leonard grabbed Scott by the back of the shirt and pulled him up and guided him around and threw him into the open door. Scott scrambled over the front seat and into the back. Leonard threw the hammer handle at one of the White Tree boys and stepped back, whirled into the car behind the wheel. He put the car in gear again and stepped on the gas. The Impala lurched forward, and with one hand on the door Leonard flipped it wider and clipped a White Tree boy with it as if he were flexing a wing. The car bumped back on the highway and the chain swung out and Rex clipped the feet out from under two White Tree boys as neatly as he had taken down the dried sunflowers.

Leonard looked in his rearview mirror and saw two White Tree boys carrying the one he had clubbed with the hammer handle to the station wagon. The others he and the dog had knocked down were getting up. One had kicked the jack out from under Scott's car and was using it to smash the headlights and windshield.

"Hope you got insurance on that thing," Leonard said.

"I borrowed it," Scott said, peeling the windshield wiper out of his T-shirt. "Here, you might want this." He dropped the wiper over the seat and between Leonard and Farto.

"That's a borrowed car?" Farto said. "That's worse."

"Nah," Scott said. "Owner don't know I borrowed it. I'd have had that flat changed if that sucker had had him a spare tire, but I got back there and wasn't nothing but the rim, man. Say, thanks for not letting me get killed, else we couldn't have run that ole pig together no more. Course, you almost run over me. My chest hurts."

Leonard checked the rearview again. The White Tree boys were coming fast. "You complaining?" Leonard said.

"Nah," Scott said, and turned to look through the back glass. He could see the dog swinging in short arcs and pieces of it going wide and far. "Hope you didn't go off and forget your dog tied to the bumper."

"Goddamn," said Farto, "and him registered too."

"This ain't so funny," Leonard said, "them White Tree boys are gaining."

"Well, speed it up," Scott said.

Leonard gnashed his teeth. "I could always get rid of some excess baggage, you know."

"Throwing that windshield wiper out ain't gonna help," Scott said.

Leonard looked in the mirror and saw the grinning nigger in the back seat. Nothing worse than a comic coon. He didn't even look grateful. Leonard had a sudden horrid vision of being overtaken by the White Tree boys. What if he were killed with the nigger? Getting killed was bad enough, but what if tomorrow they found him in a ditch with Farto and the nigger. Or maybe them White Tree boys would make him do something awful with the nigger before they killed them. Like making him suck the nigger's dick or some such thing. Leonard held his foot all the way to the floor; as they passed the Dairy Queen he took a hard left and the car just made it and Rex swung out and slammed a light pole, then popped back in line behind them.

The White Tree boys couldn't make the corner in the station wagon and they didn't even try. They screeched into a car lot down a piece, turned around and came back. By that time the tail lights of the Impala were moving away from them rapidly, looking like two inflamed hemorrhoids in a dark asshole.

"Take the next right coming up," Scott said, "then you'll see a little road off to the left. Kill your lights and take that."

Leonard hated taking orders from Scott on the field, but this was worse. Insulting. Still, Scott called good plays on the field, and the habit of following instructions from the quarterback died hard. Leonard made the right and Rex made it with them after taking a dip in a water-filled bar ditch.

Leonard saw the little road and killed his lights and took it. It carried them down between several rows of large tin storage buildings, and Leonard pulled between two of them and drove down a little alley lined with more. He stopped the car and they waited and listened. After about five minutes, Farto said, "I think we skunked those father-rapers."

"Ain't we a team?" Scott said.

In spite of himself, Leonard felt good. It was like when the nigger called a play that worked and they were all patting each other on the ass and not minding what color the other was because they were just creatures in football suits.

"Let's have a drink," Leonard said.

Farto got a paper cup off the floorboard for Scott and poured him up some warm Coke and whiskey. Last time they had gone to Longview, he had peed in that paper cup so they wouldn't have to stop, but that had long since been poured out, and besides, it was for a nigger. He poured Leonard and himself drinks in their same cups.

Scott took a sip and said, "Shit, man, that tastes kind of rank."

"Like piss," Farto said.

Leonard held up his cup. "To the Mud Creek Wildcats and fuck them White Tree boys."

"You fuck 'em," Scott said. They touched their cups, and at that moment the car filled with light.

Cups upraised, the Three Musketeers turned blinking toward it. The light was coming from an open storage building door, and there was a fat man standing in the center of the glow like a bloated fly on a lemon wedge. Behind him was a big screen made of a sheet and there was some kind of movie playing on it. And though the light was bright and fading out the movie, Leonard, who was in the best position to see, got a look at it. What he could make out looked like a gal down on her knees sucking this fat guy's dick (the man was visible only from the belly down) and the guy had a short, black revolver pressed to her forehead. She pulled her mouth off of him for an instant and the man came in her face, then fired the revolver. The woman's head snapped out of frame and the sheet seemed to drip blood, like dark condensation on a window pane. Then Leonard couldn't see anymore because another man had appeared in the doorway, and like the first he was fat. Both looked like huge bowling balls that had been set on top of shoes. More men appeared behind these two, but one of the fat men turned and held up his hand and the others moved out of sight. The two fat guys stepped outside and one pulled the door almost shut, except for a thin band of light that fell across the front seat of the Impala.

Fat Man Number One went over to the car and opened Farto's door and said, "You fucks and the nigger get out." It was the voice of doom. They had only thought the White Tree boys were dangerous. They realized now they had been kidding themselves. This was the real article. This guy would have eaten the hammer handle and shit a two-by-four.

They got out of the car and the fat man waved them around and lined them up on Farto's side and looked at them. The boys still had their drinks in their hands, and sparing that, they looked like cons in a lineup.

Fat Man Number Two came over and looked at the trio and smiled. It was obvious the fatties were twins. They had the same bad features in the same fat faces. They wore Hawaiian shirts that varied only in profiles and color of parrots and had on white socks and too-short black slacks and black, shiny, Italian shoes with toes sharp enough to thread needles.

Fat Man Number One took the cup away from Scott and sniffed it. "A nigger with liquor," he said. "That's like a cunt with brains. It don't go together. Guess you was getting tanked up so you could put the ole black snake to some chocolate pudding after while. Or maybe you was wantin' some vanilla and these boys were gonna set it up."

"I'm not wanting anything but to go home," Scott said.

Fat Man Number Two looked at Fat Man Number One and said, "So he can fuck his mother."

The fatties looked at Scott to see what he'd say but he didn't say anything. They could say he screwed dogs and that was all right with him. Hell, bring one on and he'd fuck it now if they'd let him go afterwards.

Fat Man Number One said, "You boys running around with a jungle bunny makes me sick."

"He's just a nigger from school," Farto said. "We don't like him none. We just picked him up because some White Tree boys were beating on him and we didn't want him to get wrecked on account of he's our quarterback."

"Ah," Fat Man Number One said, "I see. Personally, me and Vinnie don't cotton to niggers in sports. They start taking showers with white boys, the next thing they want is to take white girls to bed. It's just one step from one to the other."

"We don't have nothing to do with him playing," Leonard said. "We didn't intergrate the schools."

"No," Fat Man Number One said, "that was ole Big Ears Johnson, but you're running around with him and drinking with him."

"His cup's been peed in," Farto said. "That was kind of a joke on him, you see. He ain't our friend, I swear it. He's just a nigger that plays football."

"Peed in his cup, huh?" said the one called Vinnie. "I like that, Pork, don't you? Peed in his fucking cup."

Pork dropped Scott's cup on the ground and smiled at him. "Come here, nigger. I got something to tell you."

Scott looked at Farto and Leonard. No help there. They had suddenly become interested in the toes of their shoes; they examined them as if they were true marvels of the world.

Scott moved toward Pork, and Pork, still smiling, put his arm around Scott's shoulders and walked him toward the big storage building. Scott said, "What are we doing?"

Pork turned Scott around so they were facing Leonard and Farto who still stood holding their drinks and contemplating their shoes. "I didn't want to get it on the new gravel drive," Pork said and pulled Scott's head in close to his own and with his free hand reached back and under his Hawaiian shirt and brought out a short, black revolver and put it to Scott's temple and pulled the trigger. There was a snap like a bad knee going out and Scott's feet lifted in unison and went to the side and something dark squirted from his head and his feet swung back toward Pork and his shoes shuffled, snapped, and twisted on the concrete in front of the building.

"Ain't that somethin'," Pork said as Scott went limp and dangled from the thick crook of his arm, "the rhythm is the last thing to go."

Leonard couldn't make a sound. His guts were in his throat. He wanted to melt and run under the car. Scott was dead and the brains that had made plays twisted as fishing worms and commanded his feet on down the football field were scrambled like breakfast eggs.

Farto said, "Holy shit."

Pork let go of Scott and Scott's legs split and he sat down and his head went forward and clapped on the cement between his knees. A dark pool formed under his face.

"He's better off, boys," Vinnie said. "Nigger was begat by Cain and the ape and he ain't quite monkey and he ain't quite man. He's got no place in this world 'cept as a beast of burden. You start trying to train them to do things like drive cars and run with footballs, it ain't nothing but grief to them and the whites too. Get any on your shirt, Pork?"

"Nary a drop."

Vinnie went inside the building and said something to the men there that could be heard but not understood, then he came back with some crumpled newspapers. He went over to Scott and wrapped them around the bloody head and let it drop back on the cement. "You try hosing down that shit when it's dried, Pork, and you wouldn't worry none about that gravel. The gravel ain't nothing."

Then Vinnie said to Farto, "Open the back door of that car." Farto nearly twisted an ankle doing it. Vinnie picked Scott up by the back of the neck and seat of his pants and threw him onto the floorboard of the Impala.

Pork used the short barrel of his revolver to scratch his nuts, then put the gun behind him, under his Hawaiian shirt. "You boys are gonna go to the river bottoms with us and help us get shed of this nigger."

"Yes sir," Farto said. "We'll toss his ass in the Sabine for you."

"How about you?" Pork asked Leonard. "You trying to go weak sister?"

"No," Leonard croaked. "I'm with you."

"That's good," Pork said. "Vinnie, you take the truck and lead the way."

Vinnie took a key from his pocket and unlocked the building door next to the one with the light, went inside, and backed out a sharp-looking gold Dodge pickup. He backed it in front of the Impala and sat there with the motor running.

"You boys keep your place," Pork said. He went inside the lighted building for a moment. They heard him say to the men inside, "Go on and watch the movies. And save some of them beers for us. We'll be back." Then the light went out and Pork came out, shutting the door. He looked at Leonard and Farto and said, "Drink up, boys."

Leonard and Farto tossed off their warm Coke and whiskey and dropped the cups on the ground.

"Now," Pork said, "you get in the back with the nigger, I'll ride with the driver."

Farto got in the back and put his feet on Scott's knees. He tried not to look at the head wrapped in newspaper, but he couldn't help it. When Pork opened the front door and the overhead light came on Farto saw there was a split in the paper and Scott's eye was visible behind it. Across the forehead the wrapping had turned dark. Down by the mouth and chin was an ad for a fish sale.

Leonard got behind the wheel and started the car. Pork reached over and honked the horn. Vinnie rolled the pickup forward and Leonard followed him to the river bottoms. No one spoke. Leonard found himself wishing with all his heart that he had gone to the outdoor picture show to see the movie with the nigger starring in it.

The river bottoms were steamy and hot from the closeness of the trees and the under- and overgrowth. As Leonard wound the Impala down the narrow, red clay roads amidst the dense foliage, he felt as if his car was a crab crawling about in a pubic thatch. He could feel from the way the steering wheel handled that the dog and the chain were catching brush and limbs here and there. He had forgotten all about the dog and now being reminded of it worried him. What if the dog got tangled and he had to stop? He didn't think Pork would take kindly to stopping, not with the dead burrhead on the floorboard and him wanting to get rid of the body.

Finally they came to where the woods cleared out a spell and they drove along the edge of the Sabine River. Leonard hated water and always had. In the moonlight the river looked like poisoned coffee flowing there. Leonard knew there were alligators and gars big as little alligators and water moccasins by the thousands swimming underneath the water, and just the thought of all those slick, darting bodies made him queasy.

They came to what was known as Broken Bridge. It was an old worn-out bridge that had fallen apart in the middle and it was connected to the land on this side only. People sometimes fished off of it. There was no one fishing tonight.

Vinnie stopped the pickup and Leonard pulled up beside him, the nose of the Chevy pointing at the mouth of the bridge. They all got out and Pork made Farto pull Scott out by the feet. Some of the newspaper came loose from Scott's head exposing an ear and part of the face. Farto patted the newspaper back into place.

"Fuck that," Vinnie said. "It don't hurt if he stains the fucking ground. You two idgits find some stuff to weight this coon down so we can sink him."

Farto and Leonard started scurrying about like squirrels, looking for rocks or big, heavy logs. Suddenly they heard Vinnie cry out. "Godamighty, fucking A. Pork. Come look at this."

Leonard looked over and saw that Vinnie had discovered Rex. He was standing looking down with his hands on his hips. Pork went over to stand by him, then Pork turned around and looked at them. "Hey, you fucks, come here."

Leonard and Farto joined them in looking at the dog. There was mostly just a head now, with a little bit of meat and fur hanging off a spine and some broken ribs.

"That's the sickest fucking thing I've ever fucking seen," Pork said.

"Godamighty," Vinnie said.

"Doing a dog like that. Shit, don't you got no heart? A dog. Man's best fucking goddamn friend and you two killed him like this."

"We didn't kill him," Farto said.

"You trying to fucking tell me he done this to himself? Had a bad fucking day and done this."

"Godamighty," Vinnie said.

"No sir," Leonard said. "We chained him on there after he was dead."

"I believe that," Vinnie said. "That's some rich shit. You guys murdered this dog. Godamighty."

"Just thinking about him trying to keep up and you fucks driving faster and faster makes me mad as a wasp," Pork said.

"No," Farto said. "It wasn't like that. He was dead and we were drunk and we didn't have anything to do, so we—"

"Shut the fuck up," Pork said, sticking a finger hard against Farto's forehead. "You just shut the fuck up. We can see what the fuck you fucks did. You drug this here dog around until all his goddamn hide came off . . . what kind of mothers you boys got anyhow that they didn't tell you better about animals?"

"Godamighty," Vinnie said.

Everyone grew silent, stood looking at the dog. Finally Farto said, "You want us to go back to getting some stuff to hold the nigger down?"

Pork looked at Farto as if he had just grown up whole from the ground. "You fucks are worse than niggers, doing a dog like that. Get on back over to the car."

Leonard and Farto went over to the Impala and stood looking down at Scott's body in much the same way they had stared at the dog. There, in the dim moonlight shadowed by trees, the paper wrapped around Scott's head made him look like a giant papier-mâché doll. Pork came up and kicked Scott in the face with a swift motion that sent newspaper flying and sent a thonking sound across the water that made frogs jump.

"Forget the nigger," Pork said. "Give me your car keys, ball sweat." Leonard took out his keys and gave them to Pork, and Pork went around to the trunk and opened it. "Drag the nigger over here."

Leonard took one of Scott's arms and Farto took the other and they pulled him over to the back of the car.

"Put him in the trunk," Pork said.

"What for?" Leonard asked.

"Cause I fucking said so," Pork said.

Leonard and Farto heaved Scott into the trunk. He looked pathetic lying there next to the spare tire, his face partially covered with newspaper. Leonard thought, if only the nigger had stolen a car with a spare he might not be here tonight. He could have gotten the flat changed and driven on before the White Tree boys ever came along.

"All right, you get in there with him," Pork said, gesturing to Farto.

"Me?" Farto said.

"Nah, not fucking you, the fucking elephant on your fucking shoulder. Yeah, you, get in the trunk. I ain't got all night."

"Jesus, we didn't do anything to that dog, mister. We told you that. I swear. Me and Leonard hooked him up after he was dead . . . it was Leonard's idea."

Pork didn't say a word. He just stood there with one hand on the trunk lid looking at Farto. Farto looked at Pork, then the trunk, then back to Pork. Lastly he looked at Leonard, then climbed into the trunk, his back to Scott.

"Like spoons," Pork said, and closed the lid. "Now you, whatsit, Leonard? You come over here." But Pork didn't wait for Leonard to move. He scooped the back of Leonard's neck with a chubby hand and pushed him over to where Rex lay at the end of the chain with Vinnie still looking down at him.

"What you think, Vinnie?" Pork asked. "You got what I got in mind?"

Vinnie nodded. He bent down and took the collar off the dog. He fastened it on Leonard. Leonard could smell the odor of the dead dog in his nostrils. He bent his head and puked.

"There goes my shoeshine," Vinnie said, and he hit Leonard a short one in the stomach. Leonard went to his knees and puked some more of the hot Coke and whiskey.

"You fucks are the lowest pieces of shit on this earth, doing a dog like that," Vinnie said. "A nigger ain't no lower."

Vinnie got some strong fishing line out of the back of the truck and they tied Leonard's hands behind his back. Leonard began to cry.

"Oh shut up," Pork said. "It ain't that bad. Ain't nothing that bad."

But Leonard couldn't shut up. He was caterwauling now and it was echoing through the trees. He closed his eyes and tried to pretend he had gone to the show with the nigger starring in it and had fallen asleep in his car and was having a bad dream, but he couldn't imagine that. He thought about Harry the janitor's flying saucers with the peppermint rays, and he knew if there were any saucers shooting rays down, they weren't boredom rays after all. He wasn't a bit bored.

Pork pulled off Leonard's shoes and pushed him back flat on the ground and pulled off the socks and stuck them in Leonard's mouth so tight he couldn't spit them out. It wasn't that Pork thought anyone was going to hear Leonard, he just didn't like the noise. It hurt his ears.

Leonard lay on the ground in the vomit next to the dog and cried silently. Pork and Vinnie went over to the Impala and opened the doors and stood so they could get a grip on the car to push. Vinnie reached in and moved the gear from park to neutral and he and Pork began to shove the car forward. It moved slowly at first, but as it made the slight incline that led down to the old bridge, it picked up speed. From inside the trunk, Farto hammered lightly at the lid as if he didn't really mean it. The chain took up slack and Leonard felt it jerk and pop his neck. He began to slide along the ground like a snake.

Vinnie and Pork jumped out of the way and watched the car make the bridge and go over the edge and disappear into the water with amazing quietness. Leonard, pulled by the weight of the car, rustled past them. When he hit the bridge, splinters tugged at his clothes so hard they ripped his pants and underwear down almost to his knees.

The chain swung out once toward the edge of the bridge and the rotten railing, and Leonard tried to hook a leg around an upright board there, but that proved wasted. The weight of the car just pulled his knee out of joint and jerked the board out of place with a screech of nails and lumber.

Leonard picked up speed and the chain rattled over the edge of the bridge, into the water and out of sight, pulling its connection after it like a pull toy. The last sight of Leonard was the soles of his bare feet, white as the bellies of fish.

"It's deep there," Vinnie said. "I caught an old channel cat there once, remember? Big sucker. I bet it's over fifty feet deep down there."

They got in the truck and Vinnie cranked it.

"I think we did them boys a favor," Pork said. "Them running around with niggers and what they did to that dog and all. They weren't worth a thing."

"I know it," Vinnie said. "We should have filmed this, Pork, it would have been good. Where the car and that nigger-lover went off in the water was choice."

"Nah, there wasn't any women."

"Point," Vinnie said, and he backed around and drove onto the trail that wound its way out of the bottoms.